THE MOUNTAINS BETWEEN US

IMOGEN MARTIN

Storm

This is a work of fiction. Names, characters, business, events and incidents are the products of the author's imagination. Any resemblance to actual persons, living or dead, or actual events is purely coincidental.

Copyright © Imogen Martin, 2025

The moral right of the author has been asserted.

All rights reserved. No part of this book may be reproduced or used in any manner without the prior written permission of the copyright owner.

To request permissions, contact the publisher at rights@stormpublishing.co

Ebook ISBN: 978-1-80508-741-0
Paperback ISBN: 978-1-80508-742-7

Cover design: Emma Rogers
Cover images: Shutterstock

Published by Storm Publishing.
For further information, visit:
www.stormpublishing.co

ALSO BY IMOGEN MARTIN

Under a Gilded Sky
To the Wild Horizon

*For my husband Peter, without whom none of my books would ever have been written.
I feel lucky every day to have married you.*

PART ONE

ONE

JANUARY 1848: THE WILLAMETTE VALLEY, OREGON TERRITORY

As the outline of a building took shape in the Oregon dusk, Grace Randolph prayed they had finally found her brother's homestead—or this would be their last wrong turn.

If this was another false hope, Grace knew she would cry. She didn't want to, but she was cold and hungry and worn out from days on a horse.

"This must be it. Surely." She tried to make her voice bright.

Her husband, James, pulled up his horse beside hers, and together they studied the buildings ahead: a cabin and barn nestled into a wood on a low hill. "If it isn't, let's hope we don't make them jumpy, coming up on them when it's almost dark."

Grace said another silent prayer. They had spent so many weeks under canvas, she longed for her brother's roof over her head. If this wasn't his place, it would be late to start setting up camp now, even though she and her husband had gotten it down to a fine art. "People in the Willamette have been helpful so far. Maybe they'd give us a place to bed down anyway."

James Randolph grunted, suggesting he had limited faith in people's generosity. She watched as he raised his coat collar against the cold and urged his horse onward, then followed as he led the way through the field. They each had a mule tethered, carrying their worldly goods.

The homestead was dark, except for an oil light glowing in one window. A dog barked as they approached, alerted by their movement in the half-light. Grace paused. Was that bark familiar?

The dog pushed its way through a gap in the barn door, growling to defend its territory.

"That's Kane! I'm sure of it."

Before James could caution her, she slipped from the saddle and ran to the dog, calling its name. It watched her for a moment, then bounded forward, its tail beating back and forth.

Grace sank down and put her arms around the dog's neck. "Kane, it's you. It's really you!"

She brushed a tear from her eye before turning toward James, who dismounted and brought the horses and mules closer. He nodded to the front door. "Better if you knock."

Grace breathed deeply and straightened up. She took the steps up to the door, feeling sick in her stomach. What if everything had changed? She'd not seen her elder brother, Zachary, since she and James had ridden away in October 1846. Had he thrived over the past year or so, a pioneer in this new part of Oregon? More than anything, she needed to know how her beloved younger brother, Tom, was faring. They had braved the six-month journey across the Rockies together, just the two of them in a wagon, before she had left him in Zachary's care.

She tried to knock in a friendly way, and called out Zachary's name. She glanced back at James for reassurance, but his face was in darkness beneath his hat, one hand pushed deep in his overcoat pocket.

She heard shuffling behind the door and it swung open. A tall, wiry figure stood in his nightshirt, outlined against the warm light in the room.

"Who's there?" The voice was cautious.

"It's me. Grace. We're... well, we're back."

He stood motionless for a moment, continuing to hold the door. "Well, blow me down with a... Grace! What you doing, standing out there in the cold and dark? Get yourself inside. And where's that soldier-husband of yours?"

James stepped forward. "Mr. Sinclair," he said, removing his hat.

"Captain!"

Grace glanced at James and saw him grimace.

Zachary stepped aside. "Come on, both of you, quick, before we freeze the house."

Grace stepped inside and sighed with relief as the cozy warmth enveloped her. The walls of the cabin were rough-hewn from enormous logs, the floor made from uneven planks. In the half-light, she could make out a black stove to one side, its chimney pipe angled out through the wall. The rustic furniture was sparse.

She stood in the middle of the room, uncertain what to do, James's tall figure at her shoulder.

Zachary went to a door the other side of the room and called, "Maggie. You got to get up. I've got one helluva surprise for you." He returned to the stove and opened its door. "You remember my wife? Margaret?"

"Of course—"

"You both look frozen. I'll get this fire going. What in heaven's name possessed you to travel in winter? Not that I'm anything other than *delighted* to see you."

Zachary. Her brother hadn't changed at all. Although nearing thirty, he was still a bundle of energy, firing questions and not waiting for a reply, like a young boy.

Margaret entered, wrapped in a woolen shawl over her nightdress, her hair in two braids. "Zachary? What's going on?"

"It's Grace. And the captain. They're here."

Her hands swept to her mouth. "Oh good heavens above. How are you? Are you well?"

"We're..." Grace struggled to find the right words. There was so much to say, but so much to keep hidden. "Yes, we're well."

Should she hug Margaret? They barely knew each other, but a handshake seemed formal for a sister-in-law, so she stepped forward and gave the woman a tentative embrace.

Grace looked at Zachary as he poked the fire into life. "And... Tom?"

"Maggie. Go fetch Tom. Lord knows how he's sleeping through this commotion."

Margaret bustled back through the door, muttering to herself.

"And sit. Sit." Zachary urged them to the chairs.

Grace sank into the nearest one, but James remained standing, his hat in his hands.

"Our animals." He gestured with his hat to the door. "I need to fix our horses and mules."

Zachary waved a hand. "Don't you worry about that. They'll survive a little longer and then I'll take them to the barn."

Grace's mouth went dry as Tom stumbled into the room, bleary-eyed with sleep and his hair messy like hay. He'd pulled on canvas pants and tucked his woolen nightshirt into the waist band. He'd grown so much, she could hardly believe he was twelve.

"Zachary?" he asked, his eyes adjusting to the lamplight. "Aunt Margaret said you needed me."

Zachary grinned at him. "Look who's here."

Grace stood and took a step forward, her legs suddenly weak. She struggled to swallow, there was such a sharp pain in her chest, seeing him standing there. He was as tall as her now, with that same clear look in his eyes he'd always had.

Tom stared at her as if she were a mythical beast. "You've come back," he whispered.

"Of course we've come back." Grace went to him, pulling him into her arms. "Oh, Tom. How I've missed you."

He wrapped his arms round her and it felt so good when he put his head on her shoulder. She blinked back tears. It had been more than a year of wondering how he was. The newspapers on the East Coast liked to romanticize life on the frontier, but she knew the truth: it was a harsh life, where you could break bread with a loved one in the morning and have them carried away by accident or disease by the evening.

She heard Margaret come back, so she pulled away from Tom, wiping her nose.

Tom looked beyond her. "Sir. Captain." He put his hand out, as if trying to work out how to greet his sister's husband, once a commanding person who easily intimidated him when they had been traveling overland under his protection, but now his brother-in-law.

James grinned and took the outstretched hand, cupping it in both hands. "It's mighty fine to see you again, Tom. And why don't you call me James? Or Uncle James, if you prefer."

Tom frowned, but nodded.

"How many times do I have to tell you to sit?" said Zachary.

Grace returned to her chair and James took the other.

Margaret was already by the rudimentary range at the other end of the cabin. "I'll have a bowl of broth ready for you in no time."

"What about little Gracie? Shall I go fetch her?" asked Zachary, winking at Grace.

Grace looked at him eagerly. "Gracie?"

"We said we'd name her after you, Sister, if it were a girl."

Grace pushed her palms together, closed her eyes, and whispered, "Thank you." She had been fearful, as they had not yet mentioned the baby she'd known Margaret was carrying when they were last here. "I'm so relieved that you were safely delivered. Can I see my namesake?"

Margaret turned to them. "She's sleeping now. I'd prefer we let her be. If you don't mind, Grace. She's got a tooth coming through and it's hard to get her to drop off."

Grace nodded. "We'll see her in the morning."

"See her?" said Zachary. "More like *hear* her."

"How old is she now?" Grace asked.

"Thirteen months," said Margaret.

James glanced at the front door again and fidgeted.

"Say, why don't I fix your horses for you?" said Zachary.

Grace shot her brother a grateful smile as he unhooked a heavy coat from the door.

James buttoned his black overcoat and picked up his hat. "It'll be quicker with both of us. And the animals know me."

Zachary lighted a storm lantern and opened the door. The January air streamed into the cabin. "After you, sir," he said, as they stepped into the dark.

Tom drew a stool next to Grace's chair. "He looks kinda different. The captain."

Grace gave an involuntary shiver. "That's because he's grown a beard now. And you're not used to seeing him in ordinary clothes. You've only seen him in his army uniform."

"Yes. It's strange. For me, I mean." Tom watched a log burst into flame in the stove. "And there was something kinda"—he searched for the word—"stooped."

Grace sighed. How did a twelve-year-old see things so deeply? "We're both dog-tired. That's all. We've been traveling for a couple of months." She put a hand on his shoulder. "And, Tom, try not to call him the captain? Huh? Try sticking to Uncle James."

Tom looked up at her, a question in his eyes.

"He's not a captain anymore," she said, almost too quietly to hear. "But please, don't ask him about it. Just... let things be."

. . .

Randolph had piled their kit in the corner. He lay with Grace, both on their sides, in front of the stove, their bedrolls pushed together, a blanket enveloping them. Grace was closest to the heat, while he lay behind, protecting her from the chill seeping under the front door. He was satiated by the broth and was beginning to feel warm for the first time in weeks.

He put his arm around his wife and threaded his fingers through hers. He felt her push closer to him, following the contours of his body.

"Things will be good here," he heard her whisper. "A fresh start. You'll see, James."

He closed his eyes as a bolt of regret went through him. It was like a physical pain. It soothed him to see her so happy to be back with her family at last, and he wished he could share her belief that they would find peace here. Truth was, he wasn't sure if he would ever find peace again.

TWO

A month later, the cabin no longer felt cozy: it felt like the walls were coming closer every day. Randolph rankled at the mess, having lived a life of order in the army. The place was too small for two couples, a growing boy, and a toddling baby. There was only the main room, a back room where Zachary, Margaret and baby Gracie slept, and a lean-to for Tom. Randolph and Grace had talked about sleeping in the barn, but the temperature had dropped and the rainy weather turned to light snow.

It had long been Zachary's plan to extend the cabin, one room at a time, until it became a proper homestead, so the men started building a space next to the back bedroom.

Randolph worked like a man possessed, cutting logs for the new room. As soon as he'd finished his breakfast, he would shrug his overcoat over his broad shoulders, pull on his boots and gloves, and go to the barn to pick up an axe and saw.

This morning, he tramped alone into the woodland above Zachary's fields, his breath making clouds in the dawn air. The mountain range in the distance was low compared with the Rockies, and rarely visible in the mist. He liked the cold, the way it made him aware of his skin. Better than the suffocating heat of Mexico, which he had endured during the war there over the past year. He'd had such hopes of a life with Grace as his army wife, after falling in love with her so unexpectedly on the Oregon Trail. He'd been proud to serve with the oldest mounted regiment in the United States Army. Proud, until... He stared over the broad, fertile valley, trying to dislodge unwelcome thoughts of the war. He needed to root himself here, now, and put what happened in Mexico behind him.

Randolph threw down his tools by the tree he had started to chop yesterday. He walked round it: a mature Oregon white oak. Yes, this should be down in a couple of hours. He removed his coat and picked up the axe, swinging at the tree with all his might.

An hour later, he heard a mule and was pleased to see Tom bringing ropes. He was a good worker and had a quiet maturity, despite his young age. Living in Oregon over the past year and a half seemed to have been good for the boy. "You're just in time to help take this one down."

Grunting with the effort, they pushed at the gnarly gray trunk. There was a tearing sound, followed by cracking and the rush of branches breaking as the oak swooped elegantly to the ground.

Randolph looked at it with satisfaction. He removed his hat and ran his fingers through his dark brown hair, before replacing it. Without exchanging a word, Randolph and Tom started on the branches, sawing and striking, working in unison. Tom pulled the wood into a neat pile to one side, as he had watched Randolph do.

Once the trunk had been stripped, Tom fetched the mule that had been nosing through the undergrowth all morning. Randolph fixed the ropes around the massive log and attached them to the harness. He tied another so he could do some hauling himself.

"Same as yesterday. You guide the mule."

Together they heaved the trunk and didn't stop until it was down the hill, coming to a halt by the barn.

"He was out early again, your man," said Margaret, as she found a rag doll for little Gracie, who sat on the floor, her chubby legs stuck out.

Grace was stirring beeswax for candles. The smell made it a favorite job. She had borrowed one of Margaret's aprons to protect her beige woolen dress. Her brown hair was looped up under a bonnet. "Logging keeps his mind off things."

Margaret came close to sniff at the melted wax, before looking at Grace. Her eyes were kind. "Has he told you what those things are?"

Grace bit her lip. "Not much. I keep hoping the moment will come." Hoping. That seemed to be all she could do. They'd been traveling, just the two of them, for weeks and James seemed to have turned inward.

Margaret put her hands to the small of her back and leaned backwards. "I only spent a day or two with him, last time you were in Oregon. He seemed pretty buttoned-up then. But he barely says a word now. It scares me sometimes."

Grace stirred faster, bristling at the implied criticism of her husband. She felt the need to defend him. "His oldest friend was killed early in the Mexican war. Lieutenant Turner. A good man. I was at Fort Leavenworth with his wife when word came through. If I'd got that news, I wouldn't have held it together like she did. All Eunice said was, 'I'll be in the chapel, praying for his soul.' She'd been an army wife for years so maybe that helped."

Grace shuddered at the memory of the constant worry she had lived with during that period. Every time dispatches arrived at the fort, she had dreaded bad news about James.

She cut a length of twine to use as candle wick, and found

herself thinking out loud. "Maybe that unmoored James. They had served together many years. Lieutenant Turner was a steadying hand."

But Grace knew this wasn't the whole story. Something else had happened, but she didn't know what. You didn't get discharged from the army for no reason, not when you'd served faithfully for more than a decade. She'd tried asking, but he would get cross, tell her she wouldn't understand. *Shouldn't* understand. This painful distance between them was not what she'd expected from married life.

She gave the wax a stir. It bothered her that Margaret shared the uneasy feelings she sometimes felt around James. "I'll try to speak to him. This is your home. You need to feel comfortable, especially in your condition."

Margaret smiled dreamily as her hand went to stroke her belly.

Grace cut another length of twine. "How you feeling?"

"Better, now the sickness is passing. And little Gracie only wants a nighttime feed, so that's less wearying." Gracie seemed to recognize she was being spoken about and put her arms out to her mother. Margaret swung her onto her hip. "And you? I'm surprised you haven't started a family yet."

Grace concentrated determinedly on dipping the first wick into the wax and hanging it to cool. It was hard enough having Gracie tottering around the cabin, pulling herself up to her feet, balancing for a moment and plopping back down on her bottom. She was adorable, and every time Grace looked at her she felt a mixture of warmth and pain. To find Margaret was expecting another child produced yet more complex feelings. She wanted to be pleased for her sister-in-law. She *was* pleased. But she was also horribly jealous of her fecundity, the ease with which Zachary and Margaret were growing their family.

"Not happened yet. One time I'd taken. But..." A waxy twine slipped to the floor because Grace had not balanced it properly over the stick. She tutted angrily. "But a little while later, I lost it."

Margaret gave Grace a little hug with her free arm, but Grace wished she wouldn't.

"Your time will come," she said, gently.

Grace wanted to snap that it was easy for her to say, with a toddler on her hip and another baby on the way. She chided herself that she should be more generous to her sister-in-law, who had shown them nothing but kindness. She didn't want to push her away, but was relieved when the men came in for coffee and a bite to eat, distracting her from the emptiness she felt inside.

Randolph paced the area that would become the next room. "But, Zachary, the footings aren't deep enough to start on the walls yet."

"They're plenty deep enough." Zachary stood with his legs apart. "They're the same as for the rest of the cabin."

"But if the weather gets real bad, the building will be weak." Randolph fought a surge of irritation that rose up in him at the man's short-sightedness.

Zachary tucked his thumbs under his belt. "Not been a problem so far. And I've lived in Oregon four years now."

"And they won't support walls made of such thick wood."

"Then maybe you shouldn't have chosen trees so big, Mr. Randolph. Seems to me, you had something to prove."

Randolph grunted and adjusted his hat. "Don't be ridiculous."

He was aware that Tom sat on the log watching him. His eyes were big and brown, just like Grace's, and his hair had darkened to the same shade of chestnut-brown. Randolph was embarrassed by the increasing arguments with Zachary, particularly when they happened in front of Tom. He knew the boy struggled to work out where his loyalty lay. With both their parents dead, Zachary was now the head of the Sinclair family. He had taken Tom in and shown him this pioneer life. But Randolph had known the boy on the six-month wagon trail to get here: they'd come through the wilderness together. He respected the boy—even if Tom kept on calling him Captain.

Randolph's shoulders dropped. "I want it to be perfect for Grace."

"You suggesting I don't care about my own sister?" Zachary scowled at him.

He shook his head in exasperation. They were like stags in the forest, clashing their antlers. "'Course not."

"And it's not like you're gonna be here long anyway. This room will be for my little 'uns soon enough."

Would the man never stop talking about how many children he planned? Randolph had noticed how Grace delighted to play with little Gracie but would hand her back to Margaret with sadness in her eyes. Did she sometimes think, as he did, about how old their child would have been now, had the pregnancy lasted?

Zachary ruffled Tom's hair. "And Tom, of course. You've got a place here."

Tom ducked his head away, batting Zachary's hand. "You can leave me out of it."

Zachary picked up a mallet to strike the footings a little deeper into the ground. "You'll be building your own place, soon as the weather improves. Then you can dig your footings as deep as you like." He pummeled at a log. "But this is *my* house and what I say goes. And *I* say we're starting on the walls."

Randolph ground his teeth, but said nothing. They wouldn't be here for ever. Although he was at a loss to know where their future lay.

THREE

The warm April weather aired their new room. James had made a rudimentary bed from planks and leather straps, and Grace had sewn a mattress from canvas and stuffed it with straw.

Grace watched James trying to help Zachary around the farm. It was painful seeing him struggle with some of the tasks her brother accomplished with ease. He had been a captain in the army, led men into battle, and escorted many pioneers to safety over a two-thousand-mile journey. But she knew he was not faring well, sometimes unable to keep his attention on being a farmhand. She found it hard to see him so diminished.

Maybe they needed to get out from under her brother's wing. She had dropped hints about them finding their own patch of land to farm. She wanted to remain close to her family, and the soil here was deep and fertile. But it frustrated her that James avoided the discussion. If they didn't do something soon, they would miss the growing season. Why was he so reluctant to make a commitment? If he hadn't wanted to try farming, why had they come here?

. . .

Once every two months, Zachary would ride north up the long Willamette Valley to Oregon City and trade whatever they had produced, buying things they couldn't make. This time, he took the pelts from the beavers and otters that flourished in the rivers. The journey took more than a week, as he caught up on news of other settlers. The number of incomers grew every trip and yet the wide valley had plenty to share.

Grace was out front when she spotted Zachary returning, and shouted to the others that she could see him coming up the valley. The shadows were long as the sun slipped below the mountains to the west, and the land was bathed in golden light. Zachary stood in the saddle and took off his hat to wave back. He urged his horse up to the homestead, two mules tied behind him, each laden with bags.

Tom took care of the horse as Zachary bounded up the steps to greet his wife with a kiss. Grace helped James unload the mules, intrigued to see what her brother had brought back this time.

"Whoa," said Zachary, as James unstrapped a large sack. "Something extra special in this one. I'll get it myself."

He carefully carried the bag into the cabin and laid it on the table.

"Now, no one touches this 'til I'm good an' ready."

Tom dived into untying the other packages. Margaret ran her hands over bolts of cotton and calico. Grace opened the carton of coffee beans, a bitter smell filling the air. Tom unfolded a brown paper packet and grinned as he sniffed the block of sugar, handing little Gracie the paper to play with. Even James picked up the new saw, admiring the quality of the steel.

When everything had been unwrapped and stowed away, attention turned to the final parcel on the table.

"I got two special things left." Zachary grinned like the cat that got the cream. "Maggie, you open this one. Careful now."

The parcel was about two feet each side. Grace caught the sparkle in Margaret's eye and was pretty sure she knew what was inside. But Margaret played along with the game, unwrapping the canvas, then the brown paper wrapping, and finally the wool that kept the object protected.

"Oh my!" said Margaret. "Another window."

Zachary seemed even taller as he proudly stood to pick it up and held it to the wall. "This one will go in our bedroom. Just you wait. We'll have a window in every room, one of these days."

Grace admired the window. It was made of a wooden frame with a cross in the middle to support the four squares of thick glass. Zachary made it clear that they were the first in the area to have this luxury.

"You said there were two special things?" Grace asked.

Zachary went to his leather case. "Now, I usually bring the *Fort Vancouver Herald*. I know how y'all love to know the news. But I couldn't resist this one instead."

He laid out a newspaper on the table. *The Californian*.

"Everyone was talking about it. Rumor has it, they've struck gold in California."

They all leaned in closer on the table so they could learn more. Grace was pleased that James's attention was captured, and she pushed the paper to him so he could take the lead.

He read out the headlines on the front page, but there was no news of gold. It was mostly notices of goods delivered by ships: china, ale, chocolate, nails, butcher knives. He raised an eyebrow at Zachary.

"Turn the page," said Zachary, grinning. "There at the bottom. Read it out loud."

James cleared his throat. "Gold mine found. In the newly made raceway of the sawmill recently erected by Captain Sutter, on the American Fork, gold has been found in considerable quantities."

"What's that mean?" asked Tom.

"I think it means a fork of the American River," said James. "A raceway is a channel for water to drive the mill."

Grace gave him a gentle nudge. "Keep reading."

"One person brought thirty dollars' worth to New Helvetia, gathered there in a short time. California, no doubt, is rich in mineral wealth; great chances here for scientific capitalists. Gold has been found in almost every part of the country." He sat up and pushed the paper into the center of the table.

"Is that all there is?" asked Grace, pulling the paper to her to read it again.

Zachary nodded. "All that's in the paper. But people at Oregon City were saying ships are already getting waylaid."

"Surely it can't be true," said Grace, glancing at James to see what he thought. "Wouldn't it have been on the front page? Rather than tucked away next to stories about... escaped prisoners, and grizzly bears eating people."

"It's all there in black and white." Zachary tapped his finger on the article.

"What do you think, Mr. Randolph?" asked Margaret.

James rubbed at his beard. "I think it's mighty strange that the Spanish were in California for more than a hundred years and found nothing. The Spanish had a nose for silver and gold. The United States has owned California for, what, a couple of weeks? And suddenly there's gold lying around everywhere."

"You mean they're tricking people into going there?" asked Margaret.

James shrugged. "Who knows?"

"Well, all I can say"—Zachary leaned back in his chair—"is there's some folks on the Columbia River already preparing to go." He folded the paper. "Now, where's that supper I been looking forward to all day?"

. . .

Grace lay with her head on James's shoulder, snuggled in their small room. After the newspaper had been put away, he'd barely said a word all evening. Granted, that was not unusual over recent months, but Grace could tell he was musing on something. He lay on his back, studying the logs that made the roof.

"What's on your mind?" she ventured. "California?"

He paused. "What if it *is* true? It might draw people from all over. What if we got there, ahead of the crowds?"

"But... what about us starting a farm? Here, in the Willamette?"

He tutted. "Grace, I'm not a farmer. You've always known that. The last few months have proved it."

She bit her lip to hold back the sadness of hearing him confirm what she already knew, deep down. Still, he'd refused to have an honest talk for months, and she wasn't going to let him clam up again, now.

"But you're not a miner either. So how *are* we going to live?"

She didn't dare mention that there was no army pension, despite his years of service. Whatever had happened in Mexico had ended all chance of that.

He stroked her arm, but Grace felt it was more absent-minded than tender. "I don't know. But if we had some capital, we could take our time. *Choose* what we want next. Where to live. *How* to live."

It was on the tip of Grace's tongue to say she knew exactly what she wanted next: children and somewhere safe to raise them. But it was hardly James's fault that she had failed to fall pregnant. And she lived in hope that things might change.

"Thirty dollars doesn't sound much though, James. That's what it said the man earned, in the newspaper."

"It said the man earned thirty dollars *in a short time*. That's the important thing. And it said they were finding gold in almost every part of the country."

"It feels like a gamble to me. And I don't like gambling."

James shifted so he could lie on his side and look at her in the shadows. "I knew soldiers who had fought the Mexicans in California. Said it was a beautiful place. Good climate."

"There's good weather here in Oregon. And it's beautiful."

He snorted. "Dear God, it hasn't stopped raining since we arrived in January."

"James, that's not true."

He put out his hand in the dark and laid his palm on her cheek. "They said California is warm, but not hot and dry like further south."

At that moment, Grace longed for somewhere warm. She was sure she'd spent months with clothing and bedding never quite drying out.

But it was more complicated than the climate. There were other things she wanted. "What about Tom? Would he come?"

James scratched his beard. "I think he's too young. His height makes us forget he's still only twelve."

Grace searched for James's blue eyes in the darkness, but he seemed to be looking beyond her. She couldn't help but say what was in her heart. "I don't know if I could bear to be parted from him again. You know how close we became, when it was just him and me."

"Well, you could stay here and I'll go alone." He spoke slowly, but each word seemed a punch in her gut.

"Is that what you want?" The tightness in Grace's throat made her voice husky.

"Maybe better that way."

Grace turned over so he couldn't see the tears that were threatening. How could he be so cruel? She'd promised to always be at his side, and had done her best, even though it meant leaving her family. The only thing that had separated them was war, leaving her alone and anxious at Fort Leavenworth.

Now he wanted to leave her again. Didn't he know that she would endure any hardship, so she could be with him?

After a while, in the darkness, James put his hand on her shoulder.

"Grace," he whispered. "I'm sorry. That was thoughtless of me. It sounds like I'm making you choose between me and your brothers."

She needed to know the truth, even if it hurt. "But do you *want* to go to California alone?"

"There's no place on earth that isn't made better by having you there." His voice was thick with emotion. "But it's gonna be hard. If gold was just lying around, it would have been found by now."

She made fists under the blanket where he couldn't see. "You know hardship doesn't scare me."

He laughed softly. "True. The woman prepared to set off alone on a six-month wagon train is scared by very few things." He put his arm around her. "If it works out, we can write to Tom. It will be his choice if he wants to stay here, or join us."

For once, she didn't soften at his touch. She lay stiffly with her back to him. "And if it doesn't work out?"

"Then we'll come back."

Grace knew the decision had already been made and nothing she said would change it. She let out an angry breath and pulled the blanket higher, so she could pretend to sleep.

As the minutes passed, she began to wonder if he was right. Maybe the decisive captain was coming back. The man who had been dismissed from the army was very different from the captain who had led that overland expedition of wagons. Maybe searching for gold in California was what he needed: something to strive for once more.

But there was no way she was going to let him leave her behind. Not this time.

FOUR

Grace knew Tom would be dismayed when James told the family they were going to try their luck in California. Zachary didn't seem surprised though, and soon started working out the best way to get there. Probably the quickest route was to go north to the Columbia River, and then take the first ship south. James didn't like the uncertainty of how much passage would cost and she agreed: they had little money and prices may have already soared.

"In that case, it's the Siskiyou Trail to the south," said Zachary. The old trail was used by the Hudson Bay Company trappers—not that there were many fur trappers left.

James took a day to ride over to a farm further down the Valley where Zachary knew the farmer had driven several hundred head of cattle north from California last year. He returned with three pages of maps and notes, and the possibility that the farmer would go search for gold himself.

"It's like a fever," Margaret said. "One person passes it to the next."

The farmer had said the Siskiyou Mountains seemed to be

just about the only ones in North America that ran east to west: the path was winding and unsuitable for a wagon.

James said, "I told him this was no problem for me and my wife. We're used to traveling by horseback."

The next discussion was about kit. Grace checked the canvas tent that had served them so well since James's dismissal from the army. She looped rope of different thicknesses, cleaned their little oil stove, and aired their bedding rolls.

Tom sat with her in the barn and helped her clean the firearms made by their gunsmith father: an exquisite pair of pistols and a rifle with a true aim.

"Why can't I come with you?" he asked.

Grace had feared this conversation ever since she had told him their plans. "We don't know what to expect."

"But we didn't know what to expect when we traveled overland."

It was a good point, which she did her best to counter. "We knew Zachary was already in Oregon, and that lots of people had taken wagons on the trail."

Tom continued polishing for a while but then asked again about coming with them.

"We'll be back soon, with pots of gold," Grace tried to joke, but inside she was aching.

"But what if you want to stay in California?"

He paused and looked directly at her. Grace thought she could see tears gathering in his eyes. She ducked her head down as she pushed the bore rod to clean the barrel, so Tom couldn't see the sadness on her face. "Then we'll write, and you can decide if you want to join us."

Tom sniffed, seeming to understand this was the best he was going to get, and became pensive.

. . .

No one knew what gold mining would require, but Zachary was sure it would need a good set of tools, and was generous with his equipment. He insisted they take the new saw, as well as an axe, shovel, hammer, and a good supply of nails.

"You need all this. I'll replace it next time I'm in Oregon City."

Margaret was equally generous with food. She parceled up flour, dried beans, dried meat, and sugar. She ground plenty of coffee beans. "Who knows when you'll find a grinder again."

The harmony was short-lived and Grace was dismayed when the discussion over payment almost turned into an argument. Zachary thought James and Grace would need to keep every dollar they had. "You can send me payment once you're rich."

James said he couldn't accept charity.

Grace was relieved to see Tom keeping the peace, encouraging the two men to take the middle path, with James making a part payment, and signing a promissory note to pay the balance in the future.

Within a couple of days, they were ready to leave. Grace pushed down her sadness at leaving her brothers again, and told herself to be pleased that her husband was taking action for the first time since he had returned from Mexico.

Grace hugged each of the family in turn, wishing Margaret an easy confinement and Zachary an abundant harvest. She picked little Gracie up high and blew on her tummy, making the child giggle. Finally, and with a heavy heart, she hugged Tom, who put his gangly arms around her awkwardly to return the hug.

"Write me," he said when he knew no one else could hear. "You promise."

Grace nodded, kissed his cheek, knowing that if she tried to speak, she might not be able to hold back the tears that threatened. After one last rub of Kane's ears, she mounted her horse, a mule attached by a rope, once more laden with everything she owned. It was just as when they had arrived, only then it was in the cold and dark of January, and now it was a warm April morning.

She slapped her reins to urge her horse to follow James as he set off south, heading for the mountains at the end of the Willamette valley.

A week later, they were in the mountains, and the pain of riding away from her family was diminishing. Grace's spirits rose, as they traveled the stony path, taking them along river valleys and up over mountain passes where they could see pristine snow nestled in dips near the top of the highest peaks. They were surrounded by tall, straight fir trees of many shades of green, some with branches firm like arrows, others with branches looping as if they were dancing.

The air was alive with birdsong. During the day, she heard chickadees and nuthatches; at night, it was screech owls. They forded rivers full of salmon and rainbow trout. She loved following her husband's comfortable swaying gait on horseback. She was getting used to seeing him in his brown jacket and pale buff hat, rather than the dark blue from his time in the army. He seemed more at ease than he had been for months. Maybe that's what time in this wilderness did for you. At night, they lay close to keep each other warm, limbs entwined, luxuriating in the sensation of skin on skin.

During the second week, James suggested Grace shoot something for supper. One of the first things he had discovered about her when they'd met on the Oregon Trail, was her unusual skill with a gun. She put her exceptionally good aim down to the superior construction of her weapons—handmade by her father. But James often told her she was as good as any man, even with a standard-issue rifle, and she was secretly proud of his admiration.

Grace stalked and killed a black-tailed deer, which James butchered on a flat stone downriver of the camp he had set up, in case the carcass attracted bears.

Back on the path some days later, they met a group of Klamath people traveling north. Grace had never been able to shake off all those stories she'd been told as a child, that they would kill white men and steal the women and children. But James put up his hand in greeting, and spoke a few words in two of the native languages he had picked up.

He was met with blank looks and Grace wondered again at the wisdom of her husband's persistence in trying to communicate with them. They seemed to be a family group with women and children, which made her less anxious. One of the men dismounted and took a package of smoked fish from his pack. James accepted this token, and followed suit, taking a small packet of tobacco from his knapsack. He presented it to the man, who smiled and nodded as if to say it was a good gift.

To her relief, James and the Klamath man mounted their horses and the groups passed each other. She surreptitiously looked at the unfamiliar features and clothing and turned to watch them work their way northwest, before she followed her husband south.

After three weeks of traveling, the mountains gave way to hills and the valleys widened. Each day, Grace felt a little warmer as the sun shone harder. Mount Shasta loomed in the distance to the southeast, its many ridges covered in snow and ice. James rode on, keeping it to their left, entering hilly territory once more, thick with trees and fast-running rivers.

Her spirits soared as finally the land opened up and they were on the wide California plain. When they reached a small town called Leodocia, James asked if she wanted a night in the guesthouse and she gratefully said yes.

She took off her hat and scarf as the owner eyed James warily. "I can guess where you're headed."

"Many come through recently?" James asked.

"Trickle to begin with. Beginning to be a stream now." The man eyed Grace. "Don't see many women though."

James stepped closer to her and asked if the proprietor had any recommendations for where they should start their prospecting.

"Can't say I do. They tell me it all started south, where the American River joins the Sacramento. If you find anything, maybe you can come back and tell me. I'd be happy to join you."

Progress was quicker on the flat plain. Grace saw the foothills of the Sierra Nevada mountains coming into view to the east. They were tempted to leave the trail, strike out up a river and take their chances, but in the end, James decided to push on to New Helvetia, the place mentioned in the newspaper article, and find Captain Sutter.

More than a month after leaving Oregon, Randolph led the way, as they disembarked from a Sacramento River ferry. At last, he was getting closer to finding a means of making enough money to give Grace some security. They were surrounded by men—young and old, smart and disheveled. He was on high alert and kept Grace close as they rode the final few miles to Sutter's Fort, along with a dozen other prospectors.

The fort was by far the most substantial building Randolph had seen on their journey. He ran a professional eye over the high walls, the square bastions at each corner, and the heavy wooden gates which led to a wide yard, milling with people and animals. It reminded him of forts he'd seen in Mexico.

Inside, the yard was dominated by a two-story-high building with a tiled roof, its walls whitewashed and gleaming in the late-afternoon sun. A set of cannons stood testament to the fort's defensive function, but he thought they looked as if they hadn't been moved for years. Around the edge of the yard were workshops and stalls. He heard the metal clang of an iron forge, mules groaning as they pulled a grist stone in one corner, grinding wheat for flour. A woman banged blankets into shape. Yes, things were happening here.

A portly man appeared at the top of the steps which led from the upper floor of the main building. Perhaps in his midforties, he wore a straw hat, which he took off and waved at the newcomers. "Aha! The newest crew of argonauts, here to pluck gold from this beautiful land." His accent was European.

As Randolph approached, he could see the man had a cast in his left eye, and only his right seemed fixed on them. He had a well-tended mustache with a small triangle of hair below his lower lip.

"Welcome to my fort, the beating heart of New Helvetia."

The rest of the group looked to Randolph to take the lead as the man came down the steps. Was this the famous owner of the fort? He had expected someone more authoritative, less like a jovial favorite uncle. "Captain Sutter?" he asked.

"The very one!"

"I'm Mr. Randolph, and this is my wife. And, well..." He looked round at the other men and then back at Sutter. "As you say, you know why we're here. What do we do now? Where do we go?"

Sutter set his features to look mournful. "My clerk will take payment to arrange quarters for some of you, but, as you can see, my fort is *exceptionally* busy. Most of you will need to shift for yourselves outside the magnificent walls of this edifice."

Randolph was inclined to save their limited funds and sleep in their tent, but glancing at Grace, he could tell how weary she was. She would usually be excited by seeing a new place, but she had said hardly a word about the fort. He wondered if she was still sad about leaving Oregon. Maybe he should ask her.

He took off his hat and banged it on his thigh. The least he could do for her was pay for what might be their last chance to rest under a proper roof for many months.

That evening, Sutter invited Randolph and Grace to join him for supper. Randolph knew that, in earlier times, this would have been an honor accorded to him as a fellow captain. He was under no illusion that now it was the dark eyes and trim figure of his beautiful young wife that elicited the invitation. Still, their future depended on making this search for gold successful. He was eager to learn whatever he could from the famous Captain Sutter, the man who had first found gold in California.

FIVE

The food was plentiful and tableware extravagant: china plates, silver cutlery, bronze candelabras. Although Randolph was eager to gain intelligence, he started with general pleasantries.

"Where did you serve, Captain Sutter?"

Sutter waved a hand as if incorporating wide spaces. "I have traveled the world, serving in many places."

"And where did you become a captain?"

"Ah, that was in the Swiss Guard."

Randolph paused cutting his meat and raised his eyebrows. "That is... unexpected." His recollection was that the Swiss Guard were purely a militia to protect the pope.

"It is my native land. And I fought in France. I have sailed the high seas, even spent some time in the Sandwich Islands." Sutter glanced at the man serving them and leaned closer to Randolph. "I brought some of the Native fellows with me, when I sailed to California. They are *excellent* workers, when disciplined properly."

"You do not have any family?" asked Grace.

Sutter shifted in his chair. "No, no family. At least, not *here*." Sutter waved his hand in that same vague way. "There is family back in Switzerland. One day I'll send for them. Once things settle here."

Randolph thought things looked very settled for Sutter, with a whole fort to his name, and, the ferryman had told him, generous tracts of land given him by the Mexican Consul General.

"How did you know where to look for gold?" Grace asked when the conversation faltered.

Sutter laughed. "My dear lady, I didn't. I wasn't *looking* for it. And if you want my opinion, you are best not going searching for it either. It will slip through your fingers, trust my words." He pointed at Randolph with his knife. "Now, *agriculture*. That is what you should be investing in. I will take you to my orchards tomorrow."

The last thing Randolph wanted was to visit farmland the next day. "So how did you find the gold, if you weren't looking for it?"

Sutter leaned back in his chair, enjoying the chance to tell the tale once more. "I have great plans for this region. Soon I will build Sutter Town. But that takes timber, and plenty of it. We are blessed with good straight trees up in the mountains, so I thought"—he tapped his nose—"construct a sawmill there. On the American River. So, I sent my best man, James Marshall, and he spent some months doing a splendid job. In January, Mr. Marshall gets the men to dig a channel for the water to flow to the mill and one day he spies a yellow nugget in the silt. He picks it up and thinks aha! But Marshall, he is not so foolish to run around crying, gold! There are many minerals that look the same. So he takes it back to their cabin and puts it on the table. Jenny picks it up—"

"Jenny?" Grace was startled to hear a woman's name.

"Jenny Wimmer. She was cooking for the gang. Not a nice woman. Very headstrong. Well, Jenny pops it into her soap kettle and heats it up. In no time at all, out comes the nugget, gleaming even brighter. No doubt about it. Gold." Sutter topped up his glass before continuing. "The next day, all thoughts of constructing the sawmill are forgotten and every man is up to his knees in the American River, searching for more of the stuff. Which, of course, they found.

"Being a sensible chap, Marshall brought the gold straight to me. We sat at this very table, testing it. My, that was quite a day." He sat back in reverie.

Randolph glanced at Grace and gave a polite cough. "So what would you recommend? Where should we go to find it?"

Sutter looked surprised at being asked this. "Recommend?"

"What equipment do we need to take?" Randolph persisted.

"Mr. Randolph." Sutter smoothed his striped waistcoat over his barrel-like stomach. "I have *no* idea. I am leaving all that to others. I need to keep an eye on my interests here. I am already plagued with thieves and vagabonds. They think nothing of staking a claim without even asking my permission."

Randolph tried to hide his disappointment. "So, you have no advice for us?"

"As I say: *farming*. That's where the money is." Sutter relished another mouthful of wine. "Although I do have one piece of advice: don't get stuck in those mountains come winter. The snow comes in something terrible and then there's no getting out. You'll have heard of the poor Donner Party, no doubt?"

Grace shuddered. "Indeed, we have."

Randolph frowned and his grip tightened on his coffee cup. Why would Sutter raise the subject of this notorious incident in front of Grace? Two years previously, a party of overlanders had reached the eastern slopes of the Sierra Nevada mountains far too late in the year, and attempted to cross in winter. Half the party made camp, including all the women and children, while some of the men pushed on to find help. Few of the ones who had stayed behind survived. The stories of cannibalism had caused shock and fear across the West.

Sutter looked sadly at his empty glass. "I sent some good men to save those poor souls. And some of my best horses. Never was reimbursed for the outlay, you know."

Randolph was sick of Sutter's company and didn't want the pompous old man reminding Grace of such terrors. He stood and gave her a meaningful look, eager to say their farewells. He was grateful that she immediately understood, and got to her feet.

"Thank you for your generous hospitality, Captain Sutter," he said. "We will not forget it. But it is time we were abed. We plan to make an early start in the morning."

Grace stood at James's side outside Brannan's General Store. It was a substantial wooden structure—recently extended, if the new wood was anything to go by.

"Let's hope we find out some useful information here," James said, "and avoid being persuaded to buy equipment we don't need."

Grace followed her husband inside, taking in a store packed full of goods of every type. There were packets of foodstuffs: coffee, chocolate and spices. A box was printed with *Chyboongs celebrated curry powder*. Bottles of ale lay on top of mosquito netting made from hemp. As Grace stepped in further, she saw firearms gathered in the corner: rifles, pistols, guns old and new, many of them with fancy engraved detail.

A Spanish-looking woman was unpacking newly arrived boxes. She caught Grace's eye and seemed pleased to find a woman in the store. "*Señora*, you looking for something in particular?"

"I'm just..." Grace turned round slowly. "I don't think I've ever seen so many beautiful things in one place."

The woman winked at her. "Mr. Brannan ships it all up the Sacramento, straight off the boats at San Francisco. Men with gold in their pockets will buy most-like anything that catches their eye. Take that Mexican." She nodded to the counter at the far end of the building. A man with a fringed red-and-white cloth over one shoulder was being served by a tall man in a black hat.

Grace joined James watching the Mexican paying for a case of black silk handkerchiefs with gold dust. The man in the hat carefully weighed it. Grace's eyes widened: so it was true. There was gold to be found.

When the Mexican had left, the tall man introduced himself. "Samuel Brannan, at your service."

James politely shook his hand and Grace nodded to him.

"You look like new arrivals."

"Uh-huh."

"You'll need kitting out. I have everything you could need, right here." He bustled to the front of the counter and led them to the extensive array of picks, shovels and axes.

"We have some of this already," said James, his arms folded. Grace knew he was nervous about how long their money would last.

Brannan continued, undaunted. "First you need a pan." He put one on the counter. "Next: a shovel."

"Already got one."

"How big?"

"So big." James indicated with his hands.

"Ah." Brannan looked pleased. "You'll need a smaller one too. Bucket?"

James narrowed his eyes. "Which do you suggest?"

Brannan unhooked one and added it to the pile.

James held up a palm to Brannan. "Before you ask, I got an axe, saw and plenty of nails."

"All good for making stuff, sir. But you'll need a pickaxe like this for breaking up larger pieces of rock."

Grace looked skeptically at the growing pile of tools and wondered if they were being fleeced. She could tell from James's prickly responses that the same thought was going through his mind. But, last night, local folk had told James that Brannan knew his business—and there weren't any other options anyway.

"Now, what are you going to put your gold into?" Brannan asked.

James glanced at Grace, but she hadn't thought of this either.

Brannan took down a box from a shelf. "One of these strongboxes should keep it safe. Looks small, I know, but if you come back with that full, you'll be doing well. And one last thing. Scales."

"Scales?"

Grace knew that sharp tone meant James thought he was being fooled. She wished her husband might be a little warmer with Brannan, as they were still hoping he would give them much-needed practical advice.

"You need to keep track of how much you find. Most argonauts find it easier to work in teams. Then it's essential to weigh who's found what."

"Argonauts," Grace repeated. "That's the second time I've heard that name."

Brannan smiled at Grace. "Someone came up with it—seems to have stuck."

James settled the bill with the cash loaned by Zachary.

"Thing is, Mr. Brannan," Grace said, "my husband and I are still not sure what we're looking for."

"We had dinner with Captain Sutter last night and didn't learn much," James explained.

Brannan snorted. "That old fool? If he's a captain, then I'm the king of China."

James raised his eyebrows, and glanced at Grace, who caught his eye. He had said as much last night as they went to bed, and his instincts usually proved correct.

"He tried to sit on news of the find," said Brannan.

"Why would he do that?"

Brannan leaned closer to James. "So he could buy up all the land cheap, before word got out. Luckily, some of those men building the sawmill were Mormons and told me what's what."

"You're certainly doing well from it," said Grace, gathering their goods.

"Got to keep an eye out for a good business, ma'am."

"So tell me," said James, picking up the heaviest items, "we just go up any of the rivers and stake a claim?"

Brannan nodded to the door. "See that Mexican who just left?"

"Yeah."

"He'll be in the bar next door by now. Go buy him a drink and talk to him. He's got a real knack for it. Has lived in California a few years and has good English. Originally comes from the silver mines in Sonora, so I guess he knows what he's doing."

"Much obliged."

Grace picked up the strongbox and tucked it under her arm. It felt good and solid; she pictured it full of golden dust and nuggets, and felt a frisson of excitement run down her back. She hadn't wanted to come to California to begin with, but now she was here, she was darn well determined to make a success of it.

Randolph placed a whiskey in front of the Mexican. Grace had stayed outside the saloon, enjoying the sun and keeping watch on their animals and newly purchased equipment.

The Mexican nodded an acknowledgment, lifted the glass

and downed half of the gold liquid. His face was sunburned, but the long goatee beard was ash-white. He wore a generous cotton shirt, with a belt around the waist.

"I'm guessing you want to know about mining, *senor*."

Randolph sat down. "How do we know where to start panning? Or digging. There's a whole lot of mountain out there."

The Mexican looked Randolph in the eye, as if deciding whether to share his wisdom. Something made him decide to be generous. "You look at the rock above the river, for where the color changes. Like that." The man laid one hand horizontally above the other.

"You mean a seam?"

"That's right. Where the bottom level is a lighter gray."

Randolph nodded his encouragement.

"And in the river—go where the bend is. Sometimes the gold, it gathers behind a rock. Or even a tree stump at the edge of the water."

"And then?"

"Dig there. You shovel dirt into your pan, rock it with some water." He took a plate which had the remains of dinner still on it, and showed Randolph the movement. "Thing is, gold is much heavier than the dirt. It stays in the bottom of your pan, after you've washed everything else away."

"Much obliged. And should we go south? Looks like where most are headed."

The Mexican shook his head. "I'd gamble on going north. More likely to find virgin river. Ride for a day or so, then head east up a river.

"What's the name of the tribespeople up there?" Randolph asked.

"That's the Nisenan."

Randolph tried out the name. "What are they like?"

The Mexican prevaricated. "Mostly peaceable. Until more of you Americans started showing up. Sutter made things a whole lot worse. But you should have no bother, staking a claim."

"And how do we do that? Stake a claim, I mean."

The Mexican downed what remained of the whiskey and Randolph signaled to the barman to bring another. At last, he had found someone who knew what he was talking about.

"You get there first, it's yours. You mark out the area you want with stones or stakes. Put up a sign if you can. Then, as long as you're mining it, it's yours."

"And if we leave?"

"You're gonna get claim jumpers. Not much you can do about that. Ain't no law around here. No one knows who's in charge. Certainly isn't the Mexicans no more. Nor the Californians." He gave a dismissive shrug. "You Americans say you're in charge, but I don't see it."

"Isn't Captain Sutter responsible for law and order?"

The Mexican grimaced and spat on the ground. "*Escoria*. He shouldn't be in charge of a flock of hens. Evil, he is."

Randolph sat back, surprised by the vehemence of the man's response. "I'll keep that in mind." Randolph wiped a hand over his face. He didn't see any Americans in charge either, and it worried him. "You say there's no law around here. I have my wife with me. Is it safe for her?"

The Mexican stroked at his long goatee, pulling it through his palm. "Keep her close, and you should be alright. She won't be the only wife out there prospecting; one or two other miners have brought them. It's gold that is driving men crazy."

This wasn't of much comfort. Randolph wondered whether he should have insisted Grace stayed in Oregon until things were settled. But he'd married a determined woman: that was why he had fallen in love with her. He laughed softly to himself at the idea of insisting on Grace doing something she was dead-set against. She was here now, and he would take the advice to keep her close.

SIX

Randolph led the way, retracing their steps north up the Sacramento Valley for a couple of days, before heading east upriver. It had taken more than a month on horseback to get here since he'd first read about the gold find, and he finally felt close to success. He wasn't sure what their future would hold, but sometimes, in the quiet of the hills, he would find himself thinking about a safe home somewhere with Grace and the child she longed for. He would close his eyes for a minute and allow himself to picture it, and it pushed the dark thoughts of Mexico from his mind.

As they rode alongside the river early one afternoon, they passed an argonaut and Randolph stopped to study him to learn how to handle a pan.

"Any luck?" Randolph called.

The miner whooped. "You betcha."

"What's this place called?"

"Grass Valley."

"We're thinking of heading further upriver."

The man waved them on. "Plenty for everyone."

Randolph hoped some of that optimism would rub off on them.

He dug his heels into his horse's flank to urge it on faster. They worked their way into hills covered in ponderosa pine, oaks and cedars. He studied the banks of the river, looking for changes in color in the rock. They came to a peaceful spot at the bend of a river.

"How about here?" he called back to Grace.

"Looks as good a place as any to find our fortune."

They dismounted. "Set up camp first, or panning?" he asked.

Grace stroked his beard with her fingertips before going on tiptoes to kiss his cheek. "We're a team. You start panning. I'll do the camp."

Randolph smiled to himself, grateful to have his wife by his side. He took the pan and hand-shovel, and strode down to the bend on the river. This was it: his first attempt at building their fortune and a better future together. He dug the shovel into the dirt of the streambed and dropped it into the pan, then filled it with water and swirled the pan, as he had watched the other miners do. Most of the water sloshed out, leaving the pan still full of dirt.

He tried again, this time managing to let the lighter soil wash over the edge but leaving most of the water. This was a skill it was going to take time to master.

He tried a third time. The dirt at the bottom of the pan diminished until it was just a layer of slurry. He ran his fingers through the remains, looking for the glint of gold. Nothing. He smiled at his own eagerness. He was hardly likely to hit pay dirt on his first attempt.

Randolph threw the sludge away and started with a fresh shovelful.

. . .

Grace went to the riverbank, a metal mug of coffee in each hand. She watched her husband concentrating on his task, slowly moving his body as he swirled the water in the pan, then throwing away the dregs when he found nothing.

"D'you want to take a break?" she called. "I've got coffee here."

Randolph looked up and grinned. She hadn't seen that broad smile for a long time. He climbed up out of the water to sit by her on the grassy bank.

"How is it?" she asked.

"Cold. And my back is gonna ache at the end of the day." He took a sip of coffee and looked at her. "But I ain't complaining." He lay down and gazed at the sky. "Who could complain, lying in this valley, listening to the river running. His wife beside him."

He put out his arm in invitation and she lay down next to him, putting her head on his shoulder. He kissed the top of her head, and she wondered if Grass Valley was bringing back his tender side.

"Say, why don't you turn over and I'll rub your back."

He rolled onto his front and laid his head on the backs of his hands, watching her.

She pulled his shirt free from the top of his pants and slipped her hand onto his back, massaging the strong muscles. He gave a moan of pleasure.

After a while, he spoke softly. "I know it's not been easy for you. But this is the start of something new. I know... I know you wanted little ones, by now—"

She stilled her hand and took it from under his shirt. He had never spoken of this before. "Don't *you* want them? I thought we both..." She let her words fall, fearful of the possibility that he might have changed his mind.

There was a silence. He moved himself onto his elbows. "Of

course I do—and yet what sort of cruel world are we bringing children into?"

Was this what was bothering him? She tried to choose her words carefully. "I know there's cruelty. But there's kindness as well. People who want to help and to share. Like... like the Mexican. And that miner down the valley."

James made a sound in his throat, something between a grunt and a moan, and turned round so he was sitting, his feet on the grass, staring at the river. "But we have no way to *know* who is kind and who is cruel. The placid man can turn into a monster, given the circumstances." He picked up a stone and threw it into the river. "Some men can commit unspeakable terrors."

Grace's mind raced. How quickly his purposeful, happy mood had darkened, as if a cloud had passed over the sun. Was he finally going to be open with her? She knelt beside him and put her hand on his shoulder.

"Why won't you speak of it, James? Of whatever happened." He moved his shoulder to shake her off, but she pushed on. "If you could *share* it with me, maybe I could help? Maybe... take some of the burden."

He dropped his head and shook it slowly. Wordlessly, he got to his feet, picked up his hat, and made his way back to the riverside.

Grace turned face down on the grass and silently pummeled it. There he'd been, affectionate and calm, even willing to mention children. And she'd gone and reminded him of whatever it was that had haunted him since returning from the Mexican war. Could she never get it right? What sort of wife was so insensitive?

Grace washed the mugs and tended the fire but was at a loss for what to do next. She wondered about taking her rifle and finding food, but she didn't know the area yet. Perhaps there was a native tribe who would be alarmed by gunfire.

She let out a sigh of frustration. She had to do something to make things right with James.

She wandered down to the bank: the river was wide and shallow. Although the trees on the hillsides were substantial, here in the valley bottom the trunks were thin and delicate. With the sound of the water running over the rocks, James hadn't heard her approach.

"Can I have a try?" she called softly.

James stood and arched his back. "Don't see why not."

"Show me how it's done."

"Me?" he scoffed. "I haven't found the smallest speck of dust yet." He turned and smiled.

"Give it time."

She looped up her skirt so it wouldn't get wet, and he put his hand out to help her into the shallows of the water.

"You put a shovel load of dirt in like this. Not too much, mind. Then hold the pan like this."

After he demonstrated, he handed it over. She held each side of the pan; it was heavier than expected.

"Dip it in the river," James instructed.

The water was cold as it flowed over her hands and into the pan.

"Now, swirl it around."

She tried, but a whole pile of dirt flew over the edge.

He chuckled. "Like this." He stood behind her and put his arms around, his hands over hers, holding the pan. He swayed it rhythmically to move the water around.

He paused and rested his head against hers.

"I'm sorry about before," he whispered. "It's just... there are things I should protect you from. Not... giving you my burden."

She stood completely still. "You know I love you, don't you? No matter what you've seen or done."

"Yes. I know." He kissed the back of her neck. "And you know I love you, too. No matter what I've seen or done."

He put his arms around her waist and lifted her from the water. She shrieked and he let her back down.

He laughed. "Now, let's see if we've found pay dirt."

She swirled the pan once more but moved it too far and sloshed water onto James's pants. He jumped back, crying out in mock horror.

She turned to him, almost losing her balance. "You're soaked," she giggled.

He wiped his pants with his hands, having no effect. "Never mind. It won't take long to dry off. Keep going."

She swirled her pan until nothing was left, feeling a little disappointed that they hadn't magically conjured gold, through the power of their love.

Grace gave the pan back to him. "Maybe we should have bought one each from Mr. Brannan."

"I daresay we can take turns." He surveyed the stretch of river. "I'm going to try further round the bend."

Although she was pleased they had restored peace, Grace was quietly grateful to get out of the cold water and leave him to it. She returned to the beginnings of their camp and took her sewing kit from her saddlebag. There was a seam on one of James's shirts that needed repairing.

Grace had drifted asleep on the grass when a shout jerked her awake. She immediately looked to where her rifle was secured inside the tent.

"Hey! Grace."

It was James's voice that had roused her.

She stood and looked toward the river, where he was returning with the pan.

"You found something?" she called.

"I don't know. Come have a look."

She ran to him and peered in the pan. He swirled the bottom and she could hear a different note, not the squelch of mud or the thud of a small rock. This had the clink of metal. She saw a sparkle, a flash of yellow.

"No!"

He picked it out with his finger and thumb and placed it in her palm, a tiny pebble of gold. She wiped the remaining dirt from it, and it shone like the sun.

She stared at him, and James grinned. "I think it is, you know. Our first nugget of gold."

Grace squealed with excitement, jumping up and down like a child on its birthday. "What do we do with it? Where do we put it?"

"In my pocket, for now. Should be safe enough." James stowed it away and then picked her up off her feet and swung her round. "See? All it took was moving along the river a little."

The sun was setting over the hills.

"You're gonna have to stop sometime, James," Grace called. "We don't want to be eating supper in the dark."

Since finding the first tiny lump, James had continued to find flecks of gold and occasional nuggets, some larger than the first. He stored them in a leather pouch Grace had unpacked from their belongings.

He gathered his tools and strode back to the campsite. She watched him stacking the equipment neatly, thinking how his military training was still in place. As he threw himself down by the fire to warm himself, Grace spooned the bean and beef stew into a bowl. He ate fast and she was pleased to see his hearty appetite.

"So, we're staying here?" she asked.

James nodded. "First thing, we make it clear we've claimed this stretch."

"I can do that. I'll find a piece of wood to stand up, like those miners we passed."

"You sure?"

"You concentrate on panning. I'll fix up the camp." She gave him a cloth filled with chokeberries. "Look, I found these nearby. They're sweet."

He took a handful and closed his eyes. "Life is sweet, at the moment."

Grace smiled as she handed him a folded shirt and pants. "You really need to get out of those damp clothes. The air is getting cold."

She saw a glint in his eye, and a roguish smile.

"You know, honey, my fingers are so cold, I can't manage the buttons. You're gonna have to help me."

She bit her bottom lip and moved closer to him, undoing the top buttons of his shirt one by one, pulling the garment over his head. She was as captivated now by the clear definition of his muscles as she had been when they'd first made love.

He growled as her hands moved to the top of his pants and she pushed the first button free.

He tried to kiss her, but she ducked teasingly. "Maybe we should continue this inside the tent."

"There's no one for miles around," James replied.

"I'd feel more, well, private." She stood and he took her hand, letting her lead him into the tent where she had laid out their bedding rolls.

SEVEN

Grace was still half asleep as James got up at first light, the lure of finding more gold drawing him back to the river. She pulled herself out of the tent to light the fire and make a hearty breakfast. If he was going to work at this rate, he'd need plenty of fuel inside him.

When it was ready, she called to him to come back to the campsite for food. He ambled over the dewy grass, the morning sun behind him, and sat on a stool to eat.

"I think you should weigh it," James said, munching on bacon. "The gold I found yesterday."

"What, now?"

"Yes. That should be your responsibility."

She smiled at him. "I like the idea of that."

She unpacked the small brass scales they'd bought from Mr. Brannan and set them up. Carefully pouring the gold into one of the pans, she balanced it with the weights.

"That's... seven... no, eight ounces." She packed the dust and nuggets into the strongbox, and, fetching James's notebook, wrote the date and the weight. "How much is that worth?"

"Pfft. You know, I have *no* idea." James roared with laughter and strode off back to the riverbank, a spring in his step.

Today's important job was laying out their claim. Grace took the axe and searched in the nearby trees for a suitable log. Dragging it back, she chipped with the grain to make a smooth surface. Using a sharp knife, she carved the letters of their name, RANDOLPH, momentarily wishing her husband had a shorter moniker. She brushed charcoal from last night's fire into the lettering, and sat back to admire the result.

She took the shovel to where she judged was the center of their claim and dug a hole. Pushing the post vertical, she pressed soil around the bottom and gathered stones to keep it steady.

She stepped back, hands on her hips. James would have completed the job in half the time, but this was what working together was all about.

At midday, Grace asked James how far he wanted the claim to stretch. He measured it out in strides between two white oaks. She laid cairns of stones taken from the river. By the end of the day, her hands were grazed and the small of her back twinged, but she felt the satisfaction of a job well done.

After dinner, she settled down to weigh today's gold find. James showed her what he had gathered, and she was as excited as an infant being given a stick of sugar candy. It was even more than the day before, as James was getting the knack of panning effectively. Maybe they had made the right choice in coming here after all. She daydreamed of writing to Tom and sending the money they owed back to Zachary. Maybe things were going to get better now.

The next day, Grace paused her tidying of the campsite as a line of Nisenan passed their camp on horseback. Her breathing quickened as they stopped and watched James in the river. He calmly put down his tools and approached, Grace following, thinking the presence of a woman would show they wanted to be peaceable.

"Gold?" one of the Nisenan men asked James. Grace wondered how much English he spoke.

"Yes." James took off his hat and ran his fingers through his hair to push it back. "Say, Grace, why don't you get that pouch of tobacco from the tent?"

Grace hurried and returned with the pouch, which she put in James's hand. He walked to the man who had spoken and reached up to give it to him.

The Nisenan man smelled it and crumbled some in his fingers. "Good," the man confirmed.

"It's yours."

The man took out a canteen. "Water." He stretched out his arm toward James.

"You want some?" James asked and Grace caught his puzzled look.

"No. You drink this."

James took the canteen, put the opening to his mouth, and drank carefully. His eyes widened. "Hmm. That's good-tasting water."

The man nodded to Grace, indicating she should drink also.

She took the canteen from James and drank. My, the water was sweet and refreshing.

"The spring." The Nisenan man turned in his saddle. "There." He pointed to a gulley in the nearby hill.

James nodded. "Much obliged."

The man studied their campsite and shared a few words with his companions.

"This is a good place," he said, and the party rode on.

Grace stood still by James, watching them pick their way up the valley.

"They have given us a far greater gift than that tobacco I

offered," he said quietly. "A fresh water spring means we don't have to boil everything before we can drink. They've gifted us good health."

They got into a rhythm, Grace keeping the camp orderly, providing food, drying clothing, and James working his way along the river. By the evening, he was often so tired, he would go to bed early. Sometimes he sat up staring at the fire, and Grace was saddened that despite their good fortune, and the joy he seemed to take in his day's work, some evenings he would fall into a reverie, a mournful look in his eye. On those nights, he would stop speaking, and find comfort from a bottle of whiskey he had tucked away, and eked out, little by little.

Grace would take over sometimes during the day, giving James a break from the relentless panning—but neither of them were strangers to hard work.

Grace was frustrated, though. She wanted to contribute more, but they only had one pan. She had watched Randolph for a few days and over lunch shared her thoughts about the problem.

"You remember Mrs. Perriman's crib?"

James stopped eating and raised his eyebrows. "You mean the one she cried over because I said she had to leave it on the prairie?"

"Uh-huh." Grace was tentative. They rarely talked about their journey west, two years earlier.

"I thought you were crazy for rescuing it for her. Couldn't understand why you would take more weight in your wagon. But it was one of the first things that made me look at you differently." He gazed at her, lines appearing at the edges of his blue eyes.

She took his hand. "I want to help more with looking for

gold. I've been thinking how we can wash the dirt more quickly."

He stroked her palm with his thumb. "And?"

"If we had a machine, like a crib, where I could rock it to and fro—if there was a way of putting in the dirt and... pouring the water through. Using the bucket."

Saying it out loud, it sounded outlandish.

James frowned.

"It was just a thought..." Grace's voice faded and she took back her hand. Had she overstepped? Sometimes, even two years on, there were moments when she didn't know her husband's mind, especially since Mexico.

"No... I'm thinking, that's all." He threw the dregs from his coffee on the ground and put his tin mug on its side on the earth. "Something like this?" He pushed the cup back and forth.

"Yes. Somehow the water would need to get in."

"Hmm." He put his palms together and rested his fingers against his mouth while he studied the cup. "And there'd need to be something to stop the gold just flowing out at the end—"

"Like the footboard of a crib." She put her thumb across the open end of the mug.

"I see what you mean. But lower." He stood up and looked around the site. "What could we use?"

"What, now?" Grace asked in surprise.

He grinned and put out his hand to help her stand. "It's a good idea, my sweet. The sooner we can devise something, the sooner we can see if it works."

His enthusiasm warmed her, like the sun breaking through clouds. "Okay. The Perriman crib was made from planks of wood."

James scratched his beard and frowned. "I don't want to have to go back down the valley to buy planks. What if we made it from one big piece of wood. A tree trunk, I mean. We could hollow it out, like a canoe." He picked up the axe and saw. "Come on."

"But the dinner things are still out."

He waved his hand. "Leave them. Bring some rope."

She hurried to the tent. "Just let me get my boots on," she said, pulling on the laces. This was so unlike him to leave the camp disordered.

One of the advantages of the spot they had chosen was that it was surrounded by woods. She caught up with James studying different trees.

"What about using one that has already fallen?" she suggested.

"I don't want anything too rotten."

"How about this one though?" She pushed a tree trunk with her foot. It lay on its side, and must have been blown over in a winter storm.

James ran his hands over it. "Perfect."

He sawed a portion about three feet long, taking more than an hour to do so. Grace spent the time looking for berries and nuts to add to their food store. James tied a rope around the portion of trunk and together they hauled it back to camp.

Once there, Grace watched her husband hack at the log with his axe, standing back every so often to think about what was needed.

Grace tidied away the meal things. "Maybe I could carry on panning, while you work on the crib?"

James looked at the river. "We can take a break from making our fortune, just for one day. Lie there in the sun and listen to birdsong."

Grace laughed. What had got into him?

EIGHT

Every so often over the next day, Grace helped James take the half-finished crib to the river's edge to work out what to fix next. She wasn't best pleased when he said he would need one of the two metal plates.

"It's got to have a sieve of some sort to break up the dirt as it goes in at this end." He bashed the metal flat and stamped holes in it, before nailing it to the wooden frame.

The final job was to construct a channel at the edge of the stream to place it on. James then laid stones to support the crib.

They tried it out, but the water ran through too easily, taking all the silt with it. James sat on his haunches staring at it, before using narrow pieces of wood to run horizontally across the base to catch the gold. Grace could see how much James was enjoying solving each problem, and left him to it.

The next morning, James grabbed Grace's hand and took her to look at the new contraption. "Let's have another try."

They placed it on the stones in the river and James tipped the first pile of dirt in the top.

"Do you want to pour in the water?" he asked. "It's your invention."

She smiled. "I'd say it's a joint venture."

Grace poured in a bucket of water and rocked the device forward and back. When the water cleared, there was a thin layer of mud behind the pieces of wood. Over and again, James put in dirt and she the water.

"Let's see if this is working." James ran his fingers through the fine silt that had gathered behind the struts. It sparkled with gold. He grinned up at Grace. "I think we just found us a way to get gold dust."

Grace clapped her hands in joy and James kissed the top of her head.

After that, the little Randolph claim was much more productive, James continuing to pan, and often finding larger nuggets, while Grace worked the rocker. She marvelled at the golden earth that Providence had provided for them.

Over the summer months, there was a steady stream of men traveling further up the valley. They would always stop and stare, a woman being a novelty in those parts. Randolph wasn't sure whether to feel proud or concerned.

He would ask where folk were from. Men were arriving from all parts of the world: Chileans from the south, Russians from Alaska, Australians and Chinese who had crossed the Pacific. He would inquire about their country, and those with enough English would share a little about their homeland: how far away it was, whether it was mountainous or flat, hot or cold.

A trio of men from Sydney stopped and introduced themselves one afternoon. They seemed to have heard of him. One called over: "You must be the Lucky Miner."

Randolph stopped his work and approached. "We're doing alright. So will you, if you work hard."

"Wasn't meaning that. You're the only one in these parts with a good-looking woman caring for him."

"I'm not the only man who's brought his wife with him," Randolph replied, glancing over to where Grace was gutting a rabbit.

"That's true, but none of them is a pearler like yours."

The Australians moved on, leaving Randolph with an uncomfortable sensation. That evening, he checked all the firearms were primed. Just in case.

By early August, some food supplies were running low. Randolph was proud of how much meat Grace had provided through her skill with a rifle. He had sometimes taken a break to fish, but did not find it as calming as he used to, all the while wondering if gold was being carried past by the water. It was the flour and coffee beans that were depleting and Grace sometimes confessed to a longing for a cup of milk and a breakfast made with fresh eggs. Her happiness was everything to him. It was strange that they were sitting there with more riches than he could imagine, but their clothing was falling apart and they were rationing coffee.

Randolph was troubled by what would happen to their claim if they both left it. Even though the Mexican had said that leaving tools in place signaled to other argonauts that the claim was live when the miner was absent, Randolph was skeptical. Would all miners be honorable?

"I can stay," said Grace when they discussed it over dinner. "You know I can look after myself."

Yes, she could, but Randolph rubbed the back of his neck with his palm, uneasy at the prospect. "Let's sleep on it. We don't have to decide just yet."

The next morning, Grace told him she would take her rifle and see what she could hunt in the woods. Maybe a brace of pigeon would make a good change for dinner. He watched her go, knowing how much she enjoyed hunting, but was unable to shift the unsettled feeling in his gut that had started with the Australians.

Randolph was continuing with the rocker when he saw two men riding by. They stopped and one of the men got down from his horse. Nothing unusual in that.

"Howdy," said Randolph, standing by the sluice.

"You got a fine camp here," said the man who was still on his horse. He had a long beard but the wiry dark hair hadn't been combed recently. The rim of his hat looked like it had met with an accident, because it drooped to the left. The man was chewing tobacco.

American, thought Randolph.

The second man sauntered over to the tools and picked up one of the shovels, admiring it. Randolph noticed that the men weren't carrying mining gear on their horses.

"You been here long?" the man on the horse asked.

There was something in that southern drawl that alerted Randolph's instincts. "Not so long."

"You must have gotten a fair bit of gold by now."

Randolph didn't answer but, drawing himself to his full height, stepped up from the bank, and closer to the mounted man.

Almost casually, the man took a pistol from his holster. "Now, why don't you go get that gold and bring it over."

Randolph's eyes slid over to his tent, and the woods beyond, behind the strangers. He turned back to him. "And why don't you two ride on and we'll say nothing more."

The man looked down from his horse and spat a wad of tobacco on the grass. "Fella, don't you see what I got in my hand?"

"Oh, yes," said Randolph. "I see."

"So why ain't you moving?"

Randolph put his hands in his pockets. "Thing is, you've got that gun on me. And I've got my wife pointing a rifle at you." He nodded to the trees.

The man looked over and widened his eyes. Then he smirked. "Dent, you put down that shovel and go take the gun from the little lady."

"Dent, is it?" Randolph looked at him: he was fatter than his companion, the handle of the long shovel resting against a paunch which pushed the buttons of his beige shirt. "Not a wise thing to do. You see, I'm willing to wager my wife is a better shot than your trigger-happy friend here."

Dent looked from Grace to his mounted friend and back again. "Snyder?"

Snyder narrowed his eyes, seeming to be making calculations. "Woman, you put your rifle down and I won't shoot your husband."

Grace took some slow steps closer. "You thinking of shooting him?" Her voice rang across the clearing.

"If I have to," Snyder replied, his pistol still trained on Randolph.

"Well, in that case—" Before he could react, she lifted the rifle and let off one shot. The gun flew from the man's hand and he screamed in pain. The horse shied away.

"Hell and damnation, she tried to kill me!" He struggled to control his mount with one hand.

Randolph strode to where the pistol lay. "Stop your cursing. If my wife had tried to kill you, you'd be dead." He picked up the pistol. "You, Dent, put down my shovel before my wife decides you need teaching a lesson too."

Dent promptly threw it to the ground.

Randolph examined the pistol. The handle and firing mechanism were damaged, possibly beyond repair. He handed it back to Snyder, who was cradling his bloody hand.

"This is not how we do things round here," Randolph said.

"There's plenty, if you work for it. But you go round trying to steal people's hard-earned gold, you're gonna find yourself six feet under, in double-quick time."

Dent hurriedly remounted his horse.

Randolph glared at each of them. "Get out of here. If we see you again, we won't be so gentle next time."

Snyder scowled at Grace and then back at Randolph.

"And just so we're clear," said Randolph, his voice nearly a growl, "you wouldn't be the first man my wife has had to shoot."

Snyder wheeled his horse. "Don't you go thinking this is over." He dug in his spurs, Dent scrambling to catch up.

Randolph watched them ride away, and once they were far enough from camp, he ran to Grace and enveloped her in his arms. He could feel her heart thumping against his chest.

"You seemed so calm," Grace whispered.

He grunted. "I was, but only once I saw you standing there in the trees, a gun drawn on him."

She let out a long breath. "What if I'd been further away?"

He stroked her hair, knowing there was no answer. They walked back to the campfire, arm in arm. "I guess this decides things. There's no way I'm leaving you behind to look after our claim."

Grace nodded. "And if someone jumps it?"

He shrugged. "If those Americans are anything to go by, I've a feeling things are going to get more lawless here."

"We'd move on?"

"You've been weighing out less gold in the evenings, recently. Maybe we've got the easy stuff from here. We can move further up the river once we come back with more supplies."

"So when do we leave?" She looked up at him.

His heart quickened as he gazed into those dark brown eyes. He stared out beyond her and drank in the beauty of the riverside and valley that had been their home. Despite the nugget of unease he carried with him always, he had been happy here—they had been happy together.

"How about we pack up tomorrow, and set off early the next day?"

NINE

They stayed in bed longer than usual the next morning, Grace enjoying lying entwined in James's arms and legs, listening to the birdsong and trying to fix this memory in her mind. The thinness of the canvas made them feel part of nature.

While James went to pack up outside, she took out her sewing kit and sat in the tent to unpick the seams of their traveling clothes. She folded the larger nuggets into the fabric and sewed the seams back up tightly. She took her one corset—she had abandoned its use some months ago—and sewed gold into the busk and bone casing.

James returned to the tent and put his head to one side, watching her.

"Thinking about those men, yesterday," she said. "Wouldn't take much for us to be forced to hand over our strongbox. Whatever happens, we'll have something to show for the past few months."

James chuckled. "And people think I married you for your looks."

. . .

At first light the next day, they loaded their belongings onto the mules. The animals had been almost wild over the summer months and protested at the saddles and baggage. James had hidden the crib in the trees, hoping to pick it up again when they returned.

James led the way, Grace picking her way behind. The path between the undulating hills was clearer than when they had arrived in May—so many more had trod it since then.

They had got to know the miners closest to them, and called their farewells as they passed. They watched a larger group of men who had constructed a wooden sluice and were working together, clearing a good amount of dirt.

By the evening, they had reached the wide Sacramento Valley. How things had changed in a matter of months. A trading post they had briefly stopped at had been transformed into a large store, and it no longer stood alone. Buildings had sprung up around it: a saloon bar, a building with Hope Hotel painted on a sign by the door, a barber's, a rival store doing just as much good business. Tents and huts clustered around the edge, each on the best spot the owner could find.

Grace sensed something of a carnival atmosphere. People from all parts of the globe had gathered and she heard a cacophony of languages. She guided her horse to sidestep a huddle of men looking at a spot in the dirt, urging something on. James brought his horse closer. A cheer went up and the men parted, some laughing, others slapping backs. Dollars were exchanged: they had been gambling on which beetle would be first to reach the step at the door of the saloon.

As always, Grace was aware of drawing attention from the men she passed and she was grateful when James rode closer.

He leaned over. "I suggest we make camp somewhere on the edge of town, and see what's what tomorrow."

. . .

First thing the next morning, James went in search of a proper shave. Grace was glad to have time to explore. She went into a cabin, where two women were making pies.

"Just arrived?" a woman asked. She was young and plump, with flushed cheeks and a white bonnet.

"Yes. Well, no. We've been in the hills since May."

"Well, welcome to New Mecklenburg. Always good to see another woman round here. I say we're a civilizing influence. I'm Mrs. Lippincott, and this is my sister Agnes."

The other woman looked even younger. She waved briefly, and returned to her pastry.

"You by yourself?" Mrs. Lippincott asked.

"No, with my husband."

"Done well?"

Grace shrugged. "Hard to tell. This is our first time back from mining. I've got nothing to compare it with."

Mrs. Lippincott winked at her. "If you find it hard going in the mountains, there's plenty of money to be made here."

A man came in and greeted them in a language Grace did not understand.

Mrs. Lippincott handed over a prepared order. "That's a dollar, thank you Mr. Lugg."

He handed over his coin and left.

Grace's mouth dropped open. "A dollar! For just one pie?"

"These men will pay it, so I'm gonna charge it. You want one? My sister makes a tasty pie, I can tell you."

Grace shook her head. "I don't have a dollar on me."

Mrs. Lippincott smiled. "Here, sweetie. Take one anyway."

"Oh, no, I couldn't—"

Mrs. Lippincott wrapped it up and pushed it to her. "We ladies need to stick together."

"Thank you. That's very generous."

Mrs. Lippincott adjusted the straps of her apron. "How long are you in town?"

"We're planning on buying supplies and getting back into the hills." The smell of the pie was so delicious, Grace opened the wrapping and broke off a piece. It was as tasty as Mrs. Lippincott had promised. "How do we pay for supplies? I mean, we have gold. Can I pay with that?"

"You can, but you need to be careful with it."

Grace stood aside as Mrs. Lippincott served another customer.

She turned back to Grace. "Know what I recommend? You earn a few dollars while you're here, and use that."

Grace blinked, her mouth full of pie.

"There's all sorts you can offer. Men without women, they don't know how to shift for themselves. You can charge a dollar a shirt for washing. Same with repairs. There's a couple of women earning a good living on their backs, up in the saloon, but I can't see you doing that."

Grace tried not to splutter her mouthful with Mrs. Lippincott speaking so openly of such things.

"Keep an eye on your husband, though."

Grace bristled on his behalf. "He's not the sort to go looking for pleasure elsewhere."

Mrs. Lippincott rolled her eyes. "Oh, hush, now. Didn't mean to insult you, Mrs..."

"Mrs. Randolph."

"What I mean is, it's easy come, easy go. These men have made more money than they've ever known. They forget the value of it. They'll gamble on anything and everything, thinking there's plenty more, if they lose. And that goes hand-in-hand with the drinking."

A pair of men came into the shop and Grace felt it was time to let the sisters return to their business.

"Thank you for the pie. And the advice."

"Hope to see you again." Mrs. Lippincott turned to her new customers.

Grace walked back slowly to their tent. Mrs. Lippincott had touched a nerve. She was sure her sensible husband wouldn't be lured by gambling. He had always abhorred it. But drinking? They had had an idyllic time in Grass River, despite the hard work. But she couldn't deny that even there he would shrink into himself some evenings. She would find the whiskey bottle in the morning. She'd tried to speak to him, but he'd brushed her off, saying there was nothing for her to concern herself with.

Grace returned to the tent and fixed the midday meal. Her breath caught as she saw her husband striding toward her. He was always handsome, but now he was shaven, his square jaw caught her attention, and his wavy dark hair shone.

"I've been finding out how everything works here," he said, dropping down onto a barrel to eat. "You can pay for things with dollars and cents if you have them. But you can also use gold dust. The storekeeper will measure it out. Small things you can pay for with a pinch."

"A pinch?"

"I saw it at the barber's. The miner poured a little of his dust from his pouch onto the counter. The barber checked it wasn't just dirt, and then he took a pinch. His payment was the amount of dust he could pick up."

"No!" Grace exclaimed.

"I swear."

Grace put another slice of beef on his plate. "I'm thinking of laundering some shirts. I can make a dollar a piece."

"D'you need to?" James dug into the meat. "I mean, I'm pretty sure we're rich at the moment, even if we don't look it."

"Are we? Have you found what our gold's worth?"

James stretched out his legs. "I tell you, a barber always knows everything about a place. Says the government pays twenty dollars an ounce. Twenty dollars, sixty-seven cents, to be precise."

"My, that sounds good."

James took a moment to swallow his food. "Problem is, there isn't a government round here. No banks. No one to hand you your twenty dollars."

Grace raised her eyebrows. "Not even in San Francisco?"

"Maybe. But nothing here. The barber said some folks are offering fifteen to seventeen dollars an ounce."

Grace scratched her earlobe. "Where do they get *their* dollars though?"

"The storekeepers. Cash comes in from the men just arriving. And look around, there are plenty of them passing through."

Grace thought for a while. "So we might as well pay with our gold and forget about dollars."

"That's what I thought. Darling, d'you want to go shopping this afternoon?" James winked at her, and she felt a warm bubble growing in her chest. It seemed everything was going to turn out well, after all.

They entered the larger of the two stores and waited their turn. The owner fussed around Grace, making her feel uncomfortable. He was probably reckoning they had just returned from panning and had plenty of gold to spare.

She ordered foodstuffs to take them through a good few months: wheat-flour, cornflour, ready-ground coffee as she had no way to grind it in the camp. She asked for a sack of dried beans, some tins of vegetables, an earthenware jar of honey.

Grace watched James eye up another strongbox, not large, but with a more sophisticated lock. He replaced a shovel that had worn out, and got plenty of iron hardware. They had talked about the equipment they'd seen on the way back down the valley. She guessed he was planning what he could construct.

Grace's eye was taken by a neat writing set: creamy paper, pens and ink, all packed in a wooden traveling case.

"You want it?" asked James.

"I promised to write Tom." She had often found herself wishing she could tell him all about how beautiful California was, about their success in prospecting.

James nodded to the storekeeper to add it to their pile. He put a couple of leather pouches on the counter, the sort he'd seen other men store their dust in, and asked how much he owed.

"In dollars?"

"No, in ounces," Randolph replied.

The man made a note of each item in a ledger. "I'll take an ounce and a half."

"That seems rather high. I was thinking more like an ounce."

The man pulled a face. "Say we split the difference. Ounce and a quarter."

He set up a delicate set of scales with the precise weight and Randolph slowly poured in his gold dust until they balanced.

The man carefully scooped the dust into a jar behind the counter. "Much obliged."

Back at their tent, Grace stowed their new provisions and equipment. "How do we know it will be, well, safe? If we go someplace together, I mean. Wouldn't take a moment for someone to steal it."

"That's been puzzling me too. The barber said people are vigilant for each other and that's how it works. If anyone steps out of line, they face the chance of a hanging. There's no sheriff or justice of the peace. Men just band together."

Grace folded her arms. Was vigilante justice the best they'd got?

"A man waiting in line for a shave said there's a place on the American River called Hangtown. Got its name when three men were caught stealing. Only need to do that once for the fear to be effective."

Grace tucked her hand in the bend of James's arm as they ambled back to the main street through the medley of tents and shacks. Grace paused by a small wooden building with "Hobbs Tailors" painted above the door.

"I've patched most of your clothes," she said. "Why don't you buy something new?"

James had always kept himself smart when he had been a captain in the army. She sensed it pained him to be in civilian clothing.

"It would be good for you to have something new as well. I doubt there'll be anything in there, though," he said, looking at the sign.

Grace bit her lip. There was something she'd been thinking about and now seemed as good a moment to mention it. "I've been meaning to say... I'd like to try wearing men's clothing, particularly when we're back up in the hills."

Randolph took a step back and stared at her.

How could she explain without making him concerned? Or feel that he wasn't protecting her?

"I'd feel safer. Men often make comments as I pass." She glanced up at him, but he tilted his head to look at her, a frown on his brow. Maybe she should try making a joke of things. "And you have no idea how cumbersome these skirts are when working and riding."

He let out a breath. "I never thought of them like that."

"And, Lordy, I've enjoyed the last few months without a corset. Feeling free to move."

A slight smile came to his lips and he pulled her closer to speak in her ear. "I have to admit, I've enjoyed seeing your natural curves."

She laughed and ducked away from him.

James turned to the door. "Looks like this tailor will get double the business."

She whistled out a breath. That had been easier than she had feared.

The shop was hung with half-made clothing, waiting to be fitted to the customer. James explained their needs to the rather surprised tailor, who first measured James and then turned to Grace, his face suggesting this was not something he approved of.

"I need the clothing to be loose," said Grace. "To hide that I'm a woman."

The tailor sniffed and assured them the clothing would be made up and ready for tomorrow.

That evening, James said he wanted to spend time at the saloon. Grace understood his need to be in company once more. She sat up, extravagantly using candlelight to write her first letter to Tom. She felt bad that it had taken her so long, and there was much to tell him. She sealed the letter and planned to take it to the store the next day, where they would arrange for it to be carried northwards.

She went to bed early and tried to sleep, but Mrs. Lippincott's words wound themselves into her brain. James had changed so much since returning from Mexico. For all the happiness they had enjoyed alone by the riverside, and for all their good fortune, there was still a darkness inside him no gold could lighten. With money in his pocket, might he be tempted to gamble? Or to drink more than was wise?

TEN

Grace woke with a start at James stumbling into the tent and half-stepping on her. She guessed it was the early hours. He mumbled "sorry," and was asleep in minutes. Grace lay awake listening to his rhythmical breathing, and fuming that she couldn't get back to sleep.

She wondered how the hell he was able to get up at the same time as ever the next morning, as she pulled her blanket over her head.

He brought coffee as a peace offering. "There's some people I want you to meet."

She hesitated, sitting up and rubbing her eyes. "People you met at the bar?"

"Uh-huh."

Grace resisted asking more questions. She was still mad with him, even though she knew most women would find his behavior perfectly ordinary.

"So, d'you want to know more?" he asked.

"I'm sure you're gonna tell me." She scowled at him over the rim of her mug.

He sighed and cleared his throat. "I've been thinking about

how we do this. Mine gold, I mean. I get the sense things are changing. Trying to make it work, just the two of us... Well, you said yourself you don't always feel safe. I worry about that too."

But you went off to the saloon last night anyway, she thought, but held her tongue.

"With a bigger team, we could be more productive. And if it's men we know and trust, then you'll feel safer."

She felt a twinge of sadness at the idea. She'd loved the last few months, just the two of them. Even with the times he was distant, even when her bleeding knocked her low each month until she picked herself back up again, they had been happy.

"There's four men I met last night. They've been in California a couple of months, like us. They're experienced. I think we could do well with them."

Grace finished her coffee. Clearly her help wasn't good enough.

"I'd like you to meet them. This morning. See if you like them. If you can trust them."

She handed her mug back to James. "And if I don't?"

"Then we carry on as we are. Your choice."

Her choice. Really? Or had he already decided?

She dressed and traipsed after James through the warren of canvas shelters to a set of three tents under an oak tree. One of the men looked up and hailed her husband, greeting him like a long-lost friend.

"Randolph! *Buen día*, good morning." They shook hands, the man slapping James on the back. He had tanned leathery skin which told of a life outdoors. The hair poking from under his hat was the same brown as his mustache and beard, and he wore a brightly colored blanket around his neck, tied at the front. "And this must be the charming wife you spoke about."

He stood up straight, as if to salute her, but then bent over to take her hand and kissed it. Grace stepped back in surprise at these extravagant manners and glanced at James. There was a slight smile, but she gave him a look that said she hadn't forgiven him yet.

"Carlos Espinoza, at your service. May I introduce my friends?" He called out in Spanish. A large man emerged from the biggest tent. "This is Arturo Moreno, my compatriot from Chile."

He was similarly dressed and made a small bow. Built like a prizefighter, his misshapen nose suggested he had had to use his fists in the past. His blanket was pushed back over one shoulder, showing thick muscles straining at his shirt.

Another man got up from where he had been repairing kit.

"And this is Kami."

The man inclined his head politely.

Grace took a startled look at him. His face was round, the line of his chin broken by a short beard. His thick black hair was pushed back. But the thing that mesmerized her was a zigzag tattoo curving around his right eye and over part of his brow.

"Also from Chile?" Grace asked, because she couldn't think of anything else to say, but knowing the man looked very different from the first two.

"No, Kami is from the Sandwich Islands. And, in truth, his name is not Kami. But none of us could say his full name, so this is as close as we can get."

Grace wasn't sure if it would be polite to ask his real name. He didn't speak, and she realized she was staring, so she muttered, "I've heard the Islands are very beautiful."

The man nodded. His eyes were fixed on her in a disconcerting way, but then she found it hard to drag her gaze from his tattoo.

A fourth man, much younger than the others, came from behind the tents, carrying water. His skin was smooth and had no sign of facial hair as yet. His clothing was different also: a pale, loose shirt that extended to his hips, buttoned to the neck.

He wore a straw hat, the front folded upwards at the brow, which added to the youthful impression.

"And Miguel Lopez is from Panama."

"Ah, Mrs. Randolph. We were hoping to meet you," said Lopez. He gestured to the fire they had smoldering. "Please, sit and let me make you some coffee." He put a blanket on a barrel and Grace sat. "And you, Mr. Randolph."

James took a seat on a wooden packing-box beside her.

Lopez busied himself with the coffee pot, while Kami stoked the fire, adding more wood. The two other men sat on the dry ground.

"So, your husband has told you our plan to work together?" asked Espinoza.

Grace glanced at James. "Just the briefest details."

"And you have come to see if we pass muster?" Espinoza said with a wink.

She could feel color on her cheeks from being called out so plainly. "I... Well, I suppose that's true."

"*Excelente*. You need to know about us, if we are to form a joint company."

They told her how they had each heard of the discovery of gold and made their way across the sea to San Francisco. Espinoza and Moreno knew silver mining in Chile, but Kami had been a fisherman and Lopez a tanner. Espinoza enthusiastically recounted how they had each done well in their early months, but had got far more gold by working together.

"That seems very much of my mind," said James.

Grace put down her coffee. "And why are you offering to extend your partnership to my husband?"

Espinoza's eyes twinkled. "There is something about him that inspires confidence. And he looks strong. A hard worker." He threw back his poncho and pumped his own muscles as a demonstration.

Grace cast her eyes over each of the men. "Surely we have to pass your inspection, as much as the other way round."

Moreno nodded. "Your husband told us a good deal last night."

"And what would be the terms of our partnership?"

Espinoza explained that they would pool all the gold and divide it equally. "There is so much luck with gold. One man may find a nugget the size of an acorn, and the man next to him find nothing. So we all work for each other."

Grace thought about this for a moment. James was saying nothing to try to persuade her. "And if a man gets sick? Or is injured?"

Kami spoke for the first time. "We are a brotherhood, not a business. We *still* divide the gold equally. Sickness or injury could fell any of us."

Grace looked at Kami again, struck by this cooperative way of doing things. "A brotherhood, you say? How many are you including in the division of gold?"

Kami looked puzzled. "Why, five."

She glanced at James, who was watching her closely. Perhaps he guessed that she would fight for her share. "If we're to join you, I will be an equal partner. The gold will be divided by six."

Espinoza sat up and looked at Moreno who frowned in return. Lopez whistled.

"You'll be expecting me to work too, I'll wager?" Grace said. "Cook meals, keep the place tidy, wash and mend shirts? My labor means you can be more productive. Work faster. So I am as much a part of this as the rest of you."

Espinoza stroked his mustache flat against his weather-beaten skin. "Perhaps a half share?"

Grace shook her head. "I'll be working just as long as the rest of you. It's a full share or nothing." She put her coffee mug on the ground.

James lifted an ankle over his knee. "I warned you. My wife knows her mind."

Moreno shrugged and spoke to Espinoza in Spanish. It seemed to be the common language for all four men.

After some discussion and gesticulation, Espinoza turned back to Grace. "Very well. It is a partnership of six."

"In writing?" James asked.

"Indeed, Mr. Randolph. Lopez is a stickler for such things." Espinoza lightly punched Lopez's arm, who laughed and looked at his feet, embarrassed. Grace sensed a private joke amongst the men.

They agreed to gather that afternoon to agree the exact terms under young Lopez's supervision, once James and Grace had collected their clothes from the tailor.

They all stood and shook hands.

"Here's to a successful venture," said Espinoza, smiling once more.

On their way back to their tent, Grace slipped her hand through James's arm as they walked in step.

"So what do you think?" James asked.

"I think it's worth taking the risk. They seem good men."

"You didn't mind me not speaking up to support you as a partner?"

"I... Well, it might have been nice."

James gave her arm a squeeze. "I'm sorry, my love. Thing is, you were handling it so well yourself."

She looked up at his face, but it was shaded by his hat.

He threaded his fingers through hers, softly rubbing his thumb on the back of her hand. "I couldn't have been prouder."

Grace thought of the man she had first met, who had believed women to be weak things, beneath his regard. He'd come a long way in two years.

As they skirted two dogs fighting over a bone, she spoke carefully. "How much of our history did you share last night?"

"Our history?"

"Y'know. Things that have happened to us."

"I said we met on the overland trip to Oregon."

"Espinoza said something about you inspiring confidence. Did you... Did you tell them you were a captain? That you were a military man?"

Grace felt his arm tighten. "No. And I don't plan to. It's not information they need."

She watched one dog get the better of the scrap and scurry off with his prize. "Very well. I just wanted to be clear on things."

Perhaps the others were concealing their histories also. It took a certain sort of man to hightail it to California, on the basis of a rumor. She wondered whether things from the past would stay there, or would emerge to prevent this new group of six souls making the future they hoped for. Only time would tell.

ELEVEN

Grace changed into her male clothing behind the curtain at the back of the tailor's shop. It felt strange, having stiff fabric around her hips and between her legs. The shirt felt good though, and pulling on the masculine jacket gave her a sense of power.

"Now, you're not to laugh when you see me," she warned her husband.

She stepped out, swinging her thighs wider than usual in an effort to stop the pants rubbing.

James put his hand to his mouth to hide his response, but his shoulders betrayed him.

Grace slapped him on the arm. "I said you *weren't* to laugh." But she was having difficulty suppressing her own giggles.

The tailor screwed up his lips and tutted his disapproval at the use to which his tailoring was being put.

Grace turned so James could see the back. "Well? Will I do?"

"You're less obviously a woman, I grant you. More of a young boy. The hair gives you away, of course." He reached for one of the hats stocked on a shelf. "Try this."

It came down past her ears and the edge rested on her nose. She burst out laughing.

The tailor picked out the smallest hat he had: a pale, buff-colored one with a wide brim.

Grace put it on, tucking in her hair, and was pleased with the fit.

James looked at her. "You're still too beautiful to ever pass as a boy, but not much to be done about that." He kissed her on the tip of her nose and she felt her stomach clench.

He paid for the clothing as she changed back into her dress. She didn't want to make a spectacle of herself, even in this small town where no one knew her. It would take some getting used to, but she hoped she'd feel more assertive in her new attire.

The party of six rode out that afternoon, heading northeast up the Yuba River. The plan was to push on into the higher hills and find a place Espinoza had heard rumors about—a good seam opening up near a place called Deer Creek. Maybe they could get ahead of the crowd.

Grace's throat tightened with sadness that they would not return to the place where she and James had been happy. She wasn't sure why, but she felt a sliver of anxiety deep in her belly as they set off, as if some part of her feared happy times would be in short supply in the future. They wouldn't be gold miners for ever. What came next for a man who had lived for the army and a woman who failed to fall pregnant?

As they traveled, each morning Grace got a little more confident in pulling on men's clothes. The men had made jokes the first couple of days, and Grace was relieved when they stopped commenting and just accepted her.

She was grateful that the summer temperatures were a little cooler than in the Sacramento Valley. The hillsides grew steeper and greener, the pine trees denser, mixed with oak and maple. As the path twisted and turned, she could see the Sierra Nevada mountains, their tops covered with snow, even in late summer.

Each day, the number of claims they passed was lessened, as fewer miners had made their way this far. With each new possibility, she watched the men get down from their horses and pan the riverbed. Sometimes everyone would get excited by a glisten of gold dust at the bottom, but there was not enough to make it worth setting up camp.

By the fourth day, they were traveling up Deer Creek and paused at a section of river that looked promising. A smaller tributary joined the river where it was wide but shallow. Kami was the first to alert everyone that he had found gold flakes in his pan. The other men redoubled their efforts and soon Moreno had found a small nugget, followed by Lopez.

"Looks like we've found our promised land," said James.

Grace could see it was a good place to make camp with the trees close to the river edge. Kami and Lopez chose level areas nearby to pitch their tents, Espinoza and Moreno found a space a little further up for their large tent. It was agreed that the flat area near the Chileans' tent would serve as a general area for cooking and eating. James and Grace explored further and found a pretty glade between trees, giving them privacy.

"I'll build you something more substantial," James said, stroking her cheek with the back of his hand. "Just as soon as I can."

She knew that each man would be expected to pull their weight, and thought it unlikely her husband would have a break to build a cabin, any time soon. She was touched that he was thinking of her needs, but hoped he knew that she was happy as things were.

The next morning, the men took their pickaxes and shovels to the river. No panning or using a rocker this time. James had explained to her that the men were going to dig a sluice channel that would bring water to a proper long tom. She watched him naturally fall into managing the team. He'd worked out each man's talents, by listening to their conversation, as well as observation.

Moreno was a giant of a man, well over six foot, and broad with it. He broke stones with one strike of the axe. Espinoza was lithe and wiry. He energetically cleared away the broken rock to create the rough edges of the channel. James's skill was placing the rocks in the right position to build something that would not be swept away. Kami's ability as a carpenter was prodigious. Grace had wondered about the long planks that had been loaded on the mules. Now Kami swiftly constructed them into a long trough. Grace watched, rapt, and, as she was overcoming her initial wariness, asked him how he knew what to do, given he was a fisherman.

Kami looked at her steadily. "Where I come from, we make our boats from wood on the islands. A good fisherman needs to be a good carpenter so he can trust his boat. The waves that surround my island can be as high as that tree." He pointed to a ponderosa pine.

Lopez assisted, nailing together the easier sections, maneuvering the long box-like structure. He fixed small struts across the bottom. Grace admired his work.

"The water and dirt will run along here, Mrs. Randolph," Lopez said, pleased to be able to show her. "And the gold will gather behind each strut, which is called a riffle. We have worked with long toms before. Very good for catching gold."

"Let's hope so." She didn't feel the need to tell him that James and she had worked out a lot of this for themselves with their rocking crib.

Grace found cooking for six considerably more challenging than when it was the pair of them. Just boiling enough water for six coffees took half an hour. Her day was filled with finding wood, heating water, making food. She had insisted on James buying a Dutch oven at New Mecklenburg. It was heavy on the mule's back, but now she was glad to have stood her ground. It was the only way to make bread, as well as being large enough to hold broth or stew for everyone.

Grace had visited Mrs. Lippincott before leaving town and bought some sourdough, carefully stored in a crock with a tight lid. She used this to start her own bread culture, always keeping some dough back and feeding it with flour and water for the next loaf.

The men rigged up a canvas awning, tied to the branches of nearby trees. It formed a mess tent of sorts, a place where Grace could cook and the men eat, protecting them from the occasional shower.

The long tom and the sluice were completed about the same time. The men put the tom in place, eager to see if it would work. James and Moreno made adjustments to the stonework so the tom was stable and the water ran in the right place.

"Mrs. Randolph," Espinoza called, and took her hand as if at a formal dance. "You should have the honor of throwing in the first shovel of dirt. You bring us luck."

Grace was happy to oblige and threw a shovel load into the tom. Moreno shifted the stones which had formed a temporary dam and they were in business, water flowing down the wooden channel.

The men seemed happy to be organized by James and enthusiastically took their roles of shoveling dirt into buckets, bringing it to the top, tipping it in little by little as the lighter material was be swept away. They would run their hands through the dirt, breaking up larger pieces with their hands.

Three times a day, before the midday break, mid-afternoon, and at the end of the day, James would block the flow of water and they would all carefully search for gold trapped behind the bars. These were the most exciting times of the day. Most of the gold was in tiny flakes and dust, but it all added up. Everyone put their findings together.

It had fallen to Grace to weigh the gold each evening after supper and she hoped it was because the men trusted her to treat them all equally. She felt a thrill each day at the sight of the pile they had amassed between them. She would weigh the total amount and keep a record. Then she placed equal parts on six pieces of leather. The men chose which pile they wanted, taking turns to go first each night, but with James and herself always taking the last two piles. After that, each person was responsible for looking after their own haul.

As they worked together, Randolph got to know each man, and he began to look forward to the convivial evenings, with conversation ranging over matters political and social. Some nights a bottle of whiskey was produced and passed round. He knew Grace disapproved that this had taken the place of foodstuffs, or a second change of clothing. He had felt slightly ashamed when he produced a bottle himself, having concealed it from her.

The men talked nostalgically about home. Espinoza had brought a small guitar-like instrument and entertained them with ballads and drinking songs, making them all helpless with laughter. Randolph noticed how Moreno would lean back and stare at his compatriot intently, a gentle smile on his lips.

Sitting by the fire, dark shadows around them and Grace at his side, each man began to tell of why they had left their native land to travel to California. It was not simply the lure of gold, the possibility of an easy path to wealth. Each had a reason for leaving. For Lopez, it was that he wanted enough money to study to become a lawyer, rather than be a tanner like his father, and his grandfather before him. Kami told of losing his wife and child to disease spread by sailors who had sheltered on his island during a storm. Moreno had broken a man's neck after he had insulted Espinoza and the two had fled north.

"Randolph, you have a military air about you," observed Espinoza one evening after he had put down his guitar. "Would I be right?"

Randolph shifted his position on the wooden box he was sitting on. He had no desire to tell his story, but the other men had shared their pasts. He glanced at Grace, whose eyes were on his face. "That's right."

"Did you serve long?"

"More than a decade."

Espinoza let out a low whistle. "That's a lot of life to give to your country."

He took a sip from his glass. The whiskey suddenly seemed more bitter. "Indeed it is."

"Where did you serve?" asked Lopez, gently, as if encouraging a child to confess to a misdemeanor.

"In Texas at first. With General Houston in 1836. Then wherever the US government sent me."

Espinoza pushed a log further into the fire. "You don't behave like you were a private."

Randolph waited for him to take his seat and looked steadily at him. "I was a captain."

Espinoza nodded. "Makes sense."

"You fought in Mexico?" Lopez asked.

Being from Panama, had he suspected this?

Randolph nodded.

"So you only recently left the army," Lopez observed.

"Not even a year ago. End of '47." He looked at the men's faces in the firelight. They had become his trusted friends, something he had not expected to find in the rush for gold. They were honest, simple men. "There were things which didn't sit well with me. Men did things which... which weren't honorable. The US Army and me... we didn't part on the best of terms."

He could see the men had more questions, but he couldn't haul more words into his mouth. To open the box of his memories of what the army had asked of him in Mexico—that felt dangerous. Those memories might not go back into the box. Most of all, his beautiful, innocent wife sat not two feet from him. He couldn't bring himself to look at her; he had already said more tonight than he ever had before. He refused to sully her with talk of what war actually meant.

"Gentlemen, it's late," he said. "I don't know about you, but I want to get some rest, so I can spend another day making my fortune." He got up and Grace immediately rose. He was relieved that she asked him no questions as she followed him up the hill to their tent.

TWELVE

The summer slipped into fall and the oak trees between the firs turned golden. Grace had noticed a squirrel burrowing nearby their camp and how it had got bolder each day, sometimes stealing scraps of food. Now it was busily gathering acorns and pine nuts, and storing them in the burrow. Grace fancied it was female, preparing for winter hibernation and then a brood of pups to look after in the spring. All of nature seemed to easily produce its offspring. It was only she who had failed. Maybe she had to accept that she would never become a mother.

She and James would sometimes disappear into the woods to shoot animals for food. Occasionally, they met the Nisenan people. James thought he recognized one from their early encounter, in the other valley.

Grace marveled at his natural ear for languages. He could recreate the sounds, when Grace struggled. Soon, he had the basics—just the simplest terms, but she hoped James made it clear that the party wanted no trouble.

"*Ustumah*," he said to Grace one evening. "That's the name for this place."

Grace tried out the word. "What does it mean?"

James laughed. "My darling, I have no idea."

The mornings were getting cold. One day, Grace rose early to fix coffee for the men and was puzzled when they did not head straight to the riverside. Instead, they picked up their axes and saws, and went up the hill into the woods.

Grace called after them. "What's going on? Where are you going?"

James turned, grinning as he walked backwards. "Stay there. You'll see."

All morning, the sound of chopping and sawing echoed around the valley, along with the men's voices. They gathered wood and planks in a space near the Randolph tent. Grace watched in amazement as the five men constructed a small cabin.

It was almost dark by the time it was complete. Espinoza proudly fetched Grace to see if she approved. She was speechless, overwhelmed by their generosity. It wasn't just the effort of building the cabin; the men had sacrificed a day's work at their long tom.

There was no door, and inside was barely large enough for James and Grace to sleep and store their kit, but the floor was made of flat planks, the walls of logs. Intertwined branches formed the roof, with moss pushed between. A small gap let light inside.

She stepped back outside, open-mouthed. The men stood in a semicircle, the Chileans both with arms folded, Lopez looking sheepish but proud. James stood with his weight on one leg, his thumbs hooked in his pants pockets. No one had ever done anything so thoughtful for her.

Finally, she spoke. "It's beautiful."

"It was Kami's idea," said James. "He's been gathering suitable wood for some weeks. He led us in what to do."

"We are blessed to have a lady with us in our camp," said Espinoza. "You should have something better than a tent."

That night, she lay side by side with James, holding hands and absorbing the different sounds as the wood settled.

"You know, if we organized things," said Grace, "we could clear everything from our tent."

"Why would we want to do that?"

"Then we could lend it to Espinoza and Moreno, and they could have a tent each."

James turned to Grace and ran his fingers through a piece of her hair. "I think they're fine as they are, my love," he said softly.

"But then they wouldn't have to share."

A line emerged between James's brows. "Let them be as they are."

"But, James—"

"Trust me on this. Offering our tent would only make them feel awkward."

Grace turned over, disappointed that, when the men had been so kind to her, she shouldn't give something back.

Moreno and Espinoza had constructed a complex maze of sluices and long toms, and were working as hard as they could. Randolph knew the main problem was bringing enough dirt into the system. Moreno's strength meant plenty of rock was broken up, but they'd cleared the stones close to the river and each day had to carry it from further. Maybe they could get a wheelbarrow next time one of them went back down the valley. Or pick up a cart and Kami could fashion it into what was needed.

Sometimes the pickings were slow and Randolph wondered if they had come to the end of the seam. The next day, gold would glint behind the riffles in the long tom, or a glowing nugget would emerge from the sand. They were gathering more gold than any of them had hoped for, or thought possible. Randolph was slightly stunned by their success and was at a loss to decide what they should do with it to secure their wealth.

One morning in November, Randolph woke to find a dusting of snow had fallen in the night. He looked back at Grace, still sleeping in the cabin, snuggled under the blankets, and didn't want to wake her. He pulled on his coat and boots, and made the fire, putting on the coffee.

When Grace emerged, she had extra layers of clothing, and blew on her fingers to warm them.

Randolph put his hands in his pockets and looked at the sky, wondering if the gray clouds carried more snow. "Early for it."

"Hmm?"

"Snow. Early in the year."

"Beautiful though, isn't it?" Grace gazed around.

He studied her. How had he not noticed that she'd lost weight, even though she worked all day to provide wholesome food? When he touched her at night, her muscles were strong, but he could feel her bones as he ran his fingers down her spine, or pulled her legs closer. He realized with a jolt that Grace had not had a day's rest since they'd arrived, more than two months previously. The men would occasionally take a day's rest away from the sluices, time to fish, or read. But they never had a day without eating. Even now, she was already cooking breakfast.

"We should leave," he said, surprising himself with the suddenness of this thought and the strength of his conviction.

Grace looked up from the frying pan she had placed over the fire. "Leave?"

"Go to San Francisco."

Her mouth fell open. "San Francisco!"

"We've got more gold dust stored in those two strongboxes than we ever dreamed. Plenty to get us started."

"Started with what?"

He shrugged, feeling as if she had pressed on a bruise. "Not sure yet. That's why I'm suggesting San Francisco."

"But—" She looked around at the camp. "What about the brotherhood?"

"I have to put your safety first."

She threw a fatty piece of bacon into the pan. It spat. "Oh, come now. I'm safer here than I've ever been, any place."

Lopez came up the slope from his tent, further down the hill, ready for his morning coffee.

Randolph frowned, knowing the other men would be here soon. He wanted this conversation to be over.

"Did you know about this?" Grace glared at Lopez and threw in the next piece of bacon. "Thinking about going back down the valley?"

Lopez shook his head and turned to Randolph.

"Look, I'm not saying all of us. But I want to get my wife out of the mountains." He brushed the dusting of snow from a box he used as a seat. "Remember what Captain Sutter said? About not getting caught in the winter?"

"But we're not *in* the mountains." Grace angrily turned the bacon.

"We're high enough. Remember..." He took out his knife to slice a hunk of the loaf Grace had made the day before. "Remember what happened to the Donner Party?"

Grace stopped her work and frowned at him. It was a cheap shot and he wasn't proud of it. He knew the Donner name made her fearful.

Lopez poured a coffee and looked at Randolph, and then his gaze turned to Grace, as if seeing her in a different way. "Your husband is right. It would be better back in the valley."

Grace dropped a piece of bacon onto a tin plate and shoved it at Lopez. "I didn't ask your opinion. And what about the partnership? Your so-called brotherhood?"

"We can work it out," Lopez said.

"And who would keep you all fed? And stop you all smelling rank. I bet none of you would clean a shirt or long johns if I wasn't here."

Lopez mouth twisted in a half-smile. "Not saying it would be easy."

Randolph glanced at Lopez with gratitude. "We can come back, Grace. Spend winter in San Francisco and then meet up with these fellows in the spring."

"Looks like you've got it all figured out." Grace thrust a plate toward him.

The other men were emerging from their tents and she returned to making them breakfast.

She was so stubborn and determined. But it was his job to keep her safe. He'd heard mixed things about San Francisco, some good, some bad. But no matter, she deserved to be treated properly. He understood her reasoning about wearing pants and a shirt out here in the wilds. But with the gold he'd already found, he could set her up in comfort. Didn't she want just one silk dress? To have someone cook for her?

And was it possible that, if they rested up somewhere, the baby she longed for would follow?

Grace watched James load their mules again. Each time he did it, they seemed to have acquired more possessions. But the weight of the two strongboxes was gratifying.

Even after only three months, she found it hard to say goodbye to the men. She had developed a deep affection for them: Espinoza's jokes and merrymaking each evening, Moreno's quiet strength, Lopez's wisdom, and Kami's creative gifts. She suggested they draw lots for who would get the log cabin.

"Already decided." Lopez shrugged. "Espinoza and Moreno will use it. Kami and me, we'll move our tents up to the mess area. We were too near the river for winter, anyway."

James frowned. "You boys think hard about staying here all winter. Not worth risking everything for a few more ounces of gold."

He helped her mount her horse and she turned it to the path. There was a final round of farewells and then James rode out, Grace trotting behind him. Her time near Deer Creek had been more satisfying than she had expected, after the spring and early summer of just the two of them.

She had suggested returning north for the winter, to spend it with Zach and the family. She wanted to know if Margaret's second baby had been delivered safely. And her heart ached for Tom. But James said it was important to go to San Francisco, to turn all this gold dust into something secure for the future. She guessed he was right: it was the sensible thing to do.

Grace's stomach fluttered when she thought about the city. The four men had all arrived at the port, and they had told her about how busy it was, how gripped with gold fever. They'd told her about the size of the Pacific Ocean, the beauty of the coast, the power of the waves. Was it possible San Francisco would live up to the vision in her mind?

THIRTEEN

It was early morning when Randolph led their horses and mules up the gangplank and onto the steam ferry that would take them west out of the Sacramento River delta and then south across the bay to San Francisco. This wasn't the first time these animals had traveled across water, but it was by far their longest journey, taking most of the day. He and Grace each stood close to their animals, trying to keep them calm.

He was pleased that Grace had decided to return to women's dress for their arrival in the city, a shawl wrapped around her head to protect her from the November cold. He hadn't said anything, because he didn't want her to think he was criticising, and she was still bristling from the sudden departure from the mountains.

Randolph lifted his collar and buttoned his coat against the wind from the Pacific as the ferry cut through water the color of lead. It was powered by a steam engine which rattled noisily and sent black belches of cloud into the dank air. Halfway across, they met a steamer coming toward them, packed full of men, hats pulled low. Randolph remarked to one of the ferrymen how much faster the other ship was going.

"Everyone's rushing to the goldfields," said the sailor. "They act like they haven't a minute to spare, like all the gold's suddenly going to run out."

"Maybe it will," said Randolph.

The sailor was old and worked the ropes with one hand. The other arm seemed withered. Randolph wondered if this was why the man worked the ferry, rather than trying his luck himself.

The sailor was eager to talk. "That one's going with the prevailing winds, of course. The captain gets paid more if he crosses the bay ahead of time. Throws coal into the furnace and pumps up the speed like it's an old nag that he's whipping to go faster. Thing is, sometimes the nag just keels over. One of these steam-ferries exploded last week. Nearly everyone died."

Randolph glanced up at the blackened funnel and hoped Grace had not heard the old sailor's words. For heaven's sake, he was trying to get her to a safer life, but he was putting her in danger, simply by crossing the bay.

The clouds hung thickly over San Francisco so he couldn't see it until they were quite close. A forest of masts emerged from the fog, like a pine forest after a fire, where the trunks remained standing, black and erect, but without their branches.

Randolph squinted. "What are all those?" he asked the ferryman.

He snorted. "Abandoned ships."

Randolph looked at him, waiting to be told more.

"When a ship with you argonauts arrives, all the sailors jump ship and declare themselves for the goldfields. The captain hasn't enough crew to take it back out to the ocean."

"No!" said Randolph, incredulous.

The man waved his withered arm toward the ships which were growing closer. "Evidence of your own eyes, mister. Same with merchant ships. Drop off their cargo and the sailors don't go back. I heard some owners won't send their ships here no more, they're so afraid their ship will get sucked into the bay, like quicksand, held fast, never able to leave."

The ferry slowed to avoid this graveyard of clippers and brigs. The fog thinned and Randolph could see the town emerge: one-story wooden buildings near the water edge, and cabins and tents scattered on the hills behind. He laid a hand on Grace's shoulder and she looked up, wide-eyed. He knew she'd never seen so many buildings and tents in one place.

The ferry chugged until it drew up next to a schooner. A man onboard caught the ropes and secured the ferry. The gangway was thrown down onto the deck.

Randolph rubbed the scar on his jaw. "Hey, I thought we were being dropped off at the harbor."

"Close as we can get," the ferryman yelled over his shoulder. "Harbor's full of boats. There's a series of gangways to get to shore."

Randolph looked at Grace and gave a brief shrug. Following men who had hurried down the gangplank, he led his horse, the mule tethered behind. Grace did the same, her horse tentative on the wood, which was slippery with the damp.

They made their way from deck to deck, the pathway well established. Most boats were closely lashed together, but sometimes the black water slapped up between the shifting hulls. Randolph heard children and saw two boys chasing each other over the decks. A woman's voice hollered out from below-deck and the boys darted out of sight.

"Do you think people live here?" Grace asked.

"Looks like it," Randolph called back to her. "Perhaps it's as good a place as any."

They reached firm ground, but Grace called to him. "I don't feel... quite right, James. It's like the ground isn't firm."

He walked back and took her shoulders. "I've heard it happens after being on the water a while. I feel it too. Keep walking. You'll be fine soon."

They made their way along the wharf and turned inland. The street was surprisingly wide, and the buildings on either side looked new, paint glowing, bare planks still a honey-yellow. The regular thump of hammers suggested more buildings were being constructed as they went, that maybe a new one would spring up at the end of the street, that hadn't been there when they started out.

People jostled nearby, making Grace's horse shy. She patted its neck and made soft noises to settle it. "You and me both, buddy. I've never seen so many people, neither."

Randolph stopped in front of one of the few two-story buildings: a sign read Montgomery House.

"This is the place the ferryman recommended. I suggest we stay here for the night and get our bearings tomorrow."

Grace longed to rest, no matter where, nor how much of their precious gold dust it cost. James stepped inside, while she kept watch on their animals and belongings. Soon, a boy ran out to look after the horses and waved his arms to indicate she should go inside.

The lobby—such as it could be termed—was shadowy. Grace moved close to James. The owner ran his eyes up and down her, as if a unicorn were standing before him.

"My wife," James said, giving the man a firm stare.

"This way." The man bustled in front of them. He was dressed in black and his greasy hair was long enough to curl at the collar. He took them up the narrow stairs to a corridor that ran the length of the building. On either side were cloth partitions, rather than doors. "You can have the room at the back." He pulled aside the calico sheet.

Grace looked inside: to call it a "room" was generous. It was more what she imagined a ship's cabin to look like. Bunk beds filled most of the narrow space and appeared to have been taken from a boat. Grace squeezed past James to go in. Two sides of the room—the side and back—had wooden panels, the other side of the room was papered. There was a candle on a stand at the end of the space. She would have to remember to ask for a taper.

"Where will our belongings go?" asked James. "There's not enough room here..."

The man pulled on his ear. "You're in luck. The room next to this is empty at the moment. You can take that. I'll have to charge double, of course."

"Of course," James said under his breath.

Grace put her hand to the wooden slats on the bunks. Surely, in a hotel... "Where's the bedding?"

The proprietor raised his eyebrows. "You have your own, have you not?"

James breathed. "We have bedding rolls. I guess my wife just hoped..." He glanced at her.

She gave a quick shake of her head: she didn't want James to think he needed to find somewhere else.

"We'll take both rooms," he said. "I'll help your son bring up our belongings."

Grace sensed that he did not trust the proprietor, or his son, despite the ferryman's recommendation.

"I would appreciate you fixing some coffee for my wife, while I fetch our things."

The proprietor sniffed, perhaps unused to being ordered to do things in his own hotel. But her husband was paying good money, so the man shuffled back down the stairs ahead of them.

"Wait in the parlor." The proprietor pointed to the room by the lobby.

Grace entered, more in hope than expectation, and found a dim room with a single window, one table and a few chairs. The far end was hung with more calico.

"Beyond is the dining room," said the proprietor.

So, not actually a parlor, thought Grace.

The man went through the curtain to the kitchen beyond the dining room.

Grace watched as James and the boy took several trips to carry their belongings upstairs. James made sure he took the baggage containing the strongboxes. She'd offer to help, just as soon as she'd rested her eyes a moment.

Grace jerked awake as the proprietor placed two cups of coffee on the table beside her. She was disoriented for a second. The cups were fine porcelain with an intricate blue pattern.

The man saw her admire them. "Just off a boat from China. Took my fancy. Glad I bought them, given we have a lady staying."

James appeared at the doorway. "All fixed."

He sat beside her, as the proprietor withdrew.

"You can have a lie-down, soon as you've finished your coffee." He leaned nearer. "Just to warn you," he said in a low voice, "the other wall in our room. It's actually more calico, but he's glued paper to it."

Grace snorted. "How much are we paying?"

"Enough that I thought it would buy us a proper room. You know, with a door. Window. Walls."

"Space to turn round."

His blue eyes flashed in the half-light. "Now, one thing I don't mind is being close to you."

The evening meal was basic and they turned in early. James helped Grace undress, slowly unbuttoning her bodice, placing kisses on her shoulders, as soft as a butterfly beating its wing. His lips moved up until they found her mouth. He pulled her close—

And then she heard a man cough and clear his throat, before making a hearty spitting sound. Grace froze. It sounded loud enough to be in their room.

"There is absolutely *no way* anything is going to happen between us tonight, James," she hissed.

He rested his brow on hers. "This is what happens when a hotel has walls of calico and paper."

Despite their tiredness, neither slept well. Grace was kept awake by the snoring and muttering of unknown men. Some struck up conversations, and she longed for the courage to shout at them to be quiet. She was concerned about their belongings. James had placed the two boxes under their bunk beds, of course. But she wondered about the sort of men who had been drawn to this town, and how far you could trust them. When a hotel was not what it seemed, how much else that looked solid in San Francisco would turn out to be calico and paper?

FOURTEEN

Randolph awoke cold, as there was precious little heating in the hotel. He and Grace washed quickly, dressed quickly, and ate breakfast quickly. He wanted to make a reconnaissance of San Francisco as early as possible, hesitating before agreeing to leave their belongings in the care of the proprietor, for a fee.

He led the way down to the harbor first. Despite what the ferryman had said, boats were disgorging their contents, stevedores carrying the cargo from the row boats that ferried between the shoreline and the vessels. Merchants were keen to supply the luxury items the newly rich argonauts could afford. There were no warehouses, so goods piled up on the street: crates of fine wine, tins of oysters, bales of tobacco.

Grace tucked her hand into the crook of his arm and walked close. He knew she had never been in such a large town, surrounded by so many people. Was he right in bringing her here?

Randolph had experience of New York and Washington, back east. Last year, he had been with the army in sprawling Mexico City. What struck him as different about San Francisco was the range of places where the men had originated. Men from China carried bundles of silks or crates with porcelain. He recognized the round features of men like Kami who had travelled from the Sandwich Islands. Spanish was spoken by men from South America. Mexicans stood out from the crowds by their colorful blankets swept around their shoulders. Dark-haired Californian women looked on disdainfully, seeming to abhor the changes coming to their home. And there were English-speaking Americans like themselves, who had also originated from different parts of the world.

They made their way back up Market Street. Even though there were no boardwalks and the street was a muddy morass, Grace commented with amazement on how wide the street was, and that the buildings already looked so grand and substantial. Yet, they were cheek by jowl with sand hills covered with ragweed and spiky beachgrass. They walked through an area in the lea of one of the sand hills, sheltered from the wind. The ground was marked up in plots, some already filled with buildings, some with tents, some lying empty.

People huddled around a brazier, a man standing nearby with a mule laden with charcoal, as if the fire were a shop-window for his wares.

"What's this place called?" Randolph asked.

The man looked around him. "What, here? We call this Happy Valley."

"The name augers well," Grace said. "Why not here? We could put up our tent and be settled in a moment." She looked at him, her eyes imploring.

Randolph turned back to the man. "Is that how it works? Can we just pitch up anywhere?"

"Yes... and no. They have marked out squares and you can have one, if you find it free. But to keep it, you need to pay for it."

Randolph wondered who *they* were, who had plotted the streets, and how much each plot cost.

"Who would we pay?"

"You go to the *alcalde*'s office."

"*Alcalde*?" asked Grace. "What's that?"

"The man supposedly in charge." The charcoal-seller grunted. "That's what the Mexicans called him. Then the Californians. Now you Americans are in charge, you're mostly calling him the mayor."

Randolph touched his hat to thank the man. "Let's look further."

He took a few steps before realizing Grace hadn't followed him. He turned back. Her mouth was a straight line and her lips narrow.

"Mr. Randolph, is this how it's to be? Every decision made by you?"

"The plots may be cheaper further from the harbor."

"And maybe they're more expensive because they're further from the town." She placed her hands on her hips. "You decided we should leave Oregon. You decided we should leave the Sierras. Well, *I'm* deciding we're going to put our tent *here*."

Randolph took off his hat and ran his fingers through his hair, trying to tamp down the anger rising in him. He closed his eyes. Perhaps he needed to listen to his wife more. He let out a long breath. "Very well."

They led their animals out of the stables behind Montgomery House and, once again, loaded them with their belongings. Randolph settled up with the proprietor and they walked the few blocks to Happy Valley. They found an empty plot partway down the space that was nominated as a street—simply a muddy track—and set up their tent.

With both of them inside, Randolph tied the door flaps tightly as Grace measured out enough gold dust for the coming days. He picked up his shovel and dug a hole into the sandy earth inside the tent, and placed the two strongboxes inside, before smoothing the earth over them. He tossed the bedding rolls full-length so an intruder could not see the disturbed earth.

"I'm going to build us something, once we've bought a plot. But let's see if we can make this place a little easier first."

He pulled on his overcoat and hat against the light drizzle, and untied the door. Randolph had seen a place to stable their horses and mules and paid for their livery for a week. He would think about selling the mules once he'd worked out if they would still be useful.

He went to a general store on Market Street. It had everything a gold-seeker could need, and plenty more he didn't. Prices of equipment were high, but not extortionate—given it was being purchased by the newly arrived men who had barely a dollar in their pocket. The luxury goods for those returning from the goldfields, now, they were a different matter.

Randolph bought a canvas shelter for cooking and storage. He carried it back and Grace erected a mess tent, modeled on the one that had worked so well when she was feeding five men. Randolph retraced his steps to the store as Grace set things up, returning with a metal stove to replace the Dutch oven they had had to leave behind, and, after his third visit, a tiny pot-bellied stove with a long chimney.

"This one's going in the tent. We'll be snug as bugs in a rug." He made sure it was on level ground and poked the chimney through a gap in the canvas flap at the rear of the tent.

Randolph sensed their first day did little to settle Grace. Perhaps the incessant noise disturbed her: hammers on wood as yet another building went up, snatches of music from a nearby saloon, angry voices when someone lost whatever he had been gambling on. He wondered if a hill would be a better place to settle—away from the constant bustle. There was precious little flat land near the harbor edge, and as more people poured into the town, the hills were dotted with houses and tents. Maybe he could buy something for her, get a house built. But that would use up all their capital and then what would they do? No, he needed to be smart with their gold.

On the second day, while surveying the town and gathering supplies, he was struck by the lack of warehousing in the port and wondered if this was the opening he was seeking. His instinct to restore order made him itch to sort the boxes and bails lying on the harbor edge.

With Grace's agreement, on the third day, he dressed as smartly as he could and took the smaller of the strongboxes to the *alcalde*'s office in the town hall. He was shown into a clerk's office hung with maps of San Francisco, the wider bay area and California. The land had been in the hands of the American government for less than a year and word on the street was that the *alcalde* was struggling to keep up with the demands.

Randolph approached. "I was told this is the place to buy some plots."

The clerk adjusted his glasses, and pulled his vest lower over the bulging belt of his pants. He moved some ledgers off the map that extended over most of his desk. The paper was cream, with the outline of the sea traced out in dark ink, cross-hatching indicating the hills and sand dunes. Across this was plotted a regular pattern of lines showing current and future streets.

"All my own work," the clerk said, pushing out his chest. "Where d'you have in mind?"

A line ran diagonally back from the harbor. Randolph peered closer: Market Street was elegantly inscribed. On the south side of this thoroughfare, the map was marked out in neat boxes. On the north, the lines represented streets butted on at an angle. "We'd like a corner plot."

"Always popular. Not sure how many we got left."

"How about there." Randolph pointed.

The clerk waggled his head. "Corner of Fourth and Howard." He ran his fingers through papers in a drawer. "A-ha. You're in luck. Plot fifty-four on the southwest corner is available. Had sold it to a man from Alaska, but he defaulted." The clerk took out the paperwork. "Each plot is twenty-two dollars."

"Is that the same for the harbor? I want a water plot as well, to build me a wharf and warehouses."

The clerk pulled at his lower lip. "Same price. Smaller plot." He moved the map around on the desk. "What about here?" The clerk pointed to an area just west of where Rincon Point jutted into the Bay.

"Anything further north?"

"Yes, but the abandoned boats are blocking it."

"Say, what happens to those ships?" asked Randolph. "Who owns them?"

"Not quite sure. Doesn't look like anyone owns them now."

"So, if I cleared some?"

The clerk whistled through his teeth. "I know the mayor thinks anyone who can shift those ships will be doing the city a service."

"I'll take those two water plots." Randolph pointed to adjacent squares on the map.

The clerk leaned over the map. "Hmm. You done well with the gold panning, then?"

"Can't complain. Worked hard for it."

"You paying in dollars or gold?"

"Gold."

The clerk whistled as he sharpened his pen and poured more ink into his pot. He drew up a document. "Name?"

"Mr. James Barnes Randolph."

The clerk took the particulars and carefully described the three plots being purchased. "These papers stay here, so anyone can check them."

The clerk led him down the corridor to a small office.

"This is Mr. Grimes, the city treasurer. He'll measure your gold."

The clerk laid out the paperwork for Mr. Grimes, who made strange clicking sounds with his tongue as he set out the scales. He calculated how much gold would be needed. The government was, in theory, paying twenty-one dollars an ounce, and therefore each plot was a little more than an ounce of gold. But pressure on land meant it didn't work out that way. Each plot was closer to two ounces of gold. Randolph wondered if any made its way into the treasurer's own pocket.

Randolph poured the contents of a leather pouch into a bowl.

Grimes picked his way through, clicking his teeth again. "Good stuff. Glad to see you're not trying to defraud the government by mixing dirt into this. But I'll take the liberty of using the bigger pieces."

Grimes took his tweezers and picked out the tiny nuggets, leaving the flakes of gold behind. Bit by bit, the scales balanced.

"Done," Grimes announced, and poured the gold in the brass saucer into a box behind him. He signed the paperwork. "Now, this is your receipt. Anyone challenges you 'bout it being your plot, you wave this under their nose."

Randolph left the building with a lighter heart and lighter pockets. This was just the beginning. Maybe this was where he and Grace would put down roots and grow something new. He could properly close the book on his time in the army, once and for all.

FIFTEEN

Randolph stood on the rocks that formed the curved shoreline between Rincon Point and Market Street, the city's wide thoroughfare. He knew what he wanted, but getting it was proving tricky.

He couldn't build warehouses and a wharf by himself. He needed labor. The scrawny men fresh off the boats after weeks at sea were eager to travel to the Sierra mountains, even though Californians told them it was ill-advised in early December.

That left Randolph with the men living in San Francisco, who were of three sorts. Firstly, those too elderly or infirm to become miners, but who saw opportunities in the city. Secondly, men like the proprietor at Montgomery House: fit, healthy, and making good money from providing a service to the returning miners. These were generally Californians who had lived here for generations and were often resentful of the new American government. And thirdly, miners, who, like him, had decided to winter in the city. They had gold or dollars in their pockets and were disinclined to work hard for a low day rate.

If only the men from the brotherhood had followed

Randolph out of the hills. Kami would have put up a warehouse in no time; Moreno could porter all day long.

He didn't want the uncertainty of going into partnership with unknown men—and sharing the profits. No, he wanted to pay men for their labor. But there were few to be found.

He had made a start, using the skills he had learned from Kami. Most days, he found a handful of men to work with him. He paid a dollar a day—a shocking amount—yet it was impossible to pay less. He would ruminate on the labor difficulty over dinner with Grace, sitting under their awning, watching the rain form puddles around their tent. They hadn't yet moved to the plot he'd purchased. What was the point, when they were settled in Happy Valley?

"I'll build you a beautiful little house, I promise," he said. "Just as soon as the warehouses are up."

Grace's patience was wearing thin. They couldn't keep working their way through their gold dust: the gold needed to multiply through trade. She remembered the sisters in the pie shop in New Mecklenburg and all the ways Mrs. Lippincott had said a woman could make money. There was something exciting about the Lippincott sisters' independence.

Grace was determined to do something to improve their situation. She had felt overwhelmed by all the noise and bustle when she'd first arrived, but she had the sense now that James wanted to hide her away, with so many men living cheek by jowl, and no authority ensuring order was maintained. That was no way for her to live. She had lost that sense of being a partnership. She needed to prove that she could look after herself, and contribute something of value.

Once James had left for the day, Grace fetched her mule from the stables and took down the canvas shelter and rolled it. Next, she persuaded her neighbor to help her lift the stove onto the animal's back. She secured the canvas, cooking pots, a stool, and a tiny table.

On her way through Market Street, she bought plenty of vegetables and cheap cuts, and a dozen metal plates and spoons. She led her mule to the harbor and along to their water plot. A sign read Oregon Wharf. She was touched that James had chosen this name. Perhaps he did realize how often her brothers were on her mind.

Her husband was nowhere to be seen, which maybe was no bad thing. She would carry out her scheme before he could veto it. She set up her temporary kitchen, getting the fire going in the stove. When she fried the meat, the aroma sizzled into the air, attracting the attention of men nearby. A couple of them wandered over.

"The stew will be ready in an hour," she said. "Come back then."

Sure enough, an hour later a crowd of men gathered near the awning, drawn by two things: the smell of the food, and the beauty of the woman cooking it.

James still had not returned. She knew he would be working hard somewhere and bit her lower lip, worrying about whether she should have told him her plan. Still, too late now. She straightened her shoulders and clanged her spoon on the side of the iron pot.

"Now, which of you is working for my husband, Mr. Randolph?" she said in a loud voice.

The men muttered, but none was able to say they were.

"He's building the wharf just there." She pointed her spoon at the plot. "A bowl is just five cents for his workers. For everyone else, it's a quarter."

The men muttered more. They'd been waiting in line and didn't want to leave. One man pulled a quarter from his pocket. Grace blessed him with her warmest smile.

"Why, thank you, sir." She slipped the coin in the pocket of her skirt and ladled a generous helping. "Spoons are there. I do hope you enjoy it."

The man tucked in and soon others followed suit. Grace made conversation with each of them, asking where they were from and whether they had family, trying to charm as many as she could.

Suddenly, her eye was caught by the sight of James jumping from boat to boat, a pile of lumber over his shoulder. It looked like he'd been stripping one of the abandoned ships. His attention was on his feet, taking care of where he stepped. She swallowed, afraid he might be angry and think she was interfering in his territory. Only one thing for it: double or quits.

A couple of men handed back their bowls. "That was mighty tasty, ma'am."

She flashed a smile. "Ah, there he is. My husband. Mr. Randolph." The men looked over their shoulders. "If you're lucky, he may have some work for some of you. And there'll be more food at the end of the day. Only five cents for his workers, of course."

The two men exchanged a look and ambled over to where James had thrown down his lumber on the harborside and was massaging his shoulder. She couldn't hear their conversation, but she could see her husband frown beneath his hat. Two more men broke away from her kitchen and joined the first pair. She saw a man gesture to the canvas shelter.

James raised his head and his eyes met hers. His mouth was the straight line she was so familiar with from the early days on the trail when he had always seemed so aloof. She gave a little wave, uncertain if he was going to laugh, or explode in anger. He did neither, but returned his attention to the four men. It looked like they were agreeing day rates, or was that just wishful thinking? James turned and—thank goodness—the four followed him as he set them to work.

. . .

James and the men were still working when Grace packed up her kitchen at the end of the afternoon and secured it on her mule. She had left her station once her first two pots had sold out, and bought more supplies from the nearest grocery store. She found it thrilling that, even after buying more food and taking account of the provisions she had bought in the morning, she had more money in her pocket than when she had set out. As promised, she provided a pot of stew toward the end of the day—the four men paying just five cents, others the full quarter.

She was painfully aware that James had failed to come over to her canvas canopy during the day. Maybe he was too furious to come near. She put a generous helping on a metal plate and added a spoon. "Would you be so kind as to take that to my husband?" she asked sweetly of the first man who had stepped forward to work that morning.

She saw James accept her peace offering, but her heart tightened when he still didn't look over at her.

When she returned to Happy Valley, she was too tired to set up the canvas shelter yet again to cook their own dinner. She gingerly took the iron pot from the mule's back and was relieved that the portion she had left in the bottom was still there. That would feed them both tonight.

James returned at about six, and lowered himself into the armchair he had salvaged a couple of days before, who knew where from. He said nothing, but ran his hands over his face before leaning back. Grace brought him a bowl of food, and sat on her stool to eat. A light rain started. James looked at where the cooking shelter should be, where the ground was getting muddier by the minute.

He rubbed through his beard at the scar on his jaw. "If you're going to do that again, I'd better make you a second mess tent."

She looked up into his steel-blue eyes, her heart beating faster.

"Then you won't need to keep moving the one that should be here."

She nodded, suppressing the urge to punch the air in triumph, and they both carried on eating, a truce of some sort between them.

Two days later, the kitchen was doing well and more men had joined James for work. Finally, the warehouses were taking shape.

Grace stood in line at the grocery store, the money in her pocket clinking in a satisfying way. She was an entrepreneur, not just a wife. The line seemed to be moving slower than usual. Perhaps she should find out who supplied the store and deal direct. There'd be more profit in it. Her fingers ran over the coins again.

A tall woman in a wide-brimmed hat was delaying things.

"You want *how* much?"

Grace couldn't hear the storekeeper's response.

"D'you want my eyeteeth at the same time? Or maybe one of my children. A bag of flour and a basket of eggs. That's all I'm after. It's not like I'm trying to cook for the Emperor of China."

There was something familiar about the voice, but Grace couldn't quite place it.

"That's the price I'm offering," the storekeeper said loudly. Grace could tell he was beginning to be perturbed by the woman.

"And just how am I supposed to feed my husband and children next week, if you've stolen all our money now?"

"If you don't like it, ma'am, you are welcome to leave my store."

Grace reached into her pocket and pulled out a few coins. She pushed past the men waiting in line and put her money on the counter. "Look, I'm in a hurry. This should cover what the lady needs."

"I don't need *charity*," the woman said. "I need a fair price."

Now Grace knew that voice. She looked up to see the woman looking down her long nose at her. They stood for a moment, each looking the other up and down.

"Lillian!"

"Oh my good Lord. Grace!"

SIXTEEN

Lillian's hand went to her chest. "If it isn't an angel standing before me. Gracie, is it really you?"

Grace stared in wonderment. Could it be true that her closest friend from the overland crossing was standing in the same shop? Under her forthright exterior, Lillian Hollingswood was the warmest woman Grace had ever met. A staunch supporter of her husband, they had safely brought a family of six children over the prairies and the mountains to make a new life in Oregon. What on earth was she doing here?

The storekeeper coughed. "You women gonna stand there all day?"

"I can't let you pay for me, Gracie," said Lillian. "I have the money. It's the *principle* of the thing. This price is extortion."

Grace laughed. Lillian hadn't changed one bit. "You must have only just arrived in San Francisco. I'm afraid this price is usual, here." She pushed her coin to the storekeeper, as the men behind were getting vocal about the wait. "Let's take your provisions and we'll settle up outside. I can come back for what I need."

Grace helped Lillian with the brown paper packages and they pushed their way out to the muddy street.

"And this is another thing," Lillian said, lifting each of her shoes in disgust. "I didn't expect streets paved with gold, but honestly, is it too much to ask them to build sidewalks?"

Grace slipped her arm through Lillian's and steered her to the square on Post Street where things were quieter. "I thought you'd settled in Oregon. I have a thousand questions."

"And I for you. How is married life treating you? I want to see that darn handsome captain of yours."

Grace bit her lip.

"What's that look for, Gracie?" Lillian narrowed her eyes. "Something wrong between you?"

"He's not... Well, he's not in the army any more. So when you meet, please don't call him captain."

Lillian frowned and pulled her chin to her chest.

"Not in the army? I thought it was his calling."

Grace fiddled with the paper around the groceries. "Things change."

Lillian patted her arm. "Look, we need to go sit and tell each other *everything*."

Grace shook her head. "Lillian, I'd love nothing better. But I have to set up my kitchen in the harbor."

Lillian raised her eyebrows.

"Mr. Randolph is building warehouses and a wharf. It's hard to get labor round here, so my kitchen is a way of attracting folk to work for him. But where are you staying? I'll come to you this evening."

"We're all the way up near the cemetery, on the road to the old mission. Pitched a tent, even though it's like a swamp. Look, I'll come to you."

"We've bought a plot on Howard and Fourth, but it's standing empty. We're camped in Happy Valley. Come and find us on First Street. And please bring the whole family. I'm longing to see them."

Grace saw a shadow cross her friend's face.

"Lillian?"

"There's lots to talk about, Gracie." Her voice cracked. "But things will be better knowing you're here. Now, you go set up that kitchen."

"That can wait—" It wasn't like Lillian to show emotion. Grace remembered her fox-like features, with sharp cheekbones and piercing eyes. Looking closer, she noticed the cheeks were sunken, and the eyes had shadows.

"No, I insist. We'll talk this evening." Lillian leaned down and kissed her on the cheek.

It was hard to watch her dear friend disappear into the crowds, particularly knowing that something was dreadfully amiss, but Grace had work to do.

There were now six men working for her husband, and Grace could see he had them operating like a military platoon. She watched from her kitchen as he showed them how to construct the warehouses in exactly the way he wanted. Buildings were being thrown up near the harbor in such a slapdash way, but James only wanted something of quality. Grace felt a warmth inside her chest as she watched how hard he worked all day, an example to his workers.

She was cleaning the pans after the midday meal when she heard a woman's voice.

"Anything left?"

Grace spun round, excitement fizzing inside. "There'll always be something for you, Lillian. How d'you find me?"

Lillian snorted. "Not hard. Asked for the pretty woman selling dinner on the harbor. Everyone knew who I meant."

Grace blushed and knew that James worried about her

drawing male attention. Not a lot she could do about it, not if she wanted to pull her weight in their marriage.

She spotted a young girl, just behind Lillian, half hiding in her skirts. "No! Is that Molly?"

Lillian took the girl's hand and drew her forward. "Say hello to Mrs. Randolph. Is she like you remember her?"

Molly nodded. "Hello, Mrs. Randolph."

Her eyes were big and blue, just like Grace recalled them. She abandoned the pots and crouched in front of Molly, face to face. "Oh, my sweet darling girl. It does my heart good to see you. Can you give me a hug?"

Molly stepped into her arms and laid her head on Grace's shoulder.

Grace pulled her close. "How old are you now?"

"I'm eight," she said, proudly.

"A very fine age to be." Grace stood up and ladled the last of the lunchtime stew onto a plate each.

"Afraid I couldn't wait 'til this evening to see you," said Lillian. "Feels like yours is the first friendly face I've seen in a long while."

Grace set her stool behind her cooking area so Lillian could sit away from the thoroughfare. She put a box for Molly and a barrel for herself.

"I persuaded Mr. Hollingswood to look after everything for a few hours so I could come now."

Grace remembered Lillian's husband, George Hollingswood, from the six months on the trail. He was a kind and sensible man who delighted in his large family who had filled his wagon with noisy chaos.

"He's desperate to see you, of course, but was willing to wait. Unlike this one." Lillian patted Molly's cotton cap. "When she heard Captain Randolph was in the city, her eyes lit up." Molly studied her feet. "She still thinks of him as her hero."

During the crossing from Independence to Oregon, two

years previously, James had saved Molly when she was swept into a river. There had been a special bond between them for the rest of the journey.

"He's working at the moment," Grace said to Molly. "But he'll be so pleased to see you."

Molly's cheeks colored and she took a cloth doll from her pocket to play with.

"So," said Lillian, finishing her plate. "Who goes first?"

"You do. When did you arrive?"

"Just a couple of days back."

"But you've been to the goldfields?"

Lillian nodded. "We headed for the Mariposa. Maybe not the best choice. It was hard to stake a claim because Frémont owns that huge tract. Most of the time, Mr. Hollingswood was working for others. Made more money than we did farming—but not a fortune."

"Hmm. That's often the way. How long were you in Mariposa?"

"Just a couple of months. We came to California through the Siskiyou Trail in October. Seems like half the Willamette is on the move."

Grace's stomach tightened at the mention of her brothers' valley, but she decided to let Lillian's story unfold. "So you had started to farm there? In Oregon?"

"Yes, but north. Near the Cascade River. It... Well... it didn't work out for us there."

A shadow of sadness settled on Lillian's face and she fiddled with the trim at the bottom of her jacket.

"Lillian?" Grace asked gently.

"Cholera took two of the children. Our boy, Benjamin, and our next-but-youngest Lizzy."

It was like all the air had been pushed from Grace's chest and the world went still. She reached out her hand and put it on Lillian's. "That is the sharpest of pains."

Lillian sniffed. "Takes them so fast. Can be sitting at breakfast and then—" She clicked her fingers. "Gone by the evening. The rest of us caught it, but not as bad as Ben and Lizzy. Weakened the whole family. Not sure how much that was down to the wicked disease, or the grief." Lillian sniffed harder and ran a handkerchief under her nose. "By then we'd missed the planting season. Did what we could but..." She sighed and straightened herself on the stool. "So George, he decides we need a fresh start. Decides we need to follow all the others to Californy."

Grace was desperate to ask a question, but wondered if she was being insensitive. "Is it possible, when you were traveling through the Willamette, you came across my brother? Zachary Sinclair. He has a wife and young children. And—" Grace's voice was hoarse as she tried to form the words. "And Tom. He stayed with Zachary. You remember Tom?"

"Sure I do. Thought of him lots when we lost Benjamin."

Grace nodded slowly as she pictured the two boys walking beside the wagons. "They became firm friends on the trail."

"But no, I'm sorry. We didn't pass a Sinclair farm."

Grace knew it had been a slim hope that the Hollingswoods might have news of her beloved family. "Tell me more. About when you arrived in California."

"By the time we reached Mariposa, it was getting cold. The snows on the mountain peaks were already thick. We stayed as long as we could. But it's no place for little children to spend the winter. So here we are. San Francisco. Waiting for the weather to improve. At least here the weather is mild." She scrunched her nose as if smelling the air. "And you?"

"We've been in California since May. Like you, Randolph decided San Francisco is a better place to be. I have a feeling he might be looking to stay."

Lillian moved her head slowly, side to side. "Could have blown me down, when you said he'd left the army. I thought military service ran through every drop in his veins."

Grace lowered her eyes. "He was discharged."

"No! What happened?"

"He won't say. It was in Mexico. He was serving in the war there. Do you remember Lieutenant Turner?"

"Of course! A lovely man. Always ready to help us overlanders."

Grace swallowed to clear her throat. "He was killed in Mexico."

Lillian tutted. "So much death. So... the discharge... it was something to do with that?"

"That's what I guessed. I tried asking. James said 'no.' Said soldiers die in war. It's a risk they all sign up for."

"But... discharged." Lillian put her hand to her mouth as she leaned forward, and lowered her voice. "What does that mean?"

"I'm not sure. I think it means they force you to leave. No pension, no nothing. It doesn't sound honorable." She let out a long breath. "But *something* happened. Something made him... change."

"But he won't say what?"

She shook her head sadly. "If I ask, he, like... he goes into himself. Gets moody. Next thing I know, he's taking comfort in a bottle of spirits. So I've learned not to ask."

Lillian put her hand on Grace's and gave it a shake. "Oh, Gracie. That's hard."

They sat together a moment, feeling each other's pain.

Grace got up to put some coffee on the stove.

Lillian's eyes followed her. "And you haven't any little ones?"

Grace paused to compose herself and then continued to measure the ground coffee beans. "That hasn't happened for us." She returned to her barrel while the coffee was heating. She glanced at Molly who was absorbed with her doll, teaching it to ride a horse she had conjured up from some vegetables. "There was one time when I thought I had taken. But it wasn't to be. A couple of weeks later, the bleeding came again. Heavier than usual, more painful."

Lillian got up from her stool and crouched to envelop Grace in her arms. "Gracie, darlin'. Your time will come."

She buried her head into Lillian's shoulder. "Will it though? We've been married more than two years."

"Much of it with Randolph fighting south of the border, sounds like."

"I know." She sat back a little, fighting the tears. "But it aches so bad. Like there's a big hole where I'm grieving for something that never was. Each time my bleeding comes on, I feel like sitting down and sobbing."

She heard the coffee bubbling on the stove so shook herself free, got up and poured it into cups.

"And look at me, crying over this, when you've lost two of your darling little ones."

"Grief is grief," Lillian said, returning to her stool. "One person isn't forbidden to mourn, because someone else got it worse." She took a sip of the coffee. "And how does Captain Randolph feel about it?"

"—*Mr.* Randolph."

"Darn. That's going to take some getting used to."

Grace blew out a breath. "I don't know. Another thing we're not talking about. Again, I tried. But it was like..." She lowered her voice to a whisper. "Like I was blaming him for not putting a child inside me."

Lillian put her head on one side to study Grace. "Oh, my dear sweet friend. Sounds like you two have a lot to work out. And ignoring it ain't gonna make it any better."

They drank their coffee and sat in silence for a while, each deep in their thoughts.

Molly returned, growing bored of her game.

Lillian slapped her thighs. "Tell me what the plan is here."

Grace picked up the cups and gave them a wipe. "Come and have a look."

They ducked out of the canvas and onto the harborside. "We've bought two water plots. Run from there to there." Grace pointed to markers.

Lillian grunted appreciatively. "Good amount of land."

"And he's building warehouses. Then we're going to build a house on the plot in town. And *then* James wants to construct a proper wharf, going out into the water."

"My. You really do have plans."

"Come. I'll show you." Grace began walking. "And look, there's James. He'll be so pleased to see you."

James was standing by the footings of his warehouse, making sure they were ready to build on. Grace shouted and he looked over, taking off his hat to wipe sweat from his brow.

"You'll never believe who I've found," Grace called.

Molly recognized him and slipped her hand out of Lillian's. She ran forward, and then paused, turning back to her mother, an uncertain look on her face.

"Go," Grace urged. "Say hello."

Molly ran and stopped in front of James, as Grace and Lillian hurried up behind. He looked at the girl, his mouth open, then glanced at Grace and the tall woman beside her, and his puzzlement melted.

He dropped to his haunches. "Molly? Molly Hollingswood?"

She nodded.

Grace thought he would smile, or laugh. Instead, she could see him blinking back tears. He lifted her up and Molly swung her legs around him, as she had when they'd been on the trail. The girl put her arms tight around his neck, perhaps remembering that time he'd pulled her from a raging river.

He closed his eyes, and Grace saw a look of ineffable

sadness cross his face. She turned away to compose herself, before turning back and pretending to smile.

SEVENTEEN

George Hollingswood arrived that evening at their plot, followed by his family.

"Captain—sorry—*Mr.* Randolph." Mr. Hollingswood put out his hand.

Randolph hesitated. Previously, he had been responsible for this man's safety and had authority over him. Now he must get used to treating him as an equal. He shook his hand. "It's good to see you and your family."

Hollingswood bowed to Grace and then grinned. "You're looking well, Mrs. Randolph." He seemed to still be the good-hearted man Randolph remembered, well-built with strong shoulders, and thick reddish hair when he raised his hat.

Lillian arrived, holding Molly's hand as they picked their way through the sandy soil and onto the wooden boards Randolph had laid over their plot. He briefly held Lillian's elbow. "Careful where you step, Mrs. Hollingswood. The floor is uneven."

Next came the twin girls who stood close together, smaller versions of their mother, with the same narrow face, sharp cheekbones and straight nose that she had.

"You have similar names, as I recall. Harriet?"

The girls were too shy to speak, so Lillian stepped in. "Hester and Hetty."

"Of course. I do apologize. It's been more than two years since I saw you."

"Sit on the bench," Grace said. The twins settled close together. "How old are you now?"

They were still tongue-tied.

"Twelve," said Lillian. "Just last month."

Finally, a lanky young man came forward. He had the same rusty-brown hair as his father, but had not yet developed Hollingswood's confidence.

Randolph put out his hand. "Simon, isn't it? You've grown taller than your father."

Simon made a movement halfway to a salute before realizing he should take Randolph's hand.

Mr. Hollingswood slapped his son's back. "Takes after his mother with his height. Grown man now. Eighteen, if you can believe it."

Randolph had borrowed chairs and benches from neighbors to be able to sit everyone round the open fire. Grace handed out food, making sure each plate was full to overflowing.

The conversation was bittersweet, full of memories and absences. Randolph asked about the Hollingswoods' experience of Oregon, and Mr. Hollingswood tried to put a brave face on things, particularly the loss of Ben and Lizzy. He said he wanted to get back to Oregon at some point, try farming again, but with more capital behind him.

Randolph glanced at Grace, fearing deep down she hoped for something similar, but her face revealed nothing.

Despite the impression made by Lillian's haggling over prices, the Hollingswoods had done well enough in the short time they were in Mariposa.

"Simon's a good worker," said Mr. Hollingswood.

"Takes after his father," said Lillian, patting her husband's thigh.

They discussed where the Hollingswoods were living and agreed it was too far distant from opportunities in the city.

"Will you buy a plot?" asked Randolph.

"Darn right, I will."

"Why don't you buy one near ours?" Grace asked.

Mr. Hollingswood waggled his head, thinking about it. "This feels a bit too close to the harbor."

Grace waved her arm to dismiss the comment. "This is just the place we're squatting. The plot we've bought is on Fourth. That's where I mean."

"We'll start building a house there, just as soon as I've finished the warehouses," said Randolph.

"Come tomorrow and see where it is," suggested Grace.

Lillian looked keen on this suggestion. "George, you know how much I would love to be near Gracie. There're so many ways we could help each other."

"Absolutely," said Grace. "We should stick together. You don't know who to trust in this city."

A time was agreed for a visit the next day.

Randolph sat back in his chair, steepling his fingers against his lips. With Grace's proposal that the two families live close by, an idea was rapidly forming in his head; something that could benefit every soul sitting around his fire.

"Mr. Hollingswood, have you and Simon found work yet? Or are you living off your gold?"

"Haven't been here long enough to get work. But we definitely will. I want to keep hold of that capital."

"How 'bout you and Simon join me at the warehouse?"

Mr. Hollingswood sat forward eagerly. "What d'you need?"

"At the moment, it's construction. I'm trying to get that warehouse built as fast as I can."

"We'd be delighted to come work for you."

Randolph shook his head. "I don't mean that. How about we become partners? A proper partnership, I mean. Half Randolph, half Hollingswood. Split the capital, put in the work. And split the profits."

Mr. Hollingswood whistled through his teeth. "My." He looked at Lillian, who raised her eyebrows. "What d'you think, hun?"

"I think you don't look a gift horse in the mouth."

Mr. Hollingswood grinned, but just as quickly a frown came to his face as he considered Randolph's proposal. "But why would you want to do that? You'd be better off paying us a day rate and keeping all the profits. I'm right, aren't I, Mrs. Randolph?"

"I'm sure my husband knows what he's doing," Grace replied smoothly.

Randolph sat forward, closer to Hollingswood. "As my wife said, the most valuable thing in this city is knowing who you can trust. And I trust you, Mr. Hollingswood. I saw how hard you worked to get your wagon and family across the Rockies. I know you're a good, honest man."

Mr. Hollingswood muttered something about not knowing about that, and stared at his boots.

Randolph admired his modesty. He knew he needed to explain his thinking. "This city is lawless at the moment. And I think it's going to get worse. No one's in charge. The folks in Washington sure as hell don't seem interested in governing California. There're men arriving every day, and none of us knows if they're saints or sinners."

"Ain't that the truth," muttered Lillian.

"There was a code of honor in the hills when we were mining. A man could leave his tools to show it was his claim, come back a couple of days later, and no one would've claim-jumped. I doubt that's going to last. So I'm proposing we partner up the two families. You building a home close by would be a weight off my mind, thinking about my wife."

Grace began to protest. "Have I ever given cause—"

Randolph raised his palm. "Oh, I know you can take care of yourself, Grace. You're the strongest woman I ever met. Why I married you. But that doesn't stop a man worrying." He turned back to Hollingswood. "But partnering makes business sense too. Means we can build quicker. Catch this bubble before it bursts."

"What about your dream of a farm in Oregon, Pa?" asked Simon.

Randolph looked at him. It was the first time he'd heard the young man speak. "It's a good point, son. When you want to go, I'll buy out your half. Or you sell it to someone else. Aren't we all trying to make as much money as we can, before deciding what we want to do next?"

Mr. Hollingswood put a hand on Simon's shoulder. "You happy with this, son? Because if we go into it, I see it as a Hollingswood family business. Fifty-fifty. Randolphs, Hollingswoods."

Simon nodded.

"Well in that case—" Mr. Hollingswood clicked his tongue and put out his hand. "Let's shake on it."

Randolph took the hand. "Work starts tomorrow."

At last, the project was going as Randolph had hoped. The construction of the warehouse continued at an even faster pace with Hollingswood and Simon involved. They stripped an abandoned brig of anything they could; the mast was perfect to support one of the walls. They ripped up the deck, removed hardware from the quarters—all of it solidly made, much of it brass. They curled rope and folded canvas. The boat ended up looking like a skeleton washed back and forth by the tide.

The warehouses rose from the harborside, as if the ship had given birth to something new. The wood was well-seasoned and difficult to work, but Randolph hoped it would be durable.

As soon as the first warehouse was ready, Randolph filled it with goods straight off the latest ship. He knew how Hollingswood's warmth charmed people, so his job was to make contacts across the city: storekeepers who would buy sacks of grain that had stayed dry, and fabrics undamaged by being left in the streets. Business was good.

The six men who had labored expected to need to find new employment and were relieved when Randolph kept them on: he wanted them to build homes for the Hollingswoods and for Grace, before the year turned. A tall ask, but he had formed a strong team.

They selected another ship to harvest. Randolph checked with the *alcalde* for the owner, but was assured it had been stranded many months ago.

This was a clipper, and he was astonished that such a valuable ship could be abandoned. He ran his hand over the fine wood in the captain's quarters and pictured how it would look in the new house. The men carefully took the cabin apart, keeping carved embellishments intact. There were even windows, which Randolph prized free with great care. He looked forward to seeing the joy on Grace's face when he took them home.

His building crew didn't let him down. Very soon, he stood on Howard Street to admire his new house. Yes, it was small, only one story high, but there was just the pair of them still, and it was all they needed. The main door was in the middle, with a window each side. A chimney emerged from the center of the roof. It was simple enough that a child could have designed it, but Randolph thought it robust, and that was the important thing. He made sure the shutters at the windows kept out the wind, and the vertical planks that made up the walls overlapped thoroughly. He would build something larger if things went well.

Randolph was relieved that the Hollingswoods managed to buy the plot directly behind. Their home was similar but two stories high. Lillian had marveled as it took shape, swearing she'd never be able to live in such a grand place. Grace pointed out that grander villas with porches and colonnades were already being built for people who were doing well from the gold.

Both families were able to move in by January. They gathered to celebrate and bring in the New Year.

Hollingswood lavishly bought real French champagne. "To 1849! May it bring riches to each and every one of us."

The six workmen again feared they would need to find new work as the houses were finished, but the man who had bought the opposite corner plot of Howard and Fourth planned a grand hotel and wanted it built within weeks. Randolph had no need of the men, now he was running the warehouses, but he wanted to help the team. One of the crew had emerged as their foreman so Randolph brought him to meet the ambitious hotel owner.

Grace had been fetching wood from the store at the time and paused to greet the man.

"Good to see you again, Mrs. Randolph," the foreman said. "Me and the men, we reckon this town is going to boom. Hoping to stay. We'll make more money here than chancing our luck in the goldfields." The foreman turned back to Randolph. "Thank you for the introduction, Captain. We'd be pleased to build that hotel."

Grace stopped dead when she heard how the man had addressed her husband. She glanced at James's face, but saw no discomfort.

That evening, sewing by the fire in their new parlor, she asked him about it.

"I heard one of the men call you 'captain'."

James looked up from the book he was reading, but said nothing.

"I thought that was in the past."

He put the book down. "Hollingswood couldn't remember to call me anything else. Simon neither."

"And the other men? They've only known you since settling here."

"Picked it up." He cleared his throat and used a finger to loosen his collar. "I guess I treated them like they were my platoon."

She went back to her sewing before carefully asking, "Did they know about your time in the army?"

"Hollingswood told them about how we met. Traveling overland. So... yes."

Grace swallowed, wondering if at last he was ready to tell her more. "And since then? Did you tell him about '47?"

The blue of James's eyes seemed to go colder. "And why would I do that?"

"I don't know. I just thought..." She couldn't put it into words.

James picked up his book without a word and she knew the subject was closed.

Later that night, James finished the rest of a bottle of whiskey and fell into bed, falling into a noisy sleep. Grace turned to face the wall and let the tears come.

EIGHTEEN

As promised, the men completed the building opposite within weeks. Grace was briefly introduced to the owner, a Frenchman, Monsieur Albert Bernard, but was dismayed to find it was not the hotel she had been expecting. Instead, it was a saloon, with rooms to rent on the floor above. It would be noisy at night, and she feared James would spend his evenings there.

Grace and Lillian were scrubbing clothes when they paused to watch M. Bernard accompany two elegant women down the street, one on each arm. They were dressed in blue silk, and had bonnets which sat well back on their heads, showing luxuriant blond hair. The women walked with a certain poise, chins held high, backs straight.

Grace picked up a shirt. "At least it looks like the saloon will be managed by women with a certain style."

Lillian watched the two women pass. "Fair but frail."

"Pardon me?"

"Those ladies. I suspect the gentlemen will be paying for their time."

Grace's eyes widened and she looked again at the women. "But they seem so... poised."

The ladies disappeared into the saloon and M. Bernard closed the doors behind them.

Over the next couple of days, Lillian picked up the gossip. The women were from Paris, supposedly Bernard's sisters, but Lillian didn't credit that. She'd heard the women were skilful at cards, luring the customers into games of vingt-et-un and monte. More fool them, she snarked. Grace was simply relieved that James's visits to the saloon were only occasional.

Truth was, Randolph favored a small bar close to the harbor. Most nights, he bought a drink after locking the warehouse and before walking up the hill to Fourth Street for dinner. Increasingly, he returned to the bar after Grace had retired for the night. That way, he could avoid her judgmental looks. After all, he didn't drink half as much as many men he knew. What was she complaining about?

It was a Saturday night in early February and Randolph, Hollingswood and Simon sat at a table in the corner. After a hard but profitable week, Randolph felt they deserved leisure time, especially as tomorrow would be the sabbath. He drank whiskey, while Hollingswood and his son preferred beer. They talked about the latest arrivals of hopefuls, a year on from the first discovery of gold at Sutter's Mill. Each week brought a new boatful; now many were Americans who had sailed south to Panama, struggled across the isthmus and paid for a berth on the first ship traveling north.

Boats brought cargo as well as men, and Randolph's first warehouse was full to the brim with foodstuffs, building materials, and luxury goods—with the second one heading that way.

He knew their success was partly down to Hollingswood's nature. In the bar, he was talkative, eager to discuss the day, plan the future. Randolph was increasingly taciturn, despite their early business success. He would sit with his whiskey, sometimes going an hour without speaking. He lowered his hat and watched people coming and going, trying to take the measure of each man.

When he did rouse himself to speak, it was often to condemn the criminality increasing in the city. How could they build a business with such lawlessness? The authorities were too weak to control it. There was a garrison stationed to the south, in Monterey, but what was the point of that? The United States government did not see fit to move troops closer to San Francisco where they were needed.

Over his whiskey, he thought about the gangs who were taking hold. Only that morning, a man had spoken to him about the safety of the warehouses, and how it would be in Randolph's interests to hire him to keep an eye on them. Impudent scoundrel. Randolph had not liked the man's tone and sent him away with a flea in his ear. He wondered if he might need to carry his pistol when working alone. Should he suggest Grace do the same? He breathed out. Perhaps best not to put fears in her head.

A young man burst into the bar and forced all thoughts of Grace from Randolph's mind.

"Fire! There's a fire."

Randolph jerked up his head. Had he heard right, or had he drowsed off and his mind was taking him back to his past yet again?

The youth continued to shout.

"Where?" asked Hollingswood.

"Down on the harbor. We need help. Things are going up fast."

Randolph, Hollingswood and Simon leaped to their feet, pulling on their jackets and grabbing their hats. Outside, they could smell soot on the air. Randolph was suddenly sweating and his heart beating like a bird was trapped in his chest. He hesitated, not wanting to face what they might find.

Hollingswood and Simon raced ahead toward the harborside. Randolph clenched his teeth together until his jaw ached. *Get a grip, man. This is no time to...* He forced himself to follow them.

Many warehouses were already alight, golden flames against the black of the night sky. Randolph turned to his right, catching up with Hollingswood and Simon as they headed along the shoreline. He was horrified by what he could see. The roof of one of his warehouses was already burning—flames were licking down the sides, the tar which had sealed the wood as a ship now making it like tinder. By the time the three men reached the warehouse, it was fully alight. They stood dumbfounded in front, with men running to and fro on the street behind them.

"There was no one in here, was there?" Randolph asked.

Hollingswood frowned. "What d'you mean?"

"I just..."

Randolph scrambled for the key in his coat pocket. He knew his fear was irrational. Why would anyone be inside? But... He struggled with the lock, not noticing the ironwork was already hot to the touch. He pulled the double doors open and was knocked off his feet as flames leaped out, fed by the sudden rush of air from the open door.

The goods were already on fire. The woody smell took him back to his months camping. Bags of wheat produced toasty flavored smoke. Jars shattered and popped in the heat.

Hollingswood ran past. He'd found a bucket and filled it with sea water, and threw it on the growing flames.

Randolph got to his feet, stunned by what was happening. "George! There's no point." He grabbed Hollingswood by the shoulders and dragged him out to the street.

Simon was returning with another bucket.

At least the youth was doing something. Randolph had to pull himself together, overcome his fears. This was about the present, not the past.

"We should do what we can to save the other warehouse," Randolph shouted above the roar of the flames.

Simon nodded, quick to follow whatever orders Randolph gave him.

The second warehouse stood so close there was barely room for a man to pass between the two. Would it be possible to save it?

"You two, soak the walls with sea water," he yelled. "I'll get as many of our goods out as possible."

He opened the second warehouse, relieved that, so far, the fire had not reached it. It held fewer items than the first. If he could get the goods out, that would be something. He seized the crate nearest the door, with no idea what was inside it. He set it in the middle of the road.

A man ran past and Randolph reached out to stop him. "I need your help."

The man shook him off. "I have my own goods to save." He rushed into the darkness.

Randolph returned to the open doors of the warehouse and grabbed the next packing case, then a large sack of who knew what. Hollingswood and Simon threw water where they could. It hissed ominously. This warehouse was getting hot from the blaze next to it.

Randolph threw down his hat by the few items he had saved and ran his hand through his hair. What was for the best? There was no hope of saving either warehouse. Should all three of them be clearing it? Or was the water slowing the progress of the fire, to give him more time?

As if reading his thoughts, Hollingswood paused beside him. "It's useless. We don't have enough water."

Randolph nodded. "Clear what we can."

He ran back into the warehouse, but it was now alight. The roof was crackling above him. Orange flames leaped up at the back of the storage area where a spark had fallen on something combustible. He turned a barrel of ale on its side and rolled it out, through the double doors. Simon followed with a second barrel. Hollingswood hoisted a sack onto his back and clambered out, bent double. The mismatched objects gathered in a pile on the street.

They returned, even though the fire had taken hold inside. Smoke filled the space, making Randolph cough and stinging his eyes. There was a caramel smell as a barrel of molasses took light, a smell he would have delighted in at any other time. He grabbed a canvas bale, tied with rope. Simon and Hollingswood were close behind, picking up whatever they could, throwing them onto the mound of goods.

Running back to the warehouse doors, Randolph heard a crash. The central ridge beam of the roof had given way and fallen into the space. The remainder of the roof followed, crushing whatever goods were left behind, making him leap backwards.

Randolph thrust a hand on Simon's chest as he tried to return for more goods. "There's nothing to be done."

The three men stood there, mesmerized by the flames. Randolph could scarcely believe this was happening, that all those precious goods were being turned into fuel for an inferno.

Foul-smelling smoke billowed from the door and forced them further back.

Randolph returned to their pile of goods. They had saved a pathetically small amount. He kicked a bale in frustration.

Breathing hard and wiping sweat from his eyes, he looked along the street. All the other warehouses were destroyed: none had escaped the fire. Men ran back and forth, panicked witless by the disaster.

Hollingswood put his hand on his shoulder.

"I don't think this was bad luck," growled Randolph.

Hollingswood rubbed his brow. "What d'you mean?"

"For the fire to take so quickly."

"The warehouses are full of things that burn. The whole city is, when you think about it. A city made of wood and canvas, lit by oil lamps, food cooked on stoves," Hollingswood reasoned.

Randolph shook his head. "But for so many warehouses..."

"But, James, who would be so wicked to deliberately do such a reckless thing?"

Randolph thought of the man he had spoken to that morning, but said nothing.

They watched the smoke roll and swirl into the air, dark gray against the night sky, red sparks of soot floating upwards, competing with the stars.

Hollingswood was right. The whole city was a tinderbox, ready to go up. Who knew where these sparks would land...

His throat went dry. Why had he not realized it before?

"The women," Randolph cried in anguish. "We need to get to the women."

NINETEEN

Grace woke suddenly, disturbed by voices in the street. Nothing unusual in that: probably men leaving that damned saloon. She felt across the bed. Empty. Nothing unusual in that neither, these days. She couldn't tell what time it was, so she turned over and tried to get back to sleep.

The voices continued. She cursed inwardly. Didn't those men know some folk had to get up early? Or that there were children nearby?

She rose and pushed her feet into her slippers. At the window, she pulled back the floral fabric tacked up as a curtain. Maybe it was closer to morning than she'd thought: the sky to the east was pale gray, the clouds looked like they'd been dragged through filthy water.

She sniffed: the bitter smell of soot and oil, mixed with an earthy tang of wood. Dear God, they weren't clouds. There was a fire!

Suddenly, flames leaped into the air, as if breaking free of a building nearby. Then another. The fire must be leaping from building to building, pushed by the onshore wind. And it was coming her way.

She threw some clothes on, pulling a bodice and a woolen skirt directly over her nightdress. She ran into the lobby by the door and unhooked her coat, then stopped. No. Not that coat. She returned to the bedroom and lifted down her heaviest winter coat from behind the door. Only she knew why it was so heavy: she had left a line of gold nuggets sewn into an inner seam. Why had she done it? She didn't know. Maybe deep down she was afraid that disaster would catch up with them.

Then she hurried to the front door, and pulled on her stout boots. Where on God's earth was James? What if he were still at the saloon, too drunk to realize what was happening? But if anyone could look after himself in a crisis, surely it was him. Lillian, George and the children—they were her priority.

Stepping outside, the stench of smoke was stronger. Grace ran the few steps to the Hollingswood house, banged on the door and hollered their names. She dashed round to the back, trampling winter plants in Lillian's garden, and rattled the handle of the door. It opened and she darted into the darkened house, shouting at the top of her voice.

The house was bigger than her own one-story dwelling, with bedrooms upstairs. Grace reached the bottom of the stairs and saw Lillian at the top, ethereal in her white nightdress, and holding a candle.

"Lillian, it's me. There's a fire—"

"Say—"

"We need to get out. Now." Grace scurried up the stairs. "Truly! It's coming our way."

Lillian stared at Grace's face, then seemed to understand the danger and turned on her heel. "I'll get Molly. She sleeps with us. The twins: they're in there."

Grace shoved open the door to the little room, but couldn't make it out, without a candle. She felt her way to the window and pulled down the curtain. There was a narrow bed, the girls sleeping together. She shook them awake.

"Hester. Hetty."

They began to move.

"You've got to get up. We've got to leave."

They were too sleepy to understand.

"Now! Where are your clothes?"

Hester yawned and pointed to the trunk.

Grace pulled the girls upright. "Get dressed. It doesn't matter what you wear. Pull on anything."

Finally, the twins picked up the urgency in Grace's voice.

"I've got Molly," Lillian shouted and Grace could hear them clattering down the stairs.

Grace grabbed other pieces of clothing: bonnets and shawls. "Don't worry, we'll get you dressed once you're outside." She pushed them out of the room and hurried them down the stairs to the back door in the kitchen.

"Shoes?"

Hester nodded and was about to sit down to put them on. Grace glanced behind her, out of the open kitchen door—she could see everything more clearly now, as the fire lit up the sky, casting a strange glow. She gathered an armful of footwear and dragged the girls outside. They ran to their mother, who hugged them and kissed their heads.

"Where's George?" Grace asked. "Simon?"

Lillian shook her head. "Randolph?"

"Not here neither."

"Damnation. I'm guessing they're all together somewhere, then. Down near the harbor."

They stood in the cottage garden and watched the flames come closer.

"Maybe we'll be safer on the street," Lillian said. "Further from any buildings."

They made their way to Howard Street and Lillian stood in the center, too shocked to think what to do next.

Grace looked around. What if there were people who had

not been roused yet? Although the bar of the saloon was dark and empty, there could be folk asleep upstairs.

Grace called out, "Monsieur Bernard!"

She shook the main door, but it was locked shut.

"I might be able to get in round the back," she said to Lillian. "Oh, Lord. The back—the stables. Our horses. The mules."

The livery stabled horses and mules for local people. Grace took off down the alley and reached the wooden building behind. She could hear horses inside, restless and snickering as if they knew they were in danger. She struggled to raise the wooden bar that held the double doors shut. Lillian was at her side, helping to lift it.

"I told the twins to stay with Molly," she said breathlessly. "And to stand in the open on the street."

The rich whiff of hay hit Grace, replacing the bitter smell of the fire. But the place could be an inferno in moments.

Grace and Lillian ran to the stalls and opened the doors. The animals could sense something in the air and refused to leave, horses shying away as Grace tried to force them out.

A man ran in and Grace recognized the stable manager. Thank God.

The animals trusted him and as he led a stallion out into the central driveway, others followed. Grace saw it was Randolph's horse. The man slapped the rump with his hat and jeered at it. The horse bolted forward and out of the livery, into the darkness.

Grace and Lillian now had all the stall doors open and the man led and cajoled the terrified mules and horses outside.

"We need to get back to the girls," Lillian said, as they left the stables behind them. "The horses will be running free, God knows where."

Grace looked up at the back of the saloon. The windows had slats, but in between she could see a woman's face. She was shouting at her and banging on the window, but Grace couldn't hear above the roar of the fire and shouts of men. It looked like one of the elegant French women, but why on earth had she not got out? She must be trapped.

"You go," Grace called to Lillian. "I'll be there in a minute."

Grace raised the latch of the back door where she had seen the two French women lounge at odd times of the day. It didn't open, so she barreled at it with her shoulder, with all her might. The bolt fell free of the surround and the door burst open.

She was in the kitchen and found an oil lamp still lit, standing on the table. She picked it up and made her way through to the bar at the front. Grace knew the layout well enough: she'd watched it being built, and had come to find James on occasion. The stairs from the bar were wide. At the top, she hurried along the corridor to the back, past a couple of rooms. The furthest door was locked with a large padlock. She shouted through the door and heard desperate replies—two voices—as the women prayed their release was at hand. The women banged on the door as Grace pulled at the padlock.

There was no opening it. She put the lamp down and looked around for something to break it, but could see nothing strong enough.

"It's locked," she cried out, stupidly.

"The key. *La clef.* The key." The woman's voice was frantic.

"Where is it? I don't see it."

"*En haut.* Above. Above the door."

Grace slid her fingers along the top of the sill and knocked the key to the ground. It was heavy and solid, just like the padlock. She fumbled as she tried to put it in the slot.

"More haste, less speed," she muttered under her breath.

The padlock fell away and she threw open the door. The women all but flew out, panting with relief.

There was a crash at the other end of the corridor. A portion of the ceiling was on fire—but there was no other way out. They picked up their skirts, the French women their satin and silk, Grace her plain woolen, and ran for the stairs, the smoke making them choke.

"The back door is open," Grace shouted.

One of the women grasped her hand as they ran.

Reaching the door and bursting outside, the air was colder but full of smoke.

The two women hugged Grace to them, crying and laughing. "*Mon Dieu. Merci.* You save us. God knows what—"

"We're not safe yet." Grace led the way down the alley to the street.

Lillian was still there with Molly and the twins. She groaned when she saw Grace. "Dear God, I was so worried—"

"I'm here now—"

"People are going to the hill the other side of Market Street. They think it will be safer up there."

"*Mais...* Is no one trying to stop the fire?" asked one of the women, gesticulating frantically. "In Paris, we have water cisterns. We have fire soldiers."

Grace shook her head. "Nothing like that here."

She looked at her small home, not yet engulfed in flames, but it was only a matter of time. Where the hell was James? He must know about the fire. Why wasn't he *here*?

"You go. I'll follow very soon."

Lillian took her arm. "We have to leave. Now."

Grace shook her arm free.

"Your friend is right," said the other French woman. "We go to higher ground."

But that house held precious things of her father's that she had carried with her since he had died, three years ago. Dragged over the prairies, over the Rockies, over the Cascades. She refused to let that last link with her father be broken.

"I'll join you there," she said, and ran toward her house, before they could drag her away.

TWENTY

Randolph raced from the harbor, not caring that he was leaving Hollingswood and Simon in his wake. He had to get to Grace.

He dodged between men, a few trying to stop the fire, some retrieving valuables from buildings, many trying to find a place of safety.

A drunk sat on a barrel in the middle of Mission Street, stupefied by alcohol and laughing at the commotion. A storekeeper was beside himself, watching his shop and stock be engulfed in flames. Randolph ignored them all, and ran on, past Second Street, past Third. He was nearly there. A man grabbed him and asked something in a language he didn't know. He shook himself free and ran on.

His head ached as memories of battle crowded his brain. The noise, the smell. Horses galloping free, terrified and knocking over anything and anyone in their path. But it was more than that. Fire. Fire was what he never wanted to experience again. And yet here he was, little more than a year later. It was like the Devil and all his demons were chasing him, bringing the fires of hell with them.

He was approaching Fourth. A tall woman, a child in her

arms—surely that was Lillian and Molly. They were heading north, toward California Hill. If that was Lillian, then where was Grace? He ran even faster, his lungs painful with breathing in the filthy air.

"Lillian!"

The woman stopped and turned. He reached her.

"Where's George?" she cried, her hand on his chest, tears in her eyes. The twins crowded round.

"George? Why he's—" Randolph indicated to the way he'd come. "On his way."

Simon came into view and Lillian stepped toward him, calling his name.

Randolph grasped her hand. "But Grace? Where is she?"

Lillian shook her head and hollered again to Simon.

"Why isn't she with you?" Randolph insisted on a reply, the acid taste of fear rising into his mouth as Lillian failed to speak to him.

"She went back to your house," said Hester. "Ma told her not to. Maybe she thought you—"

But Randolph didn't wait to hear more. He took off left, down Fourth Street. The Hollingswood house was alight, the saloon opposite likewise. He came to the home they had proudly built together. Sparks had fallen on the roof and were starting small fires, which would soon join together.

Where was Grace? What if she were inside?

He pulled open the front door, fearful he would fuel any flames, but knowing he had to find his wife. Terror hit his gut so hard, he thought he was going to be sick.

"Grace? Grace!"

He heard a scratching noise in the kitchen. Running through, he found Grace on her knees in front of the stove, floorboards around in pieces and digging with her hands.

He stared at her in horror. "What are you doing?"

She stopped and looked up at him. "James. You're alive!"

"Of course I'm—Why are you here?"

Her eyes were wide, like an animal that has been cornered and doesn't know whether to attack or run. "I thought you were... You had to be..." She ran dirty fingers over her scalp. "Because otherwise you'd be here..."

He'd failed her, failed to protect her.

She didn't get up, but frantically returned to her digging. "That's why I had to—"

He lunged down and caught her arm. "Grace! Stop."

"I came back for Father's guns," she said, her voice taut, looking beyond him. "And then I thought: if I can get even one of the strongboxes, it will be enough."

"Enough for what?"

"Enough to start again. Me. The Hollingswoods. 'Cos I thought you'd gone."

"Leave it. It's only money. I'm here now." He pulled her to her feet. There was dirt and black smudges all over her beautiful face. Her nighttime braid fell down the back of her heavy winter coat. "The house is already on fire, for God's sake." He pulled her behind him to the lobby. He would carry her out, if necessary.

"I'm not going without these." She had already placed the pistol case and two rifles by the door. "They are all I've got of my father."

Randolph grunted. What kind of madness had taken hold of her? "Fine. We take them." He slung a rifle across his back, and Grace did the same. He took the pistol case in one hand and firmly held Grace in the other, pulling her out of the house.

On the street, they paused to look back. The roof was burning now and it would only be moments before the whole house was destroyed.

"I promised Lillian I'd follow her to the hill."

Grace didn't seem willing to acknowledge him. He couldn't understand it. "I know. I saw them."

They turned their steps in the direction of California Hill. As the ground rose steeply, the space between tents formed a firebreak. When Grace paused to catch her breath, Randolph turned and stared down at the chaos below.

It began to rain. Big, fat drops which made a pat as they hit the earth. The pattering got faster as the rain fell more heavily, rivulets running down the path. Grace already had a coat, so the only thing he could give to protect her was his hat. It sat deep on her head. They would soon be wet through, but he rejoiced at the rain. Nature would end the fire.

Randolph led the way up to the top of the hill. There were hundreds of people, wearing nothing more than what they had fled in, sitting and watching in the darkness.

They huddled on the sodden earth. He drew Grace nearer and she returned his hat to him, nestling her head into his shoulder. At last.

"You weren't there," she said, her voice hoarse from the smoke.

"I know." She couldn't make him feel guiltier than he already did.

"I thought you were dead. Or you had left me."

He pulled her closer and kissed the top of her head. "Why would you think that? I would never leave you."

She was quiet for a while and then whispered, "I think you left me some time ago."

Randolph watched the sun rise over the bay as Grace slept fitfully, her head in his lap. He had sat for hours on the leather pistol case, rather than the wet ground. The rain passed and it was bitingly cold. He put his palms on the earth, trying to cool the blisters growing on his palms. The pain of the burns was nothing to the deep ache inside caused by his wife's words, that no amount of thinking could soothe.

They needed to find shelter. He gently shook her awake. "Time to see what's left of things."

He helped her struggle to her feet, stiff from the night cold. Her face was filthy, with wisps of hair loose around her face. At least she was wearing her thickest winter coat, the one with sleeves that came down beyond her hands.

They wandered through the desperate groups on the hillside until they found the Hollingswoods. George was with them, so the whole family was safe and reunited.

"We're going to try the mission," said George.

"That's quite a walk for the girls," said Randolph.

"I know. But surely they won't turn away women and children."

The whole family looked ragged with exhaustion.

"I'm going to secure the goods we saved last night," said Randolph. "I'll see if any are good enough to sell. Then I'll dig up a strongbox. Take out enough dust to pay for a couple of tents. Some food."

Hollingswood pulled at his beard. "Sounds a good idea."

"Once the women are safe, you and Simon should come back to our plots and see what we can salvage. Grace, I'll come and fetch you from the mission when I've found a shelter."

She folded her arms. "Why would I want to go up to the mission, when there's so much to be done here."

"To be with Lillian and the girls—"

"James, I'm perfectly capable of making a start at the house."

"I thought—"

"If I go to the mission, I'll only worry about everything that needs to be done."

Randolph took a deep breath through his nose. She was not deliberately being difficult, he told himself. She was tired and cold. The night's events had shocked her. "Very well. But we stay together."

"Fine."

Randolph and Grace slung the rifles onto their backs. Hollingswood agreed to take care of the pistols until they had sorted themselves out.

They all made their way down the hill, the Hollingswoods turning south when they reached Market Street, Randolph and Grace turning north, to make their way to the harbor.

Randolph was surprised how the fire had destroyed the city in pockets. In some places, buildings were burned to the ground. In others, a row of tents stood untouched.

The warehouses beside the harbor were among the worst to be hit. Every one of them had been destroyed. He reached the remains of the two warehouses of which he had been so proud, and on which their future depended. Gray smoke floated up from one of them. There was a crunching, crackly sound, like logs shifting in a grate. A set of charred trusses fell against each other and collapsed inwards.

Grace stared at the remains, and then she turned toward him, her mouth open, as if unable to find the words, and fighting back the tears.

TWENTY-ONE

Randolph kicked his way through the charred debris that covered the road, looking for the pile of stock he had thrown together, only hours before. He couldn't see it, and widened his search, his eyes on the ground. Maybe he was looking in the wrong place. Everything was so different this morning.

"What does it look like?" Grace asked.

"An ordinary pile of goods. Barrels. Crates. Bales. But it should be so high." He indicated waist height. "We got out what we could."

Grace shucked off her rifle and pushed an empty crate with her foot.

Randolph picked up a scorched plank and threw it to the side of the road. It was still warm. Then another. Grace pulled at singed sailcloth that had got tangled in the mess.

He searched more desperately, turning over objects he knew weren't his, as if something would magically appear.

"It's not here," he said. "Nothing's here." He stood upright, staring at the remains of his warehouses. "It's all been damn well stolen."

Grace's eyes were wide and she seemed to have shrunk into

her winter coat. "Perhaps someone has taken it. For safe-keeping."

Randolph snorted and remembered the man who had accosted him the day before. He'd offered to keep watch on the warehouses. *Couple of dollars to keep it safe*, the man had said. When Randolph had passed up the offer, the man had muttered something about regretting it. So this was what he meant.

Randolph groaned and kicked at the remains of a barrel, sending it skittering across the street. "Dear God! All that work. For nothing."

Grace put her hand between his shoulders and rubbed in circles.

He needed to contain his anger. It wouldn't do any good. He took some deep breaths, trying to slow his heart as it beat hard in his chest. "No point staying here. I'll clear it up with George and Simon tomorrow. Let's go home, see what can be done there."

They made their way up Howard Street. The city was very much alive now. Some were trying to make a fast buck by selling basics at inflated prices to men who had nowhere to live. The chapel on Second Street had set up a stove and was giving out soup.

Randolph paused and looked down at Grace. When had she last eaten? Her skin had a sheen of ash and her eyes were dull. He joined the line, drawing Grace next to him. He'd never accepted charity before. It was just one meal, until he got their strongbox.

The soup was thin, little more than water, but it was hot. They drank straight from the bowl and returned them empty to the table. Randolph yearned for a whiskey: that would warm him inside. But it was still morning. That was a dangerous Rubicon to cross. He'd always despised men who drank in the morning.

They went on their way again until they reached the corner of Howard and Fourth, and stood looking at what had once been their home. Now it was a pile of blackened beams, collapsed in on itself. The Hollingswood plot next door was no better.

Grace stared at it, no expression on her face. She had not said a word for more than an hour. He looked for somewhere for her to rest, but there was nothing to sit on, and the ground was sooty mud.

The heavy rain meant the remains were warm, but not too hot to handle. Randolph started at the back of the house, methodically moving wood onto the muddy patch behind the remains. Even charred wood could be useful—could be used as firewood to keep Grace warm. Grace came to help him, moving as if she were in a dream.

He climbed over some of the beams to where the kitchen had once been. The metal stove was blackened, but possibly useable when he cleaned it. He noticed debris had already been cleared from the kitchen floor. How could that have happened?

He stepped closer, a surge of white-hot anger rising up in him. He remembered Grace on her knees, scratching at the earth to dig out their strongboxes. But she had barely disturbed the ground before he had pulled her away.

A large hole had been dug, the edges smooth. It had clearly been dug with a spade.

Randolph leaped forward and crouched by the hole, trying to steady himself. Empty. Both strongboxes were gone. Every muscle in his body tensed, his fists folding tight, his teeth clenched.

Someone had stolen everything. Someone had watched his home burn and taken a spade to steal the gold he had broken his back for. Someone had stolen their future.

He picked up a large, blackened timber and flung it back at the ground, releasing an agonized roar.

"What?" Grace asked, quickly standing. "What is it?"

She picked her way like a cat over the warm remains toward him and came to a halt when she saw the gaping hole in the ground.

"It's gone," said Randolph. "All of it."

"But..." Grace seemed to struggle to understand. "Who could have... How did they know?"

Randolph thought back over recent months, desperately trying to remember whether he could have told someone where his gold was hidden. The Hollingswoods knew. But he trusted them with his life.

Truth was, most people hid their valuables in this way. The city had no bank to speak of, so it had become common advice to put your gold underground—in a place where you would remember, such as in front of the stove. Probably the Hollingswoods had done the same.

Randolph started to sweat. The Hollingswoods. If someone had stolen his gold, then...

He clambered back out of their remains.

"Where are you going?" Grace called.

"To check..."

The mud stuck to his boots as he strode through what had once been the Hollingswood cottage garden, then to where the remains of the back door lay on its side. Being a bigger building than his, there was even more debris. Perhaps that had protected their cache.

But no. He made his way into the wreckage and saw the kitchen had been cleared of wood, down to the earthen ground. The soil had been dug in a number of places, and there was a larger hole, again with the smooth edges of a spade. This was where the Hollingswood gold had once been buried. But no more.

Randolph looked around him, fury rising. This was not one criminal, trying his luck. It would have taken a gang of men to clear the remains so swiftly, men who came armed with tools, and, no doubt, heavy boots and thick gloves. Organized. Planned.

Was there no honor left in this land? No decency? They had come to California to start something new. He had wanted to escape his memories of the worst that man could do. But here, in this fresh, new, supposedly golden land, there was more corruption and criminality. War brought out the worst in men, and gold did too.

What a fool he'd been. *Of course* California had drawn the worst of men. The lure of quick and easy money always did. The brief months in the mountains with men he trusted, who shared equally—they had been salmon swimming against the stream.

This was the reality. Some men working hard. And others taking it easy. There was no law, no society. No morality.

He made his way back to Grace, who was standing at the threshold, her beautiful, tired face questioning—hopeful.

He shook his head. "All gone as well."

Her hand came to her mouth, shaking as she tried to hold back the tears. He came to her, put his arms around her. She began to sob, the sound loud and anguished, gasping for air. Each cry felt like an admonishment. Somehow he should have stopped this from happening. He was powerless in the face of forces stronger than him—the heat of fire, the cold of rain, the evil of men.

TWENTY-TWO

Grace had experienced hardship before, and plenty of it. But she'd always had something to strive for, whether that was getting her younger brother Tom to safety in Oregon, or waiting out her husband's return from war. During the week following the fire, she experienced a hopelessness that she hadn't known was possible.

At the mission, the priests had been overrun by homeless people and at a loss over what to do. Grace, Lillian and the girls were given places inside, as they were among the few females there. Grace had asked where the French sisters were, but Lillian said they had slipped away, knowing they would find protectors in the city.

Their husbands and Simon remained outside the mission, huddled around fires, wrapped in blankets.

It was Lillian who had gathered everyone together and told them, in no uncertain terms, they needed a plan. She reminded them how much they still had: plots on Howard Street, water plots by the harbor. Grace and Lillian had saved the horses and mules. True, they didn't know where they were, but the animals were branded and could be found. Grace and Randolph had firearms with which to defend the families from more thieves.

With Lillian's admonishment ringing in their ears, it was agreed that Randolph and George would return to the city and take any work they could. Simon would search for their animals. At least one could be sold. The women and children would clear the remains of their homes, look for anything that could be salvaged, even if it was simply wood for fuel. They would clear one of the plots, ready to build a shelter, just as soon as Randolph and George had earned enough to buy tents. Until then, they would sleep at the mission.

Lillian's pragmatism impelled Grace to action. The next morning, she stood with her palms pressed to her head, in front of the charred remains that had briefly been her home. If she could clear a space in the plot, the men could build a shelter.

There was the pile of wood James had started making, before he had stopped in despair. She took up the task, pulling a plank and throwing it on the pile, and then another. Most of the roof shingles crumbled in her hands. As she cleared wood away, she would come across things that had strangely escaped the worst of the fire. A chair was blackened but useable. She found one of James's boots near where the door had been, but the other was curled up, nearly unrecognizable. An edge of curtain still had its floral pattern but fell apart as she lifted it.

As Grace looked around, she was overwhelmed by the futility of her task. She searched for the cabinet where she had stowed the two letters from Tom, but it was in ashes. The fine linen pillowcase, James's first gift to her—why hadn't she run back to save that? She grunted as she pushed some beams aside where their bedroom had been. The twisted metal bed frame mocked her. There was nothing else. All ties to the past were gone.

She was overheating from her labor and pulled off her overcoat, laying it on the ground. She would not let it out of her sight.

The knot of guilt deep inside her grew larger. She had held on to the secret that lay within the seams of that coat. She didn't know what had compelled her not to mention the gold on the night of the fire. James would have been so relieved—would have praised her for her cleverness and forethought. Every day that passed, it became harder to tell him the truth. Or to tell her dear friend Lillian.

Why hadn't she told James about it? Or the Hollingswoods, as they sat round the fire that night, making their plans? It would have made things so much easier for everyone. One day, she knew, the Hollingswoods would curse her for forcing them through this hardship, when she possessed the means to avoid it.

She sat on the filthy ground and wept, covering her face with her sooty hands. She knew she had clung to the coat as her last piece of protection. Things were bad for them, but they were hungry, not starving. The children had food and shelter, the adults had skills to trade. She needed something to save them if they truly hit the bottom of the cliff—and they hadn't reached that yet. She needed to be able to rely on herself. The awful truth was that she could no longer be sure of her husband.

So she bottled up the feelings and pushed them to a place deep inside her, forcing herself to concentrate on the task in hand. She stood up, wiped her hands on her skirt, and set to work.

Randolph's body ached from a long day unloading coal from a ship that had just anchored. He hated working for someone else, when just a week ago he'd had his own thriving business. He had a day's wages in his pocket and needed a drink. He passed a bar close to his former home, in a building that had survived the conflagration, and was tempted. There was a poorly painted sign saying The Eagle. Maybe just one on his way back to the tents on Howard Street. His wife couldn't begrudge him that.

There were a couple of barrels stacked outside. He paused: they looked familiar, the name *Jungling* stenciled on top. The wood had the smoky sheen of fire damage.

He ducked inside and let his eyes adjust to the dark. There was an oil lamp over the bar, and a candle on each table. He recognized the familiar smell of sweat and tobacco.

"Say, where you get those barrels?" he asked, approaching the barman at the counter.

"Which?"

"The ones outside your door."

The barman moved the lamp to look more closely at him. "What's it to you?"

Randolph shrugged, not wanting to show his cards. "Got something similar you might be interested in."

"Similar? You mean... recently, shall we say, 'liberated'?"

"Maybe."

"What sort of price?"

"How about... five dollars."

The barman snorted. "Five dollars? Sonny sold me those two barrels for half the price."

"Sonny?'

The barman tossed his head at a man sitting at a table in the corner where it was nearly dark. Randolph could make out another man on the other side and a woman, barely visible in the shadows.

As he went over, the candle flickered and he went cold as he recognized the companion: it was the man who had wanted payment to guard his warehouse just before the fire.

Maybe the wise thing was to return to the tent, fetch his pistol, and bring Hollingswood as backup. Yes, that was the wise thing, but Randolph could feel the blood fizzing through his veins. He couldn't walk away. He dragged a spare chair to the table.

Sonny glared at him. "Do I know you?"

The man was big and bulky with a full red beard. His nose was flat, suggesting a lifetime of fights. He pulled on a plump Havana cigar.

Randolph sat down. "Not yet. But you know my business."

Sonny leaned back and tapped his fingertips on the table, put on his guard by Randolph's tone, and seeming to weigh up the situation.

"It's simple. I want my goods back," said Randolph, keeping his voice low and smooth.

"What goods?"

"The goods you stole on the night of the fire."

Sonny slowly extended an arm over the back of the woman's chair, not taking his eyes off Randolph. "Now, strangers shouldn't go accusing upright folks."

"There are two barrels outside you sold to this man." Randolph nodded toward the barman. "They're barrels I pulled out of my warehouse."

Sonny made a strange snorting sound. "And how you going to prove it? Did you see me take anything?"

Randolph's pulse increased, causing a throbbing noise in his ears. It was true: he hadn't witnessed anything.

"Tell you what," said Sonny, sitting back and spreading his legs. "Why don't you go tell the *alcalde*? Say, how about me and Burton come with you. Who will he believe? You, a dollar-a-day stevedore. Or me? A respected San Francisco businessman."

Randolph knew the corrupt *alcalde* would take payments to look the other way. It was impossible for him to confirm the theft—and there was no one to lead a prosecution, even if he could prove it. This city was fast becoming the dregs of the earth.

These men had done far worse than theft, and Randolph

knew he couldn't walk away without confronting them. He turned his attention to the second man, Burton. "You set those fires, didn't you."

There was a rustle of silk as the woman rose from her seat. Sonny put a hand on her arm. "Cora, you sit."

She shook his hand free. "*Laisse-moi*. You've had as much of my time as you've paid for."

Randolph noticed the French accent and looked at her properly for the first time. She was one of the women who had lived in the saloon opposite. A momentary look passed between them. She gave a single shake of the head, trying to communicate something, but Randolph couldn't tell what. She picked up her empty glass and sauntered to the bar.

"Now you gone scared my woman away," Sonny said, pulling on his cigar. The tip shone red in the dark.

"You're not denying it. The fires."

Sonny put the cigar in a saucer and began to clap. "All you argonauts come swaggering into this town, pockets full of gold. You've all lost it in days, anyway. Thrown it away on cards or whiskey." He laughed. "I'm just speeding up the process."

Randolph's fists tightened. "People *died* in that fire."

"Whoa. You can't put that on me. It's up to folk to look after themselves. Me and my men, we look after ourselves."

Randolph's fury grew hot in his chest. The man was blatant that his gang had started fires so they could pick the miners' pockets, secure in the knowledge that no one was going to bring him to account.

Randolph exploded, springing to his feet, his chair clattering behind. He dragged the man up by his jacket and spun him away from the table.

Burton stood up, but Randolph upended the table, making him stagger back.

Sonny took a swing at him, so he ducked and laid a punch into his stomach and upward hook to his face.

The other man leaped onto Randolph's back, trying to pinion his arms. Randolph swung round with the fury of a wounded bear. He crushed Burton against the flimsy wooden bar, which collapsed against the impact. Burton released his arms, and Randolph threw him onto his back, where the man lay winded.

Sonny now returned to the fray. Randolph was so fired up, he was pleased to see the man run at him. This time, Sonny's punch found its target, making Randolph's jaw crunch. He ducked away from the next punch but threw his own, making Sonny stagger backwards, out through the saloon door. Randolph followed. The two matched each other, blow for blow. Sonny stumbled back into the dirt of the street, Randolph straddled him, raining down blows, feeling only his rage.

A voice shouted at Randolph to stop, that he would kill the man. Sonny was barely responding now, his face bloody.

Suddenly, Burton returned, and kicked Randolph in the ribs. Randolph groaned with the pain. The man came closer, but Randolph flipped him off his feet. Now all three men were on the ground, their breathing loud and labored, their limbs heavy.

Sonny got up, blood running from his mouth. He roared, and launched himself at Randolph, who was knocked back once more. Randolph knew he had been reckless in starting a fight with two men, but they symbolized all the degeneracy he had witnessed over recent years, and he was finally fighting back.

The growing crowd urged them on, enjoying the spectacle.

A rifle fired into the air.

"If anyone lays another hand on my husband, I swear to God, I'll shoot *at* them next time."

TWENTY-THREE

Grace stood, her feet planted wide, a rifle in her hands. She had shoved a pistol into the leather belt around her waist. "I'm not afraid to use this thing."

Hollingswood stepped forward to where James lay on the ground, pulling him to his feet and half-dragging him from the mêlée. Grace backed away behind them, her heart beating wildly, her eyes and gun on the crowd. People drifted from the street as the two men struggled to their feet and back into the saloon.

Grace washed the blood from James's face. He was sitting on a crate, his right eye swollen and beginning to close up. His blisters had only just healed from the fire and now his hands were raw from where he'd pummeled his opponents. Grace was being none too gentle with her ministrations.

"What in God's name were you doing?" Her voice was taut, she could barely keep her anger in check.

"They did it." James spat out the words.

"Did what?"

"Set the fires."

She dabbed again. "How d'you know?"

"Pretty much admitted it."

She glared at him. "And you just had to react. Then and there."

"People died in that fire. Thankfully not many. But... Monsieur Bernard? The man who owns the place opposite? He died. I heard yesterday. He was sleeping at a place near the harbor. Didn't make it out."

She paused. This added to the mystery of why the French sisters had been left locked in a room. But it wasn't her business. She tutted. "So you risk your neck, to avenge a man we barely know?"

"It's the *principle*, Grace. And I'm surprised you want me to turn a blind eye."

"That's not what I'm saying. You could have come back here. Got Hollingswood and Simon. Evened up the odds."

She finished bandaging his knuckles and looked at him, at his tired and bruised face. The man she used to know wouldn't have done anything so imprudent.

James got to his feet. "I'm turning in."

"So early? You've not eaten."

He threw her a look, like he was disappointed in her. "Not hungry."

He disappeared into the tent, leaving Grace to empty the bowl of bloody water. She let out a breath. Was he angry that she had pulled his irons out of the fire? Having your wife save you from a beating was not something a man like James would be proud of. But what else could she do, when the French woman had rushed to their plot to tell them what was happening? If she'd not gone, it looked like James might have killed that man. God knows, that would have been falling to the bottom of the cliff. Perhaps she was right to keep quiet about the gold in her coat, after all.

. . .

The next morning, she was woken by James getting up early, as usual. With barely a word, he took off down Howard Street to see what work he could find. Grace worried that he would struggle to find day-work, given he could only see through one eye and his hands were so bandaged he could barely hold things.

She was at the standpipe, pumping water, when one of the French women walked past. There was a large white feather in her bonnet which rippled as she moved. "Madame," Grace called.

The woman paused and turned. "It's *Mademoiselle*."

"Ah. *Mademoiselle*. Please wait."

The woman folded her gloved hands as she watched Grace put the lids on the two water buckets. Grace carried them to the dry earth away from the standpipe and the woman followed.

"I wanted to thank you. For fetching me last night," Grace said.

The woman chuckled. "I didn't fetch you. My plan was to fetch the man who lives with you."

"Mr. Hollingswood?"

"*Oui*. The man with the children." She put her head on one side and smiled. Dimples made her face less haughty. "I didn't think it would be *you* who would take a rifle and break up the fight."

Grace shrugged, unable to explain to someone she barely knew that her childhood with a gunsmith meant her first instinct was to pick up her gun. "You going back to Fourth Street?"

The woman raised her elegant eyebrows. Grace noticed how expressive her face was. "*Mais oui*. I am meeting a man to look at repairing the saloon. But... you want to walk with me?"

"Why not?"

"Well..." The slight smile was back on the woman's rouged lips. "I haven't found American women welcoming so far. But then, most Parisienne women wouldn't welcome my sister and me, either."

"Maybe I can put that right." Grace wiped her hand on her apron before checking her hand was clean and put it out. "I'm Mrs. Randolph."

The lady shook it gently and inclined her head. "And I'm Mademoiselle Coralie LaFonteyn. I'm delighted to meet you properly, at last. Please, call me Cora."

"Cora. And I'm Grace." She picked up the ropes of the buckets to start their walk home.

"Let me take one," said Cora.

"Heavens, no. Water might spill over your beautiful silk dress."

The outfit looked brand new. Grace guessed that Cora had it made as a priority, after the fire. In her line of work, appearances were everything.

Cora shrugged. "It will dry out." She lifted the rope handle. Even though the woman's stature was slender, Grace was impressed by the ease with which the she carried the burden.

They took a few steps toward Fourth Street.

"Your English is very good," said Grace.

"My father was French and that was where we grew up. However, my mother, she was English."

Grace nodded and carried on walking. There was so much she wanted to know about the sisters' lives. Paris was another world. But there was something more pressing on her mind. "I wonder... if you might tell me, what happened yesterday? The fight, I mean. How it came about."

"Your husband, he hasn't told you?"

Grace bit her lower lip. "Not really."

"As I'm sure you can guess, I was working at the Eagle, as

our saloon is shut down. I was at a table when your husband walked over to us."

"You were with the men? Randolph said they set the fires."

Cora grunted. "I expect that is true."

Grace frowned and wondered why Cora would risk being with such dangerous criminals.

"I could tell trouble was brewing," Cora continued as they walked. "If you work the bars and saloons, you get an instinct. There was something... on edge about your husband. *Sauvage*. A wildness. Most men give Sonny and Burton a wide berth. It was like he was itching for a fight."

They passed a smartly dressed man who lifted his hat to Cora but barely glanced at Grace. She noticed Cora gave the slightest nod in recognition.

"It was Providence that took me to the Eagle that evening."

"Providence?"

"It meant I was there, and could get someone to stop the fight. Before your husband killed, or was killed."

"I'm so grateful to you. James... Mr. Randolph never used to be the sort of man who would go brawling in the street."

"It does not matter what sort of man your husband is. Providence meant I was able to help *you*, and someone important to you."

Grace looked at Cora and shook her head. "I don't know what you mean."

Cora stopped and put her water bucket down to ease her arms.

"You saved our lives. My sister and I. The fire."

Grace put her bucket down too and wiped her brow with her hand. "It was simply chance I was there that night."

Cora looked intensely at her, her green eyes seeming to search her face for something. Grace couldn't remember being looked at in this way by a woman.

"This is not true," Cora said. "Others might have walked on

by. But you were brave. Brave enough to come and save us. My sister and I, we pay our debts. We will *always* look out for you, and yours. Forever."

"Oh!" Tears rose suddenly in her eyes. Cora spoke with such deep sincerity. They stood and stared at each other for a moment, and Grace felt slightly embarrassed by the depth of her emotion. They picked up the buckets and continued down Fourth Street as if this talk of Providence and a declaration of a bond had not happened.

Grace spoke to break the silence. "I meant to say. I am so sorry to hear about Monsieur Bernard."

Cora harrumphed. "*Boof.* I'm not."

Grace blinked in surprise. "I thought he was a relative."

"No. A businessman. That is all."

They reached the tents, with the remains of the saloon opposite. Grace called the twins, who took the water buckets back to the campsite.

Something had been troubling Grace since the night of the fire. "I wanted to ask... why... why were you locked in the room? I mean, you couldn't even escape through the window. It seems so... cruel."

"That is a long story." There was a wistful smile on Cora's lips, suggesting a past full of regrets.

Grace finally had the chance to find the answer and she wasn't going to be deflected. "I have time."

"*D'accord.* Marguerite—that is my sister—we wanted to escape the fighting in France. The revolution."

Grace frowned. "My book learning is elementary, but wasn't the revolution years ago?"

"Indeed. This is *another* one. My countrymen, they are slow to learn. It was February last year. Marguerite and I wanted to escape, so we got free passage here, on condition we paid once we arrived. We had no money, of course, but knew of M.

Bernard. He covered the debt but wanted to make sure we paid off his investment."

"By locking you up until you had made enough money for him? That's dreadful."

Cora shrugged. "Things have worked out in the end. He told everyone we were relatives. So now he is dead, Marguerite and me, we have lodged a claim for the remains of the saloon and the plot. We will have it up and running as soon as we can. Our own place. We won't have to answer to anyone."

Grace wasn't sure whether to be shocked or admiring. Admiration won out. To have such freedom must feel exhilarating.

Cora picked up her skirts to make her way into what remained of the saloon to wait for the builder. She turned back at the door. "Madame Randolph. Keep an eye on your husband. You are a good woman. And I hope he is a good man—inside. You said he was not the sort of man to brawl. But—I have known many men in my profession—your husband is troubled. I sense he can be unpredictable, reckless. Careless of his safety." That intense look came to Cora's eyes again, as if trying to make sure Grace understood what was being said, and then she disappeared inside.

The rain started again, making puddles in the mud around their plot. As Grace had feared, James had struggled to find a place for the day. He returned with not much money in his pockets.

The second-hand tent felt even smaller than usual. Their damp clothing smelt of mildew. It was futile trying to keep the groundsheet clean when James walked in yet more dirt. This place. Dust all summer, creeping into folds in her clothes, making clean dishes turn gray. Mud all winter, clinging to her boots, sliding into corners.

James's body was stiff from the fight. He moved awkwardly, his large body all elbows and knees in the confined space.

The rain continued to tap on the canvas. There was a place in the corner where the waterproofing had worn thin and water was dripping steadily. Grace put a saucepan below, with a piece of cloth inside to deaden the rhythmical sound.

They got under the blanket she had exchanged for some cleaning. She couldn't remember the last time she had felt properly warm. James didn't want to lie close at night, instead was constantly moving to try to find a comfortable position.

"I spoke to the woman who lived opposite, today," Grace said.

James grunted to show he had heard her.

"She's from Paris. Says they had another revolution there."

"Whole world seems to keep fighting," James said.

At least he had replied. Maybe he felt bad about earning so little today.

She paused and then risked saying something, hoping to be reassuring. "I'm sure you'll find better-paid work tomorrow."

He turned over to face her, frowning. "Is that it? I'm not working hard enough?"

"No—I didn't mean that. It's just—"

"Because I'm doing the best I can."

"I know—"

"Maybe it's not good enough for you," he said, almost spitting the words.

"James..."

He turned away from her.

She looked up at the canvas. "Maybe... maybe we should try going back to Oregon."

She sensed his body stiffen.

"You mean go back with my tail between my legs, like a whipped dog."

"I didn't mean that—"

"And what would we do when we got there?"

"I don't know. There's plenty of land."

"Grace, you know I'm not cut out to be a farmer. I'm not like your brother."

She was stung by this, by the implied criticism of Zachary's choice. "Farming is a perfectly honorable way to make a living."

He turned again, glaring. "Are you saying I'm dishonorable?"

"No—James, you are deliberately misunderstanding me."

"Because that's what the army says. That I behaved dishonorably. I never thought my wife would agree with them." His eyes blazed with anger.

"What do you mean?" Grace's heart beat faster. He had never spoken of this. "You weren't court-martialed..."

"Oh, Grace... I had no choice. I failed to obey orders. Worse than that, I even..." He pulled his hand over his face and took a deep breath. "The only reason I wasn't court-martialed was because the general knew me of old. I was dismissed, nevertheless. It wasn't my choice."

Grace tried to understand what he was telling her. "So you would have stayed in the army? If you could?"

"It was my calling. You know that, Grace."

"Even after... whatever happened..."

He closed his eyes. "No. Maybe I couldn't stay. Not after Mexico..."

But he wanted to go back. That's what she heard. He'd choose the army over her. He'd given things up. But so had she. Sometimes she ached to see Tom again, to see how tall he'd grown, hear his laugh. She had given up her family in the hope of creating one of her own. But that hadn't happened. She still wasn't pregnant. Perhaps Randolph no longer wanted a family. She had given up hope of it happening, and maybe he had too. Maybe...

"James," she whispered, "do you still want children?"

He grunted. "Why would anyone bring an innocent child into this corrupt world?"

She looked at his back, trying to steady her breath. He didn't want children anymore? Surely every man wanted a son to continue his name?

She scrunched her eyes shut so she wouldn't cry. James was prepared to let his name sink into the mud, forgotten by future Californians. She felt her grasp on the world slip away like a salmon wriggling back into a stream. When had this change happened? He'd said he wanted a large family, when they'd first married.

She lay there, feeling nauseous, wondering if she should ask him more. Maybe if she understood exactly what had happened in Mexico... *Something* had changed him. Or perhaps it was her. Perhaps this childless marriage she'd given him, and the difficulty of making a life together, had worn away his love for her.

A tear ran down her cheek as she listened to the rain on the canvas, to people carousing nearby. A dog was barking, and she had a yearning for her dog, Kane. Another thing left behind in Oregon.

Her mind raced through the past year, picking up scenes in her mind, trying to remember what he had said.

She opened her mouth to speak, but was aware of that slow, rhythmical breathing. James slept so poorly now, she couldn't wake him, not even to find out what he really felt. The two of them were on parallel lines, like two masts on a ship, fixed together by the deck, but not actually touching. She lay just inches from him, but had never felt so distant.

TWENTY-FOUR

Grace slept badly but dragged herself out of her tent at first light. They were surrounded by a damp mist, which turned the whole world gray. It took a while to get the little iron stove going as the wood was wet. There was not much ground coffee left in the caddy, so she skimped on the amount she spooned into the pot. Maybe she could go buy some today.

James emerged from the tent and pulled on his boots. He hadn't gone to the barber for days and his beard was growing raggedy. He ambled over to the stove, his eyes down to avoid Grace's face. She wordlessly handed him a mug of coffee. He took a sip and pulled a face.

"What?" Grace asked.

"Tastes bad," he said testily.

She tossed her head. "Well, I'm sorry I couldn't produce it to your liking, sir. Maybe if we had more money, we could buy more coffee."

"It's not easy to work with one eye and bandaged hands."

She put her hands on her hips. "And whose fault is that?"

He clicked his tongue. "You still think I should have let those criminals get away with it?"

"It wasn't your job—"

"So what *is* my job?"

Grace took a step back. It was unusual for him to raise his voice. But she wasn't going to be cowed. Overnight, her sadness had hardened into something else. She wasn't prepared to just keep taking it. "Look, James. It's not just you suffering round here. The fire happened to all of us—"

"I didn't say—"

"Look at George." She pointed to the other tent. "I don't see *him* going round with a face as dark as storm clouds. I don't see him drinking himself into a stupor of an evening. Maybe the money you spend on whiskey could have bought more coffee."

He tutted and looked heavenwards. "So, I'm not even allowed—"

She went on, like a dam had burst. "Oh, don't you go giving me that, like I'm some hen-pecking wife." She went back to the stove to tidy up the pots. "When have I ever allowed or not allowed you to do anything? When have we ever done anything other than what *you* want?"

"I'm the head of this household—"

She spun back to him. "Then why don't you act like it? Why don't you think about how to get us out of this mess? You used to lead a whole company of men. Now you can't even lead yourself."

He glared at her, unable to find the words, but his face darker than she had ever known. Her heart was beating hard: she'd crossed a line, she knew she had. But still she couldn't stop herself speaking.

"I'm sick of it, James," she cried. "Sick of the cold, and the wet, and the mud. Sick of standing in line for water and bread. But most of all, I'm sick of you and your moods."

He threw the remains of the coffee on the ground and wordlessly handed the mug back to her, his mouth a thin, tight line.

She could see his chest rising and falling as he tried to control himself. He picked up his hat.

"Tell Hollingswood and Simon I'll meet them at the harbor." He buttoned his coat. "Hell. He'll have heard every word of this anyway." He raised his voice. "George? You know where I'll be."

He turned on his heel and marched across their plot to the street.

Grace stood trembling. She'd never spoken to him this way. Never. There was so much anger, bubbling up in her stomach. She wanted to pummel his chest, make him feel the pain she was feeling. But more than anything, she wanted the old James back.

When Hollingswood and Lillian emerged from their tent some minutes later, it was clear they had heard the row. Everyone moved awkwardly, not making eye contact, but sharing lighthearted comments about the bacon in the pan, the way the fog was lifting, the days getting longer now it was February.

Grace felt embarrassed to have exposed her feelings so publicly, but she could no longer deny them. She returned to their threadbare tent and looked at how few belongings they had left. It seemed to symbolize the parlous state of her marriage, and she wondered if there was any hope of repairing it.

That night, James, Hollingswood and Simon returned earlier than usual. Grace and Lillian were peeling vegetables for dinner.

"We've made a decision," James said, Hollingswood at his side. "We're going back to the goldfields. We're never going to make up what we lost if we stay here."

Grace stood motionless and stared at him. He still wasn't

discussing things with her, even after everything she'd said that morning. "We're going—?"

He shook his head. "No, George, Simon and me. *We're* going."

"But without—?"

Hollingswood broke in to try to smooth things. "We've heard some good stuff about further south. Rivers before you get to Mariposa."

Lillian slowly put down her knife and swallowed. "When?"

"Soon as we can," said her husband. "There're more people arriving every day. One man I spoke to said people are beginning to arrive from the overland route, even with the snows."

"What d'you mean by 'soon as we can'?" Grace asked. What was James thinking? Next week? Next month?

James stared at her. "Tomorrow."

"Tomorrow?" The squash she was peeling fell from her hands. They were going to be separated again, just like she feared.

"Uh-huh. We got things fixed today. We'll take two of the horses and both the mules."

"But that leaves us with just one horse..." Grace said shakily. Why, of all the things to protest about, was it the horses...

Lillian put a hand on her arm to calm her. "We don't need the horses. Not here."

"And we'll take our tent." James looked at Grace. His face seemed to be made of granite. "You can bunk with Lillian and the girls."

Grace was speechless.

"How long?" asked Lillian. "How long will you be gone?"

Grace glanced at her. Thank goodness Lillian was keeping her wits to ask important questions.

James shrugged. "No way of saying. We'll stay until we've made enough capital again. Likely months."

Grace felt a weight inside her chest. Months. But it could

be worse than that: it sounded to her like he might never come back.

"And us?" she asked. Her throat was so tight, her words came out in a whisper.

"Us?" James's steel-blue eyes suddenly came alive again. His jaw bobbed as he swallowed.

Was he asking whether they still had a marriage?

"Me, Lillian and the girls, I mean. You've said that you think it's dangerous here."

"Dangerous everywhere," said James quietly, his eyes sliding away.

Hollingswood laughed, but it sounded hollow. "You two women together, strong as a yoke of oxen. You'll be safer here than going with us to the goldfields. People say things have changed out there."

"Yes," said Grace tartly. "Chasing after gold will do that to a man."

James glared at her and she stood her ground. "You'll have your father's rifle and pistol. You know how to use them."

She folded her arms. "Looks like you've got everything worked out."

James's eyes were locked on hers. "I seem to remember you asking me to find a way out of this mess."

Lillian coughed. "Now, come on you two. Enough of your rowing. Looks like we've got plenty to sort out tonight. Better get on with cooking dinner."

"Indeed," said James and retreated to the tent to start sorting his things.

James and Grace barely spoke all night and rose before dawn to prepare for the departure. Simon went to the livery to fetch the animals while James packed their tent. He rolled up his bedding and clothing. Grace noisily divided basic cooking and eating utensils. The men had bought some tools the day before, Hollingswood using his charm to get a good deal.

Grace handed James one of the Sinclair pistols. She wanted to say something, that her father's pistol had kept him safe in the past and it would do so again. It was on the tip of her tongue, but he took the pistol in his bandaged hand without catching her eye and tucked it into his holster. He slid his shotgun into its place on the side of his horse and the moment passed.

The horses were saddled, but Simon rode the most docile of the mules. The other mule was loaded with their belongings.

Everyone made their way to the harborside, where a steamer would take them across the bay and up to Sacramento. Molly sat on one of the horses, the twins together on the other. Lillian and Hollingswood walked close together, her arm through his. Grace watched with an empty feeling deep in her gut, aware that she and James walked side by side, but not touching.

The harbor was frantically busy with new arrivals to San Francisco, eager to get their place on the steamer.

Molly and the girls were lifted down and George said a tearful goodbye to each of them. He hugged Lillian, drawing her in for a kiss. She slapped his backside. "See that you come home with plenty of gold dust."

Grace glanced up at James to see if he had been watching the Hollingswoods' farewells. But he was staring at the charred remains where his warehouses had been. Grace took a step to stand beside him.

"Remember, we still own the plots," he said, without looking at her. "Don't let anyone take them."

"I won't," she said, quietly.

He sighed, took off his hat to run his fingers through his dark hair, before replacing it. "I will be back. I'll rebuild it."

What would he rebuild? The warehouses? Their marriage?

She wanted to tell him that she would wait, that they would

build things together. As she turned to him, to try to haul the words into her mouth, he had already wheeled, and was striding to the gangplank.

She ought to call after him, but he wasn't looking her way.

The boatsmen untied the ship, its engines shuddering into life and the paddle slowly turned, making a gushing sound.

James leaned against a rail, and finally he was looking back at her, his face stern, one side still bruised. She raised a hand and he gave the briefest of nods. The boat moved away and she could no longer see his face under his hat. His body remained motionless.

A light rain began, and Molly and the twins pulled at their mother to return home. Grace stood alone to watch the ferry disappear into the mist.

PART TWO

TWENTY-FIVE

Randolph gazed in amazement at the transformation of Sacramento. A year ago, he and Grace had been part of a steady stream of people disembarking from the ferry and trudging the remaining couple of miles to Sutter's Fort. Now there was no need. It was as if all that Sutter's Fort provided—shelter, supplies, information—had moved to the riverside.

Men hurried down the gangplank, eager to find a place for the night. Randolph, Hollingswood and Simon were near the back, leading their animals.

It was as if someone had taken the essence of San Francisco and dumped it on the lowland beside the river. A wide street had stores and saloons on either side. Men from all parts of the globe had descended, a babel of languages.

Randolph led the way to the edge of the town, where a tent village had sprung up. They pitched near a cottonwood tree, the three men sharing the Randolphs' leaky second-hand tent.

Randolph and Hollingswood walked back downtown to find something to eat, leaving Simon to look after their belongings and get some rest.

The evening was dry but cool. Next to a hotel, men sat at

trestles and benches under canvas strung between trees, eating and drinking in groups and alone. Randolph could tell the new arrivals by their hunched, intense look.

They bought a beef steak and beer, and took their place on a bench. Randolph caught Hollingswood's knowing wink as they listened to men telling stories of their daring winter overland crossing. Many had wintered in Salt Lake City, paying Mormons for hospitality. Their talk of surviving the Humboldt Sink and the Forty Mile Desert reminded Randolph of soldiers reliving old battles. He fell into a silence, remembering that the overland journey was how he'd met the wife he'd now left behind. The dull feeling inside told him he was already missing her.

A familiar South American accent fell on his ear. It sounded Chilean and reminded him of the months in 1848 on Deer Creek. Or maybe everything was making him think of times with Grace.

He looked over his shoulder and saw four men, sitting close together.

They couldn't be... Many miners from Chile wore similar brightly colored blankets.

Randolph turned round fully, as one of the men was looking over. The surprise on the man's face matched what he felt.

"Moreno!" Randolph stood and rushed over. Moreno was already on his feet, his bulk looming over him. "And Espinoza."

Espinoza looked up and gave a wide grin. "Randolph. My dear, dear old friend!"

He went to shake hands, but Espinoza pulled him close and slapped his back. He swallowed to hold back his emotion at being embraced by his friend.

Randolph turned to the other two, who had aways been more reserved, but were no less delighted to see him. "Kami. Lopez."

They shook hands energetically.

Randolph waved Hollingswood over, standing between the Chileans, a hand on each shoulder. "These are the men I was in partnership with last summer."

"Men?" Espinoza asked, punching his arm.

"Brothers," said Randolph.

"*Hermanos.* Brothers indeed," said Espinoza. "You eat with us now." He hurried to Randolph's table and gathered their bowls and beers.

Randolph made the introductions. "This is George Hollingswood. I've known him since '46. We crossed to Oregon together." Hollingswood nodded enthusiastically, trying to keep up with what was happening. "This is Kami, of the Sandwich Islands. Lopez from Panama. And Espinoza and Moreno, both from Chile."

They shook hands and took their places on the benches. Randolph threw his hat on the space beside him. This was the first good thing to have happened for weeks.

"And where is the beautiful Mrs. Randolph?" Espinoza asked, looking around for her, though there were only men here.

Randolph studied his beer for a moment. "She stayed in San Francisco."

"We are sorry not to meet her again."

"She is with Hollingswood's wife and three daughters." He cleared his throat. "Much better that she's there. Much safer. It's for the best."

"Ah." Espinoza stroked his long mustache. "For the best. No doubt."

Espinoza shared a look with Moreno that Randolph couldn't interpret. Was he surprised she was not with him, the man who had been famous for having his wife at his side?

Espinoza continued: "But tell us, why are you here? What are your plans?"

Randolph put his beer to one side as he told how they had

spent the winter in the city, that things had gone well, but the fire had changed everything.

Moreno nodded toward Randolph's face. "You look like you are using your fists to survive."

Randolph put his fingers to his swollen eye, where the bruising had changed from purple to yellow and green. "Yeah, things can get a little rough in San Francisco." He smiled ruefully, remembering Grace's reaction. "But you. You are all still together. And why are you here?"

Espinoza told him the story. They had stayed in the Sierra Hills for a couple more months, building up their gold, before going back to New Mecklenburg for the worst of the winter. It was now a booming town, so they had decided to enjoy their earnings. Now, they were going back to the goldfields. With so many men arriving, they wondered if there would be any gold left.

"We heard there were rich pickings on the Stanislaus River," said Kami.

"So did we," said Hollingswood, enthusiastically. "They say the mother lode runs straight through it."

"We're on our way to stake a claim," said Moreno.

Randolph rolled his shoulders to unknot a stiff muscle. "Still working as a brotherhood?"

"It's the only way," said Lopez, raising his glass. "All for one and one for all."

The men laughed and clinked their glasses.

Espinoza spoke rapidly in Spanish to Moreno, who muttered a brief reply.

"Say, do you want to join us?" Espinoza asked.

Randolph stretched out his legs. "Traveling to the same river, you mean?"

"No, as partners."

Randolph felt a warmth in his chest: to be welcomed back

so quickly. He looked at Kami and Lopez to see what they thought. They nodded their agreement.

Randolph scratched the back of his head. "Thing is, there's three of us. Mr. Hollingswood has a son with us..."

"Is he a good worker?" asked Moreno.

"You bet," said Hollingswood. "Eighteen and as tall as me. Strong."

"So it would be a partnership of... seven," asked Espinoza.

Randolph looked at Hollingswood, his eyebrows raised in a question but hoping he would understand how lucky they were to have this offer.

"Captain, I trust you. Always have. Whatever you think is best for me and my boy."

He looked at the brotherhood and then back at Hollingswood. "I can't think of anything better than teaming up with these men."

"In that case," Hollingswood put out his hand. "It's a deal."

They shook on it and Espinoza roared with laughter. "Your friend is easier to do business with than your wife. You remember?"

Randolph ran a hand over his head, remembering that August day in New Mecklenburg. "I married a fine woman."

He slipped into his thoughts. The fine woman he'd married seemed to doubt whether he was a fine man. He'd become a husband who let his dark thoughts dominate their lives. He kept seeing her in his mind's eye, her figure on the jetty, getting smaller as the ferry pulled away. He'd been unable to touch her this morning for fear he would break his resolve. One kind word from her, and he might have been weak enough to stay. And where would that have got them? No. Returning to the goldfields alone was the right thing to do. The only thing.

He was broken out of his reverie when Espinoza ordered another round of drinks to celebrate.

"You are miles away, my friend."

Randolph shook his head. "You know, I still can't believe the coincidence of meeting you all here."

Kami gazed up at the sky and his eyes seemed to focus on something far away. "Not coincidence. Providence. Nothing happens by luck. There is a divine purpose, even when we can't see it."

The next morning, the company of seven men boarded a ferry to take them south to the San Joaquin River. Along with many others, they disembarked at the mouth of the Stanislaus River and made their way upstream.

Finding gold had changed even in the few months Randolph had spent in San Francisco. Now it was more ambitious. Randolph and the Hollingswoods could only offer their labor, but the four original partners had gold enough to invest in equipment to help them build dams and sluices. This had been loaded onto a line of mules. When they had discovered, back in Weberville, that the three men were sharing one small tent, Kami had insisted on buying a small tent for Randolph. "We look out for each other," Kami had said.

It took the best part of a week to work their way up the river, passing many claims where men were already prospecting. Occasionally, Randolph would see a lone man up a creek, bent double over his pan, thin, with patched clothes and a wild look in his eye. Generally, he passed groups of men, hard at work to redirect creeks. His confidence grew: a team of seven had more chance of success.

The river twisted, running through narrow gorges, then opening out into a wider river. The mountains grew steeper, the tops covered in heavy snow. Timber was plentiful—another thing that encouraged him.

They decided to take the South Fork of the Stanislaus,

having heard that the Middle and North Forks were already populated with argonauts.

Eventually, they found a bend in the river that they thought could be profitable. There were creeks on either side, a flat area up the hill to make camp.

Work started immediately. The men looked to Randolph once more, even though he had less technical knowledge than the original partners. His skill was still to look at the whole task, recognize who was best doing what, think ahead to the next problem. Hollingswood and Simon habitually called him 'Captain'. Now the other four men picked up the practice. He found it didn't trouble him the way it once had; it felt comfortable, like putting on an old coat. The men seemed to use the term as an endearment, not as a way of differentiating status.

They built a dam with a race they could control and dug deep into the riverbed. They removed rocks and dirt from the hillside to be broken down and washed by the fast-moving water.

Every day their store of gold increased. Some days, there was little and he wondered if their placer had been worked out. The next, someone would find a new seam and they all reveled in the beauty of the yellow metal.

Other argonauts passed by, some asking if they could join the company, or work for a day rate. Randolph would shake his head. The brotherhood had decided a smaller operation with men who trusted each other was better than a larger one with men they didn't know.

The South Americans reminisced about Grace weighing the gold each evening, joked about how they missed her cooking. Randolph smiled and joined in talking about the memories, so none of them would realize how painfully their words pierced him.

That night, he lay in his tent, listening to an animal snuffling outside, the trees creaking in gusts of wind. He turned over and put out his arm, remembering Grace lying on the bedroll beside him. He felt cold, and it wasn't just that he missed the heat their two bodies would make. There was a cold feeling inside, a growing regret at his behavior. When had it begun to go so wrong? If he could put a pin in that moment, perhaps he could work out how to fix things.

Was it when he failed to say goodbye at the harbor? When he had failed to take her in his arms and tell her how deeply he would miss her?

Or when he had started that fight in the saloon? He had relished the feeling of losing self-control, of punching and hitting, with no thought of the consequences. When had he become a brawler?

Was the moment way back: the decision in Oregon to come to California? He had given little thought to how much Grace would miss her brothers.

Or had it started to go wrong before then? He thought of how he had failed to comfort her when her pregnancy had come to an end. Failed to tell her how his hopes had been snuffed out as well. That he had daydreamed of all the things he would teach his son. For surely she had been carrying a boy.

But as he lay there in the dark, waiting for yet another night when sleep refused to embrace him, he knew the thread went back to Mexico. To the fighting there. To what the army had done. To the things he had failed to prevent happening. Was that the memory where he should stick a pin, skewering it in place to be examined like a butterfly he had once seen in a glass exhibition case in the home of a superior officer?

If that was true, then there was no hope for him or Grace. Because that was a memory he wanted to break, like the glass in the case. To rip out the specimen, and crush it in his hand.

TWENTY-SIX

Grace knew she had to be straight with Lillian, to make a new start—even if that meant Lillian was angry at her.

The first evening, Lillian put the girls to bed and sat near the fire. Grace fetched her winter coat, sewing kit and a small bowl. She pulled a stool close, and sat. "I need to show you something."

Lillian raised an eyebrow in response to her serious tone.

"And you are likely to be very mad with me. And wonder why I hid things."

"Sounds intriguing."

Grace placed the coat across her knees and snipped open the side seam. She plucked out a tiny nugget of gold and held it in her fingers before dropping it in the bowl. Then another. And another. She worked her way up the whole seam. Lillian watched without a word.

Grace turned the coat around and opened up the seam on the other side. Each nugget was small, some barely larger than a seed, but they built into a glowing golden mass in the bottom of the bowl.

"That all of it?" Lillian asked.

"Uh-huh."

Lillian picked up the bowl. "And why exactly am I supposed to be mad?"

"I had this all along. We didn't need to be living like this since the fire."

Lillian ran a finger through the gold. "Hmm. I'm not mad. I just wish I'd been as damn smart to hide something away, too." Lillian handed the bowl back. "Randolph didn't think it enough to set things up again?"

Grace stared at the gold and took a breath. "He doesn't know I've got it."

Lillian let out a long whistle. "Didn't think things were like that between you two."

"I feel awful. Hiding it from him. Feel like I've been betraying him."

"Honey, didn't you trust him?"

Grace put the bowl on the floor and bit her lip. "I needed an escape plan. If something happened—if the very worst happened..."

"I know. If Randolph died..."

She looked at Lillian gratefully. "I'd have enough to get myself back north, back to my brothers in Oregon."

Lillian nodded slowly. "I get that. But why didn't you want him to know you had an emergency hoard?"

Grace stretched her arms above her head, her fingers laced together before bringing them to rub through her hair. "He's been so different since he came back from the war. He always was stern, sort of buttoned-up. But when we were first married —underneath he was warm and kind and, well, soft, like a handful of wool. Since Mexico, it's like... it's like someone painted varnish over him. There's something on the surface that means I can't touch the real him."

Grace took a thread and needle and began to repair the

coat. She found it easier to talk about deeply private things with her eyes and hands busy.

"And then there's the drinking," she said softly. "It's got so much worse. Every night. I never knew what he might do when he's drunk."

Lillian leaned forward. "He hasn't... he hasn't knocked you around or anything?"

Grace looked up, shocked that Lillian could suggest it. "Never anything like that! I know some men do. But I've never had a moment when I felt afraid of him. No, I mean the decisions he makes when he's had too much whiskey."

"He did get into that ruckus. The one with those lowlifes who set the fire."

"Exactly. He never used to brawl."

"George said he was pummeling that man as if he were the devil."

Grace thought back to that night. "It was like that fight released something in him. Like when you boil a kettle and the lid lifts up when you leave it too long. He was that steam, streaming out." Grace continued sewing, the coat across her knees. "I wanted to tell him about the gold. He knew I'd sewn it into our clothes when we first came here, but he thought I'd taken it all back out. He didn't know about this coat. I should've told him the night of the fire. Or the next morning. But I didn't. And then with every day I didn't tell him, the lie got worse. Lillian, it's been eating me up."

Lillian put a hand out and Grace paused to grasp it. "I can see that, hon," she said. "So, why you telling me about this now?"

"You and me, here together. It's a fresh start. I want to try again, without hiding stuff." Grace shook out the back of the coat. "And this is the time we really *need* the gold. It's important you know that you, me and the girls, we're going to be safe."

Lillian frowned. "But it's *your* escape money."

"No, Lillian. It's *ours*. We're family now. I love Molly and the twins. I never had a sister. This is for *all* of us."

Lillian puffed loudly. "That's mighty generous. So what you planning on doing with it? I mean, you're sewing that seam back up empty."

"We're going to use it. You know your Bible. The parable of the talents?"

"Yeah, the servants who were each given money. Some made use of it. One buried it."

Grace smoothed a pocket into place. "I'm not going to be the servant who buried it. When our husbands come back, I don't want to have been sitting around, waiting."

"Me neither. Plenty of things I was planning to make us some money."

Grace smiled. "*Exactly*. Now those plans can be bigger. And bigger means more profit. I'm hoping when James comes back, I'll have been *so* successful, he'll forgive me hiding the gold at the beginning."

"So you're planning on telling him one day?" Lillian stamped on a spark that spat from the fire.

"I have to. Keeping things hidden from him has felt so very wrong. It's made everything worse."

Lillian nodded. "Sounds like you've learned something important then."

Yes, she had. Although, James had left before she'd found the courage to be honest with him. And he was still keeping things hidden from her.

"So, what have you been planning?" Grace asked.

"Aha. There aren't many of us women here. Our greatest strength is providing things only a woman can."

Grace flashed her a scandalized look.

Lillian giggled. "Now, I don't mean the things the LaFonteyn sisters provide across the street. But look at you now, sewing that coat with ease, even though there's hardly any light.

Half the men here go round as a raggedy mess. We could repair clothing."

Now Grace laughed. "They're often a *smelly*, raggedy mess. We could clean shirts as well. I got used to doing that last summer."

"And when I first arrived here, you had that kitchen by the harbor. You could do that again."

Grace looked at the bowl of gold. "We could do all that, whether or not we had all this. We need to think *bigger*. I'm not sure what yet. But, Lillian, we're two smart women. We'll work it out."

"And what d'you propose to do with that gold while we decide?"

Grace frowned. "I suppose the same as everyone else does. Hide it."

"You should sew some back in that coat, before you finish."

"Yes, but I'd feel safer with it in a number of places. Some of it buried. Some in your clothing. Then if there's another fire—or if those criminals come back, we won't be left with nothing."

There was a call from the tent.

"That'll be Molly," Lillian said. "She's upset from saying goodbye to her papa today. I'll go comfort her. And you can sort out hiding that gold."

Lillian must have spent as much of the night pondering how to make a good living as Grace had, because ideas came pouring out as they prepared breakfast.

"Our biggest assets are these two plots and the two water plots," said Grace.

"Agreed."

"If we think of these plots as one, we could build something substantial. There's a constant flow of men through this city. What about a boarding house?"

"I was thinking along the same lines," said Lillian. "But there's growing competition. What if we went a step grander. A hotel. There aren't many of those in the city."

Grace snorted and folded her arms. "We stayed in Montgomery House when we arrived. It was shocking. No walls, just painted canvas." She gripped herself tighter as she remembered James being so tender that night.

"Most buildings are like that here. But if we were able to make something better—"

"And run by reputable women—"

"We could charge a high rate."

Grace clapped her hands. "It would need to have space for me, you and the girls."

"Of course." Lillian pushed a fried egg onto Molly's plate. "How would we get it built?"

"James gathered that team when he was building the warehouses. I heard they're still working together. I'll go find them and ask how much it would cost."

"Sounds perfect. And what about the warehouses? George said they were doing well before the fire."

Grace pulled at her lip. "I don't think it would work for us to set that up again. It was profitable because James and Simon did so much of the portering. And your George had a gift for making deals with storekeepers."

"You're right. Got to play to our strengths."

"So, I was thinking of renting out the plots. Until the men come back."

"Need to have a watertight contract, Grace."

"I know, but it would be useful money."

"If we're going to run a hotel," said Lillian, breaking another egg into the skillet, "we need to get some practice. What d'you say to buying a couple more tents—small ones—and putting them over there." She pointed her knife to where the Randolph home had stood. "Rent them out by the night. Provide meals."

Grace raised her shoulders and dropped them with a happy sigh. "Sounds a capital idea. It'll take a while to start work on the hotel, I guess. We could be renting tents from tomorrow." Grace sat to eat her breakfast. "I was making good money with my kitchen by the harbor. I want to get back to that. And it means I can size up new arrivals for the sort of men we'd be happy to have staying overnight."

Lillian grinned at her and shivered. "I haven't felt this excited for a long time."

As soon as they'd eaten, Lillian left the twins to look after Molly, while she took a few nuggets to exchange into dollars and went looking for tents.

Grace asked after the crew who had worked so well with James. She found them constructing a row of stores on Pine Street, energetically restoring things after the fire.

The foreman greeted Grace like a long-lost cousin. He told her how grateful he was to Randolph for putting them together, showing them how to work as a team. Of course they would build what Grace needed, just as soon as these shops were finished.

She felt a stab of guilt, remembering her words to James about his not being a leader anymore. She was wrong. James had done good things here. But now he was gone, and there was no way to tell him.

She described the hotel she had in mind: two stories, wooden walls inside, maybe even brickwork to keep it safe if there were another fire. The foreman gave her an estimate of the cost.

Suddenly, everything came clattering to a halt, like a horse shying at a fence. She smiled and nodded as the foreman told her what they could do, but inside, she knew the golden nuggets she had kept hidden weren't going to cover the cost. Nothing like it.

When she returned to Fourth Street at noon, Lillian and the girls were busy clearing the earth of the last pieces of lumber, ready to erect two tents. Grace couldn't bring herself to tell her the bad news yet and make all their plans come crashing down, but Lillian read her disappointment on her face.

"There's no way we can afford to build a hotel. Maybe we got a little wild this morning. The foreman gave me the very best rates he could, in gratitude to James. But even then, we don't have enough gold to pay for it."

Lillian put her hands on her hips. "Yet. We don't have enough gold *yet*. But we're gonna make this happen."

TWENTY-SEVEN

Grace welcomed the inaugural guests at the Randolph-Hollingswood Hotel—though it was simply a pair of tents at this time—Mr. Pringe from Georgia and Mr. Williams from Australia. She and Lillian had had a whispered discussion about whether they should accommodate Mr. Williams: many of the Australians who arrived at the Golden Gate were ex-convicts. Or had been convicts in previous generations. But Mr. Williams spoke well, and looked tidy enough. They decided they should put their prejudices to one side—at least for tonight, and see whether the sheets had disappeared in the morning.

The sheets were another thing Grace pondered. Most guesthouses didn't provide bed linen—not surprising, given how many men arrived with lice and ticks after months on a ship rounding Cape Horn, or days battling through the swamps of Panama. Grace and Lillian decided to start as they meant to continue: their hotel would be salubrious, run with care. They would provide linen and charge accordingly.

Cora and her sister, Marguerite, sauntered over to the little encampment to see how things were going.

"You are not thinking of providing competition, I hope," said Marguerite, putting her nose to a pan of soup and sniffing. Their saloon was already nearing completion. Marguerite was a little taller than her sister and just as blond. Grace found the two women together a little intimidating.

"I think it's more likely we will benefit from each other," said Grace, hastily. "We don't plan to have a bar in our hotel, just a dining room."

Cora tapped Grace's arm and the dimples appeared on her cheeks. "My sister is teasing you. We are delighted that another business will be run by women. Lillian told us all about it."

Grace cleared a couple of seats for the ladies, sweeping them of dust with her hand to protect their smart dresses. Lillian and Grace perched on a barrel and a crate. Cora took a cigar out of her reticule and lit it with a thin piece of wood she had poked into the fire. Grace stared at her.

"A habit I picked up from some Spanish ladies," she said. "They smoke cigars all the long day. Would you like one? They are very calming."

Grace put up a hand to refuse, thinking how different these French ladies were to other women she had met.

"*Bien*," Cora said, breathing out a mouthful of smoke. "How long do you think it will take before you can build your hotel?"

Grace glanced at Lillian and slumped her shoulders. "We will have to wait until we've made enough capital from our other ventures."

"And add it to the gold you already have," said Cora.

Grace flashed a frown at Lillian. She didn't want more people knowing.

If Cora noticed, she was too polite to show it. "But if you had your hotel, you could be making so much more money. Enough to build each of you a fine house. Perhaps up on Goat Hill."

Grace had daydreamed of something along those lines. Some elegant villas were already being built on higher ground. Maybe, one day.

"And if you wait, others may build a hotel before you." Cora tapped some ash on the floor.

"We don't have much choice in the matter," replied Grace gloomily, all too aware of the chance they were missing.

Marguerite sat forward, her rouged lips in a half-smile. "Ah, but you do. Because Cora and I would like to invest in your scheme."

This was unexpected. "Invest?"

"We want to loan you the money," said Cora, "so building can start immediately."

Grace glanced at Lillian again, who looked a little sheepish. "I told Cora and Marguerite about our situation."

"And you asked for money?" Grace moved her seat, uncomfortable at being ambushed.

"It seems to me like a good idea, hun. Cora's right. Sooner we get our hotel built, sooner we're going to be raking in the dollars."

Grace's mouth had gone dry. She licked her lips and wondered what to do. She wanted a private discussion with Lillian but didn't want to be rude to the sisters. She wasn't sure she wanted investors. That would mean giving up control of her future to someone else.

"I thought you'd have reservations," said Cora with a knowing look. "So why don't we put them all out in the open now."

"Well, I'm not sure—"

"First, there is the matter of taking money from women who make a living in ways some would see as immoral."

Grace knotted her hands, feeling a little awkward that Cora should think this. Truth was, she knew women had to make hard decisions sometimes, and who was she to judge another's choices?

"You have to understand, my sister and I grew up with nothing. *Rien*." Cora drew a line in the air with her cigar. "It's hard to insist on morals when you haven't eaten for a week. When you've done the deed once, the second time is not quite as hard."

Grace glanced at the tent, anxious the girls should not hear this frank conversation.

"Second, I guess you want this hotel to be all yours. You don't want someone else in charge, or to end up working for them."

This was exactly how she felt and she was intrigued that Cora understood. They perhaps had more in common than she realized.

"So, this is what we propose. You will pay us back as soon as the hotel begins to make a profit. And once you have paid back the capital, we will have no further concern."

No further concern? That sounded interesting. But still, they would want a say, surely?

"And you will hear not a word from us before then," said Marguerite, as if reading her thoughts. "We will not advise you on how to run your establishment. Unless you ask for our help."

This was becoming *much* more attractive. And the idea of building the hotel soon...

"However, there is one term my sister and I insist on," said Cora.

Grace's shoulders dropped again. Here it was: the catch.

"At first we considered gifting you the money."

"Why ever would you do that?" Grace asked, sitting upright in surprise.

Cora leaned over and took her chin in her hand, looking straight into her face. "As I told you before, Mrs. Randolph. We owe you our lives. Giving you money would be small recompense."

Grace opened her mouth, but no words came.

Marguerite broke the moment with a shrug and a wave of her hand. "But we sense a gift would not make you happy. I have come across you pioneer types before. Standing on your own feet seems to be an article of faith."

She was right. A gift would make Grace feel obligated, no matter what the sisters said. "So, what is your one condition?" asked Grace.

"That you pay us back the exact same amount as we loan. We will not charge you interest," said Marguerite.

"Even if it takes you some years to pay back the capital," chipped in Cora.

Grace put her fingers to her mouth as she thought. "But that means your money is not working for you. It is no better than burying it in the ground."

Cora shrugged in the same way her sister had. "That is the only condition we give. My sister and I refuse to profit from your work."

Grace turned to Lillian. "Did you know about this?"

Lillian wrinkled her nose and made a clucking sound. "I had an inkling."

Grace smoothed out her skirt. "I'm going to need some time to think about this."

"*Bien sûr*. Have as much time as you want. But remember, every day's delay makes it harder to build something you can be proud of, for when your menfolk return."

Grace and Lillian lay in their tent and whispered about the French sisters' offer deep into the night. Of course, they were going to accept the loan. Something inside Grace had known this from the start.

She could barely sleep with excitement. She missed James more each day; being apart from him was sharpening memories of the old James, the man she had fallen in love with and was determined to spend her life with. His regard for her had dropped so low that he had left San Francisco with barely a word. But, dear God, she was going to make him proud of her.

Grace rose at first light with Lillian to make breakfast for their paying guests. The men were eager to be away to the goldfields, so wolfed down their food and left. Lillian had taken payment the night before. The two of them admired the first dollars of their joint enterprise and then Grace hurried back to Pine Street to tell the foreman they were able to proceed with the hotel. He agreed to view the plot that evening.

She returned to collect Hester and they went to the harbor to set up the kitchen. The argonauts on the earliest boats that day pressed onward to the Bay ferry, in hope of making their fortune. A later boat disgorged weary men, desperate for a place to rest, and Grace found two respectable-looking men in need of accommodation.

That evening, the foreman arrived at Fourth Street. Grace told him what they had in mind as the man paced the site, nodding and taking notes. He commented on the ideal location and the size of the double plot. Quite the opportunity. Lillian told him she wanted space for a cottage garden at the back so she could grow fresh food to serve to guests. The foreman sketched some plans in his notebook and they agreed a price. Grace could hardly believe everything was so easy.

It would be two weeks before the crew were ready to begin. Grace and Lillian resolved to take this time to build up their earnings and get a reputation for both their accommodation and food.

Grace knew that part of the success in drawing custom was because of the rarity of being women, but she found it uncomfortable, even more so now James was gone. Each day she missed that protected feeling he gave her. Still, she had to deal with this by herself.

One evening, as they sat at the fire, Grace spoke to Lillian.

"Y'know, back in Deer Creek, I took to wearing men's clothing."

"Truly?" Lillian had started smoking a pipe under the influence of Cora. She lit it carefully.

"Indeed. Made lots of things easier."

Lillian snorted. "Can't see that husband of yours being happy with that. Always was a stickler."

"On the contrary. He thought it made me safer."

Lillian looked at the end of her pipe, which was failing to burn properly. "What was it like?"

"There were good things and bad. No skirts to get in the way of working. No cleaning the mud from my hems. But you have to get used to the strangeness of fabric between the legs."

Lillian hooted with laughter.

"Thing is," Grace continued, "I'm out and about a lot in town now. Most of the men, they're respectful. But some get leery and say uncouth things. It doesn't feel very... well... comfortable."

"I worry about that for my Hester and Hetty, as they're growing up."

"So... would you mind if sometimes I wore men's clothing?"

Lillian dropped her pipe. "You mean *here*? In San Francisco?"

"Where else would I mean? As long as I keep my hair in my hat, I pass quite well for a boy. You'd be surprised."

"Darn right I'd be surprised. I can't stop you doing as you think best. But if you start cutting that beautiful, thick chestnut hair, I'll rip the scissors from your hand."

Grace tutted. "I have no intention of cutting my hair. But tomorrow, I'm thinking of taking myself to the outfitter and buying pants and a jacket. You alright with that?"

"Alright? I'll come with you. I could do with a belly laugh."

The hardest job was the laundry: the sheets, their own clothing, their monthly rags. They offered shirt cleaning to their guests for an additional fee, and would collect more from men who lived in the area. Either Lillian or Grace would go with the twins to do the cold, laborious job.

They tied up the sheets and garments in canvas and carried the bundles on their backs to the freshwater lagoon close to the presidium. There, they would join Mexican and Native women scrubbing clothes against a board and swirling them in the water. It reminded Grace of the early days panning. Grace had heard that the local women were getting rich on laundry, charging a dollar a dozen shirts. In one area of the lagoon, a group of Chinese men seemed to have decided this was as good a way as any to make their fortune.

Grace and Lillian didn't bother trying to starch and iron the laundry. Being clean was the important thing; being smooth was a luxury too far.

As work began on the hotel, there was less space on the plot for the tents. First they reduced to just one tent to rent out. Soon, every inch was needed by the construction crew, so their little business of accommodating guests had to be suspended. Grace redoubled her efforts at the harbor kitchen and Lillian washed more shirts, now there were no sheets to launder.

Each day there were decisions to be made about the hotel. How much brick could they afford? How big should the windows be? Which wood for the internal panelling?

Grace was astonished by how quickly the building went up. The saloon opposite was being erected at a similar rate. Grace's chest swelled each time she turned into Fourth and Howard and saw what was new that day.

Within a month, the handsome double-story building was

complete. A new chapter of Grace's life was about to begin. James seemed committed to California and she was going to prove to him that she was too. Soon she would write to Tom and tell him things were going well. Perhaps when Tom was old enough, he would join them here? She got butterflies in her stomach just thinking about all being together again.

TWENTY-EIGHT

Grace was like a proud puffed-up dove as she stood on the street next to Lillian in the mid-April sun and admired their new hotel. They decided to call it Independence Hotel after the town where they had started their journey west, three years ago. They set their prices high, aiming for the men returning with plenty of gold in their pockets.

Grace was pleased that the hotel filled quickly, word spreading around the city that there was now a place with proper walls, clean bed linen and good food. Marguerite and Cora's saloon opposite was also open and Grace admitted that it was an attraction for some of the men. However, Lillian insisted on payment in advance, before any danger of money being lost at the French women's card table.

They had a set of rooms with a staircase direct from the kitchen: a room for Grace and James, one for Lillian and George, and one for the girls. Lillian thought Simon plenty old enough to live in his own lodgings, when they came back. Grace felt the emptiness of her room as she ran her hand over the new bed, but pushed away her sadness by picturing the day James would return, and showing him what she had achieved. Sometimes she would stand at the window, looking out at the city, and wonder if he was coming back. They'd heard nothing for two months now.

Work was hard and the hours were long, but Grace was used to this. With eight guest rooms, there was more laundry than ever. Grace and Hester loaded their horse and took the long road north over to the lagoon, the huge sandhills on their right protecting them from the Bay, the April air beginning to warm.

The Chinese men were always there, along with a few women. A lone Chinese woman was at the spot Grace usually used, so she moved along the slope; there was plenty of room on the shore of the lagoon, although with rising numbers, Grace noticed the water had a scum at the edge today.

The Chinese woman worked fast—far quicker than Grace or Hester. Although willowy, her hands and arms were strong as they squeezed the water out of the fabric. She looked in her mid-twenties, perhaps the same age as Grace. She wore a dark jacket with generous sleeves, buttoned at the neck and straight down beyond her knees, with wide pants underneath. Grace was dressed in men's clothes, as usual, and felt a kinship to this woman.

She heard the woman repeatedly sniff and wondered if she were unwell. Surreptitiously looking over, she saw the woman wipe her nose, and although dark hair had fallen from its clip and hid her face as she leaned forward, Grace could tell she was crying. She wanted to say something of comfort but did not know a word of Chinese.

Grace and Hester rang out the sheets between them, one at each end, twisting the fabric. The woman loaded her clean clothes into her wheelbarrow and began to push it up the slope at the side of the lagoon. A stone whistled past Grace's ear and hit the woman, who yelped, and turned on the Chinese boy who had thrown it. Another stone landed in front of the wheel, and before the woman could maneuver, the barrow had lost its balance and tipped sideways.

The woman cried out as the shirts, collars and cuffs tumbled into the dirt. She collapsed to her knees and buried her head in her hands, making high-pitched cries, like a cougar Grace had heard in the Siskiyou mountains.

Ah, this was not tears over children's stones and muddy clothes. The sound was as if the woman had lost all hope in the world. Grace went over and kneeled next to her, pulling the woman into her arms. She made no resistance, and cried against Grace's chest. Hester pulled a handkerchief from the pocket of her apron and handed it over. The woman hid her face in the linen.

Gradually, the tears slowed and the woman took great gulps of air. Grace patted her back between the shoulders. She was so thin, Grace could feel the bones of her spine.

"Thank you," said the woman. "You, kind." Her accent was strong, but the words were clear.

She struggled to her feet and righted the wheelbarrow. Stumbling, she picked up a shirt from the ground, shaking off the mud, then another.

"I start again," she said, turning back to the lagoon.

"We'll help," said Grace, standing up. "With three of us, it'll be done in no time."

The woman seemed too weary to protest, so they knelt together by the water, removing the mud and gray streaks.

When they carried the shirts back to the wheelbarrow, Grace noticed how the woman struggled up the slope.

"Are you going back to town?"

The woman nodded.

"We can walk together."

She didn't seem enthusiastic about this, but waited, her head down, as Grace and Hester tied their bundle to the horse.

They walked along the undulating road until they reached a huddle of tents pitched near a swampy area.

"I say goodbye now." It was the first time the woman had spoken since leaving the lagoon.

Grace studied the ramshackle tents. "You live here?"

She gave a movement that Grace could not interpret as yes or no.

"Where will you dry things?"

"I start fire. Hold close."

It was the usual way to dry things in this damp weather.

"Farewell, then," Grace said gently. "And take care."

The Chinese woman began to make her way, each step painful, struggling to keep the barrow upright. Grace wondered when the woman had last eaten.

She ran to catch up, touching her arm. She couldn't quite put it into words, but instinctively knew the woman should not be left alone. "Do you have a place to sleep tonight?"

The woman twisted her head, rather than answer.

"The truth," Grace said.

"When shirts dry... when I give back shirts. Then money to buy place for night."

Grace looked at the shanty town and wondered what other compromises that place might require of a lone woman, just to be out of the rain tonight.

"You're coming with us," she said, firmly.

The woman frowned and looked like she might refuse.

Grace picked up the arms of the wheelbarrow and steered it round, pushing it toward the road where Hester waited with the horse.

The woman trailed behind. "Shirts. Must have my shirts."

"You'll have them. But you can dry them with us first."

Grace reached Hester and put down the barrow. She turned to the woman.

"Tonight you're sleeping at my hotel."

The woman's eyes opened wide in alarm. "Hotel? No money. No money."

Grace shook her head. "I didn't mean... There are no rooms available, so you may be on the floor in the kitchen. But it will be warm and dry. There will be food."

Still the woman shook her head. "No money."

Grace didn't want to take away what remaining pride the woman had. "Maybe there's chores you can do in return. And tomorrow? Well, you are free to come back here." She picked up the arms of the barrow once more. "Off we go, Hester."

Hester took the guide rope and led the horse. Grace followed with the barrow, the Chinese woman shuffling to keep up.

As they reached busy Market Street, Grace glanced back to make sure the woman was still following. Thankfully she was, eyes fixed on the ground. She could sense the woman's fear and it made her sure she was doing the right thing.

Grace reached Howard and Fourth. "This is the place I run. With my friend. Hester's mother."

The Chinese woman looked up at the building, but her face was blank.

They made their way to the back, where Grace and Hester unloaded the canvas bundle and Hester took the horse to the stables in the next street.

The woman remained outside the kitchen, standing in the yard.

"Now, we haven't introduced ourselves. My name is Mrs. Randolph. And you are..."

"Ling Mei."

"Ling Mei. Hold the door open while I wheel in this barrow."

Ling Mei didn't seem to understand what was needed, so Grace pointed at the door. She pushed the barrow inside and the woman followed.

The kitchen was warm and noisy, filled with Lillian's chatter with Hetty as she clattered pans, making dinner at the large stove.

"There you are!" said Lillian. "Thought we'd lost you, been gone so long."

"We have an extra person for tonight," said Grace.

"To stay? Can't do it. Every room's taken. Why, I'm running round like a horse that's been bitten on the rump."

"She can sleep on the kitchen floor." Grace stepped to one side. "Lillian, this is Ling Mei. We met her at the lagoon."

Lillian frowned. "Met her?"

Ling Mei looked up briefly, her eyes big and dark, and then returned her gaze to the floor.

"Doing laundry."

"Well, obviously."

"She's got some shirts to dry." Grace indicated the barrow.

"You mean *more* drying?"

Grace stepped closer and lowered her voice. "Something dreadful has happened to her. I don't know what, but I'm darn sure she has nowhere safe to go. Could you just trust me on this?"

Lillian met Grace's eyes and an understanding flowed between them. She turned to the woman. "I'm Mrs. Hollingswood. Looks to me like you could do with a good meal. Sit there." She nodded to the table. "Hetty, honey. Go fix Miss Mei some bread and cheese. And there should be a pickle in the pantry."

While Hetty set about fixing food, Grace untied the rope on the pulley holding up the wooden clothes rack and lowered it from the ceiling until it hung close to the table. She draped the shirts over it. Ling Mei leaped up to help, and began to shake out the shirts, smoothing collars and cuffs. When Ling Mei was satisfied, Grace pulled on the rope to raise the rack to the ceiling.

The twins served their guests dinner while Ling Mei sat at the kitchen table with Molly, who was fascinated by this new arrival. She studied her dark straight hair, tied back, not covered in a bonnet as her mother's usually was, and then her dark blue suit.

Molly leaned back on the bench to have a good look at the blue pants. "You're like Aunt Grace. Dressing like a man. In pants."

Grace stifled a giggle.

Ling Mei said nothing, so the two sat in silence.

Once the men had been served their evening meals, the twins joined Ling Mei and Molly at the table. Lillian dished out their food. Grace said a brief prayer and the twins dived in. Ling Mei looked at the food, her hands in her lap.

Grace pushed the plate a little closer. "It's good. Try a little."

She picked up her fork in her right hand, as all the women had done, and ate a small mouthful. Then another.

"See?" Grace said. "Good."

After dinner, Grace brought down her much-used bedding roll and laid it in front of the fire. She fetched blankets.

"Best we can do. For tonight."

She showed Ling Mei where the outhouse was, and went upstairs for the night, hoping she had done the right thing.

At first light, Grace went down the small stairs to the kitchen to find Ling Mei had arranged the chairs around the stove and draped a shirt over the back of each. Some shirts were neatly folded. The hanging rack was now full with the hotel's sheets.

Grace realized that Ling Mei had been up during the night, keeping the stove warm and rearranging the clothing so it dried evenly. Maybe she wanted to get back to her people as fast as possible. Grace thought of the shanty town, of the sobs of desperation by the lagoon. Maybe not.

Grace moved the chairs away so she could make coffee and fix breakfast for the men. Ling Mei understood and helped.

"Where your..." Ling Mei mimed a movement, with both hands as fists pulling back and forth in front of her, as if rolling out a huge piece of pastry.

"Sorry, I don't—"

Ling Mei pointed to the sheets and did a movement as if laying them flat on the table, and again the pastry roller.

"Oh, an iron?" Grace mimed a small iron.

Ling Mei nodded. "Iron."

"We don't have one."

A line came between Ling Mei's eyes.

Grace wondered if she was being judged. "Sorry."

After breakfast, Ling Mei folded each shirt, taking care with the frayed edges and worn elbows, and put them in the wheelbarrow. A couple of meals and a night in the warm seemed to have restored her.

"Must give back shirts," she said. "Get paid."

"Of course," said Grace.

"But I come back."

She picked up the wheelbarrow and trundled off up Fourth Street.

Grace doubted she would ever see her again, even though she'd said she would return. She wondered what had made Ling Mei break down in such despair. Probably she'd never know. But there'd been times when she'd been close to crying in the streets herself, and her heart went out to the young woman.

TWENTY-NINE

The day was busy as always, but Grace felt a swell of satisfaction that their business was gaining a reputation. As she swept the rooms, she wondered what James was doing. Was he missing her as much as she missed him? Was he ever going to come home?

She was having a brief sit down after the midday meal when Grace heard the trundling of the wheelbarrow. She opened the kitchen door to find Ling Mei with a large metal object in the barrow and a canvas bag of starch. Without a word of greeting, Ling Mei hauled the metal object onto the kitchen table. It was a cross between a kettle and a pan, with a handle across the top and a smooth copper bottom.

"You bring blankets," Ling Mei said.

Grace was intrigued, so she hurried upstairs to fetch some. When she returned, Ling Mei had moved the pan to the edge of the stove and cleared everything from the wooden kitchen table. She laid out the blankets, then untied the clothes rack and took down the damp sheets drying there. She laid one over the blankets. Grace watched as Ling Mei opened the stove, picked out some hot coals with the tongs and dropped them into the pan, before returning the lid. After a few minutes, she lifted it to the table and pushed it back and forth across the sheet, smoothing every crease and crinkle and sending a hiss of steam into the air. Ling Mei might be thin, but her arms were strong and she pushed and pulled with speed.

She picked up the finished sheet and showed it to Grace. "You have good hotel. Need good sheets."

Grace marveled at how smooth it looked and ran her hand over it. A sudden rush of sadness brought tears to her eyes as she remembered an evening when a man she barely knew had given her a gift of his linen pillowcase. His half-smile came vividly to mind, as he had said it was his only luxury. The stern captain had been a romantic at heart.

Had that tender part of their love been destroyed, just as the fire had destroyed the pillowcase she had treasured so long, tucked away during all their travels?

Grace turned to hide her tears, and took a moment to compose herself, blowing her nose on her kerchief. When she returned to the table, a second sheet was nearly finished.

"You bring other sheets," Ling Mei said.

"But it's only these which are damp," said Grace, pointing to the pile.

"Bring clean, dry ones. I make smooth."

Grace did as she was asked, bringing the sheets and pillowcases from the laundry press.

Ling Mei held one out and pursed her lips. Grace again had the sensation of being judged for the creases. Ling Mei laid it on the blanket and got a cup of water from the pitcher by the sink. She took a mouthful, her cheeks full like a chipmunk, took the smoother in her hands and sprayed water in a sheen across the sheet.

Grace jumped back in surprise. The pan was pulled over the damp area and Ling Mei sprayed again. She did it four times before she needed to take another gulp of water. Grace had never seen anything like it.

She went to the door to the rest of the hotel. "Come here. Come look!"

Lillian came down the main stairs from where she had been cleaning, the girls just behind. They stood at the door and watched.

"My!" said Lillian. "That sure is something." She picked up the folded sheets. "And look at these. Ain't they fancy?"

They watched, mesmerized, until the sheets were done.

"She says a good hotel needs good sheets," said Grace.

"And she'd be darn right," said Lillian. "Whoever gets to use these will be paying extra."

"Mama, can't we use some of them?" said Hetty. "Just to see what it feels like?"

Lillian laughed. "Well, maybe just one. But we can make good money out of this."

Grace sat at the table with Ling Mei and put her hand over her fingers. "Thank you."

Ling Mei locked her eyes on her face and a small smile came to her lips. It was the first time Grace had seen her smile.

Lillian put a coffee pot on the stove to heat as Grace took down cups from the dresser. "Thing is," Grace said to Lillian, "we might have travelers coming back and complaining about the crumpled stuff."

"They are getting sheets, crumpled or not," said Lillian. "That still makes Hotel Independence the smartest place in town."

Lin Mei stood and gathered her things.

"You must stay for dinner," said Grace.

"Dinner?" She blinked at Grace.

"Yes. Food."

She shook her head. "Must take back." She pointed to the pan. "But I see you at the lagoon?"

"Yes."

"I do more of your washing. I not paid for sleep yet."

Grace waved her hand. "No need to do more. This," she pointed at the pile of linen, "this pays us plenty."

Lillian asked Hetty to fetch bread and dried meat from the pantry. She wrapped it and put it in the wheelbarrow. "D'you have somewhere to sleep tonight?"

Ling Mei looked at her blankly.

Lillian mimed sleeping. "Tonight."

Ling Mei shrugged. "I find somewhere."

Lillian sighed and looked at Grace. Their eyes met. They had grown so close, they seemed to know each other's thoughts.

"Say, we have a ton of laundry," said Lillian. She mimed the pile of sheets being very high. "Lots of cleaning."

Ling Mei looked at Grace, who took her arm and led her back to the table to sit together.

"And you're right," Lillian continued. "If we're aiming to be the best in San Francisco, we need the details to be right."

"Good hotel. Good sheets," Grace said to Ling Mei, echoing her words.

"Oh, honestly, Grace, you don't need to go translating every word I say." Lillian gave a light slap to Grace's arm. "I'm sure the girl can understand." She leaned on the table to face Ling Mei. "We need you here with your copper kettle and fancy water spraying." She tapped the table. "You. Live here. With us. Do laundry."

Grace put her chin on her knuckle. "Maybe Ling Mei can make more money at the lagoon."

"Hmm." Lillian thought about this possibility. "You get meals. Food. Free."

They paused to see what Ling Mei was thinking, but Grace couldn't tell.

"Do you want to stay?" asked Grace, her voice soft.

Ling Mei made that small smile again. "Yes."

"Well, that's settled then," Lillian, banging a cooking pot onto the stove. "One more for dinner."

Ling Mei began to stand. "Need to take kettle back."

"Alright," said Lillian, "but then come back here. Home."

Grace put out her arm to catch Ling Mei. "How much does it cost? The kettle?"

Ling Mei frowned. "Don't know. Uncle brought with him. From China."

"Five dollars? Ten?"

"Maybe."

"Stay here."

Grace returned a few minutes later.

"And you own the barrow?" She pointed at it. "Yours?"

Ling Mei nodded.

"Here is twenty dollars."

Ling Mei's eyes went wide and a little afraid.

"Use as much as needed to buy the kettle. Then you come back with the rest." Grace put the dollar bills in Ling Mei's hand.

Ling Mei stared at her hand. "You trust me?"

"Is there a reason I shouldn't?"

She shook her head.

"Well, then."

She tucked the dollars in a pocket under her tunic and left.

Grace watched Ling Mei settle into life at Hotel Independence with satisfaction. It was Cora's idea that they should build a laundry in the yard area behind the hotel. Lillian bemoaned the loss of some of the space for planting her vegetable garden, but Cora persuaded her that the laundry would bring year-round income.

The foreman and builders put up an outhouse with its own stove and space for a series of large tubs. They cleverly constructed a gutter to gather rainfall from the roof and fill a large water butt. Lines were tied up outside and everyone was pleased not to have laundry drying in the kitchen.

As well as hotel bedding, and guests' clothing for an additional fee, Ling Mei took in items from the French sisters. Grace gossiped with Lillian about the silk undergarments trimmed with lace. She wondered what it must feel like to have such soft fabric next to the skin all day, especially now she was habitually in pants, a jacket and a wide-brimmed hat.

Grace counted how much money they were making and felt a surge of pride. At this rate, they might have the loan cleared before James came back with gold from his months in the Sierra Nevada.

How long would that be? She feared he would stay right through the summer and into the fall. He'd refused to share what was on his mind, when he'd left. Lord, they had been so angry with each other. It seemed so foolish now. If she had her time again, she would tell him that she would wait for him, that her love was an anchor holding them fast as those ships in the harbor; it was as never-ceasing as the waves they had watched together, crashing in from the Pacific; it was as enveloping as the white fog that crept in from the bay, folding around them.

But she had let him leave without telling him. If something happened to him, he'd never know. And that was quietly but surely breaking her heart.

THIRTY

Randolph admired the dam they'd built. He pictured showing it to Grace, knowing she would appreciate their ingenuity: the interlocking embankments and sluices. How she would love this place: the mountains, the clear air, the bubbling river. He banged his hat on his thigh. He'd been so damned stupid to let their arguments come between them. He should have brought her with him, then he'd know she was safe. What in God's name was he thinking, leaving her behind? What was the point he was trying to prove?

He let out a long sigh and dragged his attention back to the river. He was proud of what a small group of men had achieved, but today things were not moving smoothly. The sprocket had lost some teeth and was no longer turning the chain to bring the spoil from the mountain. They could go back to shifting dirt by hand—but it would be much slower. What was the point of all the waterways they had constructed, if there was not enough spoil to make use of it?

The men agreed that Espinoza and Moreno should take the big iron sprocket to town and get it repaired by a blacksmith—or commission a new one. It would take more than a week for the

Chilean pair to go down the Stanislaus River, over to Weberville and to return.

Espinoza and Moreno loaded their horses and secured the heavy sprocket on the strongest of the mules. They were excited by the trip, having been here two months with barely a day's rest. They decided to take their share of the gold, rather than leave the group to be responsible for it.

They said goodbye to each of the men: a mock salute to Randolph, who rolled his eyes, but took the compliment; warm handshakes with Hollingswood and Simon; hugs with Lopez, but a more guarded farewell with Kami. There was a reserve about Kami that prevented even the warm-hearted Espinoza giving slaps on the back.

They nodded toward a new man in the group: Pasatu.

Randolph had seen Miwok people in the area, gathering acorns, fishing for salmon, setting traps. This man had shown an interest in them and returned to watch several times.

Randolph and the man had stood staring at each other one morning, at the edge of their encampment, each without a word of the other's language. The man looked strong, and his intelligent eyes seemed to appraise everything around him.

Randolph had picked up a shovel and handed it to the man.

"What you go do that for?" asked Hollingswood.

"The man looked interested in work."

Sure enough, he'd started shoveling rock onto the conveyor to be taken down to the sluice.

Moreno had stepped forward and taken the larger rocks, throwing them on the ground and breaking them into smaller pieces with a pick, before tossing them back on the conveyor.

The Miwok man had watched attentively. He followed suit, taking a larger rock and splitting it as if he'd been doing this for years.

Hollingswood had shaken his head in exasperation. "And what are we going to pay him?"

Randolph shrugged. "Looks like we're going to have to work that out at the end of the day."

Sure enough, as the sun set behind the mountains, the man had come to Randolph.

"Two dollar."

Randolph raised an eyebrow, and wondered how much English he'd understood during the day.

"We don't have dollars."

"Two dollar."

"I can pay you in gold."

"*Dos dólares en oro.*"

"Hey," said Espinoza. "That's Spanish." Espinoza came to stand by Randolph. "*Un dólar en oro.*"

The man had shaken his head and looked at Randolph, who he clearly took as the leader. "Two dollar. Gold."

"What did you say to him?" asked Randolph.

"I was negotiating down to one dollar."

"But he's stuck at two dollars?" said Randolph. "George, could you measure it out?"

"But he's an Indian," said Hollingswood.

"Who's done a day's work." Randolph had stared at Hollingswood and folded his arms.

"I'm just saying what everyone else is thinking," Hollingswood grumbled as he ambled to the tent where they gathered their gold. He'd returned with a tiny portion. "Weighed it."

Randolph handed it over. The man had put it in a pouch and disappeared into the trees. Randolph wasn't sure why he felt pleased, but it had raised his spirits none the less.

The next morning, the man had returned at first light. He picked up a shovel and started work.

"Espinoza," Randolph called. "Can you ask him his name?"

Espinoza did so in Spanish.

"Says it's Pasatu."

Randolph repeated the name and patted his chest. "Randolph." He pointed at Espinoza and said his name.

Pasatu nodded and continued to work, seemingly uninterested in anyone's names.

At break time, Pasatu had sat separately, taking out a pouch of acorns and other woodland seeds. He drank water from a bladder.

"We're not going to invite him over?" Randolph asked, looking around at the other men.

"Seems happy enough sitting over there," said Espinoza, his mouth full of biscuit.

On the third day, Randolph had taken Pasatu a plate of food. He accepted it but ate it at a distance.

The next day, he had arrived with three fresh salmon.

"Says he caught them this morning," said Moreno.

Lopez cooked them for lunch and this time, Pasatu had sat with them.

He and Moreno built a rhythm together, swinging their picks in time. Pasatu would observe something and Moreno would laugh.

At the end of the day, Hollingswood weighed out two dollars' worth of gold, even though it had not been a good day's sluicing. There was no point arguing with Randolph about this.

As they sat around the fire that night, Randolph had asked whether they should make Pasatu a partner, like the rest of them.

"Why would we do that?" asked Hollingswood.

"Seems like he's willing to work as hard as the rest of us."

"And getting paid for it," said Espinoza. "He's happy enough. Why change things?"

"Well, I guess I'm thinking, it's his land—"

"It's not his land. *We* made this claim," said Hollingswood.

"I didn't see anyone else digging for gold here." He looked around the group for support, and the Chileans nodded. Lopez and Kami made no response either way.

"I mean," said Randolph evenly, "his people have been living here, before us."

"Living off the land," said Moreno. "Just like us."

Randolph had shrugged and seen he was outnumbered. He let the matter drop.

Over the next few days, Pasatu had moved his bivouac close to their camp, rather than disappearing into the trees each evening. Randolph felt it was some sort of progress.

Randolph jerked awake. From the darkness in the tent, he guessed it was not quite dawn, but he heard boots outside, heavy and fast. Then a shout.

"Okay now, boys. Time to get up." The voice had a southern drawl. A laugh. The sound of guns being cocked.

Randolph grabbed his pistol, pulled at the pegs at the side of his tent and rolled out, but straight into a pair of boots.

"Drop the pistol." A man had his rifle trained on him.

The shouts from the gang increased as they pulled the flap to the Hollingswood tent and Simon emerged, bleary eyed, followed by his father, holding a rifle.

"No need for that," said one of the intruders. "Throw it to the ground."

Hollingswood looked around and did as he was told.

Randolph counted half a dozen men, maybe more. His mind raced through the options. *Five of us, plus Pasatu.* But they were the ones holding the guns. If only Espinoza and Moreno were still here. That might have made the difference.

Kami and Lopez were pulled to the central area of the camp where Randolph stood, barefoot and in his long johns.

"This tent's empty," someone shouted.

The Southerner addressed Randolph. "Where are they?"

"Not here."

"I can damn well see that. Where they go?"

"Weberville."

"We've seen seven of you here. When are they back?"

Randolph instinctively knew he had to cover for the Chileans. "Not coming back. We had a falling out."

"Damn," someone said, "that's two men down."

There was a commotion and a man dragged Pasatu into the clearing. "Look what I found."

"An Indian. That's worth five dollars. Will make up for the two we've lost."

The leader, the one with the Southern accent, walked up to Pasatu, raised his gun and shot him in the head. He dropped to the ground like a sack of corn.

Randolph's mouth fell open, but all that came out were guttural gasps. The gunshot was still ringing in his ears. It happened so quickly, as if the Southerner had been shooting at a rat, rather than a man. One of the men who had been holding him took out a knife.

"No!" yelled Randolph. "You can't—"

"Don't get paid unless you prove it," said the Southerner. "Got to take evidence."

The Southerner came closer to Randolph. He was short, but approached until he was looking up into Randolph's face. The sky was lightening and the features of the man emerged. A moment of recognition passed between them.

"I remember you," the man said. "Where was it now? Ah, yes. Grass River. Maybe a year back."

Randolph said nothing but continued to stare at the Southerner.

"See, I remember that wife of yours. The one with all that sass, and the rifle." He lifted his right hand and showed the two broken fingers that were curled into his palm.

"Hey, Dent," he called. "Check the tents to see if there's a woman. I got a debt to claim from her."

Randolph's heart was beating hard. He had ached with missing Grace over the past weeks, but never had he been more relieved to be parted from her.

Dent returned. "No one here, Snyder."

"She gone left you? Too bad. Could have had us some fun."

Randolph gritted his teeth, but he had to control his anger. The dawn sky was gray now. The sun would not rise above the mountains for some time yet, but there was enough light to see the gang. Each was heavily armed. Randolph and his men stood helpless, waiting to see how this would play out.

Snyder, the Southerner, came close to Kami and breathed in his face. "This another one? Got that tattoo on his face."

"He's not Miwok," said Randolph firmly. "He's from the Sandwich Islands."

"Shame," said Dent. "Could have been another five dollars just standing there."

Snyder circled the men. "Where's your stash?"

No one moved.

"The gold. You got it somewhere."

Randolph was proud that still none of his friends said anything. They had worked hard for that gold.

Snyder cocked his gun and pointed it at Kami, whose eyes opened wide in terror.

"I'll tell you," shouted Randolph.

Snyder lowered his gun.

"In the tent," Randolph nodded to the Hollingswood tent. "Simon, go fetch it."

Simon looked frightened, but did as he was told, emerging from their tent with two canvas bags and a box—everything the remaining men had mined over recent weeks, waiting to be divided equally when they left the valley.

The robbers whooped with delight.

Snyder raised his gun to Kami again, and without warning, shot him twice, in the chest and the head. The clearing echoed with the sound.

Randolph ran to the bloodied body and fell to his knees beside it. He put his hands to Kami's chest, knowing it to be pointless. His friend. His peaceful, wise friend Kami. He shook his head back and forth. "What..." he stuttered. "What did you do that for? We gave you what you wanted."

Snyder smirked. "Took your time though." He pointed to Kami with his gun. "And that's another five-dollar Indian bounty."

"You're crazy! I *told* you, he wasn't from here."

"Nobody will be able to tell that from his scalp."

All the fury he'd been trying to keep in check exploded. These were animals who cared for nothing, valued nothing. Randolph roared and launched himself at Snyder, not caring that his opponent had a gun in his hand, not caring in that moment if he lived or died. He didn't want to remain on this earth, if there was such evil in it.

He knocked Snyder to the ground and struck his jaw with his fist. Two of the robbers leaped onto his back and pulled him off. Snyder struggled to his feet.

"Do we kill him?" asked Dent.

Snyder shook his head. "No. We promised these men to Becksommer. But we can sure make his life hell."

Snyder picked up a rifle, and struck Randolph across the head with the stock. He fell unconscious to the ground.

THIRTY-ONE

Randolph came to, lying on his side. His head throbbed and there was a pain around his kidneys. The camp was in disarray, the tents flat, their precious belongings scattered. He struggled to remember what had happened, but he knew it was something bad.

Someone pulled him upright. For a moment, he was relieved to see Hollingswood, Simon and Lopez were dressed and seated, but then saw their hands were tied behind their backs, their faces blank and dazed. Then he saw the bodies of Kami and Pasatu lay on the ground, each surrounded by blood. It all came crashing back: a living nightmare.

"Get dressed," Dent shouted at him.

Randolph tried to get to his feet, but couldn't, so crawled over to where his tent had stood. His brain felt as if a heavy morning fog had filled it. He found a shirt and his pants from the mess. His hands could barely function as he pulled on his boots. Unseen, he slipped a small knife into his right one, then buckled his belt and hooked his suspenders, before finding his jacket beneath a blanket. He pulled on his hat and crept back to his friends, fearful of what was ahead for them.

The sky was bright blue, the air beginning to warm. The gang were stripping the camp of anything of value: rifles, cutlery, water canteens.

"Look at this, boss," said Dent.

It was the beautiful pistol Grace's father had made, and she had given to him.

Snyder grabbed it. "My. Fancy."

He tucked it into his belt and Randolph felt sick that something Grace had handled should now be in the possession of this thug.

The four men were pulled to their feet. Gang members linked their ankles with rope, wide enough to walk, but not to run. Dent bound Randolph's wrists and knocked his hat to the ground, laughing.

"Where you taking us?" Hollingswood asked.

It was the first time Randolph had heard him speak since the ordeal began.

Snyder chuckled. "You'll see."

They left the camp, walking about half a mile to where the gang's horses had been tied up, their hooves muffled. So that was how they had approached the camp unheard.

Randolph grunted. This was a planned attack. How long had the gang been watching them? Snyder had known how many of them there were—although thankfully he didn't realize the Chileans had left. Who was this Becksommer Snyder had mentioned, and what did he want with them?

The gang mounted their horses and Snyder led the way. Randolph, Hollingswood, Simon and Lopez followed on foot, each tied with a long rope to the saddle of one of the men. Their horses and mules were tethered at the back, saddled up—the saddles had value—but unburdened.

They followed the familiar path downstream, a route they'd taken before, and came to a place where they could cross the

South Fork of the Stanislaus. The gang urged their horses across. The men followed on foot, struggling to keep their balance, the water still icy and forceful from winter melt. Randolph lost his footing and one of the gang pulled him across, coughing and spluttering as he tried to keep his head above the water.

His clothing was heavy and cold as he emerged from the river and up the path. His boots squelched.

They followed a deer path upwards out of the valley, the pine trees thinner as they climbed higher. The ground was made of small rocks and was difficult underfoot. The sun beat down on Randolph's unprotected head. He lifted his eyes to the mountains around him, mountains he had been awed by in their size and majesty. They had given him solace on the mornings when he woke early, regretting again the empty space beside him, wondering what his wife was doing, whether she was safe. He thanked God again that he had left her behind.

They crossed a high pass, dipped down, and then the path rose again. He understood where they were going. This was the mountain that divided the South and Middle Forks: he was walking north, or northeast.

As the day continued, he had reason to wish he was back at the river. The gang drank regularly from their canteens, but he was given nothing and his throat grew rough and sandy. They paused at a small creek where the gang filled their canteens. Hollingswood, Simon and Lopez were pushed to their knees so they could drink directly from the stream.

"Not you," said Snyder with a sly grin.

He caught Lopez's eye and thought he was going to speak on his behalf. Randolph quickly shook his head: he knew it was useless to protest.

Whatever their destination, they had not reached it by nightfall. The gang set up camp. Randolph was finally given water, but none of his friends were fed. The four were sat back-to-back, unable to lie down for the night. The air grew cold and sharp. They huddled closer, murmuring encouragements. Randolph whispered that he had a knife, in hope there was some way of reaching it, of escaping, but the gang members took turns to watch them all night.

At daybreak, Randolph was surprised that he had managed a few hours of sleep. Every muscle ached. His head throbbed where he had been struck and made him dizzy.

The friends exchanged glances even though speaking was forbidden. Dent gave them each a mouthful of water and a few strips of jerky. The food made Randolph hungrier than before.

The gang set off again, each step painful for Randolph. They reached the mountain above the Middle Fork valley and the path fell away. Being tethered, making his way downwards was as difficult as the path up the mountains had been. He stumbled and struggled to keep his balance, particularly with both hands tied.

They reached the level where the pines grew stronger and closer together. Birds flitted back and forth, the air alive with song. He could hear a river in the distance.

The trees parted and there below were the biggest gold workings Randolph had seen.

The river was dammed and divided into multiple sluices. Men crawled over the site, at this distance looking like insects. The biggest shock was how much of the land on the other side of the river had been excavated. At the top, the hill was lush and green, but a gray scar extended to the valley bottom. There were horizontal steps across the scar, with men with picks working on each level. Rocks were thrown into wagons on rails and pushed to the riverside.

This was proper mining. Randolph and his brotherhood had built something substantial—but nothing like this.

As he made his way down the hill, the noise of the workings

increased. Iron clashed against the rock, wheels squealed as four men pushed a metal cart. It crashed as it turned on its side to let the rock pour out.

Men's voices shouted at the workers to move out of the way, to work harder.

Further up the river, Randolph could see a collection of tents standing close together. That must be where the men slept. There was fencing around the perimeter.

A wooden cabin stood near the river. An area had a large canopy and benches for eating meals.

By the time Randolph reached the valley floor, he was exhausted by thirst and hunger, and felt humiliated to be arriving there bound at hand and foot. But few of the miners seemed interested in them: they kept their eyes down, absorbed with their work.

The only men who took notice of him and his friends were the guards, each holding a rifle. This was ominous. If these miners needed guarding so they couldn't leave, that meant they were unpaid. In effect, slavery. One man had a whip wound at this belt. Randolph knew there were no steers nearby which would require the crack of a whip. This was for a more sinister use.

A man came out of the cabin and down the two steps to the sandy area in front. He was dressed smartly in a stone-colored long jacket with a dark-gray vest beneath, and a black tie, despite the heat. His hat was unusual: more of a bowl shape with a curved rim and made of hard felt. Snyder pushed the men forward.

"Only four?" the man asked, tsking.

Snyder dipped his head and shuffled. "Got me a couple of Indians." He nodded to the evidence hanging from his saddle. He turned to Randolph and his friends. "This is Mr. Becksommer. You better make sure you do what he says."

Becksommer examined them, one by one, for all the world

as if looking at cattle in a market. Randolph flexed his hand, wishing he could take a swing at that self-satisfied face.

"You better watch that one," said Snyder. "Something of a firecracker."

Randolph raised his chin as Becksommer stared at him. He refused to be intimidated. A look passed between them. Possibly mutual hatred.

"I'll take them. Snyder, go get your fee in the office."

Snyder hurried inside, as if eager to leave Randolph and the other three behind.

Becksommer stretched out his arms. "I am Mr. Septimus Becksommer, and welcome to Dorado Mining Company. The most advanced mine in the Sierra Nevadas. We produce more gold at a cheaper rate than any other mine."

"Because you're using slave labor," said Randolph.

Becksommer wagged his finger. "No, no, no. What's your name?"

"Mr. Randolph."

"Ah. Mr. Randolph. You malign my company. Every one of these men is paid a dollar-fifty a day—as you will be. And—just like you—they are free to leave as soon as they pay off their debt."

"What debt? We don't owe you nothing," said Hollingswood.

"You need to pay back the finder's fee I've just paid Mr. Snyder."

Randolph widened his feet and rested his thumbs in his belt. "We didn't ask to be found."

"True. But you're here now. And the fee is only five dollars a man."

"And what's the catch? Any of these men could pay that off in a week."

"As I said"—Becksommer wove his fingers in front of his

chest—"I run an advanced business. There's shelter. And two meals a day."

Dent giggled. "Shelter charged at fifty cents a night. Meals at a dollar." He seemed impressed by Becksommer's duplicity.

"That's slavery by another name," said Randolph.

Becksommer affected a hurt look. "Pfft. That word again. Now, Snyder and his gang, they're from the south. They're relaxed about that kind of thing. But me? I'm a Connecticut man. And I don't like you casting aspersions on my good name."

He stepped close and jabbed Randolph with a fist, hard in the stomach. Randolph had not been expecting the punch; he bent double, the pain around his kidneys flaring up. Becksommer hooked an upward strike, catching Randolph on his chin. He stumbled backwards, tripping on the rope tether, crashing to the ground.

Some of the laborers paused to look over, to see who was getting a hiding this time.

"Sort them out," Becksommer said, his mock-friendly tone gone. "I want them working within the hour."

Randolph had experienced hardship; he'd known what it was like to go without sleep, to live on hard rations, to work in the open. He had crossed the Great Plains and the Rocky Mountains many times. He'd lived the chaos of war, the constant anxiety of not knowing when an attack might come.

But he'd never experienced the random cruelty of the Dorado Mining Company. A guard would interpret a look and punish it with a blow, so the workers learned to keep their heads down and eyes on the ground. They were forbidden to speak to each other, so they communicated in low whispers. If overheard, a guard might withhold a meal, or water.

They were constantly urged to work harder, faster. Accidents were common: a wagon ran over a man's foot, crushing it.

A rockfall tumbled onto the heads of workers below, causing broken bones and cracked skulls.

Randolph saw one man break down from the pressure: a Mexican. He couldn't understand the man's rapid words, but read his body movements as he gesticulated. The guard shouted at the Mexican to carry on working, but the man continued to pour out all his anger and frustration. Miners nearby paused and watched. There was a moment when Randolph wondered if more would rise up against their oppressors. Indeed, this might be an opportunity for him to fight back.

Randolph knew there'd be more trouble when Becksommer marched over to the altercation. The manager exchanged a few words with the Mexican, and seemed to have calmed the situation, even shook hands, but then raised his pistol and shot him between the eyes. The sound echoed around the exposed rocks of the hillside. Everything came to a halt, Randolph included. A ripple of shock ran through the workings.

Becksommer told the two workers nearest to dispose of the body. They picked it up and dragged it away. Randolph wondered where the Mexican would be buried. Perhaps there was a pit somewhere.

He hung his head in shame as he joined the rest of the miners turning back to their digging or hauling or sluicing. The moment was over, like a coin dropped into water, making hardly a ripple and never to be seen again.

The guards noted Snyder's warning that attention should be paid to Randolph. His every mistake was punished with a blow. Early on, Simon had been singled out for an error and forfeited his meal. Randolph had protested: the boy was learning the job, he was a hard worker. The guard with the whip instructed Randolph to remove his shirt. He administered three cracks across his back. They felt like a knife being drawn through his flesh. Every move he made for the next week reminded him of the painful wheals across his back. In the evenings, Lopez tried to sooth the wounds with the inside of an aloe plant he picked nearby.

Randolph could endure the physical hardships, even as his body grew thin and the injuries took longer to heal. It was his spirit that was being broken day by day. He wondered about the Mexican. Did he have a family? A wife? Children? Would they ever know what had happened to him? Or would they think he had abandoned them, made a fortune in California but not gone home to share it?

His mood darkened. Is that what Grace would think of him? They had parted on such poor terms. Dear God, why had he not told her how deeply he loved her? Why had he not taken her in his arms that day he left, promised her he would return, that nothing in this world could separate them. He would climb the Sierra Mountains, swim a river cataract; he would always come back to her. He regretted every harsh word he had ever uttered, every night he had turned his back to her.

He had seen man's cruelty during war, but thought they were exceptional circumstances: something about the declaration of war let loose the worst instincts of ordinary men, instincts which lay below the surface. He had been sickened to see men with wives and children commit atrocities on other wives and children. Even in war he had held on, somewhere inside, to the hope that when taken out of the battlefield, soldiers' better natures might prevail.

Yet here, in the Middle Fork of the Stanislaus River, he saw the worst of man once more. Becksommer gave license to cruelty, and the guards were given free rein.

His friends seemed to sense he was close to giving up. Hollingswood urged him to get up in the morning, saying it would only get worse if he were late. Lopez put food in front of him, sternly telling him to eat, when Randolph had no interest in food. Simon would stare at him in the evening, and Randolph felt those eyes were full of disappointment.

As the days dragged on, he felt himself despairing. Surely Grace would be better off without him. He'd brought her to this godforsaken territory. It was his arrogance. She had wanted to stay in Oregon, with her brothers. If he were no longer alive, she would be free of him, free to return to the clean air and generous soil of the Willamette Valley. Free to have a future, released from the burden he had become.

THIRTY-TWO

"There's two men here to see you," said Hester.

Grace was standing at the stove, stirring a pot of fat to make into soap. "Definitely me?"

"They asked for you by name."

"Then you better take over," she said, putting the spoon down and wiping her hands on her apron. She took it off and tied it round Hester. Grace was wearing a cotton dress today, as she generally did with the warm June weather. She wondered if the men might be city officials, and whether she was dressed smartly enough. She hurried through to the front door.

The two men stood expectantly, each with a wide beige hat and a colorful blanket instead of a jacket. Although she had not seen them for more than half a year, she knew them immediately.

"Oh, goodness! Espinoza. Moreno."

Espinoza took her hand, and kissed it. Ah, still with the charming manners. Moreno towered above her, looking less certain. Grace was dismayed by how ill he looked. His eyes were sunken and what flesh she could see below his mustache and beard seemed shriveled. When he put his hand out to her, there was a tremor. What could have happened to him?

"Come in, please." She led the way to the dining room. "However did you find me?"

"It wasn't hard," said Espinoza with a nervous laugh. "We asked at the harbor. It seems everyone knows this hotel you have built."

She pulled out a chair for each of them, enjoying the familiar Chilean accent in Espinoza's speech. They sat and it took her back to good times. "You must be tired if you've just arrived." She opened the door to the kitchen. "Hester? Can you leave the soap to cool and put on a pot of coffee? And bring through a plate of the cookies your sister made."

Grace settled at the table. A warm feeling spread over her as she looked at her old friends.

"I'm so sorry, but Mr. Randolph isn't here. He would have been so pleased to see you. He's gone back to the goldfields."

"We know." Espinoza twisted his hands.

"You know?"

"We have been working with him."

She took a sharp breath. Oh, Lord, she would finally have news about him.

"We set up the old partnership."

It was as if the air in the room had gone still. "How is he? Is he well?"

Neither man spoke and both had uncertain looks on their faces.

Grace's skin went cold. "He *is* well, isn't he? Oh, please, tell me he's well."

"To be honest with you, we don't know," said Espinoza. The edges of his mouth turned down.

Grace's fingers ran over the brooch at her neck, something James had bought her when they had first arrived. "But he's... he's alive?" She could barely speak the words.

Espinoza's gaze slid to the wall beyond her. "Yes... Well, we think so."

"You *think* so!" She looked at each of them in turn, but they struggled to meet her eye. Moreno dropped his head. Her heart was beating hard. "Why are you not sure?"

"My dear Mrs. Randolph. He was well when we last saw him."

"Which was?"

"We had set up a gold operation. We were doing well—"

Grace tapped the table in frustration. "I'm not interested in that. I want to know about my husband."

Espinoza moved his seat. "Moreno and I were away. We had gone to town to repair equipment. But we heard rumors about a gang that captures men. When we returned, it seems they had taken your husband."

"Captured? Does someone want a ransom?" Grace jumped up. "I've got money. I can pay—"

Espinoza put up his hand. "It isn't like that. This gang, they take men as labor."

Grace returned to the table. "I don't understand—"

"The man who runs a crossing on the Stanislaus told us. Dr. Knight. He said it's a new thing happening. There is a big mining company. And they run it by forcing men to work."

Grace sat down on the chair again, trying to understand. "But James. He could leave, couldn't he?"

Moreno lifted his head and spoke for the first time. "The miners—they are guarded."

But this was absurd. This was California. There was plenty of gold for everyone.

Hester came in with a tray of coffee and cookies and put it on the table.

Grace looked at her. Oh, heavens. Hester's father. Her brother.

She lowered her voice. "And was my husband with anyone else? He went out with another man and his son."

Espinoza nodded. "Mr. Hollingswood and Simon were part of our company. They have also been taken."

Grace swallowed, even though her mouth was dry. "Hester. Where's your mother?"

"Buying food in town, I think."

"Go find her. Go now."

"What about the soap?"

"Forget the soap. Bring your mother back immediately. No matter what."

After Hester had hurried out, Grace turned to the men.

"And were Lopez and Kami with you?"

Espinoza nodded. "We had set up a little brotherhood. Like the old days."

"But have they been taken too?"

Espinoza hesitated so Moreno stepped in. "We think they have Lopez. But Kami... Kami was shot during the attack."

"Shot... dead?" She could hardly believe she was asking this question.

Moreno grunted to indicate yes, unable to form the word.

Grace put her palms on the table, trying to steady herself. Maybe they'd got it wrong. Maybe— "So, how do you know? How do you *know* any of this happened. If you weren't even there—"

"Mrs. Randolph, we went back to the workings, but the men were gone." Moreno's dark eyes were full of sorrow.

Grace put her fingers to her temples. "Maybe James and the Hollingswoods decided to move on. While you were away."

Espinoza shook his head.

"Had there been a falling-out?" She knew she was clutching at straws.

"The whole site was ransacked. Things everywhere."

"I don't believe it. James wouldn't have let himself be captured. He's been a soldier. He's been in battle—"

Moreno pulled himself to his feet without speaking and went outside. Grace looked at Espinoza for an explanation, but he was studying the tablecloth.

Moreno returned with a piece of baggage and slung it on the table, breathing heavily. He untied it, opening the burlap to show the clothing it held.

Grace's chest felt so tight it hurt as she picked up James's pale buff hat, her fingers tingling as she ran them round the brim. He wouldn't have willingly left it behind.

It brought to mind times when he had gazed at her, his beautiful blue eyes in shadow, but a smile playing on his lips. Her chin began to tremble.

She stroked her palms over his shirt—a green and gray plaid made of wool, with plenty of room. It had been one of his favorites.

With shaking hands, she picked up his small shaving kit with just the basics, rarely used since he had let his beard grow after leaving the army. His hands had held each of these objects.

She gave up trying to hold back the tears. "But he's alive."

"There's no need to think he isn't," said Espinoza, reaching out his hand and briefly putting it on hers. "The gang. We were told they are paid by the head. And the mine wants laborers."

This was cold comfort. But it was something.

Grace looked at the other clothing on the table. She recognized some as belonging to George and Simon.

She heard steps behind her.

"What is it?" Lillian asked. "Hester said I had to come home."

Grace turned and knew her friend was reading in her face that something dreadful had happened.

"It's George." Grace's voice croaked. "And Simon. They've

been taken. With James, and another man I knew, a Panamanian."

"Taken? Taken where?"

Grace looked to Espinoza for help.

"To another mine. As laborers," he said. "We are telling you what Dr. Knight told us. He knows the area. They will have been paid for."

Lillian stood stock-still, staring at Espinoza. "Paid for? Men being paid for? You mean, like *slaves*?"

Grace's hand covered her mouth. She hadn't thought of it in this way. But Lillian was right.

Lillian noticed the clothing. "And what"—her voice was husky—"what are my husband's and son's things doing on this table?"

Moreno stepped forward, his head bowed. "We brought back what we could."

Lillian dropped heavily into a chair. The twins stood at the door, unsure whether to enter the room. Hetty held Molly's hand.

Lillian looked up at the two men, her face hard. "Who are you? What have you to do with all this?"

Grace sat opposite Lillian and took her hand. "This is Espinoza and Moreno. I've mentioned them to you. The men from Chile, James and I mined with. Remember? They met up again and were all together."

Lillian waved her hand as if remembering such details was not important now. She pulled Simon's shirt to her and folded it neatly. She then did the same with George's clothing. She lifted it to her nose.

"Hester? Hetty? Make sure none of this gets laundered."

Grace drew James's shirt to her breast. She felt the same way. Part of her husband remained in his clothing, not just his smell, but something deeper.

Espinoza and Moreno stood nervously, uncertain what to do next. A silence fell in the room.

"I'm grateful you brought back these things," said Lillian, "but why didn't you go after my husband and my son?"

Moreno sat sideways on a chair, his head in his hands. "You are right. It is shameful that we have abandoned our brothers."

Grace thought this huge man was on the verge of collapse.

Espinoza sat back down opposite Grace. "Honestly, we thought about tracking them. It looked like it had happened only a day or so before we reached the abandoned camp. But Knight said the mine is in the Middle Fork and we thought they'd be there by then."

Moreno cleared his throat. "I promise we wanted to rescue them. But it was only the two of us, with a gun each. For Randolph and Lopez and the Hollingswoods to be taken... it must have been a large, well-armed gang."

"So we thought we needed to get a proper posse of men to go in and smoke the gang out," Espinoza continued. "We went to the nearest big town. Mr. Weber, the mayor there, would not help. Said men were being taken to the Dorado Mining Company, run by a Mr. Becksommer. Said they were armed to the teeth. We'd need an army to get them back."

Grace sniffed back her tears. "Well, thank you for coming straight here and telling us."

The Chileans exchanged a look.

"You should know," said Espinoza, "we have been delayed. Moreno has been very unwell. Dysentery."

Grace's head shot up. So that was why Moreno was half the man she remembered. What a dreadful thing to endure. "But you are recovered?"

Moreno nodded but Espinoza spoke. "No, not really. As you can see, Arturo is still very weak."

"You'll be staying here, of course," Grace said.

Espinoza demurred and muttered something about finding a place with his countrymen elsewhere.

Grace wouldn't hear of it. "You're as good as family. You'll have mine and James's room. I'll go in with Mrs. Hollingswood. I will get ready now, and you can move in your things afterwards."

"Get ready?"

"Well, there are four men and you said we'd need an army to get them back. I'm going to them for help. There's a new Governor General, just arrived from Monterey with troops. Surely he will help. I mean, California is part of the United States now. He can't let such lawlessness stand." Grace stood. "I'm going to the Presidio."

Espinoza looked surprised. "What, now?"

"Why not?" Her husband was being mistreated somewhere. She was not going to delay, even by an hour. She had never met a Governor General but was determined not to be intimidated.

"In that case, we're coming too," said Espinoza, rising to his feet.

Moreno stood but swayed and grabbed the table.

Lillian spoke. "Look, Mr. Moreno. Why don't you stay here and make sure you two have moved your gear in."

Moreno glanced at Espinoza, who spoke to him in Spanish. The matter seemed to be settled.

"I alone will have the honor of accompanying you to the Governor General," said Espinoza.

Grace ran upstairs and changed into a new dress she had bought recently: light blue cotton with a high neck and long sleeves. She brushed and pinned her hair and put on a bonnet. She called to Lillian to ask if she could borrow her cape. Grace came back downstairs looking every inch the respectable matron—except for her feet, which still had sturdy boots.

"Right. The Governor General."

THIRTY-THREE

Grace mounted her horse alongside Espinoza. It was the first time she had ridden in months. They made their way past the sand dunes, past the lagoon and on to the Presidio. The military area went back to the days when the Spanish ruled this territory, before the Mexicans, before the Californians, and before the Americans.

They went past the sentries without being challenged. Grace was struck by how slipshod the behavior was.

Espinoza asked where he could find Governor General Bennett Riley, and they were directed to a building.

They dismounted and Grace was about to follow Espinoza inside, when the door swung open and a man in dark blue uniform marched out, flanked by adjutants, one carrying a large military hat with white feathers. He was tall, well over six feet, and broad with it. His thick gray hair made a halo around his head, matched by his side whiskers, which ran in a curve from his ears to his mouth.

"Governor Riley?" Espinoza asked.

The man did not break his step. "I am."

"We need your help."

"As does everyone, it seems." Riley's voice was hoarse, as if his collar was pulled too tight.

Espinoza followed, mingling among the soldiers, trying to get his attention. Grace quickened her step to keep up.

"My friends," said Espinoza. "Their lives are in danger."

The governor slowed and looked at Espinoza. He did not even glance at Grace, who was standing at Espinoza's shoulder. "Mexican?"

"Me?"

"Yes."

"No. Chilean."

"Ah. A good many of you have settled in San Francisco. I hear there are rumblings in the camp over near Clark's Point. Is that what this is about?"

"Sir, no. It is my friends in the goldfields. Three are American. One from Panama."

"And why are they in danger?" the governor asked as he continued on his way.

Grace gave a gentle push to Espinoza's back to make sure he kept up.

"They have been abducted. They are forced labor."

Riley reached his tall, black horse. A soldier was struggling to keep it still.

"And what am I to do about it?"

"Send soldiers to release my friends and all the other men kept captive."

Riley scoffed. "You want me to send soldiers? To the goldfields?"

Grace stepped forward. The Governor General seemed about to push the problem away. "One of the men is my husband."

Riley paused and looked at her for the first time. "I am sorry to hear that, madam."

"He served in the army. For ten years." Grace hoped this might count for something.

Riley patted his horse's neck to calm him. "Then you may have some understanding of how the army works, ma'am."

"Not really. But I thought the Governor General would make sure the law was followed."

Riley took his gloves from his adjutant and pulled them on.

"Madam, I have been in post for two months and here in San Francisco for a matter of days. I would very much like the law to be followed in California. But here's the truth. I have eight companies of infantry, two of artillery, and two companies of dragoons. That's to cover the whole of California—about the same area as Washington down to Florida."

"But you can't let this just happen—"

"Now, if something had happened *here*"—he spoke over her —"or in San Diego, maybe I could have helped. But if I send a company into the goldfields, I'm never getting them back." He snapped one of his gloves in place. "My biggest problem right now? Desertion."

Grace's hands formed fists as her anger grew, realizing he wouldn't help. "You are going to let my husband rot? A man who gave so much to the United States?"

"Madam." He looked down at her, his nostrils flaring. "What was his name?"

Grace was reluctant, knowing her husband had left under a cloud. What if Riley knew of whatever it was that James had done, and that went against him?

"Randolph," she muttered.

"Say?"

"James Randolph."

The other adjutant gave him his hat, which he adjusted on his head. "Well, if Private Randolph has served so long, he ought to have the skills to break free."

"So that's it?" cried Grace.

He put his foot in the stirrup and swung himself into his saddle. "Madam, I'm late—"

"You're going to leave things so the criminals take over?"

"I have to be pragmatic—"

She folded her arms. "Because if you won't go and rescue my husband, then I darn well will."

Riley roared with laughter. "I wish you good luck in your endeavors." He touched the horse's flank with his heel and trotted onwards, accompanied by three soldiers. The feathers of his hat bobbed in the wind.

Grace watched them leave. She clenched her teeth, trying to stop herself from screaming after him, that he was a coward, a disgrace to his uniform. How could he ride away from such lawlessness? Wasn't he the Governor General?

It was the end of a miserable day. Grace had to tell Lillian that nothing would be done by the Governor General to bring back their men. They would have to sit and wait, who knew for how long? Living in hope that the men would escape and find their way back to San Francisco.

In the evening, Moreno had gone to bed early as he was exhausted and Espinoza retired to look after him. The women sat around the kitchen table, Grace staring at her plate, the remains of dinner still there. Dear Ling Mei had made dinner. She was proving to be a treasured member of their household, quietly noticing what was needed and doing things, not waiting to be asked.

Grace said Ling Mei should leave the dishes and come and join them. Cora was there and made hot chocolate for them. Lillian stirred a spoon in her cup, round and round.

Cora tried to leaven the mood. "This is the best chocolate you'll ever taste. It goes all the way from Mexico to France, and then I get it shipped from Paris all the way back here."

Grace was grateful for Cora's efforts and tried to smile, but how could she enjoy her chocolate, when James might be starving?

"We have to go and get them," she said, quietly.

"I know," said Lillian, looking at her steadily, already guessing what was on her mind.

There was a silence.

"How could you get them? When the authorities refuse to?" asked Cora.

Lillian stopped stirring. "There are things you don't know about Grace. She might look like a pretty little thing. But she's been brought up with guns from when she was a baby. Her father and grandfather were gunsmiths. She's a better shot than any man you know."

Cora's eyebrows raised.

"I'm prepared to do it," said Grace, staring at her drink. "I've killed before. Didn't want to, but I felt I had no choice. But this time." Her hand gripped her cup tighter. "These are vermin. These are men who don't deserve to live."

She took a sip of her chocolate. It was good and sweet. "So what I'm thinking is this. I dress as a man again. I travel up to the Stanislaus. Espinoza can draw me a map. And I pick them off, one by one. The gang that's got our men. Take them by surprise."

Lillian looked at Grace and knew her old friend was being perfectly serious. There might be something going on between Grace and Randolph, and she knew they had parted on bad terms, but Grace would lay down her life for that man. As she would for George and her eldest son.

But getting themselves killed was not what their husbands would want. Lillian put a hand on Grace's arm. "Thing is, my dear friend, you'd then be guilty of murder."

"Don't see why. The Governor General made it clear there's no law here." Years before, she'd shot her landlord when he was threatening her, and knew how terrifying it was to be running from justice. But she'd do anything now, to save her husband.

"Humph. There's plenty of places in the Sierras that have taken to lynching without much of a trial. I don't want that to be you."

Cora topped up their hot chocolate. "*Moi?* I'd poison them all."

Grace looked up at her. "Poison?"

"Wouldn't leave any marks behind. Couldn't prove who had done it. Not that I know how to poison a man." She sighed. "More's the pity."

The women laughed at this, relieving the tension. They relaxed into a thoughtful silence.

"I know how to poison a man," said Ling Mei in a low voice. She pushed a strand of black hair over her shoulder.

Grace had nearly forgotten she was there. Grace turned to Ling Mei with interest.

"I know what needed. To make bad medicine."

"But we're not talking about one man," said Lillian nervously. "We think there could be a dozen guarding Dorado Mine."

"One man. Ten men. Doesn't matter. Same poison." Ling Mei gave a nonchalant shrug.

Grace leaned forward. "Could you show me? How to make it?"

"No, no, no," said Lillian, raising her hands. "We can't go round killing a whole bunch of men."

"But if no one knew it was Grace—" said Cora.

"No! We can't descend to this level," Lillian insisted.

Grace put her hands between her knees and groaned. She knew Lillian was right, but this was driving her crazy. "But we have to do *something*."

"What if..." Ling Mei ran a finger over the table. "What if

you *pretended* to poison them?" She looked at Grace. "If this medicine made them very ill. Made them think they were dying."

"And I released our husbands while the guards were unwell?"

"Now hold your horses," said Lillian. "Sounds risky to me. Still a lot of them."

"What I am thinking is this," Ling Mei said. "The men think they are going to die. Because you tell them that. But you have medicine that you tell them would reverse it."

"An... an antidote?" said Lillian. "Isn't that the word?"

"You have an... antidote... in a bottle. A liquid. Guards free your men, and you give the liquid. If they say no, you will smash it and they will all die."

The women all stared at her. She was such a little thing, but had come out with such a bold plan.

Cora spoke first. "*Mon Dieu*. It sounds fantastical. Like a story at the Paris Opera."

"But Ling Mei," Grace turned fully to her now, trying to keep her hopes in check. "You can do this? You know how to make an antidote?"

Ling Mei shook her head. "No. There is no medicine that can reverse it in that way."

"Ah... but, they have to *think* it will."

Ling Mei nodded. Grace saw the cleverness.

Lillian put her head in her hands. "But we agreed we weren't going to risk being hung. You can't go killing people."

Ling Mei wagged a finger as she spoke. "I give you powder that makes a man very sick, very quick. But not kill him. In a day, it passes through. Man better. But you gone. With your husbands and son and other man."

"And how would we give this powder to maybe a dozen men?" asked Grace.

"You put it in food," said Ling Mei. "Guards at the mine,

they must eat. You said you had kitchen at harbor. And Mr. Espinoza, he say you cook for them before."

Cora's eyes began to twinkle. "She's right. I've heard of men paying women to do all the cooking and laundry at these gold mines. A good way to earn a living."

Grace nodded thoughtfully. "I remember when I first came here. We went to Sutter's Fort. He said there was a woman there, right at the beginning, when his man first found gold. Sutter said a woman called Jenny was driving the Mormon workers mad because she didn't feed them on time. And she put the first ever piece of gold in her soap kettle and it came out clean."

"I'm sorry Grace," said Lillian, "I'm usually pretty sharp on things, but I'm still not clear how…"

Grace turned to her. "I go there. Just me—"

"There's no way on God's earth I'm letting you go there alone," said Lillian. "If you go, then I go with you."

"All the better. We say we can cook for the guards. For payment."

"You put bad medicine in food," said Ling Mei.

"But *not* poison," Grace said quickly, to reassure Lillian.

"Soon, all men eat food, feel very, very ill," said Ling Mei.

"And then you produce a bottle," Cora picked up a pickle jar theatrically. "And say, 'release our husbands—or you die!'"

"Or perhaps less dramatic," said Grace, suppressing a smile. "But, yes, something like that."

Lillian pushed both her hands across her face. "It could work."

"It really could!" said Grace.

They all took a moment to think about it.

Lillian drained the last of her hot chocolate. "Look, I suggest we sleep on this. We meet after breakfast to see if it still feels like a good idea, before we tell the Chileans. Or if it's the craziest pile of hokum four desperate women ever came up with."

THIRTY-FOUR

As soon as they bid farewell to last night's guests, Grace locked the front door and Lillian asked the girls to start cleaning the rooms because she and Aunt Grace had something important to discuss.

Grace put the coffee pot on the stove, and boiled water for Ling Mei. She had learned how to make tea over recent weeks. The three women sat at the table.

"Well?" asked Grace.

"Having slept on it, it sounds like a crazy plan, just like I said. There are so many things that could go wrong," Lillian said.

Grace's shoulders dropped. She had hoped for more.

"But," continued Lillian, "I can't think of anything better. Our men are sitting there—we've gotta do *something* to bring them back."

"And no one else is going to help, so it's down to us." Grace turned to Ling Mei. "Did you have any thoughts overnight?"

Ling Mei put one hand neatly over the other on the table. "Getting so much medicine not easy. But I do it."

"If it's difficult for you..." Grace extended her hand to her.

She had come to value Ling Mei's company. She was a calm, quiet contrast to Lillian's sass and Cora's flamboyance. She didn't want to force her back into the arms of whatever she had left behind at the lagoon.

"You be kind to me, Mrs. Randolph, when everyone else be cruel. My turn to help you now."

Lillian put more water in her coffee. "So, what's the plan? You and me travel up there with the Chileans? Maybe pretend to be husbands and wives?"

The idea of having Espinoza and Moreno with them was attractive. They knew the exact path and the four might be safer. However, Grace had reservations. "It seems to me this plan works by stealth. The miners won't expect anything from women. If we have men with us, it will put them on their guard."

"And they would likely be taken by the gang anyway. Which makes everything worse."

"They will want to come, though, when we tell them the plan," said Grace. "To be honest, I'm not sure Moreno would make it. He was strong like an ox when I first met him. Now a new kitten could knock him over."

"That dysentery took him real bad," said Lillian, shaking her head.

"And one of the worst things is having to leave your girls alone. They'll be safe if Espinoza and Moreno are living here."

"That was the thing playing on my mind too." Lillian tapped her fingernails on the table as she thought. "We should close down the hotel. While we're gone."

Ling Mei sat forward and frowned. "Close down?"

Lillian nodded.

"No. No do that. I run hotel for you. With help from daughters. You say the new men stay here? Then, they help also."

Before this could be agreed, there was a rap at the back door.

"It's open," Grace called.

Cora stepped inside, followed by Marguerite, the sisters filling the room with the rustle of silk and the smell of gardenias.

"Coffee?" Lillian asked.

"*Mais, non.* We have just had one."

They took seats at the table, Cora settling next to Grace.

"*D'accord*, what have you decided?" asked Cora, studying Grace and then Lillian.

"We're going," said Grace. "Just as soon as Ling Mei can prepare us the medicine." She looked at Ling Mei for approval and saw a tiny movement of her head in agreement.

"*Bon*," said Cora. "I hoped you would have the courage."

"And Lillian and I have decided it will be better alone, without the Chileans..."

Marguerite clapped her hands. "*Voir*, Cora? I said they would agree with us. Better not to bring more men—"

"We were going to persuade you of this," said Cora. She peeled back her black silk gloves and put them on the table. "Marguerite and I, we have talked. And we have decided. I am coming with you."

Grace sat up sharply. "You?"

"*Mais, oui.*"

Lillian's mouth fell open. "Why? It'll be dangerous. Why would you want to come?"

Marguerite cleared her throat. "You two women. You are good at many things. My sister and I, we are good at other things. We are good at understanding men."

"We talk to our customers," Cora picked up. The sisters spoke as if finishing each other's thoughts. "In the saloon. Word travels quick about what is happening in the goldfields. With so many men arriving—"

"Many overland—"

"Things, they are different."

Marguerite lowered her voice. "We have found a man who worked with the Dorado Mining Company."

Cora tutted. "He was not respectful of women."

Grace put up her hand. "We know what to expect—"

"There is a leader," Cora continued regardless. "Name of Septimus Becksommer—"

"My sister Cora. Nobody is better at manipulating men, when needed."

Cora winked at Marguerite. "Making sure men listen to me."

"So." Marguerite shuffled closer to Ling Mei. "You will offer food. Something men will no doubt welcome in their camp."

"I will offer something else men want. But only to the leader. This Becksommer. To distract him." The dimples that appeared in Cora's cheeks did not seem appropriate to the seriousness of the discussion.

"You can't do that!" said Grace.

Cora sat straighter and patted a golden curl into place. "Why not? It's been my business on occasion. At times of need."

"But we can't let you use... your business... to help us," said Lillian.

"It wouldn't be right—" agreed Grace.

Cora turned to Marguerite. "I knew they would not understand. Maybe they are ashamed of us—"

"Don't want to be seen with you, Sister—"

"No! It's not that," said Grace. Truth was, there was a time when Grace felt a little uncomfortable in the French women's company in public. The way they walked drew attention, heads up and with a sashay of the hips suggesting more. Were men sizing her up in the same way she saw their eyes drinking in the sisters?

But now, Grace knew and liked Cora and Marguerite. She valued their company, the way they could find humor in any situation. She admired how they had found themselves with little, and built a thriving business. She looked forward to the evenings they sat together, watching the sun setting behind the hills, Cora telling stories of exotic places.

Cora had strengths that would help bring back the men. She was quick-witted, perceptive in a way that Lillian and Grace lacked.

But Grace knew what Cora was offering, and it was not something she could ask of a friend.

"I'm not in the least ashamed to be seen with you," said Grace. "But this rescue attempt—it is a long way to travel. Once we are in the Sierras, we will be sleeping on the ground, in tents."

"There will be nowhere to wash," added Lillian.

"There will be animals. And biting insects. And probably places where we have to get off the horses and walk."

Marguerite waved a dismissive hand in the air. "Pfft. We were two months on a boat across the Atlantic. Storms. Days of being unable to keep a meal down."

"And then crossing Panama. You remember that donkey, Marguerite?" Cora said, laughing.

"Refused to move. Probably objecting to the smell. And that time the boat capsized?"

"And we discovered the river was only waist-deep anyway."

"But *full* of snakes, and leeches, and—"

Cora shuddered.

"You see," said Marguerite, raising her chin, "we are not the pampered ladies you think."

Grace smiled at the image of these beautiful women in a Panama swamp. "But still..."

"Ling Mei's plan is very clever." Cora looked at her admiringly. "It is a confidence trick. A magic trick. The men believe something, but we know it isn't true. The success of all magic tricks relies on distraction."

"Look over here"—Marguerite shook a lace handkerchief in the air—"while the other hand is doing the deceiving."

"*I* will be the distraction—" Cora explained.

"Men's eyes will be on her—"

"While you prepare the poison—"

"Now now, Cora. *Medicine*—" Marguerite playfully admonished.

"Medicine—unseen."

Ling Mei had been concentrating hard to follow the sisters' fast speech and Parisienne accents as they finished each other's sentences. She nodded enthusiastically. "Is good plan. Will help. Yes. Cora go with you."

"Thank you, Miss Mei," said Cora, tilting her head to in acknowledgement. "I always said you were a clever woman."

Cora turned to face Grace and took both her hands. Grace felt the intensity of those green eyes once more. "*Regarde*. You saved our lives. You came into our building during the fire. You found the key and released us. My sister and I—we are alive, because you were brave. So there is *nothing* you can do to dissuade me from joining you and Lillian in bringing back your men. Even if I have to pay for a donkey and follow you."

Grace laughed at the picture. She looked over at Lillian, who raised her brows and shrugged.

Grace shook Cora's hands. "Looks like there will be three of us then."

"*Formidable!*" Cora kissed her on each cheek. She turned to Ling Mei. "How soon can you produce this poison—"

"Medicine—" corrected Grace.

Ling Mei stood up. "If you do not mind me leaving laundry this morning, I go now." She made a little bow and hurried out through the back door.

For the first time since the Chileans arrived, Grace felt something like hope.

THIRTY-FIVE

It took Ling Mei two days to gather enough of the drug. She brought it back to Hotel Independence, little by little, pouring the powder into a pot. Grace lifted the lid: it was dark brown with a rich, almost beefy smell. She ran a finger through it.

"Care!" cried Ling Mei. "Wash hand now."

Grace didn't know where the drug was coming from but feared Ling Mei was returning to the Chinese community that had mysteriously rejected her.

"The drug," she asked. "What is it made from?"

"Different plants. You call one poke root. And a mushroom."

"Which grows here?"

She shrugged. "Maybe."

Grace dried her hands on a cloth. "Where are you getting it?"

"Chinese medicine man. He sells it as a purgative."

"Is he suspicious you are buying so much?"

"I go to more than one man. And I pay gold. So no questions."

This didn't lessen Grace's concerns. She returned the sealed pot to a high shelf. "Where is the gold coming from?"

"Some I earn myself. Laundry."

"I will of course cover the cost."

"No need. Most Madame Marguerite give me."

"Oh," said Grace. Cora and Marguerite were women of the world: they would know it was easier to procure this sort of medicine with gold.

The most difficult hurdle was persuading Espinoza and Moreno to stay in San Francisco.

The men stood at the door between the kitchen and the dining room, their heads bowed. They thought it dishonorable to remain and let the women ride into danger. This was a heavy weight on top of their guilt about being away at the time of the gang's attack.

"Don't see why," Lillian replied, putting a palm to Moreno's sunken cheek. "You'd now be at that godforsaken mine as well. And we'd be none the wiser. We'd never have heard about our husbands. Looks to me like Providence took you away to mend that equipment."

Grace insisted their plan could not work if men were there. It relied on seeming harmless: almost a gift, like the Trojan horse.

Lillian pleaded with them to stay so she would have peace of mind that her three girls would be safe and well looked after, no matter what.

"And there'll be plenty of work for you, if you're going to keep the saloon and the hotel running, without Cora, Grace and me."

Cora interrupted the debate as she burst in through the back door, triumphantly holding a delicate glass bottle. "This will be perfect for the antidote." It was about the size of her hand, with floral etchings and a cork stopper. "It was for oil. For bathing."

She took the stopper off, and a smell of lilies floated out.

"What should we put in it?" Grace asked.

Ling Mei took it away and returned a few minutes later. It was filled with a vivid turquoise liquid. "Water, sugar and lye. It will fade, but you shake it and it becomes blue again."

Cora picked it up admiringly. "*Formidable*. This is what a magician would produce."

On the morning of the third day, the women were ready. They took one mule, which carried their tent, and some large pots and pans. If they were posing as cooks, they needed to look the part.

Ling Mei explained how to use the medicine one last time, how much food was needed to disguise it, how long before it would take effect. Grace repeated everything back to her.

She gave her a warm hug, appreciating how carefully Ling Mei had thought through the plan. Ling Mei was stiff at first and then softened to hug her back.

"Ling, it was a truly providential day when we met at the lagoon," said Grace.

Ling Mei whispered to her. "My name is Mei, like your name is Grace."

Grace held her at arm's length. "Oh, you mean... Ling is your family name?"

Ling Mei nodded. "Yes. The other way round."

Grace thought for a moment about how her husband would have taken the time to find this out, but she hoped it showed a bond of trust, that Mei had now put things right.

Lillian said goodbye to the girls and promised to be home in a matter of weeks, bringing their father and brother with her. She had not wanted to be waved off at the harbor; it would be too painful.

They mounted their horses and rode to the ferry, Cora riding an elegant sidesaddle. Each street they passed, Grace told herself that next time she was here, she would be riding alongside her husband. It didn't do anything to soothe the anxiety growing inside her every time she thought about the enormity of the task ahead of them.

Over the next few days, Grace appreciated the unexpected benefits of traveling with Cora. Men treated her as an exotic flower, Lillian and Grace regarded as her servants. It was a convenient fiction to uphold. They were the first ones to board the steam ferry traveling northeast across the bay, the first to disembark at Sacramento City. Men hurried to find berths to take them onwards down San Joaquin River. They were given the best room at any hotel or guesthouse—although the three women insisted on sharing each night. Grace looked at her companions as they slept and wondered that they could rest so deeply when sleep brought her visions of the awfulness of Dorado mine.

Espinoza had written detailed instructions. They spent a night at Weberville as he had recommended—after some confusion as the settlement had already been renamed, and was now called Stockton. Grace was intrigued to seek out Charles Weber. They found him overseeing the unloading of a sea-going sailing boat at the river.

Weber was something of a legend in the area, having been part of the first group of Americans to arrive in California, nearly a decade before, crossing the deserts and mountains with no knowledge of what they would find. He owned land nearby, a saloon in town, and had an interest in many of the local businesses. He was a cross between a mayor and a sheriff, although officially neither.

Lillian wanted to move on, skeptical that Weber would be of value as he was the man who had been of so little help to the Chileans just weeks before. However, Cora was expert at drawing out information. She kept their intentions concealed, of course, but established that the Dorado Mine was increasingly productive, although there were only around ten guards. *More like slave overseers,* Grace thought bitterly.

Once they left Stockton, Grace decided to change into her male attire. It made riding much easier and meant she could keep her firearms close at hand. Her father's pistol was on her right hip, and on her left, a Colt revolver she had bought in San Francisco from a soldier who had fought in the Mexican war. Dressed in a man's jacket and with a rifle slung across her back, she began to feel more confident that she could handle whatever lay ahead.

Lillian had a shotgun in a holder by her saddle. Three years before, on the overland journey to Oregon, Grace had shown Lillian how to load a shotgun, but they hoped this skill wouldn't be needed this time.

As they left the flat lands of the San Joaquin, they reached Knights Ferry on the lower part of the Stanislaus, as the terrain became more undulating. Hardly hills as yet, and the mountains still far away. Dr. Knight proudly told them that, despite having trained as a medic in Baltimore, he'd seen money was to be made in ferrying gold miners across the river, and how well he'd chosen this spot. He was perturbed to find two women and a youth using his crossing. Grace was pleased to be taken as a male, but clenched her jaw so she didn't react to the dangers Dr. Knight warned of ahead: not just the natural threats of rapids and grizzly bears. He told of men who were not to be trusted.

Once they were traveling up the Stanislaus, they slept in the tent. After Dr. Knight's words, Grace wondered if they should take turns to keep watch, but what was the point? Despite Lillian's shotgun, truth was it was only Grace who could respond properly if the notorious gang came across them. That would be one against many. Instead, they put the tent deep in the woods, covered with branches, hoping that would keep them out of sight. Grace began to realize there were many different dangers on this journey.

On the first night, Grace was woken by noises. Something had set their horses stamping. Her heart pounding, she slipped out of their tent, gun at the ready. It was a raccoon, snuffing its way through the dark. Although this one was harmless, there was no choice but to light a small fire at night to keep animals at bay.

The path grew steeper and they covered less ground each day. After a week, they reached where the Stanislaus divided. Grace thought about James and how he had chosen the South Fork when he'd arrived at this same place in February. She wished she could have taken that southern river as well, explored the mine workings Moreno had proudly described. But their destiny lay on the Middle Fork.

THIRTY-SIX

The women's jovial banter subsided as they knew they were nearing their destination. From here, they had to find their own path and Grace was fearful of taking a wrong turn. Espinoza and Moreno had not traveled this way, so they did not have a map.

It was not always possible to follow the river because the rocky earth fell right to the water's edge, or the trees were overgrown in a thicket they could not break through. Worn out and overheated, they would double back and find another way round, going on higher land.

One day they came to a clearing in the trees. It was a beautiful spot: a creek ran down a gully to their right, the main river was some distance to their left. Maybe they could make camp here for the night.

Grace pulled up her horse and put up her arm to alert Lillian and Cora. There were a couple of huts ahead, made of slats of wood, balanced together in a cone. An old woman walked slowly between the huts, her back stooped. Another woman sat to their right, a scrawny dog lying at her feet, panting in the heat. The area looked like a twister had passed through.

Cedar logs, large sections of tree bark, willow branches—they all lay scattered across the ground.

Grace wiped sweat from her brow and glanced round, uncertain what to do. It looked like their path continued the other side of the clearing. They had no alternative but to go through.

"Let's take it slow and steady," Grace said. "It's only these two old women, so far."

The place was eerily quiet, making the hair on Grace's neck stand up, the only sound their horses' hooves on the hard earth and a vulture rasping high in the sky. Not even the dog bothered to bark.

Grace saw some clothing as they passed. No, not clothing. That was a body, face down. A man's body. Grace shuddered and drew on the reins to pause her horse. Then she saw another. And another was lying face up. It was a woman. What hell had they stumbled into? They were surrounded by bodies.

"Lillian," Grace hissed.

"I see them."

Grace saw two smaller bodies, near the tree line at the edge of the clearing. They could only be children. Grace's stomach roiled.

She turned in her saddle to look at her friend and saw a face as shocked as she felt. "Do we stop?"

"I don't know," said Lillian quietly. "What would we be able to do?"

"I..." She shook her head in desperation. "Bury them?"

Cora was at the back, the mule fixed on a rope. "We ride on. There is nothing we can do."

"But maybe—"

"Three women trying to bury so many?"

Grace knew Cora was right. She felt sick deep in her belly.

"If those women had wanted them buried," said Lillian, "they would have done it by now."

Grace looked back. The older woman had disappeared, the other stroked the dog's ears but was staring straight ahead as if blind.

"Who could have done this?" whispered Grace.

"I don't know," said Cora. "But we should leave as quickly as we can."

They urged their horses to trot on, keen to be free of this mournful place.

As they continued up the river, the trees grew taller but with more space between. There were black oaks between the Douglas firs. The ground was mostly rocky. Close to the river, Grace's eye was caught by a kingfisher.

They passed small gold workings, groups of men working on the river, picking at the rock. Grace was again heartily grateful Cora was with them. She bantered with the men with ease, finding out how far it was to the Dorado Mining Company, batting back their entreaties to stay with them with jokes. She had a knowing confidence, when Grace would have been tongue-tied and embarrassed by the men's suggestions.

She noticed how heavily armed these miners were. There was always one man on guard with a shotgun. Some men frowned and looked at them darkly when Cora asked about Dorado. This boded as ill as Grace feared. A miner told them it was around three miles more, but advised them to go no further. "If we don't bother them, they don't bother us," he said. "But it's not a bear I'd go poking."

Just three more miles. Despite Grace's burning desire to see James and bring him to safety, they agreed it was better to camp at some distance tonight.

"No fires," Grace said.

Grace wanted to scout on ahead on foot and Lillian and Cora reluctantly agreed. They needed a clear idea of what to expect the next day, she said, but deep down she hoped she might simply see James, know he was alive. She left Lillian and Cora to set up camp for the night, concealing the tent and securing the animals.

Grace scrambled over rocks and deer paths in the direction the miner had shown them. She prayed her tan clothing would let her melt into the earth, if anyone was to look up. She tacked uphill and along a ridge. The going was slow and the undergrowth dense, but her heart was beating more from the anxiety of what she might soon find.

She heard the mine before she saw it, and her breathing quickened. Picks echoed off the valley walls, mixed with men's shouts and curses, and something mechanical, rumbling, metal on rock.

She crept her way to a promontory overlooking the gorge, then lay on her tummy to crawl the last few yards. She peered over the edge. She'd never seen anything like it, and her stomach tightened with fear of men who had been able to cut a slice through nature itself. The river had been dammed and parted in two. On the far side, it ran freely down the gorge. Nearer, it had been diverted into two races.

Men were everywhere, moving ponderously. They seemed dressed alike, in the same pale-gray clothing. As Grace looked more closely, she realized it was the dust from the workings making them all look the same. A few men were in relaxed positions among the workers, some sitting on rocks, others standing, each with a hat, and a rifle in their arms. These must be the guards. One seemed to be joking as he lit a pipe. She was startled by the crack of a whip and a shout, then turned her attention to a man walking toward the one with the pipe, the whip still curled in his hand. Though he was a guard, the man cowered slightly and gave the pipe to the other man.

Grace searched for James, for George and Simon. She looked desperately from man to man. Surely she would be able to identify her own husband? With her mouth growing dry, she searched for a man with broad shoulders, and a long confident stride. But the workers all had unkempt hair and beards, except for the few who showed bald pates. All were bent over, working at the rock face, or pushing the trucks.

She gritted her teeth and forced herself to remember the purpose of creeping to this vantage point. She counted perhaps thirty laboring men. Fewer than she had expected, as the Dorado Mine had grown to terrifying proportions in her imagination. There were fewer guards as well. She counted carefully. Seven, just seven. She frowned and wondered why the laborers had not risen up and overthrown their oppressors. Maybe there were more elsewhere, inside the cabin? Her holster dug into her hip as she lay on the ground and she remembered how firearms gave the guards unequal power. Her heart beat faster as she came face to face with the scale of the danger the women were walking into.

A door banged, making her jump, and a man appeared from the wooden cabin directly below. She noticed the guards straighten, even the one with the whip, a ripple running through them as the man approached. She couldn't see his face as he wore a rounded hat, but she knew the men feared him. Her hands gripped the stone more tightly; if she and her friends could overcome this man, the others would fall like dominoes.

She forced herself to wait patiently to see if any more men appeared. There was a jumble of tents further up the valley, close to the river. And, she saw with relief, a shelter for cooking. That was exactly what she and Lillian needed.

She had seen enough. Grace shuffled back, careful not to dislodge any rocks, and crept away. Her legs were shaking as she reached the deer path.

. . .

That evening, the women went over their plan once more. Lillian was bitterly disappointed that Grace had not spied George or Simon, but that spurred them on.

Grace tried to sleep, knowing she would need all her wits about her tomorrow, for their plan to work. But her heart was racing and it was impossible to calm herself enough to stay asleep for long. It was not the owls keeping her awake, nor the distant call of a coyote.

It was knowing James was close, and that his future depended on her courage. And a deep fear that she would fail him, and he would be lost forever.

THIRTY-SEVEN

The women found it hard to speak to each other when they rose the next morning. Grace folded away her pants and put on her plain beige dress. It was going to be a hot one; she wouldn't need a jacket. She tied a cream scarf around her hair and put on a wide-brimmed hat, wanting to look as homely as possible.

Cora's dress was high-necked and long-sleeved, like Grace's, but was made of dark red silk, with an obsidian brooch at her throat. She brushed her hair until it shone and pinned it high before dabbing a vial of lavender water on her pulse points. While Grace and Lillian wore practical boots beneath their skirts, Cora's patent leather ones had a heel.

They could not risk lighting a fire for coffee, so they drank from a fresh stream running nearby. Grace shared pieces of biscuit and dried jerky to give them sustenance, but no one ate much.

They loaded the mule and horses and weaved their way out of the trees, back to the main path up the valley. They mounted their horses and turned east, taking the last three miles at a steady pace. A tension at Grace's temples increased to an ache.

They passed a sign: "Dorado Mining Company," the words

carefully painted on some planks which had been nailed together. It suggested a mine of good standing, of respectability.

Grace could hear the cacophony of bangs and scrapings and yells before they reached the mine. The path turned to the right, and a guard leaped to his feet, having dozed off at the entrance. His eyes opened wide at the sight of Cora, riding at the front, her back straight, head erect.

"Well, lookie here," was as much as he could garble.

"I'm looking for Mr. Becksommer," she said, her French accent adding to her imperiousness.

"I can take you," the man said eagerly.

She inclined her head to accept his offer.

The guard stumbled ahead, sometimes turning back, a stupid grin on his face, to check the three women were following.

Grace's eyes flitted over the laborers, each of them busy with a spade or pick. Many had the dark hair and features of the Miwok. Maybe this explained the ruined village they had passed through.

The two men pushing the tub filled with rock: were they familiar? They looked like George and Simon. Or was that wishful thinking?

She tried not to draw attention by searching the men too urgently. She and Lillian needed to remain cool and detached. As they passed, more men stopped to stare at the triumvirate of women.

They steered their horses to the sandy area in front of the cabin. Now Grace was up close, she could see it was larger than she'd thought, and built to last, unlike so many structures on the Stanislaus. The porch was raised two steps and extended the width of the building. The door was in the center.

The guard hurried inside and she could hear his keen shouts, getting the attention of his boss. While they waited, Grace's eyes slid over to a tree where two dead men hung. Bile rose up in her throat and she put a hand to her mouth. One was a Native man, his head hanging forward, hands swollen in the heat. Grace thought she could see where the birds had pecked at remains. The other wore a long white shirt and leather belt she thought she recognized. Lopez. She couldn't be sure, and didn't want to look more closely. She fought back the feeling of nausea.

The door opened and a smartly dressed man strode onto the porch step, wearing the sort of hat Grace had only seen in towns: hard gray curved felt, with a small rim edged in black. He stood with his legs apart and thumbs in the lower pockets of his checkered vest, as his eyes ran over each of them. Another man stood at his shoulder, a pipe in his palm and a new-looking revolver tucked in his belt.

Eventually, the smart man spoke. "To what do I owe the pleasure?"

"Mr. Becksommer?" Cora asked, her voice clear.

"Indeed I am. Septimus Becksommer, at your service."

"I hear you are doing very well for yourself here," she said with a coquettish smile. "You cannot blame a woman for thinking there might be gold to share."

"From your accent, it sounds like you have traveled a very long way in search of gold. But, tell me, Madame, why would I want to share it?"

"If you invite me and my women in out of this heat, I will make a proposal."

He made a show of thinking about it. "Wouldn't do any harm." He looked over at the guards and laborers. "Schultz, get these damned men back to work. Behaving like they ain't never seen a woman before."

Schultz tapped the tobacco out of the bowl of his pipe and put it in his shirt pocket. He sauntered down the steps and passed them. Grace flinched at his yells and blaspheming. She dismounted and followed Cora and Lillian inside.

It took a while for Grace's eyes to adjust to the dim light inside the cabin. It was a good size with a well-made wooden floor, but with only two small windows either side of the door, too dirty to let much sunlight in. The walls were pine logs, but their smell was overpowered by the odor of sweat. She suspected too many men spent too much time in this space. There was one big table strewn with playing cards and empty bottles, a few mismatched chairs and a barrel or two repurposed as stools.

Becksommer pulled out a chair at the table for Cora. She sat with elegance, arranging her silk skirts. Clearly Grace and Lillian were not expected to sit: Becksommer assumed they were servants of some kind. This gave Grace a chance to study the room. She let out a long silent breath and lowered her hunched shoulders.

A kerosene lamp hung over the table. An iron pot-bellied stove stood near the far wall, its black chimney sticking straight up through a hole in the roof. Given the June heat, it was unlit. Two doors in the far end led to other rooms, one on the left, one on the right. She dearly wanted to know what was beyond those doors.

Becksommer sat at the table, opposite Cora. "And you are...?"

"Madame Coralie LaFonteyn."

"Pleased to make your acquaintance." His voice purred and his gaze traveled over her.

"Likewise."

"And your proposition?"

"As I said, I have heard of this mine. One of the most productive in the Sierras."

"Why, thank you." Becksommer gave a mock bow.

"It's making you rich. No one should be surprised if the delicate sex also wants to benefit from the seam of gold you have found here."

"The mother lode."

"*Bien sûr*. Even the name you have given it reminds you of women. We cannot dig for our gold as men do. But we can provide you with other things."

The man's eyes glinted. "Such as?"

"My women are excellent cooks. Experienced at providing food for a large number of men."

Becksommer chuckled. "I already have a man who cooks for us."

Grace's mouth was suddenly dry: that the whole plan could fail so easily. They might not even get the chance to cook, and then what would they do?

Cora slowly peeled off a riding glove. "Mr. Becksommer." There was a note of indulgence in her rich French voice. "I took you for a businessman. I am offering two women to cook breakfast, midday meal and dinner. But you prefer a man doing women's work? A man who could be digging for gold? Or at the very least, given what I've heard, making sure others dig quicker."

He put his head to one side and let his eyes slide over to Grace and Lillian. She dropped her chin but was in awe of Cora's easy confidence in the dangerous situation.

"You make a good point, Madame LaFonteyn. Maybe there are better uses for Simpson." He turned back to Cora. "And what of you? What are you offering?"

She took off her other glove. "Oh, Mr. Becksommer. I think you know the sort of companionship I could offer to a man such as yourself."

A lascivious smile came to his lips.

"So, as you and I are businesspeople," said Cora smoothly. "My maids would cook at a quarter ounce of gold per day. Each."

He narrowed his eyes. "Together."

She inclined her head. "Very well. Together. But on condition you provide them suitable accommodation. And assure me of the safety of their persons."

"This is a camp full of restless men. I'm not sure I can—"

"Then maybe I'll withdraw my offer."

Grace shuffled uncomfortably, uncertain why Cora was discussing accommodation, given they hoped to execute the plan and be away from this hellhole as quickly as possible.

"—But I will impress a sense of honor on my men."

"And for myself, I will receive an ounce of gold a day."

Becksommer leaned forward and opened his mouth.

"Don't try to haggle, Mr. Becksommer," Cora interrupted. "I know my value." She put her elbow on the table and placed her chin upon her hand. "You will find me worth it."

"I dare say. But what I was going to say is this: why should I pay you anything? You're here now. I can stop you riding back down the river."

Grace had feared this response and was prepared to shoot her way out if need be. But Cora was untroubled. She tutted. "Mr. Becksommer. Do you think a businesswoman like myself would not have made enquiries?" She sat back. "I know what sort of place you run here. Why it is so productive. I know the authorities show you—how do you Americans call it?—a blind eye. Maybe you give generous gifts in the right places. I know that is what I would do."

She leaned forward again and lowered her voice. "But, Mr. Becksommer, change is coming. You know this. One day soon, Washington will understand the importance of California to the United States. One day they will assert their authority. And while they may accept some of your... practices... to date, they will not ignore you if word got out that you were mistreating women. The good people of Washington, they are very conservative in that way. Instead, why don't you let me help you? I am on intimate terms with the *alcalde* in San Francisco. There are others who could smooth the way for an even larger mine."

Becksommer looked at Cora intently and grinned. "You know, you and I are going to get on very well. I like a woman who is clever, as well as beautiful. A woman of the world."

"We have a deal?"

Becksommer put out a hand, which Cora took, holding it longer than necessary.

"Indeed we do," said Becksommer, a huskiness in his voice.

Cora stood. "In that case, show my women your canteen. No time like the present: they will cook the midday meal."

THIRTY-EIGHT

Grace and Lillian followed the former cook to the canteen under a canvas awning strung between two willows. He swore and ranted over having to make way for women. Grace thought that he guessed a harder time at the mine awaited him.

They unloaded cooking utensils from the mule. Grace carefully took the packages wrapped in burlap that she would say were spit-roasting rods if anyone asked, but were actually the rifles and pistols. She hid them beside sacks of corn and beans on the ground.

Grace poked around the food stores kept by the cook, thinking what they could make to pour Mei's powder into.

"I'm sure I saw George and Simon," Lillian whispered, her eyes shining bright.

"Pushing the tub?" Grace said, under her breath.

"Yes."

Grace squeezed her arm. "We'll get them out. We can do this."

She hadn't seen James yet, but didn't want to share her anxiety with Lillian. Dear God, had they come too late?

"What if they recognize us?" hissed Lillian. "What if they realize we're up to something. And try to stop us?"

A shiver went down Grace's back. Now they were here, there were a hundred things that could go wrong with their plan. Everything had seemed so straightforward when sitting in their kitchen back home. "We have to pray things turn out right. And get this food inside the Dorado guards as fast as we can."

Lillian stoked the iron stoves to get more heat and put on three large pans. Grace untied the muslin meat pantry hanging in a tree and cut chunks of venison. She threw them in the pan, where they sizzled as the marbled fat melted and sealed the meat.

Lillian found a plentiful supply of pinto beans that had already been soaked, and boiled them. There was a jar of blood which would make a tasty gravy.

Grace had brought herbs wrapped in cotton. Their plan depended on this meal being delicious enough to tempt every man. She scattered bay leaves into each of the three pans. The cook had some vinegar, which she sprinkled in, followed by honey she had brought. This mix of sweet and sharp should make an ordinary dish more special.

It was nearly noon and the time had come. Taking a breath to calm her nerves, Grace helped Lillian pour the food into two huge pots standing on the canteen table. Mei had said that boiling stopped the drug's efficacy. Grace picked up the bag which contained Mei's powder, catching Lillian's eye. She nodded her approval. This was the moment they could not come back from. Grace carefully split the powder between the two pots and gave each a good stir until it was absorbed. The powder made the dish smell distinctive, meatier. She was careful not to inadvertently test it.

They carried the two pots to the cabin, where Cora was holding forth. As planned, she had persuaded Becksommer that every one of his men should try the food, to prove what a good deal he had made in engaging her maids. From the glassy sheen on Becksommer's eyes, Grace suspected Cora had already plied him with plenty of drink.

He was protesting that they could not all eat together. Who would guard the miners?

Grace glanced at Cora. She knew how important it was that every last guard became ill.

"Half the men will eat with you," she said with an airy wave of the hand. "And then the second half will switch when they are finished."

Grace and Lillian put the pots on the table and cleared away the detritus while the first men were fetched by Schultz. Grace served Becksommer first—a generous helping. She then served Schultz, and Lillian gave a bowl to the man who had been guarding the entrance, who was bouncing on his feet, delighted to be back in the company of women. Finally, the erstwhile cook took his bowl, a scowl on this face.

"Better than your food, Simpson," said Becksommer, waving his spoon around.

The cook grunted but ate his portion anyway.

Having eaten the venison stew, these three picked up their guns and took the places of the remaining guards.

"So few men to control such a large mine. Are you not worried about a revolution, my dear?" asked Cora, sitting on a chair beside Becksommer, a hand on his arm. "Where I come from, they happen every few years."

Even though tipsy, he fastidiously dabbed his mouth with a kerchief. "You see those two men hanging from the tree out there? That's how I deal with anyone who steps out of line. Doesn't take long for the rest to know what's good for them."

Grace kept her head down to make sure her face didn't betray her disgust.

The second group of guards were served, one of them not

much more than a boy. There was a little left in the pot. Lillian scraped more into Becksommer's bowl.

"Are you not eating any?" he asked Cora.

She ran her hands down her bodice with a wink. "I am careful what I eat. I have to protect my... assets."

Lillian and Grace took the empty pots back to the canteen area, relieved to be out of the crowded cabin.

A half-starving laborer looked on hungrily, his eyes wide. A guard kicked him away. "This isn't for the likes of you."

No, thought Grace. *It isn't.*

They thoroughly cleaned their pots and utensils, tidying the cooking area. They packed things away, ready to leave quickly when the time came.

Now, they waited.

Mei said the powder would take an hour to take effect. Maybe more. Grace and Lillian sat close together, their heads bowed as if in prayer, not wanting to risk being seen and recognized by their husbands, even though Grace was yearning to search the camp to find James.

With every passing minute, she became more anxious. She sprang to her feet, unable to sit still any longer. What if the powder didn't work? What if Mei had got it wrong? Or *they* had got it wrong? Not given enough food. Or cooked it too long, or too hot.

She looked to where her guns lay. If everything failed, she would take Becksommer hostage, hold him at gunpoint. Force him to release James, George, and Simon. She would not let him go until the men had ridden out of this gorge with Lillian and Cora.

Maybe she wouldn't let Becksommer go at all. A bullet to the head. The man deserved it. And as Grace wouldn't be able to get out alive, she might as well take this brute with her to the gates of hell.

Lillian took her hand and pulled her back to her stool.

Grace's foot tapped the ground as her mind ran wild through every possibility. She twisted her wedding band on her finger, over and over. Lillian tried to give her an encouraging smile but looked as anxious as she felt. Cora remained in the cabin with Becksommer. The rest of the gang were each back at their posts. Nothing out of the ordinary had happened. They had failed, Grace was sure of it.

What must have been an hour later, Grace noticed a guard call to one of the others. He made his way over, walking slowly, wiping sweat from his brow. The two men had an argument of some kind, the second guard shooing him away, back to his position. When the first man turned, Grace could see his face was red and blotchy. Was this the start? Had the powder taken effect?

The man sat on a rock, close to Grace. She'd heard someone call him Tate. He let his gun drop on the ground and bent double with a groan. Sweat seeped through the back of his shirt. He called to the other guard again. This time, the second guard came over, anxiously trying to keep the laborers in sight.

"Thatch, I'm sick," the first man said. "I... I can't..."

"What's wrong with you?"

"I don't know... it's come on sudden..."

Thatch looked uncertain. "You know what the boss will do if you're not guarding."

"But I can't." Tate vomited onto the ground.

Thatch twisted his face in disgust. He disappeared out of Grace's sight. She heard him shout at a miner at the nearby sluice.

"You. Here, now."

A man came into view, young and thin, a hint of red hair among the dirty gray made by the stone dust.

It was Simon.

His eyes locked on Grace's and then he looked to her side

and saw Lillian; she watched him trying to make sense of what he was seeing.

If he said anything, the game was up. The guard would know these women had not arrived by chance. Maybe they would search them, find the guns...

The guard's back was turned and Grace put a finger to her mouth, trying to communicate with her eyes, desperately hoping Simon would understand that he had to stay quiet.

"Help Tate to his tent," Thatch ordered.

Grace glanced at Lillian and could see she was barely containing her need to rush to her son. Grace had to do something.

"Say, Thatch, isn't it?"

The man looked surprised she had addressed him.

"How about my friend helps? Take the man to the tent, I mean. She can keep an eye on your worker."

Thatch seemed eager to get back to his post, particularly as they were a man down. He waved angrily to Lillian to indicate she should help.

Lillian darted forward, helping the sick guard to his feet. Simon took the other arm over his shoulder and they dragged Tate away. Thatch picked up the spare rifle and stormed off.

Grace lifted her eyes to the sky. Thank God. Lillian would be able to whisper why they were here, and hopefully make Simon promise to sit tight.

The door to the cabin opened and Cora stepped outside briefly, looking over to the canteen. She gave a movement to wave her to the cabin before disappearing back inside.

Grace looked round anxiously. Lillian should have been back by now. The plan needed both of them.

She puffed out a loud breath as Lillian hurried back.

"It's happening," said Grace.

Lillian nodded, her face grave.

"Everything alright with Simon?"

"He's alive and so's his father. And will wait out our plan, even though I didn't have the chance to explain it."

"And James?"

Lillian bit her lip. "He didn't say anything. But I didn't have time to ask, so that doesn't mean nothing." She picked up a knife and the long length of cord they had brought with them.

Grace uncovered the firearms and tied two belts around her waist, a pistol on each hip. She unwrapped the precious rifle her father had made, and checked once more that it was properly loaded.

Lillian unwrapped the glass vial and gave it a shake: the turquoise liquid still looked startlingly bright.

This was the moment Grace had waited for. They exchanged a glance and walked smartly to the cabin, up the porch step and opened the door.

THIRTY-NINE

The smell was putrid and Grace saw vomit on the floor. Becksommer was on a chair, writhing in pain. His jacket had been shed and his smart vest had sweat marks round the armpits.

Cora feigned concern, trying to loosen his necktie. "Does that make it better?"

Becksommer pushed her away. "You're making it worse, woman."

His right-hand man was there, but sitting on the floor, his head between his knees, and his pipe and tobacco beside him.

"Schulz," Mr. Becksommer shouted. "Get me something. Anything."

"I... I can't," Schulz said.

"What d'you mean? I'm ordering you..."

The other man simply shook his head helplessly.

"Septimus, *chéri*. I'll go fetch someone. Bring one of your men."

This time, Becksommer waved a hand in agreement, but couldn't speak.

Cora went to the door and smoothly passed Becksommer's

revolver to Grace. "He was too ill to notice," she whispered and slipped out.

Neither Becksommer nor Schultz seemed to have noticed that Grace and Lillian had quietly entered the cabin. Nor that Grace was armed. They waited in the shadows of the room by the door, Grace breathing through her nose to keep herself calm. Now the success of the plan would rest on whether she could keep the men under control.

Cora returned in minutes with two more guards. They both looked unwell, but had not yet begun to feel the gut pain. Grace recognized Thatch; the other was the youth. *So, that's four men in here*, she thought, *one lying ill in his tent, and one back at the entrance to the mine. Six men.* That meant there was just Simpson the cook unaccounted for, somewhere. Was that right? She couldn't shake off the feeling she was missing something.

Thatch went to his boss. "You too? I'm scared, Boss. I think it could be cholera. That comes on fast like this."

Becksommer grabbed the man's lapels, his eyes wide. "Cholera?"

For the first time, Lillian spoke. "It's not cholera."

The men turned to stare at her.

"But it's going to kill you, just the same."

In the half-light, they finally noticed Grace had a pistol in her hand and that it was raised in their direction.

"You," Grace said to Thatch. "Take your gun out and put it on the floor."

Thatch hesitated.

"Don't go making me madder than I already am."

He held up one hand, and with the other did as Grace told him.

"Go sit on that barrel." She nodded to one at the far end of the room. "And you," lifting her chin to the teen. "Same thing. Gun, and then over that side, there. Where I can see you."

Once the youth had done so, Grace nodded in Schultz's direction. "Cora?"

Cora gingerly retrieved the final revolver, avoiding the rank substances on the floor.

Good. None of them armed.

Grace lowered her shoulders and cricked her neck where she'd been holding it stiff.

Cora now took her place next to Grace by the door, three women looking back at the four men. Grace was on full alert in case the cook suddenly appeared, but they needed to move on smartly to the next step in their plan.

Lillian tapped the glass bottle with a fingernail to get their attention and handed it to Cora. "Now you'd better listen up to what I'm saying," said Lillian, loud enough that they could all hear. "You ever heard tales of the Black Widow? The woman who poisoned her husband? Well, think of us as a variation on that tune. But we want our husbands back." She put her hands on her hips. "Each of you has eaten enough poison to kill you. Yes, that includes you, Thatch. You can feel it coming on, can't you? The sweating, the thumping head, the stomach cramps."

Grace admired Lillian's thinking. Thatch was the guard least affected by the purgative. Now his eyes were wide and his hand went to his stomach.

Suddenly, Schultz, the man on the floor, vomited between his legs. Looking up at his boss, there was blood on his chin. Becksommer stared at him in horror.

"That's going to be all of you soon. Coughing up blood," said Lillian. "Unless... see this?"

Cora held up the bottle of turquoise liquid. "This, *mon cher* Septimus, this can save you. All of you. A few small drops, and it will reverse the deadly poison. But look how fragile this bottle is." Cora pretended to fumble. "Oops! I nearly dropped it."

Lillian strode from one side of the room to the other, looking at each of the men. "We'll give you this cure, just as soon as you give us our men."

Becksommer gritted his teeth against the pain. "Which ones?"

"Mr. Hollingswood and my son, Simon."

"Yeah, I know them."

"And Mr. Randolph," said Grace.

Becksommer snorted. "Christ, the captain. I should have guessed."

Grace trained her gun on him.

"Should have known that troublemaker would have a bitch for a wife." He spat on the floor.

Grace kept her breathing steady, despite fearing the worst. "Where is he? If you've killed him..."

Becksommer shook his head from side to side. "Not dead yet. Though, the devil knows, I've been tempted."

Lillian stopped in front of the young guard. "How you feeling, boy?"

He stood wide-eyed and unblinking. "Not so good," he gasped and bit his lower lip to fight back tears.

"You know the men we're talking about?"

The youth nodded.

"You go find them. Tell them to pack their belongings. To get a horse each. And you bring them back here. And you don't speak to anyone else, you hear me? Or you and these men are all dead."

The boy looked at Becksommer, his eyes beginning to water.

Becksommer nodded. "Go, son. We need to play along with these witches a little longer."

"But the captain, what if he can't—"

"Use the Hollingswood men to help you."

Grace's mouth went dry. This sounded bad. Real bad.

The boy shuffled toward the women so he could reach the door.

Thatch seized the moment Grace couldn't see him and pulled a small pistol from inside his shirt. He pointed it straight at her, but she ducked as he pulled the trigger. She fired back at him, the sound of two bullets thundering round the hut. Thatch yelled in pain, as his gun skittered across the floor. Becksommer lunged for it, his arm outstretched, just as Grace secured it with her boot.

"I swear to God," spat Grace, "if you pick that up, the next bullet is going between your eyes."

Her pistol was pointed down at his face. Becksommer froze and the other men waited to see what he would do. In the pause, she could hear men's heavy breathing. Becksommer stared up at her and pure hatred flowed between them as their eyes met.

He moved back slowly and then doubled over in pain again, his hands around his gut. "Damnation! What have you women poisoned us with?"

"She shot my arm, boss," said Thatch with a whine. "She shot my arm."

The boy stood trembling at the door, uncertain what to do. Cora had backed against the wall, clutching the bottle.

Lillian took control once more. "Now, that was a darn stupid thing to do. My friend Cora nearly dropped the bottle. That goes, and... *pooft*"—she made an exploding gesture with her hand—"you're all dead by evening."

Grace heard footsteps on the porch and turned.

"Boss? I heard shots—" The door opened and Simpson stumbled in, holding a rifle but his hands shaking. "I'm sorry, boss. I'm feeling real sick—"

He stopped as soon as he was in the cabin and tried to understand what he saw.

Lillian closed the door behind him. Smoke from the fired pistols added to the gloom in the room.

"Five," said Grace, counting off the men. "The cook. That's just the guard at the gate we haven't seen."

He stood there, dumbfounded. Grace took his rifle, and his pistol from his holster, before he knew what was happening.

There was another long groan. This time it was Thatch, lying on his side, clutching his belly.

"Go sit," Lillian ordered Simpson. "And you, boy, you go fast as you can, before the bloody flux hits you too."

The boy stared at her.

"Scat." Lillian stamped her foot to jolt him into action.

As soon as the boy left, Lillian started tying up each of the men. She cut lengths with her knife, Grace keeping a close watch. Again, she had the feeling she was missing something in the confusion.

"Remember, gentlemen," said Cora in a mocking tone. "Any move from you and I will drop this bottle."

As the powder took hold, each of the men was getting sicker. Most were shivering, with sweat drenching their skin. Schultz was losing consciousness, the whites of his eyes showing as they rolled upwards. Grace wondered if Mei had given them real poison instead of their purgative drug.

Back in San Francisco, it had seemed important that they left this gorge without having killed anyone. Now, that seemed like a nicety, a piece of morality plucked from a distant place. Grace no longer cared whether these men lived or died. All she wanted was to find James and get him as far away from here as possible.

With Lillian's task of tying the men finished, she opened the door a crack to peep out and see what was happening. She took a sharp breath. "George and Simon. They're here. And they've got Randolph. But, Grace, he's—"

"Don't tell me," said Grace sharply. She needed to keep

every ounce of her attention on the four men tied up in the room. "You go out and tell them what's happening. And send the boy back in."

Lillian slipped out of the door.

And then it hit Grace.

The man with the whip.

A shudder ran down her back. She went to Becksommer and lifted his head with one hand. His eyes were bloodshot and a line of vomit ran from his lips.

"There's one more, isn't there? The man with the whip? Where is he?"

Becksommer laughed despite his pain. "Thought you were so clever, didn't you? I sent him out surveying, but he'll be back any minute."

Grace turned to Cora. "We need to leave, quick as we can. There's a guard somewhere we haven't drugged. And there's none of Mei's powder left."

"*Mais, non,*" Cora said. "We're not leaving without a final piece of business." She stepped into the center of the room with a swagger. "How much gold did you steal from my friends? You didn't think we'd let you keep that as well, did you?" She went to Becksommer, lifting the bottle high in her left hand and slipping a set of keys from his belt with the other.

The youth came back into the hut, beads of sweat on his face, his mouth hanging open.

"We need to tie the boy up and go," hissed Grace.

Cora pretended not to hear. "Perfect timing. Now, *mon petit*, take this key to open the room there. And *this* key, I believe, will open your gold box. I want three one-pound bags."

"Cora!" This wasn't in their plan.

Cora turned with a mock-innocent look on her face. "I'm not coming all this way without recovering what's yours, my dear."

The youth put his hand to his mouth to suppress the sickness, and took the keys.

"Fast," said Grace. "Make it fast, boy."

Becksommer managed a growl, showing that he knew what was going on.

"Now, now," said Cora. "We're being more than reasonable. We're not thieves. We are taking what my friends' husbands have mined. No more. No less."

Grace let out a breath as the boy returned with the canvas bags.

Cora took the three bags and held them up. "Do you think this will be sufficient?"

Grace nodded. "Looks about right to me." Anything to get them out quickly.

Lillian came back in, her eyes blazing with excitement. The light from the open door briefly made the glass bottle glint. "The men are all saddled up out there."

"Just the boy to tie up, then."

Lillian took a final piece of rope and tied the boy securely. She slipped her knife into a pocket in her skirt and gathered all the firearms. "I'll go get our horses."

She went back outside and Grace heard the guns clattering onto the porch where Lillian dropped them.

Cora set a stool in the middle of the room and placed the delicate bottle on it. "Now, gentlemen, while you are trying to free yourselves, take particular care not to knock over the stool." She smiled at each of them, but they could barely hear. "And when you are free, don't be greedy, make sure each man has a mouthful of this liquid. Otherwise, the blood will be on your hands, not ours."

Grace was breathing so fast, her chest hurt. They'd done it. They'd really done it.

Then she heard a shout and a gunshot.

She rushed to the window. He was there, the man with the whip tied to his belt. And he had a revolver pointed at Lillian.

FORTY

"Whatever's going on in there, you need to give yourself up. Then I can get the men back to work and let this woman go."

Grace looked at Cora with horror. Lillian's life was in danger. She noticed the rhythmical crashing and pounding of the mine had stopped.

"Is there another way out?" Grace begged Cora.

For once, Cora looked at a loss. "No, there's... Yes! There's a window in the room through there." She pointed.

Grace took a couple of paces. "You go out front, slow as you can, and keep him talking."

"Talking?"

"Anything. Just give me some time."

Before Cora could object, Grace had picked her way through the tied and slumped bodies to the door on the right, at the back of the cabin.

Inside was a room, a bed to the right and a small window. This must be where Becksommer slept. She moved the chair, gathered her skirts, and climbed out as quietly as she could, sweat sticking to the bodice of her dress.

She crept low around the rear of the cabin, hidden by rocks

and shrubs, praying she could not be seen, until she reached where her horse was tethered to a tree. She needed her father's rifle.

She could hear Cora speaking to the man, her soft French tones drifting in the hot summer air. *Keep going, Cora*, she thought. *A little longer.*

Grace slipped the rifle from its long holster by her saddle and crouched behind a rock, where she had a good view of what was happening in front of the cabin.

There was the man, still with Lillian held in front of him, a revolver in his hand. Beyond, three horses, one with Hollingswood, one with Simon.

And James. Her James. Alive.

Usually he was so comfortable in a saddle, his back straight, arms relaxed. Now he was bent forward, hatless, his left arm tucked into his shirt, clutching the reins with his right hand.

None of the men dared move.

Cora seemed to have calmed the guard, but she wouldn't be able to keep him talking for much longer.

Grace rested the barrel of the rifle on the rock and put the man in her sights. She needed to distract him so he would move from Lillian, but she didn't have a way of doing so.

Then there was a crash—a rock fall somewhere.

The man turned for a moment to see what the noise was. It was all she needed. She pulled the trigger and felt the powerful kick of the stock.

The man fell to the ground.

Lillian dropped to her knees in relief as Cora ran to her down the steps, and pulled her up by her elbow. Grace heard Cora shouting to the men to stay saddled, that they would be out of here soon.

Grace untied their horses and pulled them as fast as she could to where the men were waiting. She saw Lillian gather some of the guns she had thrown on the porch. Cora briefly returned to the cabin to retrieve the three bags of gold.

Grace caught her breath as she finally came close enough to touch James. His clothes were covered in the gray dust of the mine. His hair was matted, his beard longer than she had ever known. She moved to the horse's flank and laid a hand on her husband's thigh.

"James," she said, softly.

He turned his face to her. The right side was swollen, his eye shut and bruised. She would have barely recognized him.

"I've come to take you home."

He looked down, his left eye fixed on her. There was a slight frown, but he did not speak.

She unbuckled the second belt that secured the Colt on her left hip. "Here."

He tried to take it from her, but struggled with only one arm able to move. She reached onto her toes to pull the belt round him and fasten it, making sure the pistol was secure.

George Hollingswood and Simon seemed in better shape. Lillian gave them belts with holsters and pistols, and rifles to balance across the saddle.

"There are two more guards," said Grace to Lillian. "One who got sick and went to the tents early on. But if the one guarding the entrance hasn't come by now, we can be sure he's as ill as the others. But maybe we should tie them up."

Lillian shook her head. "Look around. We didn't figure out what would happen once we disarmed the guards."

The miners had already drifted away from the workings.

Lillian laid the remaining firearms at the feet of the two hanged men. Grace understood the message she was giving to the miners.

She finally found the courage to look more closely at the bodies, to confirm what her gut had already told her. Yes, one was dear, gentle Lopez.

"Saddle up," said Cora. "We need to get out of here. The laborers will deal with any remaining men. Possibly with a vengeance."

Lillian rode first, followed by her husband and son. Next came Cora. Then Randolph, with Grace close behind, her pistol at the ready.

They cantered out of that godforsaken gorge, following the path they had used just hours before. Grace felt like a week had passed.

She kept a close eye on James. He seemed in such discomfort, she feared he might slip off. Maybe she should try to share a horse and hold him upright. And, dear Lord, she wanted to wrap her arms around him. But that would mean stopping, removing a saddle and both riding bareback.

No, it was best to keep moving, putting as much distance as possible between them and the Dorado Mine.

They rode past where they had made their camp last night, past the smaller workings further down the river. The miners stopped and stared, seeming to realize something was amiss. There was no lighthearted jesting with Cora this time. Now, the three women were accompanied by three men.

The mountains being so high, the sun slipped out of sight, but the sky was still pale blue. They pushed on, the air losing its fierce heat.

Finally, Lillian reached a clearing and pulled up her horse. "Here?"

"Looks as good as anywhere," said Grace. "But let's go up the slope a little. Off the track."

In the trees, Grace dismounted and hurried over to James. She put her arms up to help him down, but he shook his head. Keeping his right hand balanced on the pommel, he swung his right leg back over the horse and lowered himself to the ground.

He stood before her, his left arm still tucked in his shirt.

Even in pain, he tried to stand tall. She wanted to step forward, to put her head on his chest. But something held her back.

"Can I help with that arm?" she asked, tentatively.

He looked at it, as if he had forgotten about it. Again, a single shake of his head.

"You must be thirsty," she said and took the water canteen from her horse. She must be able to do *something* to ease his suffering.

He took it from her with his right hand and raised it to his lips, putting his head back to drink.

He gave it back to her and laid his hand on her cheek, his left eye searching her face. He lifted her chin and leaned forward. Grace longed for him to kiss her. Instead, he whispered her name.

"Grace."

Before she could reply, Lillian called to her: "Do we light a fire?"

Grace turned quickly, tears pricking at her eyes that she didn't want James to see. She needed to remain strong. At least until she got him to a place he was properly safe and could have his injuries treated.

"Yes, let's light a small one. Keep everyone warm. Make some hot food."

Lillian and Grace gathered wood while Cora sat the men together under a bull pine. Light was failing, so they moved fast.

"What do we do about sleeping arrangements?" Lillian asked Grace. "We've only the two small tents."

"The men need rest more than us," said Grace. "But we can't ask Cora to forego cover."

"How about George and Randolph share the other. Simon can sleep under a blanket."

Grace put up the two small tents while Lillian lit the fire and made food. Cora fetched water from a creek.

They ate by the light of the fire, blankets around the shoulders of each of the men. Grace noticed how thin George and Simon were, how the exhaustion showed on their faces. No one spoke much; certainly no one talked about the dramatic rescue that day. It was as if they were all in a daze from the enormity of what had happened.

George pulled Lillian close and stretched the blanket around them both.

Grace's heart ached: pleased her truest friends were reunited, but desolate that James was so distant. She looked across the fire at him, but his gaze was fixed on the flames.

Cora laid out her blanket on the ground.

"I heard what you two old crones said earlier. And if you think I'm going under canvas when these men have been suffering in Dante's hell, then you don't know me at all. *Pas d'argument*. No arguments."

Grace helped James take off his frayed jacket but thought it too cold for him to remove his shirt or pants. And who knew if they would be disturbed and need to escape. She noticed swelling and a lump around his shoulder and realized that was where he was injured.

"You get some sleep now. I'll be in later," she said, backing out of the tiny tent.

She knew she wouldn't return: there wasn't room for both of them, particularly with his injuries. But she hoped it might help him settle, thinking she would come back.

"I'll keep watch first," she said to Lillian. "I'll wake you in a few hours."

She sat close to the fire, throwing on a log when needed. The flames would keep animals at bay.

Simon emerged from his two-man tent a few hours later. He was in the best shape of the three men. "I'll take over the watch, Mrs. Randolph. You get some rest."

Grace gratefully rolled out her blanket and closed her eyes, sinking into a deep sleep.

Birdsong woke her early, the sky beginning to brighten. Her back was surprisingly warm as she lay on her side and she felt the weight of an arm over her waist. She turned her head slightly. James was wrapped around her, a blanket spread over them both. She could not resist snuggling a little closer to him and closing her eyes.

"You said you'd be in later," he whispered, his mouth near her ear.

His voice was hoarse. But he was speaking, at last.

"I didn't want to disturb your sleep."

"Did you ever intend to come in that tent last night?"

"No, I don't suppose I did."

He let out a long breath. "You and me. We got to start telling the truth to each other."

It was on the tip of her tongue to say, *I will, if you will.* But that sounded like criticism. She needed to be gentle.

"Could you... could you turn over?" he asked.

She was surprised, and began to shuffle.

"Careful though, particularly that arm."

She lifted his left arm and rolled over to face him.

"Just wanted to be sure," he said.

"Sure?"

"That it was really you."

"Who else could it be?"

"Oh, some angel visiting me in my sleep." His one good eye studied her: her eyes, her nose, her mouth. "That's what I kept thinking yesterday. This was some sort of dream. That I was going to wake up and it would all be the same. Still at that hellhole." The left side of his mouth raised in a slight smile. "To be honest, it still could be. A dream. So I might as well make the most of it. Enjoy looking at you while I can."

Grace carefully raised her hand to his cheek. "I'm not going anywhere." She traced her fingers over his eyebrow. How could someone have damaged that noble face? "Does it hurt?"

"Not anymore."

She smiled, and, moving closer, put her head to his chest, where she longed to be. They remained facing each other, side by side, and she pulled the blanket up over her shoulders. They slipped back into sleep until woken by Lillian making coffee.

They needed to get out of the mountains, so packed camp and were on their way as quickly as possible. Grace insisted to Lillian that they find a route that didn't take them through the massacred village. She wanted to understand what had happened, wanted to talk about it with James, the one person she knew who seemed to care about the Native people and notice what was happening to them. But instinct told her that he should not be exposed to yet more bloodshed now.

They followed the Stanislaus River, crossed at Knights Ferry and in a few days were at Stockton, taking three rooms at a guesthouse.

At last, Grace felt she could properly care for James. He had remained mostly silent over recent days, trying to make sure he did not fall behind, despite the pain he was in.

She sat him on the bed and knelt to remove his boots. His socks were threadbare. She helped pull off his jacket; it fell loose over his left arm, which was supported by a sling Grace had made from a shirt, the arms tied round his neck. She unbuttoned the top of his shirt and pulled it over his head and could not prevent a gasp when she finally saw his back, criss-crossed by red wheals caused by a whip.

She stood. "I'll be back in a moment."

The guesthouse keeper seemed to think she had asked for champagne rather than warm water. Why could she not use cold, like everyone else? Grace persisted and even persuaded him to part with a clean cloth.

Upstairs, James was already lying down, in the early reaches of sleep. She hesitated to wake him, but thought it important to clean his wounds. He sat back up and allowed her to bathe the marks on his back, cleaning away dry blood and dirt.

She then moved to his left arm. The shoulder was swollen and bruised, with a lump that told her it was dislocated. He must be in such agony. There was little she could do, other than support it. She had to get him to San Francisco quickly—surely a bonesetter there would know what to do.

Finally, she took his face in her hands and gently wiped dust from the lines in his skin. The right side was already improving. The bruising was purple and blue but changing to yellow at the edges. The swelling had gone down enough for him to be able to see from his right eye. She worried his eyesight might have been damaged.

"Close your left eye."

He did so.

She lifted a hand in front of him. "What can you see?"

"A wedding band I placed on your finger." He opened his other eye again and took her hand. "I should've replaced it with one made of gold."

"I don't want a gold one. This is worth more than all the gold in California."

She laid him down to sleep, thinking how hard it must be for him to get comfortable, with wounds on his back, swelling on the right side of his face, and a broken left shoulder. But he was so exhausted, he was in deep sleep in no time.

Grace went downstairs and found George and Lillian sitting together on the porch.

She pulled over a chair. "I don't understand. Why is James in such bad shape?"

"Why is he worse than Simon and me, you mean?" asked George.

"I guess so." It sounded insulting, put that way. Either James was weaker, or the Hollingswoods had cowardly ducked out of the worst.

George leaned forward. "What you got to understand is that even though Randolph is not in the army, he still behaves like a captain. He can't help it. People follow him. Becksommer recognized this and knew it would be a threat. And Randolph was making trouble. He'd argue back. Couple of times he got stuck in when someone was getting a raw deal. And they couldn't let that go unpunished.

"That's what happened to Lopez. A truck of stone had tipped over onto a miner. That guard was using his whip to get the man to stand and carry on, even though the leg was broken. Lopez and Randolph both took him on, managed to take the whip from him. The other guards took control pretty fast, of course.

"Becksommer decided to hang Lopez as an example. But he knew Randolph was a strong worker. So he needed to control him. To break him. Kept him away from all the other miners in a hole somewhere, hardly anything to eat. And the physical attacks, as you can see."

They sat in silence in the half-light as the gravity of what George had related sank in.

Grace rubbed her fingers at her temples. She might have wished James had kept his head down, but she knew this was not in his nature. It would be like asking an eagle not to fly. But he had been so quiet since the rescue, she couldn't help fearing Becksommer had succeeded in breaking him.

FORTY-ONE

The bed was narrow, so Grace slept on the floor, hoping James would at least get one night's deep sleep. The next morning, they took a boat north on the San Joaquin River and then a paddle steamer across the bay to San Francisco.

As she stood on the deck with her hands on the rail, Grace thought about the same crossing, not much more than six months before. So much had happened. The weather had been chilly then, but even in the July sunshine, the water of the bay looked black and cold. Last time, they had arrived in a spirit of hope. This time, Grace wondered what future was ahead for her dejected husband.

She was surprised by the warm feeling that bubbled up inside as the hills behind San Francisco grew taller and the buildings clearer. It had become her home, a place where she had proudly built a business, looking forward to the day when she would show her achievements to James. She did not have the settled life with children she had dreamed of—perhaps that dream was gone forever—but Hester and Hetty, Molly and Lillian had become her family. In a town of men, the few women had formed a community.

And now she was bringing her husband back. They had succeeded in rescuing him, against all the odds. He was not yet himself. In truth, he had not been the bold and confident man she first knew for a long while, not since his return from Mexico. Whatever had ailed him then, seemed to have returned, to have burrowed deeper into his soul.

She would be patient. She would stand by him for as long as it took. Never again the anguish of parting on bad terms, of him going away and not knowing how much she loved him.

At the harbor, they took a large carriage, all six tucked in close, and paid a boy to bring the horses and mule to their stables.

James stared at the buildings as they made their way up Howard Street. "You San Franciscans. You don't let the grass grow under your feet, do you?"

Simon shook his head in wonder. "You'd hardly know there'd been a fire six months ago."

Lillian and Grace exchanged a glance. They'd told their husbands about the hotel, and were looking forward to seeing their reactions when they reached Fourth Street.

As the carriage pulled up, the women climbed out first. Cora bid Grace and Lillian farewell and promised to return later to collect her belongings, once the boy arrived. "I'm going to see if Marguerite can fix me a long bath."

Grace turned back to the carriage. James winced as he carefully climbed down and stood on the street, his legs firmly apart, looking at the structure in front of him. He adjusted his hat so he could look upwards and turned his head so his good eye could scan across the building. Grace watched nervously, unable to tell if he approved.

Hollingswood stood beside him and let out a long slow whistle. "That sure is something! And you ladies did all this yourselves?"

Lillian clucked her teeth. "Best hotel in the city, even if I say it myself."

James slowly nodded. "Hotel Independence. I like the name." He looked at Grace and finally gave a crooked smile, the right side of his face still injured. "You've done good."

Lillian led the way. Grace's chest tightened as James took her hand and they went through the double doors, into the lobby.

"Sitting room to the left," Lillian said, waving to a door but leading them on. "This is the dining room."

Lillian called out to her daughters.

The three men barely had time to admire the furnishings before being taken through to the kitchen, the heart of the hotel.

Ling Mei dropped the mallet she was using to tenderize some beef. She was wearing the same tunic and pants as ever, and Grace was warmed by the familiarity.

"Miss Lillian. Oh, Miss Grace!"

She hurried to embrace them, pushing back strands of straight black hair that had fallen in her face. Grace had never seen Mei show such emotion. Words she didn't understand poured from her, and Grace could only surmise their meaning.

Mei stepped back as Lillian introduced her husband, son and Randolph. She returned to the respectful young woman Grace remembered, making a low bow, her hands before her, not raising her eyes to the men's faces.

Grace heard a clatter of feet on the stairs and the sound of young voices. The three girls burst into the room.

"Pa. Papa, you're home!"

Hollingswood wept as he took his daughters into his arms, trying to squeeze all three tight.

Grace quietly maneuvered James to a chair and stood beside him, allowing time for the Hollingswoods' longed-for reunion.

They all gathered round the table, sitting on benches and chairs, the six Hollingswoods, and Grace and James. Mei provided coffee in next to no time and brought out plate after plate of cold meats, of fresh bread and butter, of sweet Chinese almond cookies.

Grace found she could only pick at the food, still feeling unsettled. "Where are Espinoza and Moreno?"

"A steamer arrived last night," said Hester. "They're seeing if they can get a good deal on a load of coal to take us through the winter."

Eventually, Grace persuaded Mei to sit with them. "Your plan worked like clockwork."

She smiled shyly. "I worry every day. Maybe the powder too strong. Maybe too weak."

"The powder worked perfectly," said Lillian. "Not a man standing."

"But conscious enough to get what we came for," said Grace.

They had told the men the bare bones of what had happened that day in Dorado mine, and now had to give more detail, for the benefit of the girls.

Grace could see James was tiring, so suggested she take him upstairs to their room.

Mei ran up ahead of them. "You need guest room," she said. "Until Espinoza and Moreno find somewhere to live."

Grace had forgotten she had told the Chileans to use her room.

Mei opened the door to the best appointed of their rooms and checked the bedding was smooth. She helped Grace undress James, frowning at his swollen shoulder. She discreetly gathered clothing from the floor as Grace took off James's underwear.

A look of understanding passed between the women as Grace lifted the cotton sheet up over James's back.

"He finds it easiest to sleep on his front," Grace murmured.

"I bring doctor," said Mei, as Grace quietly closed the door behind them.

When Grace returned downstairs, the Chileans were back and everything was in uproar. Their joy and relief knew no bounds. Espinoza laughed and wept and gave her a warm hug, lifting her off her feet. She felt a fleeting hollowness at the contrast with her husband, who showed so little emotion it worried her.

To Grace's disappointment, they insisted on leaving the hotel that day, now they were no longer needed as protectors of the girls. "There are many Chileans at Clark's Point," said Espinoza. "Our own little community."

Mei returned within the hour and introduced Grace to the elderly Chinese man she had brought with her. He held a case in his bony hand. The three of them went upstairs to James's room.

She stood close by as the doctor looked first at James's face, touching the bruising around the eye. He spoke and Mei translated.

"This will heal. Maybe scar. But will heal."

He then looked at James's back, carefully examining each weal. Grace saw her husband flinch at times. The doctor went to his bag and produced a jar of white salve, giving instructions to Mei.

"This will heal also. Put this on back, every morning, every evening."

Finally, the doctor looked at James's left shoulder. Lines were deep on the doctor's brow as he ran his hand and fingers over the swellings, speaking as he went.

Mei's face became increasingly grave. "This not heal. This not right and will always be painful if not fixed now. You want fixed now?"

Grace touched her husband's hand. He had not said a word since the doctor had arrived. "James?"

His gaze was rooted on the wall opposite. "Let's get it over with."

Mei translated. "I get whiskey. And spoon."

Grace was puzzled, but helped James to sit with his back against the headboard.

Mei returned and offered a slug of alcohol. "Maybe help with pain?"

He glanced at her and drank it down.

She gave him the wooden spoon. "And you bite on this while doctor sets bone. You not move while he do it."

Grace watched the Chinese man prepare. James grimaced as the doctor lifted his arm, felt around the area again, and with a sharp shove and a crunch, slotted the bone back into the socket.

James groaned in agony, his teeth clenched around the wood, taking rapid, sharp breaths.

The doctor wrapped a bandage around his arm and abdomen, holding the bones in place.

"That hurts worse than before," growled James.

Mei spoke to the doctor. "He say, it hurt more now, but less later."

The doctor returned to his case and gave Mei a brown glass vial as he solemnly explained the contents.

"This stop the pain," said Mei. "Will make Mr. Randolph feel good. But we be careful. Only three drops at one time. Only four times through day."

Grace nodded. "I'll see to it."

The man spoke again.

"The doctor say you needing to understand. No more. No matter how much your husband want it. And in few days, only three times, then one. In one week: no more."

Grace put the vial on the chest of drawers, and then thought better of it: this should be kept in a safe place. She slipped it into her pocket and led the Chinese man to the dining room where she paid him generously.

Mei guided him out through the front door. Grace heard voices raised on the street and looked through the window. Words were being spoken between Ling Mei and the old man, who gesticulated to the hotel.

When she returned, Mei's complexion was pink and her mouth a fixed line.

"Mei?" Grace asked.

She looked a little awkward. "He not happy with me."

"The man?"

Mei nodded.

"What's it got to do with him?"

"He my grandfather."

"Your grandfather! Mei—"

But she had already disappeared into the kitchen.

FORTY-TWO

Randolph breathed in the smell of sawn wood and oil varnish. The room was a generous size with a window overlooking the street. The bed was comfortable; the most comfortable he'd slept in for years. He never dreamed this is what he would find when he came home. His wife had managed to get a whole hotel built. If anything proved that she didn't need him, it was this. His warehouse business had burned to the ground. Her business thrived.

Lying in bed gave him time to reflect on their life together. The bed linen was ironed smooth. Grace had told him something about the Chinese woman doing it. Ling Mei. The pillow smelled of fresh Pacific air and he remembered his shared joke with Grace that a soft pillowcase was his one luxury. That felt like a lifetime ago. Something that had happened to someone else. Now, there was no thread that connected him to that happy, romantic man. Even the pillowcase he had given her had been destroyed by fire. Everything they shared had gone.

The bed might be wide, but his wife showed no inclination to share it with him, and he didn't blame her, not with his shattered body and spirit. It broke his heart that he would never give her the child she longed for. She sat with him during the day when she could, and sometimes in the evening read a book by the oil lamp. Those quiet times were bittersweet. He liked that he could pretend to sleep and know she was close. Or watch her, wordlessly.

But she never stayed. She had a hotel to run. At night, he heard the heavy steps of miners, returning from the fields with plenty of gold in their pockets. Perhaps one or two new arrivals, fresh off a sailing ship, although they could rarely afford the rates that George had told him their wives were charging.

She was probably making as much here as he'd done in the Sierras. Before he'd lost everything for a second time, of course. She was better off without him. Why on earth had she risked her life to come and find him?

Randolph was roused by a knock at the door. Espinoza put his head round, grinning from ear to ear. He was followed into the room by Moreno.

"Captain!" said Espinoza. "Never has my heart been so overjoyed to see someone. My old friend."

Espinoza grasped his right hand and enveloped it in both of his. Randolph was knocked back by a surge of affection for his friend. Espinoza had been the glue that held the brotherhood together. He had feared he'd never see him again.

Espinoza pulled a chair close to the bed and dropped his head.

Moreno sat further away, by the window. Randolph was taken aback by how thin and ill his friend looked.

"We have been waiting until you are stronger. To visit, I mean," said Espinoza. "We have come to ask your forgiveness."

"Forgiveness?"

"That we weren't there—"

"You couldn't help that—"

"And that we didn't come after you. Maybe, if we'd set off immediately—"

"Espinoza. You had no way of knowing how many men had taken us." Randolph patted his hand, but it seemed a feeble gesture compared with what he wanted to convey. "Speaking as an army captain, you did the right thing. You tried to get reinforcements."

Espinoza looked up at him, his lips and chin trembling as he fought back his tears. "I could not believe the mayor at Stockton. He wanted nothing to do with freeing you. And then Moreno got sick..."

"Hollingswood told me." Randolph looked toward the window and spoke quietly. "How are you, my old friend?"

Moreno lifted his palm horizontal and swiveled it. "Good days. Bad days."

Espinoza glanced at him and sighed, before returning his attention to Randolph. "And then when we got here, still no one wanted to help. Your wife: she like a tigress. We rode over to the Presidio."

Randolph raised his eyebrows.

"You not know this? Yes, Mrs. Randolph dressed up smart and we went to the Governor General."

"And what did he say?" Was this yet another example of how capable she was, how little she needed him?

Espinoza shrugged. "Excuses. Got no troops. Can't help."

Randolph tutted. "What's going to become of this place? Washington can't ignore us forever."

Espinoza dropped his head. "I am so ashamed. Moreno, he is too. We let women go in our place. We ask your forgiveness." He let his head sink into his hands and muttered in Spanish what sounded like an incantation.

When he finished, they sat in silence and Randolph thought about what he had said, about forgiveness.

"Look, help me up," Randolph finally said. He continued as

Espinoza helped him sit. "You don't need forgiveness. It was my fault we were there at all. I couldn't make a go of it here. I couldn't keep hold of my gold. Me and Hollingswood, we were there to make back the gold we lost in the fire." He snorted with disgust as he swung his legs over the edge of the bed. His thoughts began to overwhelm him. "Instead we got captured," he muttered to himself. "And now I'm a wreck who can barely use my arm. So how can I earn a living here? It would have been better if they'd left me there—"

"Captain—"

"I break everything I touch."

He painfully pushed himself up and went barefoot to the window, barely aware his friends were still there. He stared out at life that was carrying on outside without him.

"She should've married a farmer. Should be settled in Oregon, with her brothers. Should be with a husband who could give her children. Not a..." He paused and spat the final words. "A failed soldier with a dishonorable discharge."

Where had all this come from? He never talked about personal things. Perhaps it was because Espinoza felt he had something to ask forgiveness for.

Randolph put his brow to the windowpane. "I need to fall at her feet and beg her forgiveness. And then to find the strength to walk away, out of her life. To let her have the life she deserves. With someone else."

Moreno was sitting close, staring at him. "You want to *abandon* her?" he asked forcefully.

"She's better off without me..."

"You truly think this?"

"Moreno. Look at me..." He turned back to them both.

Moreno folded his arms and grunted. "And I thought you were a man I could look up to. Listen to your words. '*Me, me, me.*' That's who you are thinking of. I see this in men many times. But usually at the end of the night, when they have drunk too much. Stop thinking about yourself. Think about her."

"But I *am*—"

"You're not." Moreno raised his hands to the heavens and growled as he searched for the words. "She loves you. She loves you fiercely, like no woman I've ever seen. She is part of you. Like the albatross my father told me about as a child. She is never going to leave you. Never. And you are allowing yourself to sink." Moreno got to his feet and jabbed his finger at Randolph. "You have to pull yourself out of this... this self-pitying hole you are in. Because you will drag her down with you."

Randolph sat heavily back on the bed, a familiar hot feeling running up inside him. Insubordination. This was how he felt if one of his men questioned an order. How dare Moreno say this to him. He said he was his friend. "Can't you see, I'm trying to *release* Grace. Give her her freedom."

"For God's sake! Do you think she risked her life getting you *your* freedom, because she wanted you to walk away, as soon as you were home?"

"Well, no—"

"And you are right." Moreno paced to the bottom of the bed and leaned on the rail. "She didn't need to do it. She could have left you. When Governor Riley said he couldn't help, any other woman would've given up. But she walked into the lion's den. For you." He pointed at Randolph. "So you had better start living up to the man she thinks you are."

Randolph felt as if he'd been slapped on the cheek. There was a tentative knock at the door and he felt relief that they would be interrupted, that Moreno would have to stop.

Hester looked around nervously. "Mother said I should ask if you wanted anything? Coffee brought up?"

Moreno spun round to look out of the window.

Espinoza stood up, looking embarrassed that the girl had

heard them. "We have stayed too long already." He picked up his hat and ran his fingers round the brim before glancing over at Moreno. "Said too much."

Moreno turned back and fixed his eyes on Randolph. "I am now, and will always be, your friend. I hope one day you will see that I have been a true friend to you today."

The door closed behind the two men and the room was quiet once more. It seemed smaller, the air thick.

Randolph swung his feet back onto the floor and felt the rug beneath him. He went over to the window and struggled with the sash with just one arm but managed to open the window a few inches. The street was full of sounds: a cart rattling past, two men laughing at a joke, a pedlar selling peaches.

Evening was falling so he went to the oil lamp on the chest and lit a taper. Glancing at the window, he caught his reflection. He stopped dead.

He barely recognized the man. His hair was dark but had grown long. His beard was wiry and untidy, like one of those Mormon preachers. He was so thin. He looked down: he was wearing the bottom half of some long johns, and a woolen shirt.

"No wonder she..." he whispered. And then he shook his head. *A self-pitying hole.* That's what Moreno had said. And he was right.

Randolph wasn't quite sure how he was going to do it, but he needed to start climbing back out.

Randolph woke at daybreak and pulled himself out of bed, stiffly taking the stairs to the kitchen and outside to the laundry. Ling Mei was already there.

"Miss? Might I trouble you for some hot water?"

Ling Mei looked at him with wide eyes. "Water?"

"I'd like a bath."

She busied herself with stoking the stove and putting a large pan on to heat. She pulled over the largest of her tubs, into the middle of the stone floor.

"And would you have scissors?" he asked.

Ling Mei frowned.

He mimed what he needed and she hurried off to fetch them.

"I help?" She pointed to his beard.

"Thank you."

She pulled a stool over for him, while more water was heating.

He measured with his finger how much of his beard she should leave and she snipped away at it. She then tidied his hair. He ran his hand back over the crown of his head.

There was enough water to fill the tub. Ling Mei put a bar of soap nearby.

"I leave you now," she said, her eyes on the floor. "Later I bring towel. I knock on door."

He took off his clothes and lowered himself into the tub. Sweet Lord, it felt good. The warm liquid enveloped him. Being tall, he had to scoop water over his chest and shoulders. He leaned forward and plunged his head right under, pulling his fingers through his hair. Sitting back upright, water sloshed onto the stone floor.

He took the soap and brush Ling Mei had laid out for him, and started to scrub. Every part of his body needed a thorough cleanse. When he had finished, he sat back again, the wounds on his back stinging against the side of the tub. He closed his eyes and circled his hands through the warm water.

He heard a knock at the door.

"Enter," he called, expecting Ling Mei.

He took a sharp breath when he saw it was Grace, her arms loaded with a thick towel and clean clothing he recognized from before he'd left.

Her eyes were large and dark, her lips slightly open, as if

about to ask a question. He never failed to be captivated by her, but this morning he felt a flush of embarrassment. He was not the strong army captain she'd fallen in love with. He was a wreck of that man.

"Ling Mei said..."

She seemed hesitant.

"I hope you don't mind. I brought you..." She indicated the clothing in her arms.

Why should he mind? Oh, there was such a distance between them.

"Thank you."

She put the clothing on a shelf and the towel on the stool nearby.

Moreno had said it was *his* job to make things right. Not hers.

"Perhaps... if you wouldn't mind... you could soap my back?"

She paused for a moment, her eyes locked on his, and then she moved the towel and sat close on the stool. He gave her the soap bar and turned his back to her, feeling uncomfortable about the marks the whip had made.

Maybe this was what Moreno had meant. Maybe he had to show her his wounds, in every possible way.

Her hands were soft and tender, delicately running over the scars. She took a bowl and poured warm water over his shoulders and back.

"Would you like me to clean your hair?"

He nodded, a tightness in his throat making it hard to form words.

She rubbed the bar against his hair and massaged his scalp with her fingers. He closed his eyes, and a sigh escaped from his lips. She ran her fingers through his hair to loosen the knots.

"Ling Mei cut it for me."

"I'm glad. It looks much better."

He moved his body to turn toward her. "The beard too."

She smiled and stroked it with her fingers. "Also much better."

Her thumbs ran up over his cheeks and her gaze lifted to his eyes. He held it for as long as he dared. She did not look away. He lifted his arm to the back of her neck and she willingly drew close until their foreheads touched, their breath mingling.

He closed his eyes and the world evaporated into this one spot. He wanted to kiss her but feared that would be like letting a butterfly settle on his palm, only to fold it into his fist.

She pulled back a little, her eyes still on his face. The noises of the city seeped into the laundry room. He heard Lillian calling to her girls. A seagull squawked, just outside the window.

"The water's getting cold," whispered Grace.

He nodded. "And Ling Mei needs her laundry back."

Grace gently laughed. "Do you want me to help...?" She lifted the towel.

"No, I'd prefer... And you've got work to do, I'm sure."

Was he still uncertain of her seeing him, so thin and broken? He had to be brave.

"But later... I don't know quite when... I have things I want to tell you."

She put the towel on the stool and closed the door behind her.

It was a start. He had shown her his physical wounds. He now had to find the strength to show the wounds inside.

FORTY-THREE

Grace brushed her hair harder than was necessary and twisted it into its nighttime braid. All of the Chileans' belongings had gone from the room and she rattled around in a room planned for two. More than two. A crib beneath the window. Or had that dream gone forever?

She plumped the feathers in her pillow and smoothed the quilt.

This was ridiculous. She had helped wash James; they had shared a tender moment. Granted, he had been quiet for the rest of the day. But that moment counted for something, didn't it?

She had told herself she would be patient, would go at his pace. What if she'd got that wrong, what if he needed a little more—well—encouragement?

Grace pulled on her silk dressing-gown—a gift from Mei— over her nightdress and picked up the candle in its holder. She opened the door carefully: everyone had already gone to bed. She padded down the corridor and through the door to the public part of their hotel.

There, she stopped dead, almost colliding with a tall man in the dark.

"James!" She put a hand to her throat. "Oh, thank God it's you."

"What are you doing here?" he whispered.

"I came... I came..." She looked up at him, but the shadows cast by the candle meant she couldn't interpret his face. "Hey, what are *you* doing here?"

"I..." He put a hand to the back of his neck. "I know that room is comfortable, but, truth is, I don't know what I'm doing in a guest room."

"I thought it would be better for you."

"Better?"

"Quieter."

"Would you *prefer* I slept there?"

Grace coughed and dropped her gaze. "Well, no. That's why I'm here. I thought maybe, after this morning, maybe you'd want to come back. Back to my room. *Our* room... the room I planned for both of us."

She was garbling for fear he would say no, but stopped when she peeked up and saw his lips curling in a soft smile.

He gave a slight shrug. "That's what I was doing. Thought maybe I... Darn. What are we doing standing here? We both want the same thing."

He reached round and opened the door behind her and she led the way down the passage to their room, her stomach fluttering from excitement and nerves.

Grace put the candle on the dresser. A mirror reflected its light. She transferred the flame with a taper to the oil lamp on a small table. The room was honey-colored and cozy.

James paused a moment, leaning on the doorjamb, drinking it in. "May I?" He indicated the chair.

Grace nodded and he entered and sat to remove his shoes.

She opened a chest and pulled out some pillows, placing them on his side of the bed.

She saw him hesitating and then pulling his shirt over his head. She glanced at the red marks.

"Are they still painful?" she asked softly.

He gave a little shake of the head. "Getting easier each day. Like my arm."

She slipped off her indoor shoes—silk slippers she had bought from a schooner from China—and folded back the quilt. She hung her dressing gown on a hook, turned down the oil lamp and blew out the candle. As he undressed, she slid between the sheets, the room lit by moonlight.

He got in next to her, the mattress dipping with his weight. How she had missed that sensation over the past months.

"Can I... Could I hold you awhile?" he asked.

At last. The tenderness she longed for. Her heart raced as she lay close, him on his back, her head in the warm hollow of his right shoulder. It was so familiar—how they had always slept. She listened to his breathing, felt his heart beating beneath her cheek.

After a little while, she moved as gently as possible so as not to disturb him.

"Still awake?" he immediately asked.

"Sorry, I didn't mean to wake you."

"You didn't. I haven't been sleeping well..."

"Me neither," she said.

He took a deep breath. "Espinoza and Moreno visited yesterday."

"I know. It must have been good to see them."

"Good? Perhaps. Moreno had a lot to say." His thumb stroked back and forth at her hip. "I never told you what happened in Mexico. Why I was discharged."

She hardly dared move. "I know, darling. I always hoped you'd tell me when you were good and ready."

"I'm ready now. If you want to hear."

She laid her hand on his torso. "I'm listening."

"I disobeyed an order. More than that, I told my men they could disobey it. And the army can't work like that. It requires unconditional obedience. But I suddenly didn't like what I was being obedient to."

He took a breath, seeming to prepare himself for what he had to say.

"I've been in many battles and skirmishes over the past ten years. And as time's gone by, I've been finding it harder. You know how I felt about that Cayuse attack on our wagon train."

"It was them or us," she said quietly.

"Was it though? That's what I'd been struggling with. Is it really our... our manifest destiny? Like the politicians and the churchmen tell us?"

He'd always had this unusual questioning about how the world ordered itself. "Is that what led to the discharge?" Grace asked.

"Yes... Well, no. Not exactly." He coughed.

She could feel him hesitating again. If he sank back into concealing his true feelings, she might never get the chance to understand. She pushed herself up and got out of bed. By the light of the moon, she poured a glass of water and returned to the bed.

"Here. Take this."

She rearranged the pillows so they could sit upright. He shuffled until he could lean his back against them, and she got in to sit next to him, putting her head on his good shoulder.

"Now, tell me what happened. In Mexico."

He took a sip of water. "It was the same as all wars. Bloody. Chaotic. No one knowing what's happening. Orders coming through that make no sense. Acts of heroism that make you feel you wouldn't want to be anywhere else in the world, the bond with your fellows is so strong.

"Everyone knew we were winning. Even though the Mexicans knew the land, we had better weapons, better trained men. It was all but over, and the order came to attack a village. I didn't understand. We didn't need the village. The people there hadn't been involved in the fighting. So I questioned the order. Not disobeyed. Just, y'know, checked we had the right place.

"The answer came back that there were a pair of important generals hiding here. But I had reliable intelligence that those men were ten miles away. It made no sense.

"Then the order came back stronger. Scorched earth. Not a building to be left standing, punish the villagers for hiding the generals.

"So I took my company of soldiers and approached the village on horseback. In the open. No one fired back. I rode right into the town, where I was met by an old man. I said the names of the generals we were searching for. He shook his head. I got down from my horse, ordered my lieutenant and some of the others to do the same. I slowly took out my pistol and approached one of the houses—it was a small pueblo-type thing.

"The old man, he went ahead, talking all the time, and opened the door. I went in, followed by a private, and checked the house. There were just women and old people there. The next house the same. Women. Children. Anyone of fighting age had left.

"My men spread out. I told them to take it slow and steady. Methodical. We put forks through hay bales. Checked among the scrawny farm stock they had." He sighed. "And finally the little church. It was made of mud and straw bricks like everything else, but painted white to make it look like a proper building. Inside, there were a few high windows. An altar with gold candlesticks. Even in this little place with next to nothing, the church still had gold. An image behind the altar of Madonna and Child. There were two old women at the front on their knees, rosaries in their hands. They looked up at me, scared. Praying we'd all leave, I reckon.

"And that's what we did. Leave. Rode back out and sent a message to my commanding officer that the generals weren't there." He ran his fingers back through his hair. "It was like I'd lit the fuse for an explosion.

"He came galloping back to where my men were camped, a whole company behind him. Roared at me that my orders were to destroy the village. Not search it. I said it was just women, children. Old men. He said the generals were old men. That they could've been hiding anywhere. He ordered me to take my company back to that village and not leave until every building was razed."

James took another sip of water. "And I refused. The major was furious with me. Got back on his horse and rode his company down the hill to the village.

"I turned to my men. Told them it was their choice. They could follow the major but I wouldn't be doing so. They could say they were following my orders, but I couldn't guarantee they wouldn't face discharge also.

"A handful of men rode on back to the village, but most stayed with me. Perhaps my proudest moment in the US army." He let out a breath, and paused as he remembered.

"But we could see what was happening. We weren't that far away. Could hear it.

"In the end, I couldn't bear it any longer. I got on my horse. There had to be something I could do, rather than standing by.

"When I rode into the village, every house was on fire. Livestock lay slaughtered. But not people. There weren't any bodies in the pathways between the houses. I was hopeful they had all run away."

His voice croaked so he finished his water and Grace put the glass on the cabinet beside her. She settled back next to him.

"I rode on to the church. The major had got his men to lay

straw and wood around it, close by the walls. He said the villagers had all fled inside. He said it with a smile.

"He positioned his men around the church and lit the fires himself. The building went up in no time.

"I could see the villagers were pushing at the main doors to escape, but the soldiers had put a cart in the way. I ran forward to move it, but was brought down by some soldiers.

"The men standing guard weren't needed. No one could get out, other than through those doors. The windows were too high."

James paused. There was really nothing else to be said. Grace stroked his chest with her thumb and waited in the dark. She heard a half-strangled noise, caught in James's throat.

"The sound. Oh Grace, the sound. I hear it even now. The cries of women, of children."

Grace reached up her palm and felt the wetness on his cheeks. She sat up further and pulled him to her. His head sank onto her chest and she stroked his hair. She couldn't find the words to comfort him. Anything she said now was meaningless. Her heart ached for him, for the burden he had been carrying. Now, she finally understood his behavior since his return.

"The fire... here in San Francisco..." she said, "you must've been in torment."

He nodded. "To be honest, it didn't bring things back to my mind, because the memories have never left. But when I found out that some of the fires had been set deliberately..." He whistled. "I saw red. I admit, when I was punching that man in the street, I was thinking as much about my army major. I'm not proud of it, Grace. But it's the fact of the matter."

At last, she felt she was really getting the truth. It might be ugly, but she could live with that.

They moved themselves back down the bed until they lay close together. James was quickly in a deep sleep and Grace hoped it might be because he had found a sense of peace, now he had told her. She tried not to disturb him as she settled for the night.

Grace woke to find James sleeping on his front, his head to one side on the pillow, his arm stretched over her, as if trying to keep her close. She studied his face as he slept. The lines around his eyes were deeper. The shade of his skin was darker from weeks in the sun without a hat. There was still a wave in his hair, but a few grays grew at his temple, among the dark brown. The beard was shorter than when she had brought him back, but still untrimmed. She wanted to kiss his eyelids as he slept, to stroke his hair with her fingers, to run her thumb along the lips that were slightly parted as he breathed.

Instead, she gently lifted his arm and slipped out of bed, pushing her feet into her slippers and wrapping the silk dressing gown around her.

She returned a few minutes later with two cups of coffee, closing the latch as quietly as possible, but turning to find his eyes upon her.

"Coffee?" she asked.

"Later."

She put the cups on the cabinet.

He sat up and swung his legs over the side of the bed, facing her.

"Come here." He put a hand out for hers.

She took it and stood close, between his thighs. He untied the belt of the gown and pushed it apart, then slid his hands up to her shoulders to push it back. It fell, pooling on the ground behind her. Her heart beat faster: they had been separated so long—physically, emotionally—that she felt nervous of what was ahead. She longed for him, wanted to kiss and touch him, but there was something fragile between them.

He took the ribbon at the bottom of her braid in his fingers and untied it, then released each of the three tresses. Pushing his fingers through each tress, he divided it, then repeated the movement, until all her hair was free and spread across her back, regular rows of kinks from the nape down, where it had been folded in the braid.

He leaned forward to put his hands below her nightdress, and slowly let his palms slide up each leg. Her breathing quickened and she parted her feet further, resting her hands on his shoulders. He took the white cotton in his hands and bunched it up, lifting it, until she raised her arms so he could thread it over her head and remove it completely.

Although he was her husband, she felt embarrassed to stand naked before him. His eyes ran over every part of her body, as if reminding himself of each curve and contour. She closed her eyes, as he caressed her hips, pulling her closer to him. His fingers fluttered over her breasts and then down between her legs. He leaned to her and kissed her torso.

She laid her lips on the top of his head, and stroked the muscles of his shoulders. He reached his arms around her waist and pulled her to the bed. Pushing back the coverlet, Grace lay on the white sheet as he removed his underwear.

She wanted to be joined with him quickly, to feel that closeness she needed. But she wanted this to last forever, to never be parted from her husband again. He kissed her deeply, passionately. The urgency of his desire swept them onwards as she pulled him close, felt the weight of him.

As he entered her, she stifled the moans she longed to release. Tremors ran through her and then waves, building, one after the next. He thrust into her, and she opened her eyes to find his fixed on hers. There was an intensity she had never seen before and it made her feel they were one being. As he pushed repeatedly, she closed her eyes and then suddenly felt as if she were a boat crashing over a waterfall. Each hand gripped onto the top of his arms as she shuddered beneath him, before he collapsed on top of her, his breathing ragged.

They lay entwined, spent, panting in rhythm with each other. He rolled onto his back and she ran her fingers through the dark hair on his chest and down his sweat-sheened torso. Even after weeks of ill treatment, the outline of his muscles remained below his skin.

They listened to breakfast being made in the kitchen beneath them. A seagull landed on the roof, its feet making scratching noises as it ran across the wood. It made a plaintive and insistent call, reminding them how close they were to the ocean.

He turned to her and traced a finger over her eyebrow and down her cheek. "I'm not saying I'm better, Grace. That, somehow, it's all forgotten now. But I am saying I'll try. I'll try to be the husband you deserve."

She opened her mouth to speak, but thought better of it and kissed his palm instead. In time, she hoped to persuade him that it was not about deserving each other, as if there were a ledger keeping record of their merits. It was about accepting all the flaws, and enveloping those flaws in love. He already was the husband she deserved, and he always would be, because she loved him.

FORTY-FOUR

Randolph lounged in a wooden chair in the backyard, his legs stretched out and barefoot, a book on his chest where he'd given up on it, preferring to enjoy the mid-July sun. He liked that Grace was within arm's reach, next to him. She had received another letter from Tom—poorly spelled and brief—and was writing a very long letter back.

He heard someone running and Simon burst through the gate, disturbing the peace of the Sunday afternoon.

"Got to come," he gasped. "Espinoza. Moreno."

Randolph sat bolt upright. "What's happened?"

Simon bent forward, resting his hands on his knees, catching his breath. "The Hounds." Simon stood up, drawing more breath. "Attacking the Chileans."

"Where?"

"Down by Clark's Point. Their camp."

Randolph was on his feet. "Wait there."

He quickly strode inside and returned with his boots and hat.

"Where's Pa?" asked Simon.

"Not here," said Grace, packing away her letter. "Gone for a walk round Mission Bay with your mother and Molly."

"Come on, son," said Randolph.

"Shouldn't Simon stay here?" Grace asked. "It could be dangerous."

"He's a man, now. And these Hounds need to be stopped."

The gang known as the Hounds had been growing in strength for months. Most Sundays, they paraded up and down, pipes and drums making a racket, and shouting about how California was for the Americans, and that all foreigners should take the first boat home to where they came from. Recently, they'd taken to provoking brawls and breaking furniture. The mayor seemed powerless to stop them.

Grace was pacing the yard. "Maybe, just in case things turn ugly, I should—"

Randolph knew exactly what she was thinking. He stood close, taking her face in his palms. "Promise me you'll stay here."

"But if our friends—"

"The Hounds have never used guns. Only their fists. You mustn't bring firearms into it. And I don't want you in danger. Not again. Please, my love, promise me."

She looked up into his eyes. "I promise."

He pecked her on the lips. "I'll make sure Simon keeps his head down."

"And yours, too."

He nodded. "I'll be careful."

He took off at a steady pace, Simon at his side.

Over the past fortnight, much of his strength had returned under Grace's love and care, although there were still scars, and his shoulder was tender. He saw why this place meant so much to her: the hills, the views of the bay with sun glistening on it. They had taken trips across the peninsula to the coast and watched waves roll in from across the Pacific.

He had begun to appreciate the community they were building, the sense of everything being possible. In the East, he'd been brought up with a belief that you made your way in the world through hard work. The dark side was that people who were finding life tough were blamed for their misfortunes. Here in California, people knew luck played a part in life. The luck of finding a rich seam, of digging a large nugget. And the ill luck that could take it from you—a fire, or a sinking ship. Instead of feeling shame that they had fallen to the bottom of the ladder, Californians simply shrugged, picked themselves up and climbed up again. It was a revelation to Randolph that he was beginning to feel comfortable with this philosophy of life.

But the lawlessness was making a good life impossible. Six months ago, after the fire, Randolph had raged against the lack of action by the mayor or the governor. He had been frustrated that Washington continued to ignore their newly won territory.

Over recent weeks, he had recognized he needed to take action to make this a place his beloved wife could be happy. He wasn't sure what that action was, but knew taking a stand against the Hounds was a start—particularly if he could help his dear friends. He owed Moreno more than he could say.

He heard the riot before he saw it. Men's shouts and groans, wood being snapped, glass broken. They turned into Broadway. The Chileans, Mexicans and Peruvians had gravitated together in this area but lived in tents and had not yet put down roots. There was a violent mêlée, with knots of men, some entwined on the ground, punching and pummeling. Many of the Hounds had batons and were using them to beat the Latin Americans, not caring where the blows fell. Tents had been torn down, belongings ransacked and scattered into the dust. Randolph was alarmed to see women and children among the fray. His military tactics would be of no help here: it was simply a mass of brawling men. There was no alternative but to pitch in.

He glanced at Simon. "Stay close. Make sure we look out for each other. And yell if you see Espinoza or Moreno."

He pulled the nearest Hound off a Mexican on the ground, and swung a punch with his right arm, keeping his left protected. Simon helped the Mexican to his feet. Then Randolph grasped a wooden baton being used to bludgeon a man close by. He wrenched it from the Hound's hands and swung it into the man's abdomen.

Moving forward through the brawl, he saw a tall, broad man slamming two Hounds into each other.

Randolph grabbed Simon. He jutted his chin in the man's direction. "Moreno. Work our way toward him."

They did so, dodging fists and kicks. There was Espinoza, close by, throwing a man to the ground.

Randolph shouted to Moreno as he came close.

There was blood on the Chilean's face from a blow to the head. He managed to grin. "Couldn't keep away, eh?"

"Looks that way."

The Latin Americans were winning the day, spurred on by defending their location and their families. The Hounds were melting away. This would soon be over, thank God.

Then a shot rang out.

There were yells and screams.

Then another shot. A man dropped to the ground.

With horror, Randolph realized one of the Hounds was firing into the battleground, not caring who was struck, knowing that most of the Hounds were lying injured on the ground.

"We need to leave," shouted Randolph. "Everyone. There's nothing we can do now. Not if they're ready to use guns, and fire into a crowd."

Espinoza nodded his agreement. People had begun to scatter.

"The sand dunes," said Randolph. "Get people to make their way there."

This took them away from where the gun was being fired, and into a landscape where the Hounds were unlikely to follow.

Randolph picked up a child, grimacing as he strained his shoulder, and encouraged others to follow.

They eventually slumped down in the steep sand and grass, catching their breath. Randolph had taken a blow to his lower ribs, which aggravated an injury from the Dorado mine. Espinoza saw to Moreno's head wound. Simon was untouched. All in all, not bad, considering the violence.

From the dune, Randolph could see that not a tent was left standing in the camp. Belongings had been broken or stolen.

Randolph insisted Espinoza and Moreno came back to the hotel for the night and, after some polite hesitations, the offer was gratefully received. Randolph was pleased to have a chance to help his old friends and show Moreno how profoundly his stern advice had changed him.

In the kitchen, Grace washed Moreno's head, getting grit out of a wound. It looked worse than it was, and she gave a thankful prayer that none of the men was badly hurt. The last few hours had reminded her of the agonies of living at Fort Leavenworth, waiting for news of her husband. After everything they'd been through, she found it hard to stop fearing the worst.

Mei brought ointment and rubbed it into the skin beneath Moreno's thick black hair.

"She's a good one, this one," Moreno said.

"Many's the day I give thanks for her coming into our lives," said Grace.

Mei colored a little. Grace had always suspected she understood more than she spoke, but Mei was pretty much fluent now.

Grace took Moreno and Mei into the yard, where everyone had gathered in the warm evening air, sitting in mismatched chairs and on cushions, drinks balanced on upturned crates. All the Hollingswoods were there, and Cora had come over from the saloon, leaving Marguerite in charge. She was dressed in a light summer gown, an arrangement of flowers in her hair, making the other women look plain in comparison. Grace sat in a chair close to James.

"What are we going to do about these thugs?" said George, shaking his head.

"We need to send a deputation to the mayor," said Cora. "Tell him it's his responsibility."

Lillian waved a fly away that had been bothering her. "The useless old goat will say he's got no one to enforce law and order."

George banged the arm of his chair. "Then we tell him it's his job to get people to do it."

There was a mutter of agreement.

"*D'accord.* Who will lead this deputation?" asked Cora.

James took his feet off the bench where he had been resting them.

"I'll do it." He sat forward. "I'll tell that worthless mayor what's needed. And if he wants volunteers, I'll sign up." He glanced at Grace. "You agree?"

She fought the desire to jump up and hug him. This was more like the James Randolph she had first known. A man willing to take the lead, to put his shoulder to the wheel.

Instead, she kept her voice even. "If that's what you think is best, James, you have my full support." Their eyes met. "As you always do."

Grace suppressed a smile as she caught Cora rolling her eyes at them, before returning to her theme. "*Zut!* The problem is deeper than that. This is a new country. I come from a place with centuries of governance, of kings, and emperors, and republics. And it always comes back to who has got the power."

"But no one has power," said Lillian with a grimace. "It's every man for himself."

Cora smiled knowingly. "It's not just Captain Randolph who rails at Washington for forgetting us. I hear plenty of men saying the same thing, every evening. So"—Grace recognized the way Cora would pause to make sure everyone was listening—"a plan is afoot for Californians to take things into their own hands."

"How?" asked Grace. Her clever friend always knew what was going on behind the scenes and she was eager to know more.

"A constitutional convention."

Grace saw Cora's glass was empty and filled it with white wine. "That sounds very French."

"It's exactly what revolutionary France would do." Cora lifted her glass as if toasting her country.

"What does it mean though?" asked Simon.

The twinkle in Cora's eye told Grace how much she was enjoying sharing her gossip. "Governor Riley's adjutant is a regular customer at our saloon. He says they are going to ask for representatives from all parts of California. They will gather and write our constitution. Instead of waiting for Washington to give one to us—we give it to them."

"Now, I like that idea," said James, leaning back and putting both hands behind his neck, elbows wide.

Cora turned directly to him. "Good, Captain Randolph. Because you are exactly who should be representing San Francisco."

James snorted in response.

Cora looked around the gathering, her eyebrows raised. Her eyes settled on Grace, and although neither spoke, Grace knew she was offering them a different future.

"She's right, Randolph," said George. "I'd vote for you."

"Got my vote," said Espinoza. "And Moreno's too."

"I'll vote for you," said Lillian, raising her glass.

Everyone laughed.

"Don't think you'll be getting a vote, sweetheart," said George.

"Well, maybe—sweetheart—our good friend Randolph can get some women's rights written into this new constitution."

There was more laughter until all eyes settled on Randolph again. Grace wondered how he would react, but dearly hoped he would consider the idea.

He looked round, open-mouthed. "Oh, come now. You're serious?"

"Why not?" said Moreno.

"I don't know the first thing about the law, or governance."

George picked up his pipe. "Last thing we want is a bunch of lawyers sorting it out. If Californians are going to write their own constitution, then I want someone who knows what a scourge this lawlessness is."

James stared at George, and then his eyes moved around the women: Lillian, Cora, Ling Mei, and finally to Grace. She kept her counsel for the moment.

He sat forward, his hands together, elbows on his thighs. "If we're going to write our own constitution, we can do it our way. Lillian, why shouldn't you have a vote? You're a part of California. Cora, you own a business." He looked round. "Why not?"

Grace knew no one was quite sure if he was joking.

He looked up at her. "What do you think?"

Her skin prickled as she realized he was truly asking for her opinion. She held his gaze again. His eyes seemed bluer in this evening sunshine. "About women getting a vote? Or you going to a convention?"

"Either. Both."

"Well, on the first..." She paused. "It's a big turnaround for a man who used to think that a woman shouldn't be allowed to take her own wagon across the Rockies."

He grinned and sat back. "Well, I'm still not sure about the wisdom of—"

"And for the second..." Grace looked at Cora, an understanding passing between them. "Where did the adjutant say this convention would take place?"

"The old capital. Monterey."

"Monterey?" Grace arched an eyebrow. "I hear it's beautiful. I'd be happy to accompany you, if you get enough votes."

PART THREE

FORTY-FIVE

Randolph wouldn't have acknowledged it out loud, but he was pleased to have Grace on his arm as he approached Colton Hall in Monterey. For one thing, he always felt that frisson of pride when he caught other people looking admiringly at his wife. But today he felt apprehensive. He wanted to do a good job for everyone who had voted for him to represent San Francisco, even though he had never done anything like this before.

He looked up at the handsome building, his hat shielding his eyes from the sun.

"My!" said Grace. "This must be the grandest place in all of California."

The September sunlight reflected off the oatmeal-colored stone, making it shimmer white. Colton Hall was wide, two stories high and, architecturally, completely balanced. A central portico was held up by two white columns, sheltering a pair of substantial doors. There were three sash windows, right and left, on each of the two levels. Two broad white staircases led up on either side to the center of the upper level, where another pair of doors led into the main hall. If Randolph could cut this building in half, he would find either side identical.

Men streamed past him, all smartly dressed, some in pairs and threes, talking animatedly.

He paused and faced Grace. "Time to go in. I'll tell you everything when I get back to our lodgings tonight."

"You better had." Grace straightened the front of his jacket. It was a sober blue, and longer than he was used to. Grace had insisted on a new suit from the tailor. He wore a waistcoat and a starched white shirt. Ling Mei had come with them to Monterey and promised to help him look the part of a delegate to the Constitution Convention. He'd spent a decade wearing a military uniform, but over the past year had enjoyed soft cotton and no collar.

Grace reached up and tucked in his black cravat. He'd thought it unnecessary, but now saw all the other men wearing them. He would have to adapt to a different sort of uniform. She touched her hand to his chin. "I was getting used to the mountain-man look, but I do like having you clean-shaven." She ran her thumb over the old scar on his jaw. "Interesting to see this once more." She took a quick look around and bounced up on her toes to give him a kiss on the lips. "Remember, I want to know *every* detail."

He joined the other men making their way up the stairway and glanced back down before entering back toward their rented house. Just knowing she was there gave him all the strength he needed.

Inside, the hall was as impressive as outside. The large windows meant it was full of light, which reflected off the polished wood floor. There were large iron chandeliers and Randolph wondered how often they would be working into the night.

He took off his hat and looked around the room. It was already nearly full and the sound of voices echoed off the freshly painted walls. Men stood in huddles, making small talk.

It reminded him of officer training back at West Point. He'd come through that; he would come through this.

He felt relief when he saw a familiar face, near the unlit fireplace at one end of the room. He strode over.

"Gilbert. Good to see you. How is the newspaper business going?"

"Can't complain. Can't complain."

Gilbert pumped his hand. A young man, not yet thirty, he had boldly set up a newspaper earlier in the year.

Randolph glanced around the room again. "Looks like a good number are here."

"I'm told there'll be nearly fifty of us."

A man clapped for silence.

Gilbert whispered to Randolph, "That's Dimmick. From San Jose. The chairman until we can get ourselves sorted."

"Gentlemen," said Dimmick, his voice hoarse. "Please take your seats."

One half of the room was roped off for observers. In the delegates' half, long tables extended either side. Across the short side, in front of the fireplace, a table and chair had been set up for the chairman.

"Are we supposed to sit anywhere in particular?" Randolph whispered to Gilbert.

"Who knows?"

The San Francisco delegates sat together. A clergyman stood by the chairman's table and coughed. Randolph and the others stood again, bowing their heads as the reverend intoned a prayer, asking for God's blessing on the proceedings.

With much scraping of chairs, the men sat once more. Randolph settled into the curved back. At least the chairs were comfortable. There were notepads, quills and ink pots along the tables. No expense had been spared.

Randolph looked forward to getting down to business: writing a constitution for the newly formed state. However, the proceedings immediately ran into the ground, with a long debate over the representatives from San Joaquin. For reasons lost on Randolph, some had been elected on the wrong day: should they be accepted as delegates? Randolph thought that as they were here now, they should get on with things. But he kept his counsel. The debate raged back and forth, proposing and amending resolutions until a special committee was appointed to look into it.

Randolph sighed. If this was how they were going to proceed, it could take months to write and agree a constitution.

The chair proposed a motion to take a recess until three o'clock, which was swiftly agreed. Randolph looked around in amazement as the men adjourned to the rooms downstairs for food, drink and cigars. They'd not done anything yet.

Gilbert nodded to the rotund man standing by the window, whose face was familiar to Randolph. "That's Captain Sutter."

"Ah, of course. I knew I'd seen him before."

Gilbert raised his eyebrows.

"When I first arrived, what, eighteen months ago. I went to his fort near Sacramento to seek advice. Quite a character."

The delegates returned to the hall in due course, but business got not much further. There was another recess until eight o'clock, by which time many of the delegates were feeling the effects of a day with plenty of food and alcohol freely available.

When Randolph returned to the little Spanish-style villa they were renting, Grace leaped from her seat in the parlor.

He threw his hat on the chair by the fire. "Sorry it's so late."

"What happened—"

"There might be a lot of late nights if we're ever going to get this constitution written."

"Come and sit." Grace led him to the chair and pulled her seat close as he told her about the day's frustrating proceedings.

"Tomorrow's another day," she said, rising from her chair and kissing his brow. "It will get better. Bide your time and choose your battles."

Tuesday passed much as the first day, with more wrangling over who would sit on which committee, what were the limits of authority, and—a particularly heated debate—how much they would be compensated for their time.

And so it continued for the rest of the week. Randolph tried to keep his frustration in check as the room got stuffier with cigar smoke hanging around the chandeliers, floating on the hot air of speeches from men like McCarver, a delegate from Sacramento, who liked nothing more than the sound of his own voice. Randolph sat back, extending his long legs, loosening his neck cravat and listening to the delegates. He rarely spoke, preferring to keep his powder dry for the things that really concerned him: law and order, and, above all else, the slavery question.

Would California be declared a state free of slavery? Delegates had carefully refrained from mentioning the issue, some fearing the southern-born delegates would object and prevent the work from continuing. But everyone knew the moment would come. Randolph needed to find his allies.

A smaller committee had been appointed to draw up a bill of rights and they returned on the Friday to present their work.

Mr. Shannon, representing Sacramento, stood to read out the sixteen items the committee was proposing. A New Yorker, whose Irish accent told he had not been born in the States, he had often spoken sense in the previous few days, Randolph thought, despite being another of the younger delegates.

Randolph pulled his notepaper and a pen closer. At last, they were getting down to business. The items covered many of the issues important to him: trial by jury, freedom of religion, and freedom of speech.

Shannon rose to his feet again. "But before we vote on the items, I move that the following becomes the first section of the bill of rights." He cleared his throat and lifted the paper he had prepared. "That all men are by nature free and independent, and have certain inalienable rights, among which are those of enjoying and defending life and liberty; acquiring, possessing and protecting property; and pursuing and obtaining safety and happiness."

For the first time, Randolph felt excited by the work. This was more like it. Safety and happiness: wasn't that what he wanted for Grace?

Immediately, men rose to propose amendments to the wording, substituting one phrase with another, making it more mealy-mouthed with each change.

Randolph rose. "The wording is just fine as it stands. I move we accept this as our new first section."

The vote went in Randolph's favor and the business moved on. Inside he felt proud of this small victory, but, as Grace had said, there were battles ahead.

It was mid-afternoon and the windows had been opened to let the gentle ocean breeze flow through the hall. Delegates were sleepy after a good lunch.

To Randolph's surprise, Shannon rose again. "I propose a further section to the ones we have agreed." He read from his prepared notes and spoke clearly so everyone would hear. "Neither slavery, nor involuntary servitude, unless for the punishment of crimes, shall ever be tolerated in this state."

He took his seat, the look on his face showing that he knew he had let the cat inside the chicken coop. Randolph admired Shannon for throwing down the gauntlet but wished he'd discussed it first. They needed to have lined up their supporters.

The chairman appeared ambushed by Shannon's addition and was assured it had not been discussed by the committee.

Mr. Wozencraft urged that a vote be taken immediately. He

was a thickset man from Louisiana. Surely this was a wily political move: Randolph feared the delegates in favor of slavery would band together and defeat the motion before it had even been discussed. The chairman decided to take the vote.

Randolph held his breath as he looked round the room at the raised hands. He was astonished when Mr. Shannon's item was agreed unanimously to form part of the bill of rights. There was some backslapping among a few of the anti-slavery delegates, but Randolph studied Wozencraft closely. What was a slave owner like him doing, voting in favor?

Grace and James sauntered along the seafront on their way home after Sunday church a week later. They had settled into life in Monterey and Grace was proud to be stepping out with her tall, smartly dressed husband.

She held onto his arm as she was wearing heeled shoes and the boardwalk was uneven. She had had some dresses made up for their move, and was wearing a green frock of light wool, and a long jacket. She enjoyed the swish of the petticoats and hoops of her skirt. She wore a bonnet tied with silk ribbons at her throat, judging her usual wide-brimmed hat inappropriate for the elegance of the old capital.

The September weather was still warm, although the sea breezes came in strong over the Pacific. Boats and ships of many different sizes were anchored in the bay. Seagulls called, high above, soaring on the air currents.

As ever, their conversation turned to the constitution. James was still troubled by the response to Shannon's amendment.

"It was too easy," James said. "I know some of those delegates want California to join the South and accept slavery."

"Perhaps you should celebrate a victory when it comes," said Grace.

James grunted. "The slave owners are plotting something. I'm not sure what. But they won't let this stand without a fight."

Their discussion was interrupted by a gangly man walking toward them. He raised his hat to greet James.

"Mr. Randolph," the man called.

"This is Mr. Halleck," said James, introducing him to her. "The delegate for Monterey."

He took Grace's hand and bent over to kiss it gallantly. "Mrs. Randolph. Now I understand."

"Mr. Halleck?"

"Why your husband argued so strongly for women's rights."

She raised an eyebrow at James. "Did he?"

"Indeed. He proposed that women should keep control of their property on marrying."

Grace looked at James and saw his half-smile. "And did the proposal pass?"

"Of course. When it is enshrined in our constitution, I have high hopes it will encourage women of means to come to California. Speaking as a bachelor."

Grace struggled to suppress a giggle. "And what about property created by a woman *after* she has got married?"

"Ah... oh... I'm not sure." The man's cheeks flushed red.

James stepped in to save Mr. Halleck. "I'm sure that can be decided by the legislature, once it is established."

Grace caught his eye. "Let's hope so." She returned her attention to Mr. Halleck. "Thank you for telling me of this success." She leaned closer. "Mr. Randolph was once a notorious misogynist—"

James feigned outrage.

"You know it's true, darling." She patted Mr. Halleck's arm. "And I wish you luck in catching one of those rich single women who will be beating a path to our state."

They made their farewells and continued with their walk.

. . .

Randolph had to wait another week to find out what the delegates who had originated in the southern states really had in mind. A concerted attack was launched.

When Mr. McCarver stood to speak yet again, there were some groans as he never failed to contribute, whether he had expertise on the matter in hand or not. This time, his words were more serious. "I propose that no free Negroes should be allowed into the state."

So that's what they were planning. He exchanged a look with Shannon. No slaves, but no Black men either.

Mr. McCarver continued. "Free Negroes are idle in their habits, thriftless and uneducated. If we do not prohibit *all* Negroes, our whole country will be filled with emancipated slaves, the worst species of population—prepared to do nothing but steal, or live upon our means as paupers."

Randolph was relieved when Shannon leaped to his feet and fought back. "Free men of color have just as good a right to emigrate here as white men."

"And what about the rights of those white working men?" railed Mr. Wozencraft, clearly in alliance with McCarver. Randolph guessed Wozencraft was the man behind the sudden proposal. "If we let free Negroes work beside them, we would degrade their labor, and greatly impair the prosperity of the state."

Randolph felt heat rising around his neck as he listened to the arguments being made back and forth. His heart was beating faster and he knew he could no longer remain silent. He rose to his feet and drew the attention of the chairman.

"Mr. Randolph."

"I wish to remind all here that we are forming a constitution for the first state of the American Union on the shores of the Pacific. We have said, right at the beginning of our bill of rights, that all men are by nature free and independent. That *all* men have the right to pursue safety and happiness.

"We have already unanimously agreed that slavery shall not exist here. We are acting in accordance with the whole civilized world. And yet, are we to say that a free Negro—or an Indian—shall not enter the boundaries of California? Is it because he is a criminal? No, sir—it is simply because he is Black."

Mr. Wozencraft banged the table in front of him. "I assure you that my constituents have every expectation of this provision being in the constitution. They won't vote for it, without it."

"And I assure you, Mr. Wozencraft," said Shannon, "the people I'm representing in Sacramento *don't* expect it."

Randolph returned home that evening, exhausted, and longing for some time with his wife. Grace took his coat and brushed it down. He leaned back in a chair in the parlor, pushing his fingers through his hair. She brought his supper through, and placed it on a small table in front of him.

"Grace, if I'd known it was going to be like this, I might never have stood as a representative."

"Tsk. Come now. You've survived the battlefield. Crossed the continent many times. I hope you're not going to let a bunch of functionaries defeat you."

He swallowed a mouthful, appreciating his wife's cooking. "Still the slavery debate. Day after day. We nearly lost today, Grace. The vote was on a knife-edge. We came close to prohibiting free slaves from entering California."

Grace drew her chair close. "But you won?"

"We won. Eventually." He sighed. "The battle but not the war. I fear they plan to bring it back to the lawmakers once we have a constitution."

She reached out and took his hand. "But it is a battle worth fighting."

FORTY-SIX

"Mei," Grace called, from the bedroom. "Where's Mr. Randolph's shirt? I hung it in the closet a few days ago and it's not there."

"It's in the kitchen, ready for when Mr. Randolph returns."

"But why did you even move it?"

"Mrs. Randolph, a grand ball, it needs proper starched shirt and collar."

Grace hurried to the kitchen. She really must keep her patience. Her nerves about the coming evening were making her short-tempered. And something more, that she really needed to talk to James about.

The delegates had worked for six weeks and now, finally, the constitution was complete. James had confided that there were times he feared the work would never be done.

Tonight, the delegates were throwing a ball for the cream of Monterey society in gratitude for the town's hospitality. Each delegate had contributed twenty-five dollars, and the ball was expected to last until the morning when the formal signing of the constitution would take place.

James's clothes were hanging tidily, just as Mei had said.

Grace had managed to borrow a black formal coat and made adjustments so it fitted James's broad shoulders. He had polished the patent-leather boots to a shine the night before. Grace had searched the town for white kid gloves, but could not find any, for love nor money.

Mei came in behind her. "See? All prepared."

Grace put out a hand in apology.

"You need to dress now," said Mei, leading the way back to the bedroom. "Ready for when he come back."

Mei helped Grace out of her day clothes and brought a newly made corset. Grace put it on over her shift and Mei began lacing the back.

"Not too tight, now," warned Grace.

"You think I don't know that?" asked Mei, gently tying the threads.

Grace caught Mei's knowing look in the mirror. Dropping her chin to hide her smile, she stepped into a set of hooped petticoats and Mei helped her into the ball gown a seamstress in the town had made.

Grace had balked at the expense, but James had reminded her that they were no longer struggling for money. Hotel Independence was a success; he had begun to rebuild the warehouses during August; and, most of all, the bags of gold Cora had insisted on bringing from the Dorado mine represented a small fortune. If she was truly concerned, he had assured her, the dress could be worn again when they returned home.

It was midnight-blue velvet, with a low scooped neckline and embroidered details in gold. Grace wondered how often a dress with such a revealing neckline would be suitable in San Francisco, but she kept those thoughts to herself.

She brushed her chestnut-brown hair and Mei braided and twirled it into an elegant arrangement, twisting through flowers she had picked that afternoon.

When Grace angled her small mirror to see what she could,

her mouth opened. Never had she seen herself so sophisticated, so glamorous. She took the pot of rouge Cora had given her as a gift and she had barely used, and dabbed tiny amounts that she rubbed across her cheeks. She put more onto her lips. She closed her eyes and Mei ran a narrow line of kohl on her eyelids, delicately smudging it.

"What do you think?" Grace asked nervously as she opened her eyes.

Mei stepped back. "Perfect."

"Not too much? Not too—"

"You are perfect."

Grace heard a knock at the door, followed by James's boots in the hall. He was home earlier than expected.

"Everything was wrapped up on time," he called. "For once."

"I'm in the bedroom," Grace called back.

"I think everyone decided—" He halted at the door and raised an arm above his head to lean against the frame, staring at her.

She smoothed the velvet on her skirt. "It's not right, is it? I've got it wrong—"

"It's..."

"Perfect?" said Mei with a raised eyebrow.

"Perfect," said James.

"She not believe me," said Mei with a toss of the head as she left the room, closing the door behind her.

They exchanged a smile.

"Your suit is in the kitchen."

"I'll fetch it in a moment." James opened a drawer in the cabinet. "But first..." He took out a box and opened it, revealing a sapphire and gold necklace.

Grace bit her lip, uncertain whether to touch it.

"I'm glad I went for sapphires. I didn't know your dress would be blue."

Her eyes widened. "And you *bought* this?"

"They are insisting on paying us delegates to be here, so I can't think of a better way to spend it than on my beautiful and loyal wife."

He picked it up and she turned so he could clasp it behind her neck. She felt his lips touch the skin between her shoulders, his hands on the tops of her bare arms. She shivered with the sensation. He turned her to him, holding her gaze, and stepped forward, inclining his lips to hers. She tasted a slight saltiness from his walk back in the sea air. She felt the graze from his end-of-day stubble. His hands encircled her waist and he drew her to him.

She pulled away, laughing. "No, no, no. Mei has only just fixed my hair—"

"Can't she do it again?"

She caught his grin and gave him a gentle push. "You need to wash and shave." She stepped back. "There's water in the pitcher. I'll bring through your suit. Mei has starched your shirt like marble."

At eight o'clock, Grace stood in front of Colton Hall, her hand tucked into James's elbow. The Spanish Californians would be fashionably late, but James would not countenance an untimely arrival. They followed other couples up the right-hand flight of grand steps leading to the upper floor. James had described the hall and she was anxious to finally see it for herself.

It was magnificent. Grace had never been in a room so fine, and rarely been in a space with so many people. The three chandeliers lit the hall, which had been decorated with young pine trees. At each end hung swathes of red, white, and blue fabric.

"So, this is where you've been spending so many hours," she said, her voice awestruck.

"Here, and in the committee rooms below. It seems strange to have all our tables moved out."

James led her to the knot of San Franciscans, most of whom she had got to know over recent weeks.

A portly man with large whiskers and a cast in one eye entered the hall.

"Oh," said Grace, "Isn't that—?"

"Captain Sutter." James spoke into her ear. "He's a delegate for Sacramento."

"I wonder how he has fared over the past year and a half since we met him."

"Not as well as one might have expected, I fear. Given it was his land where the gold was first found."

Mr. Shannon appeared with a glass of aqua vitae for each of them. "Let's celebrate a job well done. And I'm hoping you'll join me in an Irish jig, Mrs. Randolph. If I can persuade what passes for a band to play one."

Grace glanced at the corner, where two violins and two guitars were being tuned. She looked at the ladies around the room and felt more comfortable in her choice of dress. There was a mix of styles: a dark-haired Californian woman had chosen scarlet velvet and gold buttons; a fair-haired woman with a light complexion was in a dress of pink satin and gauze.

There was a break in the crowd and Grace saw Governor Riley at the far end of the hall. She swallowed nervously, remembering him from the Presidio in San Francisco. Even now, she felt embarrassed by the way he had dismissed her as he had ridden away. Here, he was in full dress uniform, with a yellow sash in honor of the battle he had won in Mexico. He was surrounded by majors and captains.

Grace glanced up at James. He looked impossibly handsome with his dark hair combed back, his tall bearing. He'd regained most of the weight he'd lost in the mine and was as muscular as when she had first met him. She wondered if he regretted not being able to wear his uniform. Did he feel lesser in his civilian clothes?

The musicians struck a long chord and Don Pablo de la Guerra, the master of ceremonies, stepped up to the dais to encourage everyone lucky enough to have a partner to take their places for the first waltz.

"I hope your shoes fit well," James said with a smile. "I think you'll be in much demand tonight."

"Well, James, lucky I enjoy dancing then."

"I'd better take my chance when I can."

He led her to the central area. She was glad neither of them had been able to find gloves: now she could feel her hand in his.

They began to move around the room in time with the lilting music. She wished it was acceptable for her to dance just with him, all night. There were things she wanted to talk about: their future, now the convention was over. But she would bide her time.

It had been too long since she had danced with her husband. He had always been an excellent lead, although he'd not felt inclined to dance much when they'd first met. But oh, how she missed it. Missed standing close enough to him she could see the pulse in his neck, even though they were surrounded by people. He pulled her near as they spun, her left breast pressed to his chest. He glanced down at her, a smile playing on his lips. Yes, he was enjoying this dance as much as she was.

The music ended much too soon and they returned to their friends. James fetched some lemonade for her. When he returned, the San Franciscan group was interrupted by the governor, who had made his way to them, a captain following in his wake.

James made the introductions. "Brigadier General Bennett Riley, this is my wife, Grace."

She dropped a low curtsy as she had seen the other women do. He bowed in return.

"Delighted to meet you Mrs. Randolph. Have you recently arrived in the city?"

Thankfully, he gave no indication of recognizing her. "No, I came with my husband. We have been in Monterey since the first of September."

"Your husband is to be congratulated, along with the other delegates."

Grace felt a warmth inside to hear her husband being praised by the Governor of all California.

The guitars and violins were ready to play again.

"Mrs. Randolph, may I have this dance?" he asked in a commanding tone.

She looked up at James in alarm. Maybe the governor did remember their last meeting after all. Why else would he want to dance with her, other than to comment on the outcome of her request? But then, she'd been rather rude to him. So why would he...

The governor interpreted her silence and glance at James as asking his permission. "Mr. Randolph, may I?"

James inclined his head. "I did warn my wife she would be in much demand as a dancing partner."

The governor put out the crook of his arm and Grace took it, glancing back at James, with her eyes wide.

He gave a wry smile and shrugged. "Enjoy it," he mouthed.

FORTY-SEVEN

Governor Riley led Grace to the center of the hall, although he kept a more respectable distance than her husband had.

"Have you been in Monterey throughout the convention?" she asked. Grace didn't want to let James down by appearing a mouse, unable to conduct polite conversation.

"I have only recently arrived. Thought it best to let the delegates do their work without me looking over their shoulders."

The rasping, slightly strangled voice was familiar from their meeting at the Presidio.

"You must be very busy, sir."

"Indeed, I am."

"Eight companies of infantry, two of artillery, and two companies of dragoons, I recall."

Governor Riley stared at her. "You are very well informed."

She might as well get this out in the open. Their encounter might come to his mind later in the evening and that would be equally embarrassing. "That's what you said last time we met. I'm afraid I was very impertinent."

"Now I am intrigued. When was this?" He tilted his head toward her.

"April."

"Ah." Riley nodded. "I had only just arrived in San Francisco."

"My husband had been captured by one of those rogue mining companies. I came to ask you to send a company of soldiers to rescue him and his companions."

"Hmm, now I recall." He peered at her more closely. "I thought it a brazen thing to do: a woman to come and ask my help. But it showed great affection for your husband. Didn't you say he was a private in the army?"

"I... I said he served. I didn't say he was a private."

Governor Riley glanced over to where James stood with his friends. "He has an officer's bearing."

"That he does."

The music came to an end and he escorted her back to James's side. He had a drink in his hand and raised it to her, silently congratulating her on having survived the dance.

"Well, that was unexpected," Governor Riley said with a tight smile. "Your wife was reminding me that we have met before."

James glanced at Grace before seeming to make a decision and responding to the governor. "I believe it was while I was forced labor on the Stanislaus."

Grace looked at James in surprise that he mentioned that period.

Governor Riley shook his head and tsked. "A bad business. Nevertheless, I recall her final words. 'If you don't go rescue my husband, then I will.' Something like that, was it not?"

Grace said nothing. A note in his voice suggested he was mocking her. She opened her mouth to move the conversation on by involving Shannon or Gilbert. The last thing she wanted was for James to be reminded of that dreadful time.

"But all's well that ends well," the general said, his voice becoming louder so he addressed the whole group. "Clearly you managed to escape without my intervention, or your wife's." The governor laughed and clapped Randolph's shoulder. "You must be a resourceful man. I suspect that came from your military training."

This was getting worse. If James thought Grace had been prattling about his military career...

James looked Riley straight in the eye. "I learned much from my time in the army, Governor. But I cannot take credit for my escape. It is my wife who is the resourceful one."

Governor Riley pulled his yellow sash straighter. "Oh?"

"I owe my freedom entirely to her. She did indeed come and rescue me."

"Now, buddy, you can't leave the story there," said Gilbert with a newspaperman's nose for a story. "I'm sure we all want to hear more." He looked at Shannon and winked.

"Very well." James shifted his weight and pointed to Grace with his glass. "My wife rode into the mountains, right into the lion's den, and she released me through her own... I find it hard to find the right word, sir—courage? Ingenuity? Tenacity?"

"Not exactly on my own, James," Grace said quietly.

James looked at her and paused. "True. She came with the wife of a friend I'd been kidnapped with. And another very good woman-friend of ours."

Grace looked downwards and felt a heat rising up her neck.

James found her hand and squeezed it. "So, sir, I'm not sure how much California needs its constitution. With women such as my wife and her friends, it already has a bright future."

Governor Riley laughed awkwardly. "Well. An inspiring story." He nodded to the group. "Enjoy your evening."

All the men made polite bows and Riley moved on.

Gilbert began to ask for more details, but Grace flapped a hand by her face. She'd never had need of a lady's fan before. "I wonder, James, if I might get a little air."

"Of course." He nodded to his friends, and steered her to the balcony that stretched between the dual staircase.

The setting sun had turned the sky shell-pink and the air had a salty tang. A gentle breeze cooled Grace's skin.

"I've spent a good amount of time standing here," James said, looking at the Pacific on his left, waves rolling into the distant bay.

Grace stood next to him, shoulder to shoulder. "You didn't need to say all that..."

"D'you mind that I did?"

"No. But, James, I think it is better if you forget that time, forget all—"

He turned to face her, leaning his hip against the balustrade. His face was serious. "I'll never forget what you did for me, Grace. And I'm sorry if I haven't said it before. Or, not said it clearly enough. I owe you my very being. You risked *everything*. For me."

She looked up at his blue eyes. "I would do it again, in a heartbeat."

He took her hand. "Everything... everything, it's all for you. I will spend the rest of my days trying to give you security and happiness."

She took a breath. "I already have everything I could ever need, as long as we're together."

They stood quietly together as the band struck up its next dance. They both turned to look at the ocean. Grace knew she had never been happier, but one more thing would make this moment perfect.

"James, there's something I need to tell you. I've been meaning to for a while." She glanced up at him and found his eyes were on her face. "I'm expecting our child."

For a moment, his expression didn't change. Then a slight crease between his brows. "You're sure? I mean, I know before, we hoped—"

"I'm sure." Her hand instinctively went to her belly. "I've even begun to feel it in the last few days."

His eyes widened. "*Feel* it?" His hand cupped hers.

"It's like... It's like a kitten is deep inside you and every so often it moves."

His mouth broadened to a grin. "That sounds... Is that a *good* feeling?"

She giggled. "It's a wonderful feeling. We are creating a new life. It's—"

His lips were on hers and he pulled her close, as if he didn't care that others could emerge onto the balcony at any time.

"I love you," he laughed between their kisses. "God, how I love you!"

The dancing continued until midnight, when supper was served in the committee rooms below the main hall. The tables were laid high with turkey, tongue, and pâté. Grace was aware of James holding her a little closer, using his arm to guard her from people crowding too close.

"I've not turned into glass overnight," she whispered, but was secretly delighted by his care.

There was a warm look in his eyes. "I know. But please allow me... It's hard not to be protective."

A patrician-looking man approached as they ate. He had a full head of hair, brushed back from his brow, grays among the brown. His eyes were such a pale blue, Grace wondered if he had cataracts.

"Mr. Gwin," said James, and introduced Grace.

"I hope we can meet as soon as we return to San Francisco," said Mr. Gwin.

"Meet?"

"There is much to be done."

James frowned. "I thought our work on the constitution was complete."

He vigorously shook his head. "This is just the beginning. It must be approved by congress. We will have elections very soon."

"I guess so."

Mr. Gwin looked at James intently. "I've been mightily impressed by you, Mr. Randolph. Every time you spoke, it was to good purpose."

"Well, thank you, Mr. Gwin. That is generous—"

"I will be running for senate." He leaned closer. "And I want you to be my running mate."

James looked stunned.

"The two of us, senators together. What d'you think?"

"I'm not sure I think anything. I'm too surprised."

Mr. Gwin turned to Grace. "I'm sure I can count on your support, Mrs. Randolph."

"I... I have never doubted my husband's talents. I will support him, whatever he chooses to do. But, sir, I'm afraid I will not seek to persuade him to—"

Mr. Gwin stepped closer to her. "You must agree that Mr. Randolph would make an outstanding representative for California."

James suppressed a snort. "Mr. Gwin, I'm flattered by your suggestion. But if being here has taught me anything, it's that I'm not cut out for committee work and debating."

Mr. Gwin harrumphed. "I'm sure the people would vote for you—"

"I would make a very poor senator. I do not have the patience."

Mr. Gwin frowned. "Well, if you are sure—"

"I am—"

"I still want to call on you in San Francisco." Mr. Gwin

tapped James's chest with a knuckle. He bowed and stalked away out of the committee room.

Grace stared at James. "Were you... expecting that?"

James rubbed the back of his neck. "I'm amazed. Not least because he is from Tennessee. He must know I could never support his position on slavery."

"But were it not for that... I mean... if it were a different party, would you...?"

James took both her hands. "I'm sorry if it disappoints you. I will *never* stand for public office again. These past six weeks... The number of times I've had to stop myself from leaping up and yelling *can we just get on with it?*"

Grace giggled.

He gave her a peck on the brow. "But there is something I want to discuss with you."

He led her outside. Night had fallen and the stars were bright, spread across the sky. There was enough of a chill for Grace to be grateful to James for removing his coat and draping it around her shoulders. They wandered toward the gardens and sat on a bench under a young sequoia tree.

"William Shannon and me. We've been talking about what California needs so it can grow."

She looked at him. "People are pouring in from all parts of the globe."

"Indeed. But it takes a month to reach from the East Coast through Panama. Longer if you go round the Horn. And you and I know better than most how hard it is to travel overland."

"So, what's on your mind?"

"A railroad. We're thinking about a railroad that would go right across from the Pacific Coast to the Atlantic."

Grace couldn't help but laugh. "You can't be serious."

"They've already got from the East Coast to the Ohio River."

"But, darling, a railroad needs flat land. How would you ever cross the Sierra Nevada? The Rockies?"

"Tunnels. Bridges."

This sounded crazy to Grace's ears. "Think of the cost. Even with all the gold in California, it still couldn't be built."

James set his jaw. "You don't think we can do it?" There was doubt in his voice.

She put her hand on his. "I'm sure if *anyone* in California can do it, you can. As I said earlier, I will support you, no matter what you choose to do."

The music started up again, with a baritone bursting into song.

James looked back toward the hall. "I think we have entered the entertainment part of the ball. D'you want to stay?"

"It's such a special night, I don't want to go home. But I confess, I am a little sleepy."

"Wait here."

James strode off back to the rooms on the lower floor. He returned with cushions and blankets.

"Let's make a camp. Right here under the stars. It'll be like when we first started prospecting together."

It was the perfect idea. They settled on the grass, a cushion under her head, wrapped close to him under the blankets. She drifted in and out of sleep, sometimes waking and studying the sky, each time different as the stars moved across the black canvas. As she watched, she could see more and more stars emerge, until she felt awed by the number.

The first birds sang while it was still dark, followed by others as the sky to the east became an iridescent blue. She snuggled closer to James, his arm tight around her.

He stirred and they heard voices around them in the

gardens: men who had spent the whole night drinking and telling tall tales.

James helped her rise, and brushed down her velvet dress.

"I must look a sight." She patted her hair where tresses had fallen from their pins.

"You've never been more radiant."

She gave him a playful tap and did what she could to put her hair back up, knowing it was no longer smooth and ordered. She reached up to help James with his collar and necktie. He struggled with the stud.

"Y'know, I'm going to leave it." He let the ends of the tie hang loose and his shirt open at the top. His jaw was dark with stubble. He picked up the blankets and cushions and they returned to Colton Hall, drawn by the smell of bacon. "The staff have started breakfast."

A cup of strong coffee in the committee room soon revived each of them.

"We're due to sign the constitution at nine," said James. "D'you want to stay?"

"Are ordinary folk allowed to watch?"

"I think so."

"Then I wouldn't miss it for the world."

At nine o'clock, all the delegates crowded back into the hall upstairs, surrounded by as many citizens as could fit in. Candles had burned down, leaving melted wax of strange shapes. In places, the floor was sticky from spilt drink.

A large table had been set on the dais with two copies of the constitution laid out: one in English and one in Spanish.

The chairman took control once more. "I call upon all forty-eight delegates present, who have been elected by the people of California, to sign the constitution and discharge their duty of creating a State Government."

One by one, they went forward to sign the two documents.

Grace's heart beat with pride as James took the quill, dipped it in the ink, and signed his name. The clerk blotted his signature, before the next delegate came forward.

James looked into the crowd, seeking her face. Their eyes met and he gave a slight nod and a half-smile.

As the final delegate signed, a cannon went off in the Monterey fort. Someone, somehow, had got the message to the commander that the document was finished.

James grabbed her hand, pulling her out to the balcony. Another cannon boomed its salute, echoing around the bay. Then another. Someone started counting.

Twenty-nine... thirty.

Everyone held their breath.

One more cannon salute.

"And that one's for California!" someone shouted. "The thirty-first state."

People started to clap and cheer. Grace saw Captain Sutter had tears running down his face.

"Time to go home?" James's mouth was close to her ear.

She put her arm around his waist. "Time to go home."

FORTY-EIGHT
MARCH 1850: SAN FRANCISCO

Randolph was directing the construction of a new wharf out into the bay. He had rebuilt his warehouses and the pace of ships arriving at San Francisco was still increasing. Bigger and better wharfs were needed and Randolph could see how this could make him plenty of money. Money that would be invested in his long-term plan: the railroad.

He heard the boy's voice before he saw him.

"Mr. Randolph? Is Mr. Randolph here?"

He stood up and stretched his back. "Over here."

The boy must have been around ten, an eager look on his face. "Mrs. Hollingswood said you'd give me ten cents if I gave you a message."

Randolph pulled the coins out of his vest pocket.

"Said Mrs. Randolph's time has come."

He thrust more coins in the boy's hand and called to his foreman: "I'm away home now."

"Captain, I wanted to ask you about—"

"It will have to wait until tomorrow."

Sweeping up his overcoat and hat from the planks, he

hurried from the harbor, dodging people, animals and carts on Market Street, and turned north. He and Grace had moved out of the room above the hotel kitchen and begun to build a smart villa on the lower slopes of Goat Hill, with views across the bay.

His breathing became heavy as he pushed himself up the hill as fast as he could until his house came into view. He was frustrated by how little was complete. Maybe he shouldn't have prioritized the warehouses after all. But workmen and timber were hard to come by.

He slammed open the front door. "Grace!"

Lillian was with him in a moment. Her sober dress was covered by an apron. "Hush, now. Don't want a commotion at this important time."

"How is she?" he asked urgently.

"She went into labor this morning."

"This morning! But it must be near four o'clock now. Why didn't you send for me at once?" He threw his hat on the console table and shrugged off his coat. The March air was warm and the rush home had left him overheated.

Lillian took his coat and folded it over her arm. "No point in having a man hanging around here all day. It's her first. It could be hours yet."

Randolph put his hands to his head and paced. He didn't care how many hours he waited, as long as he was with Grace.

"And yet you sent that boy to fetch me. Is something wrong?"

"She's doing well. But she kept asking for you. I thought, if I could assure her that you were downstairs—"

He heard a long groan from upstairs and stepped toward the staircase.

"There's really no need for you to disturb her," Lillian said, a hand on his arm. "Come and have some tea."

He ignored her and took the stairs, two at a time. He opened the bedroom door as softly as he could and stepped inside. Lillian followed.

Grace was standing in her nightdress, her bare feet firmly apart, leaning forward over the high mattress. Her hair was in one thick braid, but tendrils were stuck to the sweat on her face. Her skin had a damp sheen.

She let out a long, low sound, something almost animal.

A tiny Chinese woman stood beside her, rubbing the small of her back in circles. She was dressed in a blue tunic with pants, just the same as Mei wore.

Now he was here, Randolph didn't know what to do. This was female territory, a foreign land he should not invade.

"Who's that?" he whispered to Lillian.

"Mei's mother—"

"Her mother? I didn't know—"

"None of us did. But Mei promises she is an expert midwife."

Grace looked up.

"James," she groaned. "You're here." She put out her hand.

He sprang forward to take it. "Of course I'm here. As soon as I—"

She shook her head and looked like her thoughts were angled inwards. The sound of lowing came again, almost a growl, and she crushed his hand in hers.

Mei entered carrying a pitcher of water. She moved with smooth confidence. "Ah. Mr. Randolph." She spoke to her mother. "She say your wife doing very well. Is very strong."

He nodded and felt the room was suddenly crowded with people. Surely Grace could do with some air.

Grace dropped her head. "I'm going to be sick."

Mei brought a bowl. Her mother asked a question and Mei translated. "You feel hot?"

"Yes, so hot." Grace loosened the ties at the top of her nightdress.

Mei continued to translate. "Mother say this very good. Things start moving now. Not long."

"Not long?" asked Randolph.

"Maybe an hour."

"That seems long."

"Maybe half that."

Grace vomited into the bowl.

Lillian put a hand on Randolph's arm again. "Randolph... James... it really would be better if I made you some tea downstairs. She knows you're here now, so..."

He left the room, bewildered, and followed Lillian downstairs. He had never felt so helpless, so surplus to requirement.

In the kitchen, Lillian placed a china teacup on the table in front of him. She slid a pack of playing cards across.

He frowned. "Cards?"

"My George swore by them. He played patience through each of my six." Lillian took up the water butt and looked back at him from the kitchen door. "Otherwise the next hour is going to be the longest of your life." She left to fetch fresh water from the street pump.

Lillian was right. Time went slowly. Randolph had recently bought a smart long-clock which stood in the lobby, the seconds ticking away, loud and rhythmical. On the hour, there was a whirring sound and the time rang out.

Through the floorboards, he could hear footsteps, the springs of the mattress, firm instructions from Mei's mother, not a word of which he understood. And, in between, he heard Grace's laboring. He had expected screams and calling out. But this was more like the long growls of a mountain lion, before it pounced. And then the panting of a horse after galloping long and hard.

Lillian sat with him, talking about nothing in particular. The sound of the two Chinese women reached a crescendo, but he heard nothing from Grace.

The bedroom latch opened and Mei called from the landing: "Mr. Randolph. You come."

He leaped to his feet. Things were too quiet. There had been no cry of a baby. It had been born dead, and taken Grace with it. He rushed upstairs and stood at the open door, his fingers on the jamb of the frame. "Grace...?"

Mei put one hand on his chest and a finger to her lips.

Grace was sitting up in the bed, supported by pillows. Her hair was loose and falling forward. She was completely absorbed in the dark-haired baby in the crook of her arm, its head moving back and forward against her breast. Mei's mother leaned over, talking in a low voice and helping the baby to latch on. The baby seemed to settle and Grace's shoulders lowered.

"I... I didn't hear anything," Randolph stuttered. "No crying. I thought—"

"Not all babies cry," said Mei. "This is good sign. Very content baby."

Grace looked up and saw him. A smile spread across her face. How was it possible she could look so beautiful?

She put out her arm to him. "James, come and meet our son."

He crossed the room in a moment to sit on the bed and leaned over, but could only see the dark hair and the ball of a cheek. The baby's eyes were closed, but his jaw was moving. He lifted his son's hand and spread his fingers. Such a miniature hand, red and creased.

The baby stopped and fell into a slumber, his lips still open.

"Do you want to hold him?" Grace asked.

Randolph didn't know what to say. With all his being, he wanted to hold his son. But he didn't want to disturb his wife.

Mei stepped forward before he spoke. She took the baby in both hands and wrapped him in linen. The baby's arms jerked out, fingers splayed, but then the hands curled in again and he continued sleeping.

"Sit there," Mei said, nodding to the only chair in the room.

Randolph settled and Mei carefully put the baby into his arms, like a valuable china vase. He leaned back and studied the boy. The feeling that hit him like a Pacific wave was like nothing he had experienced before: a rush of awe, pride and protectiveness.

Mei and her mother continued to bustle around the room, collecting towels and bowls. Randolph was alarmed by how much blood was on the cloths. One bowl had a dark substance, almost like liver. Again, he felt like an intruder from another land.

Mei lit the oil lamp and a couple of candles as the evening grew darker. The room was full of shadows and golden light. The two Chinese women left, quietly closing the bedroom door behind them.

Randolph continued to marvel at the boy. He glanced over at Grace, who looked exhausted but content.

"Have you decided on a name?" he asked.

"What else could he be but 'James'?"

"Won't that get confusing? He'll need a middle name."

"I guess. What d'you think?"

Randolph paused. "What about James Thomas? After your brother."

"That's a fine idea." Grace yawned deeply and stretched out her arms. "I hope he doesn't make up for his quiet birth by crying for the next few months."

Randolph chuckled. "D'you need some sleep? I can sit here with James Thomas while you rest."

"If you're sure?" Grace settled down further on the pillows, her hair spread out on one side.

Randolph moved the baby so his head lay next to his chest, feeling the warmth on the skin at the open collar of his shirt. He looked down at James Thomas and across at Grace. She was already asleep.

California wasn't the place he had hoped for yet. San Francisco was still struggling to keep law and order. But Randolph knew, with every fiber of his being, he would do everything he could to make it a place of peace and prosperity. A place fit for his family. Because this—his beloved wife and his baby son—*this* was worth fighting for.

A LETTER FROM THE AUTHOR

Dear Reader,

Thank you so much for reading *The Mountains Between Us* and I hope you enjoyed finding out what happened to Grace and Randolph after they got married. If you are intrigued to know how they fell in love in the first place, I hope you'll read *To the Wild Horizon*.

If you would like to join other readers in keeping in touch, here are two options. Read about my new releases and bonus content by following this link:

www.stormpublishing.co/imogen-martin

Or pop over to my website and sign up to my monthly newsletter. You'll get giveaways, sneak peeks and historical snippets:

https://imogenmartinauthor.com

Or do both! I look forward to meeting you.

Your email address will never be shared and you can unsubscribe at any time.

If you enjoyed this book and could spare a few moments to leave a review, that would be hugely appreciated. Even a short review can make all the difference in helping other readers discover my book for the first time, and every single review helps. Thank you so much.

I have been fascinated by the United States all my life. When I was a teenager, I took a Greyhound bus from San Francisco to New York. Over those three days of staring out of the window at the majestic mountains and endless flat plains, stories wound themselves into my head: tales of brooding, charismatic men captivated by independent women. My first novel, *Under A Gilded Sky* is set in 1874—the dawn of the Gilded Age. You'll find out more if you sign up to the newsletter.

I have, of course, done years of research and this book draws on real places and events that happened. But it's fiction: an imagined story.

If you want to make contact, the best place is my Facebook page or the feedback page on my website. I love hearing from readers. I can also be found on other social media platforms. Come and say hello.

Thank you again for being part of this amazing journey with me, and I hope you'll stay in touch—I have so many more stories and ideas with which to entertain you.

Imogen

- facebook.com/ImogenMartin.Author
- x.com/ImogenMartin9
- instagram.com/imogenmartinauthor
- bookbub.com/profile/imogen-martin

ACKNOWLEDGMENTS

I have a habit of flipping to the end of a book: not the final page of the book, mind you—I'd hate to know what happens before I read it—but I like to know more about the author and how the book came about. Thank you for joining me in appreciating the acknowledgements page!

This is my third book, and, as with the previous two, I am endlessly grateful to my editor Vicky Blunden for making it so much stronger. I feel lucky to have what I'm sure is the best editor in the business.

I also feel lucky to be published by Storm. Every person in the team is professional and helpful—a standard set by Oliver Rhodes. And it does take a team to produce a book. As well as my editor, I'm grateful to Jade Craddock and Abi Fenton for further editorial input, to Elke Desanghere for marketing and Anna McKerrow for publicity.

This book tells what happens to my characters after *To the Wild Horizon*, but I wanted to make sure a reader could pick it up without having read the first book. Thank you, Katie McDermott and Ella Matthews for reading an early draft. If you're a reader new to Randolph and Grace and it was easy to get to know them, then that's down to Katie and Ella. Thank you to Jo McGill for her eagle-eyes when reading a final draft.

I am grateful for the ongoing support of RNA Cariad—who will meet for coffee and cake at the drop of a hat—and to the Bookcamp Mentees, each with their own publication journey.

My debut was dedicated to my elder daughter Becky and

my second book to my younger daughter Naomi. This third is dedicated to my husband Peter. If every writer had a husband like mine, there would be so many more books in the world! He is my first, and most enthusiastic, reader. He tells me everything I write is "brilliant." As I have bouts of imposter syndrome, this helps me get back to writing and editing. Peter makes sure there's food on the table and shoos me back to my desk when I'm flagging. Thank you, Peter, I really couldn't do it without you. You are my Happily Ever After.

Made in the USA
Coppell, TX
01 July 2025